"There are no horses here, my dear."

"I've heard them twice now," I said firmly. "Galloping."

"Ah." Quinnell nodded, smiling faintly, a parent amused by an obstinate child. "Perhaps you've been hearing the shadowy horses. In Ireland, our sea-god, Manannan Mac Lir, is also the god of the otherworld, riding his chariot over the waves in the wake of his magical horses. They carry men off—over the water and into the mist, to the land where the living can't go."

Small wonder the Irish were poets, I thought, when their gods were as close as the waves on the sea. And anyway, the horses that I heard at night were either real or dreamed, not phantom creatures born of Irish folklore . . .

THE
SHADOWY
HORSES

Susanna Kearsley

JOVE BOOKS, NEW YORK

THE SHADOWY HORSES

A Jove Book / published by arrangement with
the author

PRINTING HISTORY
Originally published in Great Britain in 1997
by Victor Gollancz, an imprint of the Cassell Group
Jove edition / March 1999

ISBN: 0-515-12464-8

A JOVE BOOK®
Jove Books are published by The Berkley Publishing Group,
a member of Penguin Putnam Inc.,
375 Hudson Street, New York, New York 10014.
JOVE and the ''J'' design
are trademarks belonging to Jove Publications, Inc.

PRINTED IN THE UNITED STATES OF AMERICA

10 9 8 7 6 5 4 3 2 1

To the People of Eyemouth

So many of you have had a hand in the creation of this book, and I have spent so many hours in your company that now your streets, your homes, your harbor have a warm familiar feel, and I no longer feel a stranger to your town. But I do not belong to Eyemouth. Despite my best efforts I'm sure there will be places in this book where you will find I've got some detail wrong, or used a turn of phrase that's not your own. I can only hope that you'll forgive me any errors. And I hope that you will all accept this novel as a gift of thanks, from one to whom you've always shown great kindness.

I hear the Shadowy Horses, their long manes a-shake,
Their hoofs heavy with tumult, their eyes glimmering white; ...
O vanity of Sleep, Hope, Dream, endless Desire,
The Horses of Disaster plunge in the heavy clay:
Beloved, let your eyes half close, and your heart beat
Over my heart, and your hair fall over my breast,
Drowning love's lonely hour in deep twilight of rest,
And hiding their tossing manes and their tumultuous feet.

W. B. Yeats, "He Bids His Beloved Be At Peace"

FIRST HORSE

> ...that delirious man
> Whose fancy fuses old and new,
> And flashes into false and true,
> And mingles all ...

Tennyson, "In Memoriam", XVI

I

The bus had no business stopping where it did. We should have gone straight on across the Coldingham Moor, with Dunbar to the back of us and the English border drawing ever nearer, but instead we stopped, and the shaggy-faced cattle that lifted their heads on the far side of the fence appeared to share my surprise when the driver cut the engine to an idle.

A fierce blast of wind rocked the little ten-seater bus on its tires and drove a splattering of cold spring rain against the driver's windscreen, but he took no notice. He shook out a well-thumbed newspaper and settled back, humming tunelessly to himself. Curious, I shifted in my seat to peer out my own fogging window.

There seemed, at first glance, nothing to stop for, only the cattle and a few uninterested sheep, picking their way across a ragged landscape that was turning green reluctantly, as if someone had told it only yesterday that spring had come. Beyond the moor, lost somewhere in the impenetrable mist, rose the wild, romantic Lammermuir Hills I'd read about as a child. And in the opposite direction, although I couldn't see it either, the cold North Sea bit deep into the coastal line of cliffs.

The wind struck again, broadside, and the little bus shuddered. I sighed, and watched my breath condense upon the chattering window glass.

Impulsiveness, my mother always said, was one of my worst flaws, second only to my habit of speaking to strangers. After twenty-nine years I'd grown accustomed to her heavy sighs and shaking head, and to her firm conviction I'd end up a sad statistic on the nightly news. But now, as I squinted out at the bleak, unwelcoming scenery, I grudgingly admitted that my mother had a point.

It had been impulse, after all, that had brought me from my London flat to Scotland in the first place. Impulse, and the slick, persuasive writing-style of Adrian Sutton-Clarke. He knew me too well, did Adrian, and he had phrased his summons craftily—his promise of "the perfect job" set like a jewel at the center of a long letter that was so deliciously mysterious, so full of hints of grand adventure, that I couldn't possibly resist it. Adrian, for all his faults, had rarely steered me wrong. And if today was anything to go by, I decided, he hadn't been lying about the adventure.

Not that one could really blame British Rail for what had happened. My train had certainly set out from King's Cross cheerily enough, and even after we'd spent twenty minutes on a siding waiting for a points failure to be corrected, the engine had pushed ahead with vigor, determined to make up the time. It was only after our second delay north of Darlington, because of sheep on the line, that the train had begun to show signs of weariness, creaking and rolling from side to side in a rocking motion that lulled me instantly to sleep.

I had stayed sleeping right through Durham, then Newcastle, and finally Berwick upon Tweed, where I was meant to get off. When the train lurched to a stop at Dunbar, I'd scrambled down onto the platform with the familiar resigned feeling that told me I was lost. Well, not so much lost, really, as diverted. And the fact that my train had been an hour late coming into Dunbar proved something of a complication.

"You might have taken the 5:24," the stationmaster had informed me, in an effort to be helpful, "or the 5:51. But they've both gone. There'll not be another train to Berwick now till 7:23.''

"I see." Nearly an hour and a half to wait. I hated waiting. "I don't suppose there's a bus?"

"To Berwick? Aye, there is, at . . ." he'd searched his clockwork memory for the time, ". . . 6:25. Just around the corner, there, and up the road a ways—that's where it stops."

And so I'd wrestled my suitcase around the corner and up the road to the small bus shelter, my spirits lifting somewhat as I read the posted timetable telling me the bus to Berwick travelled via Cockburnspath and Coldingham and Eyemouth.

Eyemouth, Adrian had written in his letter, *pronounced just as it looks, and not like Plymouth, if you please. You'd love it here, I think—I remember how you waxed rhapsodic about the north coast of Cornwall, and this is rather better, a real old-fashioned fishing town with smugglers' ghosts around every corner and the added lure of . . . but no, I shan't give the secret away. You'll just have to come and find out for yourself.*

I'd have been only too happy to oblige, I thought wryly, but for the fact that I was now stuck in the middle of Coldingham Moor, with the bus idling on and the driver still reading his newspaper.

There seemed little point in questioning the stop; apart from a couple of lovestruck kids fondling each other at the rear of the bus, I was the only passenger. And the driver was bigger than me. Still, my curiosity had almost reached breaking point when he finally folded his paper with a decisive rattle, sat himself upright, and pulled on the lever to open the door.

A man was coming across the moor.

It might have been the fogged window, or the wild weather, or the rough and rolling landscape that, like all the Scottish Borderlands, held traces of the harsh and violent past—the echoed din of charging hooves, of chilling battle-cries and clashing broadswords. Whatever it was, it tricked my senses. The man, to my eyes, looked enormous, a great dark giant who moved over bracken and thorn with an effortless stride. He might have been a specter from a bygone age, a fearless border laird come to challenge our rude intrusion on his lands—but the illusion only lasted a moment.

The stranger pulled his collar tighter against another punishing blast of wind and rain and jogged the final few steps to the bus door. No border laird, just a rather ordinary-looking man in his mid-thirties, fit and broad-shouldered and thoroughly modern in jeans and a leather jacket. Well, I amended as he smoothed back his curling black hair and grinned at the bus driver, maybe not *exactly* ordinary-looking . . .

"Heyah," he greeted the driver, swinging himself up the final step. "Saw me coming, did you?"

"Aye, well, ye do stick out, lad. Thought I might as well wait for ye, save ye the walk back." The doors swung shut and, joy of joys, the bus sprang forward once again as the new passenger dropped into the seat across from me, planting his feet wide apart on the floor to brace himself.

He and the driver chatted on like old friends, which I supposed they were, about the state of the weather and the latest rebellion of the bus driver's daughter and the health of the younger man's mother. It had been some years since I'd spent time in Scotland, and I'd forgotten just how musical the accent was. This was a thicker accent than I was accustomed to, and I couldn't catch each word as it was spoken, but I did my level best to follow the conversation. Just for practice, I told myself. Not because I was interested.

The bus rattled noisily over the moor, dipped into Coldingham town and stopped for a moment to let off the teenagers. Shifting around in his seat, the bus driver sent me a courteous glance. "You're for Eyemouth, lass, aren't ye?"

"Yes, that's right."

The man from the moor lifted an eyebrow at my accent, and glanced over. For a moment, my mother's face rose sternly in my mind. Never talk to strangers . . . But I pushed the image back and sent the man a friendly smile.

The bus driver carried on speaking, over his shoulder. "Are ye up here on holiday?"

Having received little response from the man opposite, I

turned my smile on the driver instead. "Interviewing for a job, actually."

"Oh, aye?" He'd politely modified his speech, as most Scots did when talking to a non-Scot, and though the accent was still there I found him easier to understand. "What kind of job?"

Well, that was just the question, wasn't it? I didn't really know, myself. "Museum work, of sorts," I hedged. "I'm interviewing with a man just outside Eyemouth . . ."

The dark man from the moor cut me off. "Not Peter Quinnell, surely?"

"Well, yes, but . . ."

"Christ, you don't mean to say you're Adrian's wee friend from London?" He did smile then, and the simple act transformed his rugged face. "We'd not expected you till tomorrow. David Fortune," he held out his hand by way of introduction. "I work with Quinnell as well."

I shook his hand. "Verity Grey."

"Aye, I ken fine who you are. I must say," he confessed, leaning back again, "you're not at all as I pictured you."

Everyone said that. Museum workers, I had learned, were supposed to be little old ladies in spectacles, not twenty-nine-year-olds in short skirts. I nodded patiently. "I'm younger, you mean?"

"No. It's only that, with Adrian recommending you, I'd have thought to find someone . . . well, someone . . ."

"Tall, blond, and beautiful?"

"Something like that."

I couldn't help smiling. I was, to my knowledge, the only dark-haired woman who'd ever received so much as a dinner invitation from Adrian Sutton-Clarke, and I'd only held his interest until the next blond came along. But while our romance had proved temporary, our separate paths, by virtue of our work, kept crossing and re-crossing like some fatalistic web. Truth be told, I probably saw more of Adrian now than I had when we were dating. When one wasn't actually in love with the man, he could be a quite enjoyable companion. Adrian, at least, understood the restless, independent streak that had made me chuck my British Museum job and strike out on my own to freelance. And he'd learned I never could resist a challenge.

I studied the man across from me with interest, bringing all my powers of deduction to bear. I had already assumed, since Adrian was involved, that the job for which I was being interviewed involved some sort of archaeological dig. Adrian was one of the best surveyors in the business. I glanced at David Fortune's hands, and ventured to test my theory. "How large is the excavation, then?" I asked him. "How many field crew members are on site?"

"Just the four of us, at the moment."

"Oh." For a moment I was tempted to ask what they all were digging for, and why, but I held my tongue, not eager to let on that I'd come all this way not knowing.

He looked down, at my single suitcase. "You've just come up from London, then?"

"Yes. I'm a day early, I know, but the job did sound intriguing and I really couldn't see the point in waiting down in London when I could be waiting here, if you know what I mean . . ."

His eyes held understanding. "Aye. I wouldn't worry. Quinnell's an impatient man himself."

The sea was close beside us now. I could see the choppy froth of waves beyond the thinning wall of mist, and the jutting silhouettes of jagged rocks. The rain had stopped. Between the racing clouds a sudden gleam of sunlight flashed, and disappeared, and flashed again, and finally stretched a searching finger out to touch the clustered houses curving around the coast ahead of us.

The town of Eyemouth looked to me like a postcard view of a fishing village, its buildings tumbling in a tight cascade down to the sea wall while a gathering of gulls wheeled and dipped above the rooftops, marking the place where the harbor, yet unseen, cut back into the greening cliffs.

The sunbeam, I decided, held a pleasant sort of promise. And somewhere, not too far away, the mysterious Peter Quinnell was looking forward to meeting me. I leaned forward as the bus dived in among the houses. "Where would you recommend I stay?'' I asked my new acquaintance. ''Is there a guest house, or a nice hotel?''

''You'll not be staying in the town?'' He raised his eyebrows, clearly shocked. ''Christ, Quinnell wouldn't hear of it. He's had a room made up for you at Rosehill, at the house.''

I stared at him. ''Oh, but I couldn't . . .''

''You want the job?''

''Yes.''

''Then don't offend the management,'' was his advice. He softened it with a smile. ''Don't worry. They're all nice people, out at Rosehill. They'll make you feel at home.''

The bus driver flicked a glance up at his mirror, met my eyes, but didn't say anything.

I frowned. ''It's just that I prefer to stay on my own, that's all. I don't like to impose . . .''

''You'll not be imposing. Quinnell loves his company.''

''I'm sure he does. But if he doesn't hire me, it might prove awkward.''

''Oh, he'll hire you,'' said David Fortune, with a nod of certainty. ''That is, he'll offer you the job, make no mistake. Whether you accept or not, well . . . that's for you to say.''

Something in the offhand way he said that made me tilt my head, suspicious. ''Why wouldn't I accept?''

''Have you eaten, yet?'' he asked, as if I hadn't spoken. ''You haven't, have you? And it's Thursday night, this— Jeannie's night off. There'll be no supper on at the house.'' He turned to the bus driver, who was following our exchange with interest. ''Danny, do us a favor, will you, and drop us at the harbor road.''

''The Ship Hotel?'' the driver checked, and glanced again at me. ''Aye, it'd be no trouble. It wouldnae do for the lass to face old Quinnell on an empty stomach.''

My suspicions growing, I slowly turned to look at David Fortune, but his expression was charmingly innocent. So charming, in fact, that I scarcely noticed when the bus stopped moving. It wasn't until I felt the sudden blast of chill from the open door that I finally stirred in my seat. Gathering

up my suitcase, I tossed a word of thanks to the driver and
clambered down the steps to solid ground.

The wind had grown colder. It struck me like a body blow
and might have knocked me over if the man at my side
hadn't taken the suitcase from me, placing a large hand at
my back to guide me up along the harbor's edge. The tide
was very high, and the fishing boats creaked at their moorings, masts and rigging swaying with the motion of the water.

If my mother saw me now she'd have a heart attack, I
thought. She'd always had a thing about the seamy side of
harbor life—a half-imagined paranoiac world of smugglers,
cutthroats, pirates and white-slavers. I took another look up
at the great dark figure walking at my shoulder.

David Fortune did look a shade piratical, come to think of
it, with his black unruly hair curling in the wind and the flat
gray light of early evening sharpening the line of his stubborn jaw. His nose, in profile, was not quite straight, as
though it had been broken in a fight. And I only had his
word for it, after all, that he had anything to do with Peter
Quinnell, or with Adrian Sutton-Clarke, or with . . .

"Here we are," he told me, as a sprawling white pub rose
at the next corner to welcome us. He had leaned down so
that his voice would carry through the wind, and I caught
the swift warmth of his cheek close by my face. Oh, well, I
thought. Pirate or no, he was easy to look at, and I was, to
be honest, in need of a drink and a plate of hot food.

There were two doorways in to the Ship Hotel—one that
led into the main public bar, and the other to the dining
lounge. David Fortune steered me through the latter.

I felt instantly warmer, out of the wind, with the light
bursting clear and inviting from rose-tinted fixtures hung
high on the cream stuccoed walls. Round wooden tables
hugged the wainscoting and nestled in padded alcoves that
enticed one to sit and relax. Through an open door behind
the bar I could just glimpse a larger, less fancified room
where coarse cheerful voices competed with piped-in music,
but on this side of the door even the bar held a touch of

elegance, its gleaming rows of bottles artistically illumined by a line of recessed lights.

A few of the tables were already occupied. David Fortune plucked a menu from the bar and chose a table for us in a window alcove. Leaning back against the padded bench, he stretched his legs out so his feet disappeared under the bench on my side. "Take a look at that, then," he offered, handing the menu over. "And order what you like, the bill's on Quinnell. He'd not want to see you starve."

The mention of Peter Quinnell's name brought my earlier misgivings sharply into focus. "Listen," I began, frowning slightly, "there isn't anything *wrong* with the job, is there?"

He raised his eyebrows, but before he could respond the barmaid came through from the other side and sent us a welcoming smile. "Heyah, Davy. How's your mum?"

"As much of a witch as she ever was." His tone was indulgent. "Is Adrian about?"

"Upstairs, I think. Do you want me to fetch him?"

"Aye, if you would. But first, give us a . . ." He paused, looked at me, eyes enquiring. "What'll you have?"

"Dry white wine, please."

"And a pint of Deuchers for me, there's a love."

As the barmaid departed, I gave in to my curiosity. "Adrian's upstairs?"

"Oh, aye. We both have rooms here. There's just the one spare room at Rosehill, and Quinnell wanted to save that for you, so he's put us both up here instead."

Our drinks arrived. I watched him down a mouthful of the dark foaming beer, and frowned again. "Isn't that rather inconvenient?"

He shook his head. "It's only a mile out to the house. I like the walk."

I tried to imagine Adrian Sutton-Clarke walking a country mile to work each morning, and failed. Adrian, I knew, would use his car.

A door from the corridor opened and closed and a tall, lean-faced man with mahogany hair shook his head and came, smiling, toward us. "Verity, my dear, you really must learn some respect for schedules," he teased me, bending down to brush my cheek with an affectionate kiss of greeting. "Friday, last I checked, comes after Thursday, and you did say Friday."

"Hello, Adrian." It always took me a moment to adjust to the sheer impact of his handsome face, even now. Each time I met up with him I kept hoping, rather foolishly, that he'd have chipped one of his teeth, or that his dark, long-lashed eyes would be puffy and bloodshot, but each time he turned up just as perfect as ever, a six-foot-two package of pure sex appeal, and invariably knocked me off center. Only for a moment, and then memory reasserted itself and I was fine.

David Fortune had misinterpreted the involuntary change in my expression. He drained his pint and rose politely. "Look, I'll leave you to it, shall I? I could do with a shower and a lie-down, myself. See you both tomorrow." Slanting a brief look down at me, he stabbed the menu with a knowing finger. "Try the lemon sole, it's magic."

Adrian slid into the vacant seat opposite and favored me with a curious stare. "Just how," he asked me, when we were alone, "did you come to meet Fortune? Or do I want to know?"

"We were on the same bus. We got to talking."

"Ah." He nodded. "The bus from Berwick."

"Dunbar, actually."

The waitress came. I closed my menu, and ordered the lemon sole.

Adrian leaned back, contentedly. "I know I'm going to regret asking this," he said. "But how, if you came up from London, presumably on the train, did you end up on a Berwickshire bus from Dunbar?"

I explained. It took some time, and I was nearly finished with my meal by the time I'd told him everything, beginning with the sheep on the line at Darlington. Adrian shook his head in disbelief and reached for his cup of coffee. "You see? If you'd waited until tomorrow, like you were supposed to, none of that would have happened."

I shrugged. "Something worse might have happened. You never know."

"True. Confusion does rather seem to follow you around, doesn't it?"

"So tell me," I changed the subject, balancing my knife and fork on my empty plate, "what exactly is this job you've recommended me for?"

Adrian folded his arms and smiled like the devil. "As I recall, I told you I'd explain everything on Friday."

"When I arrived, you said."

"On Friday. And today's only Thursday."

"Oh, give it up . . ."

"But I'm sure Quinnell will be happy to tell you anything you want to know, when you meet him."

"That's hardly fair," I pointed out. "I'm meeting him tonight."

"So you are. Finished with that, have you? Good. Then let's get you out to Rosehill so you can settle in."

"Rat," I called him, holding back my smile.

Ten minutes later, seated in his car and speeding inland from the harbor, I tried again. "The least you can do," I said evenly, "is tell me what's wrong with the job."

"Wrong with the job?" He flashed me a quick sideways glance, eyebrows raised. "Nothing's wrong with the job. It's a great opportunity, wonderful benefits—Quinnell's a disgustingly wealthy man, so the pay is obscene. And you get room and board with it, holidays, travel allowances . . . it's a marvelous job."

"You're certain of that?"

"Lord, yes. You don't think I'd have lured you up here otherwise, do you?" Again the rapid glance. "Why the sudden lack of trust?"

I shrugged. "Just something your Mr. Fortune said, in passing."

"Oh, yes?"

"He was sure that I'd be offered the job," I explained. "He wasn't so sure I'd accept."

Adrian digested this thoughtfully. We were well out of town, now, and the road was dark. I couldn't see his eyes. "I suppose," he said slowly, "that he might have been thinking of Quinnell himself. Of how you'd react."

"React to what?"

"To Quinnell."

I sighed, tight-lipped. "Adrian . . ."

"Peter Quinnell," he told me, "is a fascinating old character—well-read, intelligent, one of a kind." He turned his head so I could see the half-apologetic smile. "But I'm afraid that he's also quite mad."

II

"I beg your pardon?"

"Darling, you can look positively Victorian at times,"
was Adrian's response. He was grinning. "Those eyes . . .
and anyhow, it isn't what you think. He's not the murderous
sort of madman, nor even the creeping-round-the-back-stairs
sort."

I lowered my eyebrows, cautiously. "What sort is he?"

"You'll be able to judge for yourself, in a minute. That's
Rosehill up ahead."

I looked, but only saw a tiny, low-slung cottage set practically at the road's edge, its windows blazing warmth and
light. "What, *that*?"

"No. That," he said, with a tutor's patience, "is the
groundskeeper's cottage. The drive runs up from there, do
you see? It runs right up the hill to that *big* house, there in
the trees . . ."

"Rosehill," I guessed.

"Correct."

It didn't look like a house at all, to begin with—just a
looming block of darkness screened by darker, twisted trees,
but then the wind blew and the branches shifted and I saw
a twinkling gleam of yellow light. It wasn't as welcoming

as the light coming from the cozy little cottage at the foot of the drive. There'd be a family in that cottage, I thought, as Adrian turned the car in and we swept on past the beaming windows. A young family, perhaps, all cuddled around the telly.

But the light from Rosehill wasn't like that. It spoke to me of work, of intellect, of solitude—a student's candle burning in a lonely garret. It didn't want us there, that light. It wanted privacy.

The strange impression was made stronger by the simple fact that, though the house was huge, a great square fortress of a place, only the one ground-floor window was showing light. I frowned. "It looks as if he's gone to bed."

"At nine o'clock? Not likely. No, I'd be willing to bet that since it's Thursday—the cook's night off—our Fabia's gone out somewhere, to have supper, while the old man makes do with egg and chips in his study."

"Fabia?"

"Quinnell's granddaughter. Quite a fetching young thing. Blonde. At least," he amended, "Quinnell says she's his granddaughter." He saw my face and grinned again, urging the car up the final gasping bit of drive. "Don't worry, darling, the old boy's as harmless as I am."

"Ah."

"And don't go saying 'ah' in that superior little tone." He killed the engine, shifting around to face me. "Really, Verity, your lack of trust in me is quite appalling. Whatever did I do to deserve this?"

It was my turn to smile. "You want a list?"

"Ooh," he inhaled, feigning pain, "a fatal blow. My ego doesn't stand a chance when you're around, does it? Still," he conceded, leaning over to reach across me and unlatch my door, testing the physical power of his close contact with my body, "I am glad we're going to be working together again. We did make a wonderful team." The dashing smile came close to my own mouth, in the near-darkness. Three years ago I might have fallen for it; now I was quite blissfully immune.

"Yes, well," I said, "I haven't got the job yet." I pushed

open my door and the cold night air swirled in around us both, breaking the intimate mood. He laughed and made some comment that I didn't catch because the wind stole it, and then I heard the slam of the driver's door as he came around to join me on the level sweep of ground approaching Rosehill House.

I was grateful that I didn't stumble as I walked toward the great solid shadow looming just ahead. Without the benefit of light, I couldn't see the house in any detail. I had to rely on Adrian to lead me up a sideways flight of stone steps to the front door. At least, I presumed it was the front door, because he knocked on it, and after what seemed an age I heard the bolt slide back and watched the door swing heavily inward. An elegant curse, a sharp click, and the hallway beyond exploded into brilliant light.

It was fitting, I suppose, that in the instant I first saw Peter Quinnell my eyes were dazzled.

I tried desperately to focus in the sudden blinding glare, while spots flashed crazily across my vision and the tall black figure at the door leaned in closer still, and spoke. An English voice—a smooth poetic voice that made me think of West End theaters, of words that floated upwards from a semi-darkened stage and built an image with their melody alone. "What . . . Adrian, my boy," the voice said, in delighted tones. "Do come in. The wind is foul tonight, you'll both be blown away if you're not careful. Please." The figure stepped aside, in invitation. "And dare I hope that this lovely young woman is who I think she is?"

"Verity Grey," confirmed Adrian, as we moved from darkness into light and shut the door upon the violent wind.

Visible at last, my host reached down to take my hand, and smiled. "I am so very glad to meet you, my dear. I'm Peter Quinnell."

My first thought, on the step outside, had been that I'd been misinformed, somehow—that Peter Quinnell wasn't old at all. He fairly towered over me, loose-limbed and lean, not stooping, and the voice and movements were those of a much younger man than the one I'd expected. Only now, standing in the clearer light of the hallway, could I see the weary lines the world had carved into the long, still-handsome face; the whitened hair that might once have been gold; the evidence of age upon the beautifully formed hand clasping mine. His eyes, too, were the eyes of a man who had lived for many years. They were long, like the rest of him, and languid, and the lids drooped as though the effort of holding them open was too much for him.

I wasn't fooled. Behind the languor burned an intellect that could not be disguised, and though his eyes moved slowly, they were sharp. They wouldn't miss much, eyes like that.

I smiled back. "How do you do?"

"I was about to ask you the same question," Quinnell said. "You must be rather tired, if you've come up today from London. We actually weren't expecting you until to-morrow."

I flushed a little. "I know. Sorry. I just . . . well, the truth is, I'm not very good at waiting. I've been packed and ready to come since Monday, and when I woke up this morning it felt like such a good day for traveling . . ." I stopped, aware that I was rambling on. "I thought, you see, that I'd be staying at a B & B, or something . . ."

"What?" His look of horror was quite genuine. "Oh, my dear girl, that would never do. No, no, we have a room all ready for you, and my granddaughter's been fussing over it for days, buying curtains to match the coverlet, and that sort of thing. You'd not want to disappoint her, surely? Besides," he added, "I was rather hoping to hold you captive here until I'd managed to persuade you to join our motley little team." The hooded eyes touched mine, with stunning charm, and he smiled again. "You have your luggage with you?"

"Just one bag. It's in the car."

"Good." Still charming, the smile slid to Adrian. "Fetch it for her, will you? There's a good chap. You can put it in the guest room at the head of the stairs—you know the one? Then come and join us for a drink in the sitting room."

Adrian hadn't planned on staying—I could tell as much from the tiny frown that creased his forehead for the span of a single heartbeat. He had simply meant to deliver me, and make the necessary introductions, and then get back to whatever it was he'd been doing when I'd interrupted him. Chivalry, I thought dryly, was a word that Adrian Sutton-Clarke had never learned to spell. He'd been the same when we were dating, always vanishing from parties when it suited him, and leaving me to find my own way home.

He hesitated, looked at Quinnell, looked at me, and turned away obediently. "Right. Won't be a moment."

When the front door had opened and closed again, Peter Quinnell drew back a pace to study me with interest. I pretended not to notice the appraisal, letting my own eyes wander around the little hallway in which we stood. There was nothing in it, really, save a few pairs of tumbled boots and shoes and a leaning stack of empty flowerpots. I gathered that the proper entrance hall lay somewhere in the dark behind my host, beyond the French doors flanked by matching window panels that reflected my own image back to me. My reflection, thankfully, didn't look the least bit nervous.

Peter Quinnell finished his inspection and tipped his head to one side. "I must say, I am surprised. You don't look anything like I expected."

I smiled. "That's just what Mr. Fortune said. I met him on the bus," I explained, as Quinnell raised an enquiring eyebrow. "I gather everyone thought I'd be tall and blond, and more . . . well, more . . ."

"Quite. Our Mr. Sutton-Clarke does have a certain reputation," he agreed. "And he did say, my dear, that he knew you rather well, so naturally one builds a certain image in one's mind . . ." He smiled, and shrugged.

"Sorry to disappoint."

"Good heavens, I'm not at all disappointed. And no more, I suspect, was David Fortune. You met him on the bus, you say? Out visiting his mother, was he?"

I admitted I had no idea where he'd been. "Is he a local man, then?"

"David? Oh, yes. Eyemouth born and bred, is David. He hasn't lived here for some years, mind, but his mother has a cottage on the coast, north of St. Abbs." He turned away to pull the French doors open, letting the light creep uncertainly into the large front hall beyond. "Please, do come through.

I'll put the light on . . . there.'' A switch clicked somewhere
and a warm lamp glowed as if by magic from atop a Spanish
chest; glowed again within the mirror hung behind it, and in
all the frames of all the prints and sketches grouped around
the great square entrance hall.

In fact, one scarcely saw the wallpaper, there were so
many pictures, and with the weathered Oriental carpet on the
floor the overall effect was one of cultured and eclectic taste.

Ahead I saw the glimmer of a window, and a gaping darkness that might have been a stairway, and the corner of a
passage, but my host didn't force me into a guided tour. Of
the three closed doorways leading off the entrance hall he
chose the nearest on my left. ''The sitting room,'' he told
me, as he fumbled for the wall switch. ''Not the posh one,
I'm afraid—that's over there,'' he nodded across the hall,
''but it isn't very comfortable for sitting. I much prefer this
one.''

When the light snapped on, I saw why. Deep red walls
hugged around on every side, set off by more Oriental carpeting and a leather sofa, creased and weathered from years
of use, on which two cats were curled around each other,
sleeping. A matching armchair sat surrounded in its corner
by bookshelves crammed with volumes old and new, and
more prints and drawings hung haphazardly about the room.
The one large window had been simply hung with panels of
a floral-patterned chintz, worn in spots and faded from the
sun. When the curtains were open, I thought, one would be
able to look out over the drive.

Even as I formed the thought, the front door banged and
Adrian went thumping past with my suitcase. His footsteps
faded up an unseen flight of stairs.

''Please, do sit down.'' Peter Quinnell waited until I had
settled myself on the sofa beside the cats before he folded
his own long frame into the armchair, slinging one loose-
jointed leg over the other and tilting his head backwards to
rest against the leather.

This was his room, I thought—it had the stamp of him,
somehow, in all its corners. Not pristine and tidy, but comfortably masculine, the sort of room that men of old had

taken refuge in when wives began to scurry around the house with purpose. Here papers could be left spread out on chairs without reproach, and one could smoke, or drop a biscuit crumb onto the carpet.

"Don't mind the cats," he told me, "they're quite harmless. Stupid creatures, really, but I'm fond of them. Murphy—that's the big black beast, there—he's been with me seven years now, and his girlfriend Charlie came to us last winter, when we bought this house." A sudden thought struck him, and he frowned. "You're not allergic, are you?"

I assured him I was not.

"Good. I had an aunt once, who was. Most distressing for her. Ah," he said, as Adrian appeared in the doorway, "that's done, is it? I don't suppose, my boy, that you'd be kind enough to fetch us all a drink? I'm afraid I am forgetting my manners, and no doubt Miss Grey is parched."

I caught the faint stiffening of Adrian's shoulders, but again he surprised me by taking the request in his stride. Peter Quinnell's pay, I reflected, must be very good indeed. Adrian hated playing butler. Still, he sent me a winning smile. "Gin and it for you, darling? And Peter, what will you have? Vodka?"

"Please. And perhaps a cheese biscuit or two?" He waited until Adrian had gone again before he slid his long eyes slowly back to me. Once again I was reminded of an actor in the theater, not just because of the artistic setting, the elegant arrangement of man-in-armchair and the rolling, cultured voice, but because I had the strong impression more was going on behind those eyes than I was meant to think. "Adrian," he said, "did mention, I believe, that you and he were once an item."

Adrian, I thought, deserved a swift kick, sometimes. I forced a smile. "Yes, of sorts."

"But not now?"

"No."

"I thought not. Friends, though?"

"Yes, great friends."

He paused, and narrowed his eyes as though trying to remember something. "You met in Suffolk, did you not? On one of Lazenby's digs?"

"Yes. Though I'm afraid I didn't spend much time at the dig, myself. I'd just started working for Dr. Lazenby, then, at the British Museum, and I was rather green when it came to fieldwork."

"Suffolk," he said again, thinking harder. "That was the Roman fort?"

"It was. They built a bypass over it."

"Ah." The great black tomcat stretched and shifted, looked about, and arched to its feet, yawning. With a placid look in my direction it stepped neatly to the carpet and marched a little stiffly toward Peter Quinnell's corner. Quinnell moved his hand aside so the cat could jump onto his lap, but he didn't take his quiet gaze from my face.

"How much have you been told," he asked, "about the job?"

I answered honestly. "Not much."

"And about myself?"

"A little less."

The shrewd eyes smiled. "You needn't spare my feelings, my dear. Surely someone will have mentioned that I'm mad?"

What did one say to that, I wondered? Luckily, he didn't appear to expect an answer, for he went on stroking the black cat and speaking pleasantly.

"It was your work with Lazenby, you see, that caught my attention in the first place. He only trains the best. Adrian says you did most of the cataloguing yourself, for the Suffolk dig—and the drawings. Is that right? Impressive," he said, when I nodded. "Very impressive. I'd be thrilled if you could do the same for us, here at Rosehill. Of course, we won't have quite the range of artifacts that Lazenby turned up—the Romans weren't here that long—but we're bound to find a few good pieces in among the everyday, and a battlefield does have an interest all its own, don't you agree?"

I didn't answer straight away. I was too busy trying to sort out my whirling thoughts. A battlefield? A . . . good God, not a *Roman* battlefield? Right here in Eyemouth? It seemed incredible, and yet . . . my stomach flipped excitedly. I took a breath. "I hope you don't mind my asking," I began, "but what exactly is your team excavating?"

The hand upon the black cat stilled, surprised. "I am so sorry," Peter Quinnell said. "I thought you knew. It's a marching camp, my dear. A Roman marching camp. Early second-century. Though in actual fact I suppose it's more of a burial ground, really." His eyes captured mine, intense, and for the first time I believed, truly believed, that he might indeed be mad. "We've found the final resting place of *Legio IX Hispana.*"

III

If he'd told me they had found the Holy Grail, I couldn't have been more astonished. The Ninth Legion—the *Hispana*—here! It hardly seemed credible. Not when so many people had searched for so long, and in vain. I myself had come to believe that the fate of the lost legion would remain one of the great unsolved mysteries of our time.

Historians the world over had hotly debated dozens of theories, but the facts themselves were few. All anyone could say for certain was that, some time in the reign of the Emperor Hadrian, *Legio IX Hispana* had been ordered north from its fortress at York.

The soldiers of the Ninth, already veterans of the long campaigns in Wales and the brutal war with Boudicca, were crack troops, rarely called upon to deal with minor skirmishes—the task of day to day front-line defense was left to the auxiliaries. It took a true emergency to set a legion on the march.

And when several thousand men marched out to do battle, the spectacle would have been stunning. At dawn would come the auxiliary units of archers and cavalry, forming an all-seeing shield for the legion behind. Then the standard-bearer, holding high the sacred golden Eagle of the Empire,

symbol of honor and victory. If an enemy touched the eagle
he disgraced the legion; if a legion lost the eagle it disgraced
Rome. Close around the eagle marched the other standard-
bearers, followed by the trumpeters, and then, in ordered
ranks, six men abreast, came the legionaries, ripe for war.

They'd been trained to march twenty-four Roman miles in
five hours, fully armored, weighted with weapons and tools
and heavy packs, and then at the end of the day's march to
build the night's camp—no small task, since a camp needed
trenches and ramparts and palisades to protect the leather
tents inside.

These were hard men, hard fighting men, and a legion on
the march with all its baggage train and brilliant armor would
have been a sight that one remembered.

Which made the disappearance of the Ninth Legion all the
more puzzling, I thought. Because nobody *had* remembered.
At least, no one had bothered to keep a record of what became of the Ninth in its northern battle, and the legion itself
had been struck from the military lists. Modern historians
offered several explanations—the men of the *Hispana* might
have mutinied, or disgraced themselves by losing the eagle
in battle . . . or else, in that barbaric wilderness, they'd met
an end so terrible that the survivors could not bear to speak
of it.

Those few survivors—a pitiable scattering of them, identified by stray tombstones crumbling at the farthest corners
of the fallen Empire—had kept their secret well. So well, in
fact, that nearly two thousand years later, the full fate of
Legio IX Hispana—all those thousands of men—continued
to elude historians like a ghost in the mist of a barren moor.

I looked at Peter Quinnell, cleared my throat. "The *Hispana*? Are you sure?"

"Oh, yes. Quite sure. Adrian can show you the results of
his initial survey, can't you, my boy?"

"What?" Adrian, just coming through the door with our
drinks, glanced around in mild enquiry.

"Your radar survey," Quinnell elaborated, "down in the
southwest corner."

"Ah." His eyes came to rest on my face, trying to gauge my reaction. "You've told her, then."

"Well, naturally. Quite unforgivable, your keeping her in the dark like that. I was just telling her that you could show her what you'd found."

"Certainly," said Adrian. "It's all on computer. I'll show you tomorrow," he promised, pressing a glass into my waiting hand.

He must have known I'd hear about the *Hispana* while he was out of the room—he'd made my drink a double. Relaxing back into the sofa, I took a long sip of cool gin and vermouth and looked across at Peter Quinnell. "You have a lab set up, then, here on site?"

"Oh, yes. I've converted the old stables, behind the house. Plenty of room up there."

"You'll die, you know," Adrian warned me. "Not one but two microscopes, *and* computers—I've never seen anything like it, on a field excavation."

Quinnell's eyes slid sideways to Adrian, and again I caught the canny glint behind the old man's indulgent gaze. He knew, I thought, exactly what made Adrian tick—the clink of coins, the smell of money, the promise of a comfortable position. "Yes, well," he said, in a mild voice, "I do like my little gadgets, you know. Sit down, my boy, for heaven's sake—you're making my neck stiff. And mind the cat," he added, as Adrian narrowly missed sitting on the still-sleeping tabby. I shifted over, making space on the sofa.

"You realize, of course," Adrian informed me, "that we'll have to shoot you, now, if you don't join our little digging team. Can't risk having our secret leak out."

They had kept the secret remarkably well, I thought, and told them so. "I haven't heard so much as a whisper of it, in London, and I don't remember reading anything in any of the journals."

"The journals, my dear, are singularly uninterested in where I choose to dig." Peter Quinnell stroked the black cat's ears, smiling. "Forty years ago they thought my theories fascinating, but now most of my colleagues couldn't care less. The ones who shared my faith are dead, and the younger set are slaves of modern science, I'm afraid. No place for instinct, in their books. No place for hunches." His lazy eyes forgave my youthful ignorance as he lifted his glass of vodka. "These days, I'm considered a rather less successful Schliemann, chasing after fairy tales. Except where Schliemann had his Homer, I have nothing." He paused and drank, letting his chin droop thoughtfully down to his chest. "No, that's not exactly true," he said, at length. "I do have Robbie."

Adrian shot me a watchful glance, and leaned back against the cushions of the sofa, nearly crushing the sleeping cat. Indignantly, the little gray tabby stood and stretched and marched straight over Adrian onto my knees, where she settled herself with an irritable thump.

Adrian glanced pointedly from my face to the cat, and back again. "I don't know which of the two of you looks the more exhausted," he commented. I had the oddest impression that he was making a calculated maneuver, and a moment later, when Quinnell looked over and said, "Oh, quite," in tones of vague concern, I knew my suspicions were right. Adrian, in his smooth and wholly manipulative way, was trying to bring the evening to a close.

No doubt he'd had something more exciting planned for his own Thursday night, and since Quinnell seemed fully capable of chatting on for hours yet, Adrian had boldly decided to move things along.

I sent him a guileless smile. "I'm not the least bit tired."

Undaunted, he tried another tack. "You want to be sharp for your interview tomorrow, don't you?"

Quinnell appeared shocked by the idea. "My dear boy," he cut in, eyebrows raised, "there isn't going to be an interview. Good heavens, no. No," he said again, with emphasis, as I raised my startled gaze to his, "the job is yours, if you'll have it. But I expect you'd like to take a day or so to look around, to think it over. You can give me your answer this weekend, all right?"

The job was mine, I thought. A legendary battlefield and steady pay besides. I already knew what my answer would be, but I tried to keep my reaction professional. "All right," I said, and nodded.

"Good. And now, though you've been terribly polite to sit here listening to me, I'm sure you really are quite tired from your travels. I'll show you to your room."

"I'll take her up," Adrian offered.

"You most certainly will not." Quinnell's voice was firm. "I'd be a thoughtless cad to deliver any woman into your clutches, even one familiar with your Casanova ways. No, you may say goodnight to her, and *I* will take her upstairs, when she's ready."

Adrian was still smiling several minutes later, as he shrugged his coat on in the vestibule and bent to brush my cheek with a chaste kiss. "So," he murmured, with a quick glance over my shoulder to where Quinnell stood waiting in the entrance hall, "what do you think?"

"I think he's rather marvelous."

"I'm glad. Verity . . ."

"Yes?"

"Nothing." He tossed his dark head back and fastened the final snap of his coat. "Never mind. I'll see you in the morning, then."

I watched him go, then turned and followed Peter Quinnell through the hall and up a winding stone stairway to the first floor. My footsteps dragged a little on the hard steps, and I realized that I actually *was* tired. By the time Quinnell had shown me where the bathroom was and introduced me to the plumbing, I was stifling yawns. And although his grand-daughter had no doubt taken great pains to match my curtains to my coverlet, I'm afraid that when the door to my spacious back bedroom swung open, I only saw the plump twin beds.

Quinnell fussed around for a few minutes longer, dem-onstrating drawers and cupboard doors and making certain I had everything I needed for the night, and then with a final weary smile he gallantly withdrew and left me on my own.

Well, not entirely on my own.

One of the cats had come upstairs with us, and when I'd finished in the bathroom I returned to find it perched upon my window ledge, long tail twitching as it stared transfixed

at the ink-black pane of glass. It was the tomcat, the big
black one, and not the dainty gray tabby that had slept on
my lap earlier. The gray one was Charlie, I remembered,
and . . . oh, *what* was the black one called? The name was
vaguely Irish, I thought. Mickey? Mooney? "Murphy," I
pronounced, with satisfaction, and the cat flicked an ear in
response.

"You like that window, do you, Murphy? What is it you
see?"

I myself could only see my own reflection, and the cat's,
until I switched the lamp off. Even then, the view looked
ordinary enough. Close by, a large tree shuddered with the
wind, above a sea of ghostly daffodils that dipped and danced
in waves. And beyond that, the fickle moonlight caught a
sweep of field that slanted gently up to meet a darkly cresting
ridge. "You see?" I said. "There's nothing . . ."

The cat's hair bristled suddenly as it arched itself upon the
window ledge, eyes flaming as its lips curled sharply back,
fangs baring in a vicious hiss.

I know I jumped. And though the hiss had not been aimed
at me, I felt my gooseflesh rising in response and fought to
calm the jerky rhythm of my heart. "Murphy," I said sternly,
"stop that."

He swiveled his head to stare at me, eyes glowing, then
turned away again to watch the night. The second hiss came
fiercer than the first, and rattled me so badly that I snapped
the window blind down and nudged the black cat from the
ledge with a less than steady hand.

Murphy settled benignly at the foot of my bed and blinked
without expression. Stupid animal, I thought. There had been
nothing out there, nothing at all. Only the tree and the daffodils, and the dark, deserted field.

Nevertheless, I was glad of the tomcat's company when I
crawled beneath my blankets, having chosen the twin bed
further from the window. And for the first time since my
nursery days, I didn't reach to turn off the bedside lamp.

"Do you always sleep with your light on?" Fabia Quinnell
asked me next morning, at breakfast. Waiting for me to finish

my toast and coffee, she leaned an elbow on the kitchen counter and nibbled a dried apricot.

I hadn't yet made up my mind about Fabia. She was of an age with my sister Alison, not quite twenty, but where Alison was sensible and unaffected, Fabia Quinnell wore the deliberately bored look of an adolescent, and called her grandfather "Peter."

She was, as Adrian had said, a fetching young woman— quite stunning, in fact. And decidedly blond. Her pale hair, baby-fine, swung against her soft jaw at an artful angle, leaving the nape of her fragile neck bare. Small-boned and doe-eyed, she looked nothing like her grandfather. Nor did she appear to share his hospitable nature. The greeting she had given me was anything but warm.

I rather doubted she'd done anything to decorate my bedroom, despite what Quinnell had told me last night. More likely the old man himself had selected the curtains and coverlet, made things look comfortable. Fabia, I suspected, wasn't the sort of young woman to concern herself with someone else's comfort.

It surprised me that she'd even noticed my bedroom light, last night.

In answer to her question I replied, through a mouthful of cold toast, that I normally slept in the dark, like everyone else. "I just have a foolish imagination, sometimes—things that go bump in the night. Especially in strange houses. So I find it helps to leave the light on."

"Well, you gave me quite a turn, last night," she said. "I thought it might be Peter, waiting up for me. He drinks, you know, and then he wants to talk." She rolled her eyes with feeling. "A typical Irishman."

I wouldn't have guessed Peter Quinnell was Irish. He had, after all, that beautifully elegant voice, with no trace of a brogue whatsoever—but now that I'd had the fact pointed out to me I could recognize that indefinable quality, the faint hint of horses and hounds, that marked a certain segment of the Anglo-Irish gentry.

Taking another sip of coffee, I turned in my chair so I could see out the narrow kitchen window. From the treeless

ridge behind the house a lush green field sloped gently downwards, bounded at its bottom edge by the thick tangle of
thorn and briar that hid the road from view. Two men were
standing in the center of the field, eyes fixed upon the ridge.
One of the men was Peter Quinnell. The other was larger,
broader about the shoulders, with curling jet-black hair.

"They've started early," I commented.

"Who?" Her uninterested gray eyes flicked toward the
window. "Oh, Peter and Davy, yes. They're always puttering
around."

"What does David Fortune do, exactly?"

"He's an archaeologist, the same as Peter. Lectures at the
University of Edinburgh."

"But surely . . ." I frowned. "I mean, wouldn't your
grandfather prefer to manage the excavation on his own?"

"I doubt it," she said, flatly. "And anyway, he needs
Davy. Or rather, he needs Davy's name on his publications,
to make the dig legitimate. Peter's name simply doesn't impress people, these days," she explained, her tone offhand.
"Most people think he's past it." Pushing herself away from
the counter, she nodded at my empty plate. "Are you finished with that? Good. Come on, then—I've been ordered
to give you the grand tour."

Shrugging on my crumpled anorak, I followed Fabia outside. The morning was crisp for late April, clear and sunny,
with a brisk breeze blowing from the southwest.

I turned my back to the breeze for a moment, and took a
good long look at Rosehill, pleased to find it looked less
ominous by daylight. Pinkish-grey plaster that in places
didn't cover all the rose-colored brick made the plain house
seem prettier. A graceful flight of steps curved up sideways
to meet the front door, trailing a delicate handrail that softened the sterner angles, and the narrow white-painted window frames held an abundance of little square panes that
reflected the sunlight like glittering faceted gems.

"Why is it called Rosehill?" I asked.

Fabia Quinnell shrugged. "You'll have to ask Peter about
that, he has his own theories. There aren't any roses, to speak
of. Plenty of daffodils, though." She pointed behind me, at

the little hill that edged the drive. It was yellow with daffodils, hundreds of them, all nodding their heads in agreement. Like the daffodils that grew beneath my bedroom
window, these gently blew beneath a spreading horse chestnut whose tender folded leaves were freshly green.

Fabia idly plucked a leaf as we passed, and smoothed it
between her fingers, turning her head to look beyond the
house to a corner of the sunlit field just coming into view.

"*Did* anything go bump in the night?" she asked me,
slowly. "Last night?"

I glanced at her. "Only the cats. Why?"

"Just curious." She pulled her gaze from the field with
another shrug and let the flattened leaf fall from her fingers.
"This way," she said, and started up the hill toward the
stables.

IV

The dark wooden stables crouched long and low on the ridge above the house. From their wide arched entrance one commanded a view that stretched forever, across the roofs of Rosehill and the little cottage by the gate, across the rolling fields and the narrow road and the river that wound through a purple mist of trees, all the way to Eyemouth's distant chimneys and the icy blue North Sea.

"No horses, anymore," said Fabia beside me, gloomily.

Pulling my eyes from that marvelous view, I followed her over the threshold. There hadn't been horses for quite some time, I thought. The smell of them was gone.

Still, I forgave Quinnell for their absence the instant my eyes adjusted to the indoor lighting. "My God," I said, and meant it.

He had worked wonders here.

I was used to doing fieldwork in makeshift labs set up in tents, hauling water back and forth to wash the artifacts and battling my colleagues for table space. Now, as I looked around, I was made stunningly aware of just what sort of money was involved in the Rosehill dig. The cleaning of the place alone must have cost a minor fortune.

To my left, the double row of wooden stalls had been

stripped and refinished, their clay floors carefully levelled and swept pristinely bare. One stall, ringed around with free-standing metal shelves, held the microscopes Adrian had raved about—not just the ordinary sort, but a dissecting microscope as well, complete with its camera attachment. Another stall housed packing materials—boxes of all shapes and sizes, self-sealing plastic bags and bubble pack and even silica gel for packing metal. I was suitably impressed.

"It's all right," Fabia conceded with a shrug. "Mind you, we've had no end of trouble with those computers. The programs keep crashing. And the—"

"Good God." I interrupted her, my head poked around a half-open door leading off the wide stone passageway. "You have running water!"

"Hot and cold." Fabia nodded. "That used to be the tack room, so there was already a sink in there, but Peter had to have a larger one, of course."

My admiration for Peter Quinnell grew stronger still. There would be no messing with hosepipes on his excavation, I thought. No tedious lugging of buckets and tubs. And while the hot water bordered on frivolous, the rest of the room was perfectly functional—the ideal place for washing and sorting artifacts. Quinnell had stocked it with dozens of screens, to dry things on, and brushes of every size and shape, right down to the tiniest toothbrush. Long tables had been set up along the end wall, and beneath them waited stacks of trays and shallow sorting boxes.

"The finds room," Fabia identified it, looking round. "Not that we're likely to find much. I'd have had this for my darkroom only Peter thought it better if I had the cellar at the house. More space, he said, and not so dusty."

I felt a spark of interest. "Your darkroom? Are you the site photographer, then?"

"Peter had to find some use for me, didn't he?" Turning, she led me toward the dark end of the stable building, away from the refinished stalls. "And this is the common room," she told me, flipping up a switch to flood the space with light.

I stared. "The common room?"

"For the students."

All the stalls here had been removed, and the walls painted bright creamy white above green pub-style carpeting. In one corner, a large television and video faced two angled sofas. A narrow bookcase held an assortment of paperbacks, board games, and jigsaw puzzles, and the wall beside sported a professional-looking dartboard. And at the center of the room a massive snooker table rested, rather smugly, as though it judged itself the most important furnishing.

Fabia folded her arms. "Showers and toilets are out back."

"Showers?" I echoed, incredulous.

"Oh yes. Nothing's too good for the students, you know." Her mouth quirked. "Not that we *have* any students working here. Peter's little fantasy, that. He thinks he can convince the university to support his excavation."

Her tone implied that he might as well tilt at a windmill. I looked at her, curious. "But you said David Fortune's from the university."

"Well, yes. But Davy's known Peter for years; he's hardly impartial. Having him associated with our dig might make us more respectable, but it still doesn't solve Peter's problem. To hire students for the summer," she explained, "he needs the approval of the head of the department. And I'm told the head and Peter have a history."

"Oh, I see. Still, it's not such an obstacle, surely? If your grandfather's very determined, he could always hire regular workers to help with the dig. They don't have to come from the university."

"Ah, but that," she said, in a patronizing tone, "would mean he wouldn't get the recognition he deserved. It's his golden scenario, getting those students."

She'd lost interest in the common room.

"Your office," she said, "is down here, with the others."

I followed her back toward the renovated stalls at the other end of the stables, past the finds room, past the shelves and microscopes and packing boxes, to the last stall but one. It put me in mind of a monk's cell, clean and efficiently organized down to the tiniest detail.

The gray filing cabinet and metal-topped desk were gleam-ingly new, as was the state-of-the-art computer in the corner, and the orthopedic office chair, upholstered in soft green fab-ric that cleverly matched the desk accessories and litter bas-ket. A calendar above the desk displayed a glossy yellow field of April daffodils.

"It's lovely." I delivered my verdict honestly. "Really lovely. All of it."

"You're right across from Adrian," she pointed out. "And Davy's office is in the corner, there, but he's only here a few days a week."

David Fortune's office looked abandoned, actually, and gave no clue as to the personality of the man who worked there. Adrian's workspace, on the other hand, was easy to identify. He was not the most tidy of men.

I shifted a coffee-stained cup from a stack of his papers, and peered with interest at the computer-generated image that topped the pile. It looked like something a child might pro-duce by rubbing a stick of charcoal over a bumpy block of granite, only I knew it was nothing so amateurish. It was, in fact, a plotted section of a ground-penetrating radar survey.

Adrian had already been here a few weeks, I knew. He'd have completed his initial topographic survey of the site, us-ing the measurements to create a detailed contour map of the field where Quinnell wanted to dig. But digging, by its na-ture, was destructive, and archaeologists didn't do it blindly. There were other ways to see beneath the ground.

Geophysical surveying, Adrian's speciality, relied on highly sensitive instruments to measure minuscule changes in the underlying soil. A resistivity survey passed a current through the ground to measure its resistance—walls and roads, much drier than the earth around them, showed up clearly. Where the soil was not well drained, as I suspected might be the case here at Rosehill, Adrian usually opted for a magnetic survey.

But ground-penetrating radar was his favorite. It often proved prohibitively expensive, but then Adrian loved spend-ing other people's money. And he loved the high technology, the physical precision. I'd seen him spend days in a field, on his own, dragging the little wheeled radar device behind him like a child dragging a wagon, moving back and forth across the same bit of ground with a thoroughness that would bore most men rigid.

The results were usually worth the effort. His readings could reveal fascinating things beneath the most uncooperative of surfaces. And when the results were plotted on a computer, they produced a stratified landscape of black, gray, and white, like the one I was looking at now.

Incomplete, the image showed a definite anomaly, a sharp dip spearing down through the black and gray bands. It certainly might be a ditch, I conceded. And those smaller blips off to the right could be buried features, as well. I picked the paper up and brought it closer for a better look. Funny, I thought, how these things all started to look alike, after a while. This one put me in mind of an image I'd seen only last year ... they were very similar ... very ... and then I saw the tiny black smudge of a fingerprint to one side of the "ditch," and I frowned.

Not merely similar, I corrected myself—exactly the same. I'd made that smudge myself; I could remember Adrian ticking me off for doing it. This wasn't an original printout at all. It was a photocopy, with printing on the top edge changed to read: ROSEHILL, EYEMOUTH, BERWICKSHIRE.

"What the devil is Adrian playing at?" I asked, still frowning. I turned to Fabia. "Do you know anything about this?"

Her eyes slipped warily away from mine, to the paper in my hand. "Yes, we think that may be some sort of ditch in the southwest corner. Adrian found it last week."

David Fortune's voice surprised us both.

"It's no use, lass," he advised Fabia. "She was in Wales last year as well, with Sutton-Clarke. She'll not be so easily fooled."

We both turned around to see him standing square in the passageway, just inside the arched stable door, his arms folded complacently across his broad chest.

Fabia Quinnell shot him an angry look, then turned to me, defensive. "It's not ... I mean, we didn't ..."

"I'll do the explaining, if you don't mind," the archae-ologist cut her off. "Why don't you go and keep your grand-father company? He's back at the house, somewhere."

Defeated by the determined tone of his voice, she brushed past him, head high. David Fortune ignored the petulant toss of her fair hair. His eyes held firmly to my face.

I looked down, feeling robbed. "I gather this is why you said I might not answer yes, when Quinnell offered. There is no Roman marching camp at Rosehill, is there?"

"I didn't say that."

"But this," I challenged him, holding up the incriminating image, "is a fake."

"Aye."

The fact that he didn't seem at all put out disappointed me, and I held the paper higher still, accusingly. "Your idea?"

"Fabia's, I think." He smiled, faintly. "Adrian shouldered the blame when I caught him, but it's not the sort of thing he'd do on his own. And he has a hard time saying 'no' to Fabia."

I sighed, and dropped the paper to the desk. "You knew about this," I said, slowly, "and yet you didn't tell Quin-nell?"

"I didn't see the point. He'd already seen the image, by the time I learned what Adrian had done. I wasn't pleased about it, ken, but since it didn't do much harm . . ."

"Didn't do much harm?" I echoed, disbelieving. "How can you say that? Quinnell's digging for something he's not going to find."

"You don't understand." He shook his head, and with a tight-lipped sigh he looked away. "You don't know Peter Quinnell. He'd dig anyway."

"Why?"

"Because of Robbie."

It wasn't the first time I'd heard that name. Quinnell him-self had mentioned it, last night, and I struggled to recall the context. Something about Schliemann having Homer to guide him to the ruins of Troy, while Quinnell had only . . .

"Robbie," I repeated, shaking my head slowly as I tried

to comprehend. "But who is Robbie? And what does he have to do with this?"

David Fortune took a long time answering. He seemed to be weighing something in his mind. "Best come and see for yourself," he said, finally, and with that invitation he turned and went out.

I was plainly expected to follow, though it was all I could do to keep up with his long, rolling strides. As we passed the big house, moving onto the drive, I mustered enough breath to speak. "Where are we going?"

"Rose Cottage," he replied. "You'd have passed it last night, by the road."

Even in daylight, the cottage looked warm and welcoming, built long and low of some blood-colored stone. The path leading around from the drive to the back door was lovingly trimmed and kept clear. Daffodils grew here, as well—an explosion of yellow in the deeper green of grass, and David Fortune took care not to trample them as he stooped to knock at the white-painted door.

The woman who answered the summons was young, my own age, with short chestnut hair and a fresh cheerful face warmed by freckles. Her large brown eyes widened in mild surprise at the sight of us.

"Davy!" she said, in an accent as rich as his own. "Is something wrong? Is Peter . . ."

"Nothing's wrong. Is Robbie about?"

"Aye." She pushed the door wider, her gaze sliding past him to me, and the surprise melted to a quieter interest. "It's Miss Grey, isn't it?" she greeted me, extending a firmly capable hand. "I heard you'd arrived. I'm Jeannie. Jeannie McMorran. I keep house for Peter." Before I could respond, she took a quick step backwards, shaking her head. "Och, I'm forgetting my manners. Come inside, the both of you."

David Fortune ducked his head to squeeze through the narrow doorway. The kitchen was narrow, too, and long, and though the sunlight couldn't quite break through the small, old-fashioned windows, the lace curtains—so white it almost hurt the eyes to look at them—and gaily patterned china plates propped up along the old oak dresser, made the room homely and bright.

David Fortune looked around, and sniffed the fragrant air. "Been baking, have you?"

"Apple tart for Brian's tea."

The big man's eyes flicked briefly to the closed door at the far end of the room. "He's back, then, is he?"

"Aye. He came in late last night. No need to be quiet, though," she added. "He'll be sleeping it off for a few hours yet."

Jeannie led us past the closed door and along a tiny passageway toward the front of the cottage. "Robbie'll be fair glad to see you. He's off school today with the smit." Then, suddenly remembering I wasn't Scottish, she rolled her eyes, smiled, and translated: "He has a cold. Nothing serious, ken, but I'll not send a son of mine to school when he's ill."

Her words had only just sunk in when, after a confident knock and reply, I was ushered through a second low doorway and into the presence of Peter Quinnell's Homer.

My first thought was that I'd been brought to the wrong room. The face that looked up from the bed in the corner was a child's face, around and questioning, sprayed with freckles and topped by a shock of unruly black hair.

Robbie McMorran could not have been older than eight.

"Heyah," David greeted the boy, glancing around as though something were missing. "Where's Kip?"

"Out with Grandad."

"Oh, aye?" The blue eyes swung to Jeannie McMorran. "Where's Wally away to this morning?"

"He didn't say." She seemed unconcerned. "Brian comes in, and Dad goes out—you ken how it is. It's only my wee sodger, here, who gives me a moment's peace." She laid one cooling hand on the boy's forehead, then rumpled his hair with a smile. "He's not dead yet," she pronounced. "I'm sure he'll survive a short visit. But just a short one, now. And no Nintendo." Fixing David Fortune with a stern look, she left us to return to her kitchen and the fragrant apple tart bubbling in the oven.

"No Nintendo!" The Scotsman pulled a face of mock

dismay, which he shared with the bedridden boy. "How's a lad meant to get well?"

Robbie McMorran giggled. "It's not so bad. The electricity's going off, anyway, sometime soon."

"Is it, now? Did you tell Mr. Quinnell?"

"Aye. Mum rang him up, just afore you came." The frank around eyes looked up at me, eagerly. "Is this Miss Grey?"

"It is. Verity Grey," he introduced me, "I'd like you to meet Robert Roy McMorran."

For such a little, gangly thing, he had a solemn handshake. "She doesn't look at all like what you said," he told the archaeologist, accusingly.

David Fortune chose to let the comment pass. He hiked a straight-backed chair closer to the bed, inviting me to sit down, and settled himself on the edge of young Robbie's bed. "I think Miss Grey would like to know what part you played in bringing Mr. Quinnell here, to Rosehill."

"Wasn't me," the boy replied. "It was Granny Nan. She wrote to Mr. Quinnell, like."

"Aye. She wrote to him, to tell him what?"

"About me seeing the Sentinel."

I interrupted, with a faint frown. "The Sentinel?"

"Aye." Robbie nodded. "On the hill. Kip found him, first. And then Granny Nan showed me this book with pictures in it . . ."

"Granny Nan being my mother," interjected David, for my benefit. "She's Granny Nan to everyone, around here."

". . . she showed me this book, and it had a picture of *him* in it, and she got all excited and wrote to Mr. Quinnell. She let me keep the picture." Rolling onto his stomach, Robbie stretched to reach the lower shelf of his bedside table, and I heard the rustle of paper. He rolled back, clasping a colorful sheet with ragged edges. "I ken you're not supposed to tear a book, but Granny Nan said most of the pages were missing anyway, and the rest were all runkled like this, so it was OK." He pressed the crumpled page into my hands.

Bending my head, I smoothed the torn picture with careful fingers. "And this is the man you saw, then, is it? Here at Rosehill?"

"Aye. His name's right there, and all. He walks up on the hill, just there." The boy pointed at the rear wall of the bedroom, in the direction of Rosehill House.

"I see."

Schliemann had his Homer, I thought, and now at last I understood what Quinnell meant when he said he had Robbie. Understood, too, why David Fortune had told me that Quinnell would dig here anyway, no matter what the surveys showed. If I were a less doubting person, I might dig, too.

My fingers flattened the wrinkled image once again, more slowly, as I read the printed caption:

"The Sentinel At His Post"—A *Roman Legionary; Early Second Century*, AD.

V

Adrian snapped a bit of thorn from the low hedge at the roadside and twirled it absently around in his fingers. "The man *is* six sandwiches short of a picnic, darling. Surely you noticed."

"Oh, so that's all right then, is it? Lying to someone because he's deluded?"

"Lying," said Adrian, "is a relative term." The thorn drew blood and he threw it away, then tucked himself behind me as a car went whistling past us. "Look, just stop walking, will you? We're far enough from the house, no one will hear."

I stopped, at a shaded place where the road bridged a shallow stream before beginning its curving downwards slope. Here, instead of hedge and fencing, low stone walls edged the road to keep the unwary from toppling into the briskly moving water below. On either side the trees rose tall and thin and ghostly pale, their naked branches faintly smudged with fuzzy green. They grew at all angles, like straws set into shifting sand, forming a screen that blocked our view of Rosehill House.

Adrian turned to settle himself against the stone barricade. "It wasn't even my idea, to begin with," he defended him-

self. "It was Fabia's. She thought it might be nice to give
the old boy some encouragement."

I sent him an icy look, unsympathetic. "Can you even
spell the word 'ethics'?"

"I don't know why you're so angry about it."

"I'm not angry. I'm bloody furious. You're supposed to
be a professional, for God's sake. Professionals don't fake
their data."

"They might if they worked for Quinnell. Saves effort,
really, because he'll dig the field up anyway, no matter what
the tests show. Quinnell doesn't need me, or my surveys, to
tell him where to dig. He'll use his little psychic friend for
that."

"I don't believe this." I rubbed my forehead with a heavy
hand. "I really don't believe you dragged me all the way up
here from London, for nothing. Of all the rotten—"

"Who says it was for nothing?"

I glanced up, irritated. "Oh, come on, Adrian! Roman soldiers walking on the hills?"

"I'll admit it's a bit weird to dig a field up just because
some kid watched *Ben-Hur* one time too many, but—"

"Did anyone take aerial photographs?"

"Yes."

"And did you see a marching camp?"

"No, but that field is in permanent pasture, and you know
as well as I do that pasture hides quite a lot. It can take years
of photographing—different seasons, different times of day—
and even then you might not see a thing. Doesn't mean that
nothing's there."

"Look me in the eye," I challenged him, "and tell me
you honestly believe there's a Roman camp at Rosehill."

In a way, it was a trick question. I knew Adrian well
enough to know that if he looked me in the eye at all, he
was lying.

Instead he surprised me by looking away, squinting
thoughtfully into the shadowy tangle of leaning, leafless
trees. "I believe," he said, "that Quinnell believes it. And
for the amount he's paying me, I'm prepared to play along."

"Of course, I should have known. It all comes down to

money, doesn't it?'' I studied him. ''Do you know, I'm almost tempted to take the job, if only to protect Peter Quinnell
from the lot of you.''

Adrian smiled at my disapproving expression. ''Is that
why poor old Fortune wasted no time disappearing, when I
met you in the drive? Did you tear a strip off him, as well?''

''I don't know the man well enough to tear a strip off him.
But he's well aware of what I think.'' He hadn't kept me
long at Rose Cottage, not after I'd seen the picture of the
Roman legionary. Jeannie McMorran had offered us tea and
biscuits, but he'd merely flashed his handsome smile and
made some excuse about work to be done and guided me
out of the warm little house, out into the crisp morning air
that smelled cleanly of fresh earth and flowers and sunshine.

He had known, of course, that I'd be disappointed. Known
it all along, and still he'd taken me to meet Robbie, had let
me hear the whole fantastic tale. And as we'd trudged back
up the curving drive, he'd offered no apology. ''So now you
ken as much as I do,'' he'd told me, and his eyes had held
an understanding. ''It's your choice, to stay or to go, but I
will tell you one thing: Quinnell's set his heart on your staying.''

He'd said that last bit almost . . . well, almost as if it went
against his better judgment, and I'd had the curious impression that David Fortune would be happier if I *didn't* stay.
But before I'd fully registered the thought, a sleek red sports
car had roared up the drive—Adrian's car—and with a final,
unreadable glance, the big dark Scotsman had turned to
climb the final hundred yards or so to the low-slung stables
on the ridge, where that perfectly appointed office waited
patiently for my answer.

''Damn, damn, *damn*.'' I spoke the words aloud now with
a vehemence that brought Adrian's head around. ''It's all
your fault,'' I told him, and because he deserved it I shoved
his arm, for emphasis.

He bounced back like a punching-ball, unperturbed.
''What is?''

''I like him.''

''Who, Fortune?'' The idea seemed to shock him.

"Quinnell. I like him, Adrian, and I don't want to see him disappointed."

"So take the job, then, like a good girl."

"Yes, but don't you see? If I do that, if I just go along with his fantasy like the rest of you are doing, then I'll have to actually stand by and watch him digging trenches, finding nothing. I don't know which is worse."

Adrian shrugged. "One of them pays better."

"Oh, damn the pay," I started to say, but my words were drowned by an urgent squeal of tires on the road, followed by the unmistakable thud and crunch of metal slamming into metal and the sound of splintered glass. In the second of silence that trailed the crash, something began to crack and tear like a tree branch ripped free in a storm, and a softer thud echoed the first.

"That sounded bloody close," said Adrian.

His reflexes were better than mine. By the time I caught up with him, he'd reached the scene of the accident and was wading into the thick of things, playing referee between a red-faced man with wild eyes, and a smaller chap with spectacles who clutched a road map to his chest, staring dismayed at the wreckage of his car. I had difficulty making sense of the colorful language spewing from the larger man, but I gathered the driver with the map had stopped suddenly on the road to get his bearings, with predictable results.

Quinnell came hurrying down the long drive, his expression concerned, and a moment later Fabia came, too, to stand by the road and watch. Jeannie McMorran appeared briefly in the doorway of Rose Cottage, took one look, and withdrew with a practical, purposeful air. She's gone to ring the police, I thought, and a few minutes later the wail of a siren proved me right. I moved well back, out of the way, against the cottage wall.

The curtains twitched in a nearby window, and I caught a glimpse of Robbie's small pale face. A road accident, I thought, must surely be a spot of unexpected brightness in a sick child's boring day. And the boy was, at any rate, getting a lesson on language. The large, red-faced man—who seemed to have grown somehow larger and more florid—

had used nearly every curse invented and a few I'd never heard, in explaining his side of things to the beleaguered-looking police officer. "Ah mean," he raged, in a Scots dialect so thick it sounded like a foreign tongue, "will ye just look at what the daftie's done to yon great pole! The dampt thing's cowpit ower!"

I listened with a frown, intrigued. "Daftie" was simple enough, I thought, and "dampt" was clearly "damned," but "cowpit ower?" And then I looked where he was pointing, and my frown cleared. Fallen over, I decided. That's what he must mean. The huge wooden pole had indeed split on impact and toppled into the field across the road, crushing a section of hedge in a tangle of thick black power lines.

Power lines . . .

I froze a moment, tried to think. What was it Robbie had said to David Fortune, only an hour ago? I could see his bright-eyed, freckled face, and hear the confident young voice proclaim: "The electricity's going off, anyway, sometime soon . . ."

I couldn't help the chill. My head turned slowly, cautiously, as if I were compelled to look, yet didn't want to see. Beside me, the curtains at the window twitched once more and then lay still, and though I went on watching them, they didn't move again.

"It's quite remarkable," said Quinnell, "what the boy knows. If I weren't bothered by ethics I'd take him to Newmarket, make a small fortune." Smiling at the prospect, he leaned forward to take a chocolate digestive biscuit from the tray between us.

The electricity was on again, and he'd taken advantage of the fact to brew a pot of tea. One steaming sweet sip chased away the lingering chill of the old house and made the red-walled sitting room feel cozy in spite of the west wind that rattled the windowpanes. To one side of me the big black tomcat, Murphy, lay draped along a bookshelf, lazy-eyed, while his girlfriend Charlie slumbered on the armrest of my chair. I stroked her thick fur and she flexed one paw in what might have been a protest or a gesture of contentment. One never could tell, with cats.

I would have felt a whole lot better myself, I acknowledged, if Quinnell hadn't used that one word: *ethics*.

"My mother," he went on, "fancied herself a spiritualist, but then it was all the rage, in her day—seances and table-knocking, that sort of nonsense. I didn't believe in it, myself. Still don't, in many ways."

"But Robbie McMorran . . ."

"Robbie is rather a special case." He took another biscuit, settled back. "For one thing, he was introduced to me by an old friend, whose opinion I very much value. And for another, he has told me things that . . . well, let's just say he's convincing." He smiled gently, watching my face. "You're not convinced, I take it."

I hesitated, searching for words that would give no offense. "I've only just met the boy, really, and we didn't talk much, what with him being poorly."

"No, no, it's quite all right," he forgave me, crossing one long leg over the other. "It is the natural response, you know. I think I'd worry about someone who simply accepted the idea, no questions asked. Ghosts and goblins, spooks and psychics—they're so far removed from science, and we are all children of the scientific age."

Again I felt a twinge of conscience, and I turned my eyes away, feigning an intense interest in the sleeping cat. "Mr. Quinnell . . ."

"Peter, please."

"Peter . . . there's something I must tell you."

"Yes?"

"About the radar survey . . ."

"Yes?"

My teacup clattered in the saucer with a force I hadn't intended, and Charlie the cat half opened one eye accusingly. "I saw the results today, up at the lab, and I think that there's been a mistake. I don't think the findings are accurate." There, I thought, I'd said it. Said it, moreover, without actually coming straight out and calling Adrian a liar, without telling Quinnell his granddaughter had orchestrated the deception. I held my breath, waiting for him to ask me why I didn't trust the survey. When the question didn't come, I raised my head.

The long eyes met mine levelly, with deep approving warmth. "It is a rare commodity, these days," he told me. "Honesty."

I stared. "You knew."

"Suspected. Did he take it from another site, then? One that you and he had worked on?" The answer must have shown in my face, because he nodded, satisfied. "And you recognized it. Bit of bad luck, for Adrian, although it can't have been his idea, in the first place. I expect he was led astray by Fabia. My granddaughter has rather a knack, I fear, for leading young men astray."

So the shrewdness I had glimpsed last night had not been an illusion. Those languid eyes saw more than they revealed. Which didn't mean he wasn't mad, I told myself. It only meant that Peter Quinnell was no fool.

He smiled at me again, and said: "Of course, I shan't let on. And you mustn't tell them that I know. That would upset them terribly. I'm sure they did it with the best of intentions, after all, and it's always wise to let young people feel that little bit superior."

"But your excavation . . ."

"Oh, I intend to begin in the southwest corner, regardless. Robbie's very certain that there's something there, and it's as good a place to start as any."

He sounded so certain, I thought. Frowning, I scratched Charlie's ears. "Mr. Quinnell . . ."

"Peter."

"I'm sorry to be such a skeptic, but I just don't see what proof you have that the Ninth Legion was ever here."

"No proof," he admitted, amiably. "Though it's not quite as random as it may seem, my choosing Rosehill. I've been chasing the Ninth for fifty years, now, and I've developed something of a sixth sense myself, where the *Hispana* is concerned. You know, of course, most modern historians believe the Ninth was simply sent to Lower Germany, that it wasn't destroyed at all—at least, not here on good old British

soil. But I feel it in my bones, my dear. I feel it in my
bones." His mild eyes moved past my shoulder to the window, where the chestnut tree shaded the gravel drive. "The
Devil's Causeway came this way, the Roman road from
York. For years, I thought the *Hispana* must have marched
northwest, but now I don't believe that. They came along
the east coast," he said calmly. "They came here. Even if
Robbie hadn't seen his Sentinel, I'd still have found this
field. It was the name of the house, you see, that intrigued
me."

I failed to grasp the connection. "Rosehill?"

"Not after roses," he explained. "There's not a rose in
sight, and I have it on good authority that there never have
been roses here. No, one of the locals told me that this used
to be called 'Rogue's Hill,' until the seventeenth century,
when the house was built. The family didn't care for the
name, I suppose. Wanted something more genteel. So Rosehill it became."

"But I don't quite understand," I said, "how even
'Rogue's Hill' . . ."

"Well, there weren't any rogues, either, that's the point.
Not even so much as a hanging tree. But," he added, "it
struck me that the word 'rogues' could have been derived
from *rogus.*"

Beside me, the cat started upright as though I had slapped
it. Sending me a quick look of alarm it leapt to the carpet
and vanished beneath the leather sofa. "*Rogus,*" I repeated,
slowly. The Latin word for "funeral pyre."

It was a possibility. Place names could often give one
clues about the past, and if the Ninth Legion had, in fact,
perished here, there would of course be bodies, thousands of
them—or ashes . . . Did the Romans still cremate their dead,
in the reign of Hadrian? I was struggling to remember, when
Quinnell's quiet voice interrupted my thoughts.

"I must admit, I chose you for your name, as well."

"I'm sorry?"

"Verity." He smiled. "The truth. It's what we're searching for this season, here at Rosehill. It's what I hope to find.
And I thought, if you would join us . . . well, I rather viewed

you as a talisman, you see. A good luck charm.''

Damn the Irish, I thought. They could be so incredibly persuasive. Stoutly, I reminded myself that he'd given me the weekend to decide, and this was only Friday afternoon. Plenty of time to consider things, before I gave my answer. Atop the bookshelf by Quinnell's shoulder, the black cat Murphy stirred and stretched and stared at me with placid, knowing eyes. *You're going to say yes, anyway*, he seemed to be saying. *You like the old man, you haven't the heart to refuse him.* Which was quite right, of course, but still, I wanted to wait a day or so, to make it appear that I'd given the matter some thought.

Quinnell leaned forward again and reached for the teapot. ''No need to make your mind up yet,'' he said. ''Here, have another biscuit.'' He offered the plate with a casual hand, but his eyes, like the cat's, sensed victory, and I knew full well that when I finally answered ''yes'' on Sunday, when I finally accepted the job, it would come as no surprise to Peter Quinnell.

I sighed, and took a biscuit, and the black cat closed its eyes.

VI

The train lurched sideways and slowed, and my nodding head bounced against the window as we rattled over the points. Above me a speaker popped with static and a cheerful voice announced that we would shortly be arriving at Berwick, and would I please remember to take all my belongings with me, when I left the train.

Forcing myself awake, I rose to stand in the swaying aisle, steadying myself between the seats. The woman behind me looked up and smiled. "Good thing you woke up," she said, kindly. "The train doesn't stop again till Dunbar."

I smiled back. "Yes, I know." And I had no intention of repeating my ordeal of . . . heavens, had it only been a week ago? It seemed longer. But no, it had definitely been last Thursday, and now here I was on the following Friday, taking the same train north, having settled my affairs in London and packed enough clothing to see me through the summer season at Rosehill.

Well actually, I conceded, as I edged my way along the aisle, my sister Alison had done most of the packing. Very organized, was Alison, which explained why I was lumbered with three suitcases. The smallest, the size of a briefcase, was for toiletries; the next largest held shoes and odd-shaped things, and then came a giant-sized one that I felt sure contained my entire wardrobe. I was half afraid to look. Together the three cases took up nearly the whole of the racks at the end of the second-class carriage.

They were murder to move. Even the porter, who'd offered to help, looked rather winded by the time he'd wrestled the last case down onto the platform. "D'ye need . . ." he wheezed, then sucked in air and tried again, "d'ye need a hand up the stairs?" It was gallant of him to offer, but I shook my head.

"No thanks, I'm being met." I released him with a generous tip, and settled down to wait for Adrian.

Behind me the train slid smoothly out of the station, leaving me in peaceful silence, save for the occasional soft flutter of a pigeon flapping against the sheltering roof.

This was a pretty little station, open to the air and filled with sunlight; built upon the very spot, a sign assured me, where once had stood the Great Hall of Berwick Castle. Half-closing my eyes, I tried to imagine the place without the trains, perhaps with stained glass coloring the strong afternoon sunlight, and a few hunting dogs dozing around the still smouldering hearth. I was about to add the people, men in doublets and soft leather breeks and ladies in whispering gowns, when an all too familiar voice hauled me ruthlessly back to the present.

"Good God!" Adrian stared in horror at the mammoth suitcase. "What *have* you got in that?"

"I haven't the faintest idea. Alison packed it. Her way of thanking me, for letting her have the flat this summer."

He raised an eyebrow. "You're trusting your flat to a university student? That's awfully liberal of you, isn't it? All those wild parties . . ."

"What, Alison? Don't be daft. She'd never think to throw a wild party. In fact," I told him, grinning, "she'll very likely see to it my neighbors don't throw any, either." Alison had always been the responsible one of the family. I knew she'd keep my plants watered and my windows clean and my salt cellars filled to the exact level at which I'd left them.

"Is she still in engineering?" Adrian asked me, and I nodded.

"One more year to go. She's got a job lined up for the
summer with a firm in Westminster, so the flat will be perfect
for her. She won't have to waste all that time on the tube.
And she'll take good care of my things."

"She seems to have sent most of them up here with you,"
he commented, looking down again at the suitcases.

"Oh, that's just Alison. She believes in being prepared.
She'll have put an evening dress in there, and probably my
winter coat . . ."

"Pity she didn't think to include a small pack mule,"
Adrian quipped, testing the weight of the biggest case.
"Christ, you're sure this is only clothes?"

"Pretty sure. Why?"

"Do you have any idea how heavy it is?"

Patiently, I reminded him that I knew precisely how heavy
it was. "I dragged it all around King's Cross station, on my
own. So a big strong man like you should have no problem."

"Why is it," he wanted to know, as he hoisted the case
a few inches off the platform, "that women only call us big
and strong when they want us to do something?"

I shrugged. "Men like lifting things. It makes them feel
useful."

"Is that a fact? Then hand me that little one, as well . . .
no, not that one, the *little* one. Right. The car park's this
way."

In normal circumstances, it would have been a short walk
up and over the tracks, and down again into the small station
building, where a corner news-stand and a quiet information
booth were the only diversions offered to the rail traveler.
By the time we reached the car park, Adrian was breathing
like a man who'd run a marathon. Shoulders heaving, he
dropped my cases unceremoniously onto the pavement and
sent me a murderous glance. "It's a good thing I brought
this," he panted, nodding at the dark green Range Rover in
front of us. "We'd never have been able to fit everything
into my car."

"Does this belong to the boss, then?"

"More to the boss's granddaughter."

Lucky Fabia, I thought. I'd given up my own car ages ago. There was nowhere to garage a car where I lived, and parking in the city proved a constant headache. Easier to take the bus or the tube, and simply hire a car when needed. But I couldn't help running a covetous hand along the dashboard as I nestled into the passenger seat.

Adrian noticed, and smiled. "The advantages of being rich."

"Says the man who drives a Jaguar."

"Yes, well." He shrugged modestly. "If I can't be rich, I might as well be stylish."

"You could always marry up. Fabia's rather young for you, perhaps, but—"

"Darling, I'm shocked," he cut me off, "that you would think I'd so much as notice another woman, now that you're here."

"Adrian."

"Yes, my love?"

"Don't be a brat."

Grinning, he buckled his safety belt and reversed neatly out of the car park.

The drive from Berwick to Eyemouth, along the motorway, took less than a quarter of an hour. Adrian tuned the radio in to a station playing something with a steady reggae beat, while I looked out the window, paying rather more attention to my thoughts than to the passing scenery.

"Doesn't David Fortune drive?" I asked suddenly, surprised to find I'd been thinking of him.

"What?"

"Well, he was on a bus when I met him, and last weekend he always seemed to be walking back and forth from town, so I just wondered . . ."

"He has a little rusted Ford," said Adrian, to whom a car was a reflection of its owner's personality. "He still has teaching commitments, you know, at the university, so he's away up there most of the week, but he lets his mother have the car at weekends. Drops it off for her, usually, and then catches the bus back."

"Oh." I thought about this. "You'd think his mother would have a car of her own, living where she does."

"I gather she doesn't want one."

"But surely . . ."

"You haven't met Fortune's mother." Adrian's mouth quirked. "If she doesn't want one, then . . . hang on a minute," he interrupted himself. Braking, he pointed out my window at a greening spinney on a distant hillside. "See that?" he asked me.

"What are you doing? We're going to get hit if you stop here . . . don't you remember last week's accident?"

"Yes, well, there isn't a lay-by, and I want to show you something."

"What?"

"Rosehill." He pointed again. "Just there. You can barely see it, for the trees."

I darted a doubtful glance at the empty road behind us, then looked where I was meant to. I could see the roof of Rose Cottage, and the darker shadow of the house behind the trees, and the green broad field that still betrayed no sign of what might lie beneath it.

It should have been a peaceful view, serene and pastoral, but it wasn't. I couldn't put my finger on exactly what was wrong, but for a moment I felt the faintest shiver of foreboding, as though the house itself was warning me of something yet to come. Something evil.

I looked away. "Yes, well, I've seen it now, so could we get a move on?"

"You needn't worry." He smiled as he depressed the accelerator. "I have orders to deliver you safe and sound, in time for tea."

For once, he was as good as his word. The front hall clock had only just begun to chime half-past three when Quinnell came to meet us.

"Verity, my dear, how good to have you back again. We're just having drinks in the sitting room, do come through." Extending a fatherly arm to guide me, he raised a mild eyebrow in Adrian's direction. "What, you haven't brought her cases?"

"You haven't seen her cases," Adrian countered. "It's a miracle I got them this far."

"Heavy, are they? Well, then." Quinnell smiled sympathy, and led us through into the sitting room—not his cozy, red-walled room, but the one directly opposite, across the hall. His "posh" sitting room he'd called it on my first visit to Rosehill, and now I saw quite clearly what he'd meant.

The red sitting room, with its soft leather furniture and fading chintz curtains and shelves stuffed full of books, was designed for comfort. The posh sitting room was designed to impress.

Its walls had been papered in green, a soft sea green with pale pink roses twining upwards in a tangled pattern. Cream-colored curtains hung sedately at either side of the two large windows looking over road and drive, respectively. White painted accents gleamed against the green—white window frames, white molded cornice and skirting-boards, white mantel over the fireplace on the far wall. And around the fireplace hung an arresting assortment of framed miniatures, to complete the *House and Garden* look.

The chairs arranged on the Oriental carpet were mostly covered in pink and green as well. Fabia Quinnell had curled herself into a dark green one that set off her fair hair to advantage, while David Fortune had chosen a worn armchair of an indeterminate dun color. It didn't quite match the room's décor, but then again, neither did he. The Scottish lairds of old, I thought, must have looked like that when forced to dally at the English court—rather as if they hoped a roaring good battle might erupt to break the tedium. It gave me a bit of a jolt to realize just how pleased I was to see him again, and his coolly polite greeting came as something of a disappointment.

"David," Quinnell said, "would you be kind enough to fetch Verity's cases, from the Range Rover? Adrian can't quite manage them, he says."

Adrian hastened to correct him. "I didn't say I couldn't manage—"

"No problem." David set his glass of Scotch down with

what appeared to be relief. "I'll be happy to fetch them. She's in the back room, is she? Right."

"Be careful with the big one," I advised, as he passed. "My sister packed it for me, and it's awfully heavy."

Adrian sent me a faintly accusing look as the front door slammed behind the big Scotsman. "Why is it that he gets a warning, when all I got was 'men like lifting things''?"

Fabia roused herself from the depths of what appeared to be a sulk, and sent him a guileless look. "Well, it's true, that. Men *do* like lifting things."

"So I'm told." Adrian nodded sagely. "It makes us feel useful, apparently."

"Not useful." Fabia wrinkled her nose, her mood improving. "No, I'd have said powerful. Virile. What do you think, Peter?"

Her grandfather's glance held amusement. "At my age, I'm afraid, one must prove one's manhood in less strenuous ways." He turned to me. "How was your journey up? All right?"

"I slept through most of it," I admitted, selecting an inviting-looking pink chair with a matching footstool. It felt heavenly to stretch out my legs after a day of travel.

Adrian crossed to the drinks cabinet, grinning. "She did that last time, did she tell you? Ended up in Dunbar." I settled back and let him relate the embarrassing anecdote, consoling myself with the knowledge that he was fixing me a drink while he talked. The front door slammed again, and we all four turned our heads as David passed by in the hall, carrying all three of my cases with obvious ease.

"Ah, well," sighed Adrian, lifting the bottle of gin in a toast of admiration, "who can compete with that?"

Quinnell subsided into a high-backed chair and swung one long leg over the other. "We can't all be virile, my boy. I say, while you're there, could you make me another as well?"

"You're out of vodka."

"Plenty more in the cellar. Fabia, my dear, would you run down and fetch me a bottle?"

Fabia rose obediently. I, for my part, simply took the drink that Adrian handed me and settled back, flexing my cramped feet.

Ten minutes later, with the vodka duly fetched and poured and David Fortune reinstated in his chair beside the window, Quinnell looked around him with the air of one well satisfied. "Well," he said, raising his glass, "here's to finding the Ninth, or enough of the Ninth to make Connelly give us his blessing."

I looked at him, questioning. "Connelly?"

"Dr. John Connelly." Quinnell leaned back, a faint smile on his lips. "Head of the Department of Archaeology at Edinburgh University. He was a student of mine, once, you know." The smile grew more pronounced. "My dark angel. His own opinion of the Ninth is widely published, well supported. He claims there was no British battle; that the Ninth was simply transferred to Nijmegen, in Lower Germany, and later perished in the East, fighting Parthians, or some such nonsense."

David sent him an indulgent look. "Not a bad theory, as theories go. They did find a tile-stamp of the Ninth at Nijmegen."

"A what?" asked Fabia.

Peter, pleased by her show of interest, explained that legions didn't only fight, they built as well. Each legion, in its settled fortress, made and stamped its own individual bricks and mortar. "A tile-stamp," said Peter, "is a legion's signature."

Fabia absorbed this. "So if they found one at Ni . . . at Nima . . ."

"Nijmegen."

". . . it means the Ninth was there."

"Possibly." Quinnell shrugged. "It is suggestive, yes. But I can think of other ways the tile-stamp could have got there, can't you? One must keep an open mind."

"Like you do," David said, his blue eyes teasing.

"My dear boy, if I believed the answer lay in Nijmegen, I'd not be here at Rosehill. Anyway," he added, brightening, "we've got a fortnight before Connelly comes, to find our own evidence."

I lowered my drink. "Only a fortnight?"

"Well, a fortnight and a few days. Connelly's coming to lunch on the twenty-first."

Adrian, standing by the fireplace, turned toward me to explain. "Connelly has to approve any vacation work his students apply for, you see. Even Fortune's only here on sufferance."

"Aye, well," David said, "Connelly's very fair-minded, whatever his faults. I'm sure he'll not be difficult, if we can give him proof."

I wasn't quite so sure. "But in a fortnight?"

"And a few days." Quinnell reminded me, smiling. "Plenty of time. We've already started surveying, remember, and we only need to find enough to justify the dig."

Fabia shifted in her seat. "Not much of a dig so far," she complained. "You haven't even broken ground."

"You've seen too many films," said Quinnell, unoffended. "One does try to preserve a site, these days, not tear it to pieces." He turned to David, thoughtfully. "Of course, having said that, I do think we might start our first trial trench in the morning, if the weather holds. I'd like to see what's down in that southwest corner."

I didn't miss the flicker of a glance that passed between Adrian and Fabia. She shifted in her chair, pushing the soft fall of hair out of her eyes. "The southwest corner? But I thought we'd agreed it was best to start on the ridge, where Robbie says . . . where this Sentinel's supposed to be."

Quinnell sipped his drink and shook his head, the picture of innocence, but I caught the quiet smile in the lazy sideways slide of his eyes. He was rather like one of his own cats, I thought, toying with a weaker-minded prey. "The southwest corner," he repeated, with emphasis. "We know something's there, which makes it the logical place to begin, don't you think? And the ground's quite dry enough. We tested it, didn't we, David?"

"Aye." Unlike Quinnell's, David Fortune's eyes gave nothing away. I couldn't tell, from that impassive face, whether he knew, as I did, that Quinnell had spotted the faked image. He reached for his own glass of what looked to me like straight Scotch, and knocked it back in a single swallow, while Fabia frowned beside him.

"We can talk about it over supper," she said firmly. "What *is* for supper, anyway?"

Quinnell waved one hand in a nonchalant gesture. "Jeannie said something about a roast. She got it all ready for us to put in the oven."

"And did you?" Fabia raised an expectant eyebrow and he blinked at her, as though he didn't speak the language. "Oh, Peter, you haven't left it sitting out? A roast takes simply ages."

Quinnell didn't look too concerned at the prospect of an extended happy hour, but he did mutter some sort of apology as his granddaughter passed him, heading for the kitchen. Then, with eyes that didn't bother to hide their glee, he noticed David's empty glass and rose to fill it.

Peter Quinnell, I decided, knew exactly how to handle people. And no matter how much breath Fabia wasted tonight trying to persuade him to start his excavation on the ridge, I had no doubt that, come the morning, we'd be just where Quinnell wanted us to be—down in the southwest corner, digging for a ditch that wasn't there.

SECOND HORSE

That we may lift from out of dust
A voice as unto him that hears,
A cry above the conquered years
To one that with us works...

Tennyson, "In Memoriam", CXXX

VII

I woke in darkness, listening. The sound that wrenched me from my sleep had been strange to my city-bred ears. Train-like, yet not a train . . . the rhythm was too wild, too random. A horse, I thought. A horse in the next field over, galloping endlessly around and round, galloping, galloping . . .

My heavy eyelids drifted shut and I burrowed deeper in my pillows. My mind drifted, too, and the hoofbeats took form and became a pale horse . . . no, a dark one, a black horse, pure black like the night, black mane and black tail streaming out on the wind as it passed me by, galloping . . .

It faded and wheeled and came back again, steadily, bringing the others behind it—more hoofbeats, more horses, until it seemed the field must be a sea of heaving flanks and white-rolled eyes and steaming curls of labored breath. Snorting and plunging, they came on like thunder, galloping, galloping, and then in one thick stream they rushed beneath my window and I knew that I was dreaming, so I closed my eyes more tightly, and I slept.

I woke again in daylight. Reaching over in an automatic gesture, I flipped the switch on my alarm clock before the buzzer could sound, and heard the minute hand snap forward: eight o'clock. Yawning, I rolled onto my back, trying to work up the necessary willpower to lift my head.

This room was marvelous for waking up in. The only window faced east, over the field, but the morning sunlight edged its way in softly through the screening chestnut tree, not stabbing one in the eyes as it did in my London flat. The yellow walls danced with a dappled play of shadow and light as the tree's branches shifted and dipped against an encouragingly blue sky.

It looked a proper day for early May, warm and clear, but still I shivered in the chill outside my covers. Tugging a shapeless jumper over my standard working uniform of T-shirt and jeans, I quickly washed and went downstairs, where I found Jeannie McMorran alone in the bright kitchen, mixing a bowlful of biscuit dough.

"Do you never stop baking?" I asked. We'd got on rather well together last weekend, Jeannie and I, and I'd decided I liked her very much. She had a buoyant personality, a deliciously sly wit, and a way of putting Adrian in his place that I found particularly endearing. She turned to face me now and grinned.

"What, with all these men about? They'd never let me. Your hair-slide's crooked."

"Is it?" I raised one hand to make the adjustment, then carried on weaving the rest of my hair into its customary plait.

Jeannie sighed. "It makes me miss my own hair, watching you do that. Mine was never so thick, ken, but I could sit on it."

"Really?" Fastening my finished plait with a covered elastic band, I let it fall between my shoulder blades. "What made you cut it?"

"Brian fancied short hair on a woman," she said, with a shrug. "And I was younger then."

Brian, I had learned, was her husband—Robbie's father. Having never actually met the man I'd nonetheless managed to form a rather unbecoming picture of him. He skippered his own fishing boat, I knew, which meant he must be capable of some responsibility, yet it was hard to have a good opinion of a man who appeared to divide his odd weekend home between the nearest public house and his bed. I changed the subject.

"I take it everyone else is up?"

"Aye. Peter and Fabia were on their way out when I got here, half an hour ago. They've gone down to take some photographs, I think, before they start the digging. I've not seen Adrian's car, yet, but I know Davy's around . . . he's been down playing drafts with my Robbie since seven, if you can believe it. Eh, speak of the devil," she broke off, flapping her dishcloth toward the kitchen window to direct my attention to the figures walking down the hill outside. "There they go now."

There were three of them—four if one counted Robbie's dog, Kip. The collie ran energetic circles around David Fortune's legs, jumping up every few paces to bring its head within reach of his hand so he could rumple its ears in an absent way without interrupting his conversation with Robbie. Behind them walked an older man I didn't recognize, a short man with a slightly bent back and a dour expression.

"Who's that with them?"

"That's my dad," Jeannie informed me, in a voice that held affection. "I forgot, you've not met him yet, have you? He made himself scarce, last weekend."

Scarce, I thought dryly, was hardly the word. I hadn't caught so much as a glimpse of the groundskeeper of Rosehill, although Jeannie assured me that was not uncommon. There were, according to Jeannie, two things that Wally Tyler hated—living on his own, and living within sight of his son-in-law. Which had left him, after his wife's death several years ago, facing a dilemma. Inviting his daughter and grandson to fill the empty corners of Rose Cottage meant inviting Brian, too.

And so Wally Tyler had reached his own compromise. When Brian McMorran came home, Wally went elsewhere.

"It's not so bad as it sounds," Jeannie told me, smiling at my expression. "Brian's away to the fish most of the time—he keeps the boat out for a fortnight when the fishing's good. And Dad has friends in town." She wiped the last plate and set it in the rack to dry. "Right, what will you have for your breakfast? There's porridge made, or I can fix you some eggs—''

"I usually just have toast."

"You're never thinking to spend a whole day running around after Peter with nothing but toast in your stomach!" She fixed me with a look that made me feel about as old as Robbie, and repeated her offer of porridge or eggs.

Meekly, I opted for a boiled egg.

"Hard or soft?"

"Middling, please." Taking a seat at the kitchen table, I glanced out the window again at the disappearing cluster of men, boy, and bouncing dog. Jeannie dropped bread in the toaster and smiled.

"They won't start the digging without you," she promised me. "Peter and Davy will be busy for a bit yet, organizing things, and with my dad down there it'll be a miracle if they've done so much as break the turf by the time you finish your breakfast. Sausages or bacon?"

"You needn't go to so much trouble . . ."

"It's no trouble. This is what I do," she explained patiently, her eyes amused. "I cook the food, and you eat it. Now which will it be, sausages or bacon? Or will I give you both?"

One simply couldn't argue with a woman like that, I decided. And the plate of egg and sausages she finally set in front of me did draw a hungry rumble from my normally spartan stomach. "This is marvelous," I admitted, after the third sausage. "Thanks."

"Oh, any fool can boil an egg." From her tone of voice I knew she honestly believed that, so I chose not to disillusion her by telling her that boiled eggs were quite beyond my own skills. Instead, I speared a piece of fried tomato and watched while she wiped the newly used pans.

"You haven't always worked for Quinnell, then?" I asked her.

"What? Oh, no," she replied, with another flash of amusement. "No, I come with the house, like my dad. Afore Peter it was old Mrs. Finlay lived up here, but then she fell ill and had to go into hospital. Her son managed things after that, but he only came down weekends, from Edinburgh. And then last September Peter came and waved a stack of pound notes under Mr. Finlay's nose, and that was that.''

Money, I agreed, could be so wonderfully persuasive, and Peter Quinnell seemed to have money to burn. His family's fortune, no doubt. He had the sort of cultured look that only comes with centuries of privilege.

''Anyway,'' Jeannie went on, ''he's a good man to work for, is Peter. It's a pity that Fabia's learned nothing from him.''

I smiled, understanding. ''I don't think she likes me, much.''

''Aye, well, she wouldn't. You're a woman,'' Jeannie said, matter-of-factly. ''Still, I suppose I shouldn't be too unkind. She did lose her father, poor lass.''

''Recently?''

''Just last summer. It must have been fair hard on Peter as well, to lose his only son like that, but at least he's got Davy to lean on. They're almost like family, those two.''

I pondered this, spooning the top off my second egg. ''Was David a student of Quinnell's, or something?''

''I couldn't tell you,'' she admitted. ''I don't mind where Davy went to university—he was years ahead of me at school. But he's kent Peter all his life. Davy's mum was Peter's secretary, like. Afore she married onto Davy's father.''

''Oh. I see.''

The relationships, I thought, were rather hard to disentangle. Jeannie, growing up in Eyemouth, had known David, who knew Peter, who had once employed David's mother, who now knew young Robbie . . .

''And Peter was best man at Davy's wedding,'' she continued. ''I do mind that, because he had to come all the way over from—''

''David is married?'' I couldn't help the interruption, though it relieved me to hear that my own voice was admirably calm.

And I was even more relieved when Jeannie replied with

a shake of her head. "He was, aye, but not anymore. She left him, stupid lass."

Stupid lass, indeed, I thought.

Half an hour later, when I made my way down the gently sloping field to where the men had gathered in the southwest corner and was met by David Fortune's almost welcoming smile, I decided that stupid was an understatement.

"What kind of time d'ye call this, then?" he asked me.

"It's not my fault. Jeannie made me stop and eat a huge cooked breakfast." Something bounced at my knees and I bent to greet the collie, Kip. Scratching his shaggy mane, I took a quick look around. "Where's Fabia? I thought she was with you."

Quinnell glanced up. "What? Oh, she's gone to ring Adrian. He seems to be having a lie-in this morning, and I want to make certain I've positioned this properly."

By "this" he meant the long strip of ground at his feet, staked out with string to make a rectangle.

Every excavation took place within an imaginary grid, an unseen plan of lines and squares created by the survey, drawn over the field like a giant invisible graph. Everything we found at Rosehill, no matter how small, would be carefully mapped in relation to that graph. Quinnell had already plotted the location of what would be his trial trench against Adrian's survey markers, and set his own stakes at the four widely spaced corners, but he obviously didn't want to cut the turf until he'd checked his measurements.

Jeannie's father waited patiently to one side, leaning on his spade. In spite of the bent back he had the tough look of a man who'd done hard work his whole life and had no intention of letting up now. He looked at me with sharp gray eyes that glittered in his creased and weathered face, and raised his eyebrows. "This isnae the lass fae London?"

Quinnell assured him that I was. "Verity, this is Wally Tyler. Jeannie's father."

She didn't resemble him much. Where her features were soft, his were sharp, and his thinning hair had once been red. But his eyes, like his daughter's, were alive with canny good humor, and they crinkled kindly at the corners as he took my hand in a firm and certain grip, looking accusingly at Quinnell. "She's no blond."

"Yes, I know."

David smiled broadly. "Did Jeannie not tell you, Wally?"

"She never let dab. And Robbie only said the new lass was a stoater."

Robbie stopped poking around in the hedgerow and turned, his face coloring. "Aw, Grandad!"

Quinnell laughed, a warm melodic sound. "It's all right, Robbie. I don't think our Miss Grey can speak Scots, can you, my dear? No. So there you are, you see? She likely won't know what a stoater is."

He was quite right, of course—I didn't have a clue, but as no one seemed inclined to enlighten me I tried my best to act as though I didn't care.

Instead I looked down, at the broad rectangle marked in the grass. The pungent smell of damp earth touched my nostrils like a sweet seductive scent, and I couldn't help but feel that tiny catch of excitement deep in my chest, that tingling thrill that all explorers must have felt from time immemorial. Because you never knew what worlds were waiting underneath that ground, to be discovered. That was the beauty of it—you never really knew.

And on this perfect spring morning, with my breath leaving mist in the air and the sun warming my shoulders and a little bird singing for all he was worth in the may-blossom hedge at my back, it was easy to forget there wasn't a shred of hard evidence to support this excavation. Easy to forget that we didn't have a hope of finding anything. I simply wanted to pick up a spade and get on with it, to start the actual digging.

"Adrian's coming," Robbie announced, swinging himself down from the fencing that ran behind the hedge.

Quinnell relaxed. "Good, good. Overslept, I imagine."

Fabia's firm voice corrected him. "Car trouble."

She spoke from directly behind me, her sudden arrival startling until I realized she had come, not from the house, but from Rose Cottage, just the other side of the drive. It meant a bit of a scramble over a crumbling stone wall and a sagging wire fence, but Fabia looked as though she'd rather enjoyed the challenge, and the telephone at the cottage was, at any rate, closer than the one at Rosehill House.

"Morning," she greeted me shortly. "Finally got free of the kitchen, I see. Did Jeannie force you to eat her horrid porridge?"

"I had eggs, actually—"

Quinnell interrupted, his long face enquiring. "Car trouble, did you say?"

"What?" Fabia glanced round. "Oh, yes. He couldn't get the motor started."

Robbie, who'd been poking at a hillock with a sturdy bit of stick, looked swiftly upwards and I fancied that his large eyes held a faint reproach. My first thought was: *He's caught her in a lie*; and then I gently shook myself and smiled, remembering that no one could really be psychic.

Still, it wouldn't have surprised me to learn that Fabia was lying. She and Adrian weren't at all eager to see the southwest corner excavated, and Quinnell hadn't helped matters last night, going on and on over dinner about his plans, as though the ground-penetrating radar survey had been genuine. I, for my part, had kept my promise to Quinnell and not said a word about it, and if I didn't exactly enjoy watching Adrian's discomfort, I could salve my guilty conscience with the knowledge that it probably did him good.

"Yes, well, these things happen," Quinnell said now, with a rather deliberate innocence, and I thought I caught the shadow of a smile as he turned to talk to Wally Tyler.

Certainly, Adrian's car appeared healthy enough when he finally turned into the drive, ten minutes later. He parked at the top of the hill, by the house, and came slowly down to meet us, frowning. "D'you know," he said to Quinnell, "I've been re-examining the results of that survey, and I can't be absolutely sure, but—"

"Yes?"

"Well, that anomaly doesn't look quite the right size, you know, for what we're after . . ."

"Ah. Perhaps we ought to double-check." Quinnell smiled. "Robbie?"

Robbie, still poking about with his stick, looked around a second time. "Aye, Mr. Quinnell?"

"Mr. Sutton-Clarke's afraid we might be digging in the wrong place for our ditch."

"The ditch the soldiers dug?"

"That's right."

Robbie screwed his eyes up while he gave the matter thought. "No, it's here. It's all filled up, like, but it's here."

"Good lad." Quinnell turned back to Adrian like a proud father. "You see? There's no need to worry. If you'd just be so kind as to verify my measurements . . ."

A few minutes later, as Wally Tyler's spade attacked the toughened sod, my shoulders lifted in a little sigh.

Such a pity, I thought, that Quinnell would be disappointed. It didn't seem fair.

"The ditch is here," repeated Robbie, but he wasn't talking to Quinnell. He'd come around to stand beside me and his blue eyes tilted up to meet my doubting ones, offering reassurance. "It's OK, he's going to find it."

No one can really be psychic, I reminded myself firmly. But Robbie only smiled as though I'd told him something funny, and went bouncing off to throw his stick for Kip.

VIII

"It must be teatime, surely." Fabia pushed her hair back with an impatient hand, setting down her end of the large wood-framed screen while I reached for the next bucket of soil.

Overhead the clouds had thickened and the shadows in our sheltered place beside the trial trench had flattened into nothingness. Unable to tell the hour from the sun, I checked my wristwatch, arching my back in a work-weary stretch. "Another hour yet, I'm afraid."

"Well, this is dead boring." She glared past my shoulder to where the men, several feet away, were sinking ever lower in the trench. "You'd think with four of them digging they'd be able to go a lot faster."

I halted in mid-stretch, surprised. There were only three of them digging, in actual fact—Adrian, useless with a shovel, had been given the less critical chore of passing the buckets of excavated soil over to us to be sieved. But even without Adrian, the men were making quite good progress, I thought, their shovels scraping steadily, persistently, as they scooped up the soil in thin measured layers, moving deeper by stratified levels. If Fabia thought they could go any faster, she'd never tried digging herself.

And she'd certainly never held a sieve before today. I was beginning to think I could do the work better without her.

Leaving the sieve on the ground for a moment, I tipped over the next bucket, letting the freshly dug soil spill out onto the fine metal mesh. "I suppose," I said, lightly probing, "as Peter Quinnell's granddaughter, you've been doing this sort of thing since before you could walk."

"God, no." She tossed her blond hair back again and bent to pick up her end of the screen. "This is a first. I've no interest in dead things. I'm like my father, that way."

"Ah." Not wanting to pry, I took a firmer hold on the sieve's wooden frame and we started the shaking motion again, back and forth, back and forth, like two children tugging at opposite ends of a blanket. The clumps of soil rolled and broke and sifted through the sieve like flour.

"I can't believe, sometimes," she said, "that Dad and Peter were related. Dad was so alive, you know? So interested in everything."

I shot a sideways look at Quinnell, laboring singlemindedly in the trench, and thought I'd never seen a man look more alive. But I kept my opinion to myself.

"Peter isn't interested in anything," said Fabia, with certainty, "except this bloody dig. It's all he cares about." And then, as though she'd reached some unseen stopping-place, she switched the subject. "I can't believe you do this for a living, honestly. It would put me to sleep."

I smiled, hearing the note of complaint in her voice and knowing she'd imagined archaeology to be more glamorous. She hadn't learned, as I had, that true archaeologists were not the swashbuckling heroes of Hollywood films, dashing madly around the world from danger zone to danger zone in search of priceless treasures. True archaeologists were scientists. They moved slowly, for fear of overlooking something, damaging something, being inaccurate. For most of them, a single broken bit of pottery—what we in the field called a "sherd"—could be as great a find as Agamemnon's mask.

Hollywood, I reasoned, rarely concerned itself with getting things right. And who could blame it? Who on earth would want to make a film that showed the reality of excavation work, with all its repetition and tedium and endless note-taking? More to the point, who on earth would want to *watch* it? There was only so much interest one could muster in the act of sieving soil.

"What's that?" Fabia asked, as I picked a small drooping thing up from the sieve.

"Earthworm." I gently set it back where it belonged, on the ground at my feet. Bad enough, I thought, that he'd been shovelled from his peaceful home in the first place, and rattled all around. Tipping out the few remaining pebbles onto the spoil heap, I lowered the sieve and hefted the next bucket, smiling encouragement at Fabia. "Last one," I promised.

The heavy tread of footsteps heralded Adrian's approach. "Last one?" he echoed. "Then you must have more. That spoil heap's not nearly high enough." Cheerfully, he swung two full buckets beside the growing mound of sieved soil and rested, hands on hips, waiting for us to call him names.

Fabia, to my surprise, chose not to call him anything. Instead she ran a hand through her hair, in a self-conscious, womanly way, and her swift upward glance was designed to bewitch the observer. "Adrian, darling, I wonder . . ." She paused, as though embarrassed, and approached from a different angle. "It's only that I desperately need to go to the loo, you see, and I wondered if you might be a prince . . ." With a hopeful smile, she held up her edge of the framed square of screening.

"Certainly." Gullible as always, he stepped in to relieve her, watching fondly as she flounced away toward the house. When she'd disappeared from view, he brought his head around to meet my pitying eyes. "What?"

"You ought to have remembered your Greek myths."

"My what?"

"Hercules and Atlas."

"What about them?"

"Didn't they teach you anything at school? Atlas was the chap who had to hold the sky on his back, remember? So it didn't touch the earth. And then Hercules took over for a bit, while Atlas went to fetch the golden apples. Only when Atlas came back, he wasn't keen to take the sky again, so Hercules said: 'Fair enough, old boy, only I haven't got my shoulders set quite right. Could you just hold this for a moment while I get a better grip?' ''

"And then he buggered off, right?"

"Oldest trick in the book."

"You are a cynic, aren't you?" Adrian commented. "Fabia's coming back."

By the time we'd started into the second bucket he'd brought, his frowning glances up toward the house had grown more frequent and his voice held none of its former confidence. "She *is* coming back."

"Of course she is. Could you hold your end up properly, please? You're spilling all the soil."

"Sorry. I'd really forgotten how much I disliked . . . hang on, what was that?" He stopped shaking, peering closely at the sieve.

"What was what?"

"Blast, it's gone under again. I shook too hard. A piece about this big," he identified the mystery object, making a circle with thumb and forefinger, "a sort of triangle. I think it's down near you, now."

It took me a moment to find it. Frowning, I held the hard flat lump with careful fingers and gingerly brushed away most of the clinging dirt. It was a small potsherd with still-sharp edges and the worn remnants of a fine glaze. On any other site, I would have been excited by such a find. But now, as I stared down at it, I felt the pricking of irrational anger.

Adrian held out his hand. "Can I have a look?"

In stony-faced silence I passed him the sherd and watched him weigh it in the palm of his hand. Head bent, he lowered his eyebrows in the frown of concentration that I still found more attractive than his smile. "It's Samian ware, isn't it?"

"It certainly appears to be."

"But that's encouraging, surely? I mean, one expects to find Samian ware on a Roman site."

"Yes. How clever of you to remember."

He glanced up. "What?"

"Were you planning," I asked him coldly, "to fake the whole of this excavation?"

"Verity . . ."

"Just so I know."

"Verity . . ."

"Mind you, it's not a perfect plant. Samian ware might have been scattered throughout Roman Britain, but I'd think it more common to villas and forts than to marching camps."

"Verity, I swear." He raised his right hand in defense. "This is not my doing."

"Please. Fabia may have the brains, but she doesn't have your access to artifacts. Where'd you nick this from?"

He sighed, and sent me a look that mingled exasperation and amusement. "What makes you so bloody sure it's not a genuine find?"

"Oh, don't play the innocent. You know as well as I do that there's nothing here *to* find."

Quinnell, I thought later, could not have had a better cue. I'd barely finished my sentence when his shout of delight went rolling up the green hill like a thunderclap. Forgetting Adrian, I turned toward the sound. Robbie and Kip had returned to crouch near the far edge of the deepening trench, and I saw Robbie lean forward excitedly, pointing.

"Good God," said Adrian. He set the potsherd back on its bed of dirt and let go his end of the sieve, forcing me to shift my grip or drop the thing altogether. "They've found something."

"Damn it, Adrian," I began, staggering beneath the weight of the framed square of screening, but he was already gone, hurrying over the grass to investigate. With a muttered curse I lowered the sieve to the ground and creaked upright again, massaging my strained back muscles as I rounded the edge of the trench.

The collie met me halfway, feathered tail waving a welcome. "Careful, Kip," I warned as he bumped against my legs, but the dog just drew its lips back in a grin and danced a few steps further on, urging me to follow.

Quinnell looked up, beaming. "We've found the ditch," he announced. "Right where we expected it to be."

Adrian was plainly stunned. "Right where we expected it . . ."

"Yes." Quinnell beckoned me closer. "Just there, do you see? I'm afraid the rampart itself has been levelled at some point, there's nothing left of it at all, but you can clearly trace its edge against the dark fill of the ditch."

I looked, enthralled. They'd done an expert job of excavating, and the line where ditch and rampart had once met stood out quite clearly, running crosswise at the bottom of the trench.

The Romans had dug ditches all the way around their marching camps, great ditches nine feet wide and seven feet deep, piling the earth and turf to one side to create a soaring rampart. It must have looked a daunting obstacle, to any barbarians trying to attack the Roman camp.

And now nothing was left but a line in the soil.

Wally Tyler hoisted himself out of the trench, and David's eyes tipped up to scan the waving rim of grass. "Wally, would you hand me down that brush, there?"

"Aye." The old man complied, nearly tripping over his grandson in the process. "A body canna move with ye aboot," he complained. He gave the boy a nudge with one foot. "Shift yerself forrit a wee bit."

Robbie obligingly shifted himself forward, careful not to get too close to the edge of the trench. Someone had obviously explained to him how important it was not to collapse the trench wall and lose all the information contained in its various strata. Leaning over cautiously, he watched the work below him. "Davy . . ."

"Aye, lad?"

"How could *that*"—he pointed one shoe at the eroded rampart—"keep anybody out?"

David smiled. "Well, it used to be much bigger, lad. Like a hill, ken—nearly ten feet tall. And on top the Romans built a wall of wooden poles, to make it taller. And all this," he added, waving his trowel over the darker area, "this was a ditch then, like the moats you see around castles."

"Filled with water?"

"No, just dry. It made it difficult enough, to scramble up."

Robbie pondered this a moment. "Where'd they get the wood from?"

"What?"

"The wooden poles. Where'd they come from?"

"Oh." David's face cleared, and he lowered his head to concentrate on brushing loose dirt from the leveled rampart's edge. "The Romans were like Boy Scouts, lad. They came prepared. The legionaries carried two poles each when they were on the march."

"What, on their backs, like?"

"Aye. Along with their armor and their weapons and the things they used for cooking—"

Adrian cut him off abruptly. "We found a sherd," he said, as if he'd only just remembered. Not that one could blame him for forgetting, really. Our find had been so small compared to this one, and if the sight of the ditch had astounded me, it must have stunned Adrian speechless. It wasn't every day one's lie turned out to be the truth.

Quinnell brought his head round, interested. "What did you say?"

"A sherd," repeated Adrian. "Samian ware, we think."

"Oh, yes? Perhaps, David, you might take a look at it? You're so much better with pottery than I am. And I do want to get this trench photographed, in case it starts to rain. Wally, do you think that you could bring the stepladder round, so Fabia can get a shot from higher up?"

"Aye." The wiry Scotsman rolled a cigarette between his stained fingers, placed it in his mouth unlit, and shuffled off, no doubt glad of the opportunity to leave the field for a smoke. Most archaeologists didn't allow smoking on their sites, as radio-carbon dates would be contaminated by the ashes.

"And Fabia . . ." Quinnell paused, his eyes resting rather vaguely on Adrian and myself. "Where is Fabia?"

Adrian informed him she'd gone back up to the house. "Shall I fetch her?"

"Please. And Verity, if you wouldn't mind showing this sherd of yours to David?"

Robbie, still crouched beside the trench, looked up hopefully. "And what can *I* do?"

"You," David said solemnly, handing over his brush,
"can lend a hand to Mr. Quinnell, lad."

"Really?"

"Aye. He likes a bit of help, don't you, Peter?"

"What?" The older man glanced round. "Oh, yes, indeed
I do. Come down here, Robbie, let me show you . . ."

David Fortune smiled. In one easy motion he pulled himself out of the trench like a swimmer stepping out of a pool,
and wiping his hands on his sturdy cotton trousers he came
across to join me. "Peter does love teaching things," he
confided. "He had me out on digs when I was half Robbie's
age."

I couldn't imagine him at half Robbie's age. I looked behind me at the small dark tousled head bent close by Quinnell's in the trench, and thought: impossible. A man as big
as David Fortune could never have been Robbie's size. He
must have sprung from somewhere fully grown.

He towered beside me as we walked, our silence broken
by the thump and scuffle of our shoes falling on the thick
green grass that cloaked the pitted ground. Kip came with
us, tail wagging, eager to be off on some adventure, but when
we stopped a few yards on at the end of the trench, the collie
lost interest and trotted off on a new course.

The sieving screen was right where I had left it, balanced
on the spoil heap, and David bent to examine the small bit
of broken pottery lying nestled on its bed of dirt.

"That was in the last load of soil Adrian brought over,"
I told him.

"Careless of us to miss it in the digging."

I studied the back of his head for a moment. "You weren't
at all surprised, were you?"

"That we found something, d'you mean?" He glanced
round, his eyes touching mine with level honesty. "No."

"But it's . . . I mean, it seems so incredible, when you
think about it—Adrian and Fabia going to all that trouble to
fake the survey results, and in the end the bloody ditch is
exactly where . . . exactly . . ." My voice trailed off ineffec-

tually as I brushed a hand across my forehead, smoothing a small frown. "Incredible," I said again.

"Not so incredible." His voice held the gentle insistence of a teacher reminding his pupils of a lesson they'd forgotten. "Robbie said there was something there."

"Yes, but . . ."

"When you've known Robbie longer, you'll understand. I'm not a man of faith," he said, "but if Robbie said the flood was coming, I'd build myself an ark." He turned the sherd over carefully in his fingers. "Is this all you found?"

"That, and a few fragments of animal bone—birds and mice, mostly, I think."

"Right then, let me fetch my notebook, and we'll get this properly recorded. I won't be a minute."

Left alone by half-empty sieve, I folded my arms across my chest and frowned harder at the pottery fragment, without really seeing it. I ought to have been pleased, I told myself. It was, after all, beginning to look very much as if there really was a marching camp at Rosehill, and Ninth Legion or no, the discovery of a Roman camp was *something*. So why, I wondered, was I suddenly feeling uneasy?

I stood there a long moment, thinking, so absorbed in thought that when the footsteps rustled through the grass behind me, I didn't turn round. It wasn't until I heard the half-sigh of an indrawn breath close by my shoulder that I realized someone else had come to join me. Shaking off my foolish fancies, I fixed a smile of welcome on my face and turned to say hello.

My greeting fell on empty air.

My heart lurched. Stopped. Began again. Over the sudden roaring rush of blood that filled my ears I heard a herring gull cry out its warning high above the twisted trees, and then the whispering footsteps passed me by and faded in the softly blowing grass.

IX

"You look as if you'd seen a ghost," said Adrian, surveying me over the top of his drawing tablet. "Are you feeling all right?"

"Fine."

"Because you don't need to stick around for this part, if you're tired. Robbie and Wally have gone home for tea, and as soon as I've done this rough map I'll be taking a break myself."

"I'm fine," I repeated stubbornly.

My hands had finally stopped trembling but I kept them clenched deep in the pockets of the windcheater David had insisted on fetching for me when he'd returned to find me shaking from what he'd assumed was the cold. Not that the afternoon was particularly chilly, but when the sun ducked in behind the passing clouds I found myself grateful for the windcheater. The breeze had developed a bite.

I blamed the breeze, as well, for what I'd heard, or thought I'd heard. The wind could have a human voice, sometimes. It had fooled me often enough in childhood, setting the front gate creaking on its hinges and drawing the branches of our walnut tree across the roof until I would have sworn a gang of thieves was creeping up the old back stair behind my room, while I lay cowering in darkness with the blankets around my ears, too terrified even to call out loud for my mother.

My mother, come to think of it, would have been a welcome sight just now. She was a large, no-nonsense woman with a voice that brooked no opposition. "There are no such things as ghosts," she would have told me, and of course I would have believed her.

But at the moment, surrounded by strangers in a wild landscape, with the remnants of a long-dead civilization spread at my feet, such things as ghosts seemed possible.

Below me in the trial trench David sat back on his heels and dug the point of his trowel into the damp soil, resting a moment. "Feeling any warmer now?" he asked me.

He had beautiful eyes, I thought vaguely. It really was unfair how nature always gave the longest eyelashes to men. His were black, like his hair, and made his eyes look brilliant blue by contrast.

"Much warmer, thanks."

Adrian sent me another assessing glance. "Not got a headache, have you?"

I sighed. "No, I'm fine. Honestly."

"But you've got that little line, just here." He touched a forefinger between his eyebrows. "And usually, when you get that little line, it means you have a headache."

Quinnell, at the far side of the trench, raised his head in enquiry. "Who's got a headache?"

"Verity," supplied Adrian.

David, not to be outdone, explained to Quinnell that I'd just got a wee bit chilled, and I was on the verge of explaining to the lot of them that I was, in actual fact, *fine*, when the sun abruptly vanished behind a gathering bank of gray cloud.

Quinnell turned, and sniffed the air. "Rain," he pronounced, in a mournful tone.

"Aye." David stood. "I'm done for the moment, at any rate. It's all down to the one level." He looked at me. "That's the last of it, for now," he promised, pointing to the three full buckets to one side of the trench. "I'll just take them up to the Principia for you, so they'll not get rained on. You don't want to be sieving mud.''

I smiled at his casual use of the Latin word. ''The Principia? Where's that, the stables?''

''Aye.'' He smiled back. ''The nerve center. Quinnell named it, and the name stuck.''

Most appropriate, I thought. Every Roman fort had its *principia*—the large headquarters building at the center of the complex, where the legionaries gathered to receive the day's commands.

Our own commander, Quinnell, climbed with great reluctance from the trench and watched while David gathered up the heavy buckets. ''Taking those up, then, are you? Good lad. Time for a drink, I suppose. There's not much we can do here until the rain passes. We'll meet you back up at the house.'' Turning, he put a fatherly hand on my shoulder to walk me up the hill. ''And I'm sure Jeannie could find some aspirin for you. Bound to be a bottle or two around, somewhere.''

It seemed pointless, really, to protest, and after all the arguing about my health it was heaven to sit in the quiet kitchen at Rosehill and let Jeannie serve me my aspirins with a nice hot cup of sugared tea. ''Is it very bad?'' she asked.

I sipped my tea, uncertain. ''Is what very bad?''

''Your headache.''

''Oh.'' My expression cleared. ''I don't have a headache, actually.''

''But the aspirins . . .''

''Adrian's fault. He saw some line between my eyebrows, which he claims beyond a doubt means that I have a headache. Mr. Quinnell suggested the aspirins.''

''Peter,'' she corrected me. ''He'll want you to call him Peter. The only one who calls him Mr. Quinnell around here is my Robbie.''

''Well, anyway, the point is it's a waste of breath,'' I told her, ''arguing with Adrian. I learned that ages ago. Far easier to take the tablets and be done with it.''

She smiled and sat down in the chair opposite. It was, I thought, the first time I had seen her sitting still, not doing something. "Of course," she said. "You went with Adrian at one time, didn't you?"

I nodded. "Ancient history, that."

"Was it serious?"

"With Adrian? Never. He's not the serious type. Besides," I added, "I've the wrong hair color for Adrian. He likes blonds. I rather fancy he's cast his roving eye on Fabia, poor girl."

Jeannie shrugged and reached for the teapot to pour herself a cup. "Nothing odd about it, she's a beautiful lass. And not nearly so helpless as she lets on. Care for some shortbread? Quietly, though, don't rattle about in the tin, or the men will be in here before you know it."

I mumbled my thanks through a crumbling mouthful of biscuit. "Your father," I informed her, "seemed surprised I wasn't blond."

"Aye." Her eyes danced. "He had his doubts, ken, when Peter said he'd hired an old girlfriend of Adrian's. Full of dire warnings, was Dad. What did you think of him?"

"I barely saw him all day," I admitted. "He was digging with Quin—with Peter and David, while I sifted dirt with Fabia, but what I saw of him I liked."

I could tell she was fond of her father by the way she swelled with pleasure at my words. "He's a grand old man," she said, "but you want to watch him. He can be a right bugger when he wants to be."

"Talking about me again?" David Fortune filled the doorway as he walked through it. He had cleaned himself up a little, washed his hands, and his walk had a cocky, self-satisfied roll to it.

Jeannie sent him a motherly look. "If you were chocolate," she told him, "you'd eat yourself." By which I gathered she was calling him conceited.

Unconcerned, he smiled and looked around the narrow kitchen. "Speaking of food, did I hear you open a tin of shortie?"

"Certainly not."

"Liar. Verity's eating it now . . . aren't you?" His cheerfully accusing eyes swung from me to the tin on the table, sparing me the effort of replying with my mouth full. I went on munching while he helped himself. The unfamiliar Scots terminology reminded me of something I'd meant to ask Jeannie earlier. Chasing down my shortbread with a sip of cooling tea, I casually inquired what a stoater was.

"A stoater?"

"Yes. Someone told me I was one, so I just wondered."

"Oh, aye?" Her mouth curved in spite of her obvious attempt to keep a straight face. "And who was it said you were a stoater?"

Behind her shoulder David smiled and cupped a hand beneath his chin to catch the shortbread crumbs. "Your son," he said. "That's who."

"Cheeky," she laughingly pronounced judgment on her absent son. "That's his father coming out in him, poor lad. A stoater," she explained, to me, "is a very good-looking woman."

"Oh," I said. Because, after all, there seemed very little else *to* say . . .

David angled his gaze to meet Jeannie's. "We'll need to be getting her a wee Scots dictionary, so she can understand us. D'ye still sell them at the museum?"

"Aye, I think so."

I looked from one to the other of them, intrigued. "There's a museum here in Eyemouth? I didn't know that."

"A good museum," David confirmed. "Not a big one, ken, and it shares space with the tourist information service, but the exhibits are nicely done and they give you a feel for the past of a fishing town."

Jeannie nodded. "I can take you through, if you like. I work there Thursdays, on the desk." She sent a teasing glance up at the big archaeologist. "We'd best pick a day when your mum's not there, though, or we're liable to get stuck."

"Aye." His smile flashed a faint cleft in one clean-shaven cheek as he leaned across to take more shortbread, and I marveled at how much more relaxed he was in Jeannie's presence than when we were on our own. He had lost that faintly rigid and reserved air I'd grown used to, and his eyes laughed easily, engagingly. "My mother," he informed me, "can be a bit of a blether."

"She likes to talk," Jeannie translated.

I smiled. "Don't all mothers?" Mine certainly did. My father had developed a habit of daydreaming in self-defence, occasionally rousing himself to murmur, "yes, yes of course" or "quite right, dear," to keep my mother's monologues running. When I'd asked him once if he wouldn't prefer silence, he'd said no, he quite liked the sound of my mother's voice. He just lost interest, now and then, in what she was actually saying.

"My mum was quiet," Jeannie put in. "Like a mouse. But then living with Dad, she'd not have been able to get a word in."

"Trade you," David offered.

"Och, you don't mean that. Your mum's a lovely woman." She lifted a curious eyebrow. "Is she still being difficult, then, about having someone to help her?"

"Difficult," he said, "is not the word."

"She'll soon come round," was Jeannie's optimistic pronouncement. "And if you want difficult, Davy, you can have my dad any day. It's the funny thing about life, isn't it? If you're not taking care of your kids, you're taking care of your parents."

"Aye, well, Mum's enough for me, thanks." Grinning, he brushed the crumbs from his shirt and glanced at me. "How's the headache, now?"

"I'm fine." For a moment it occurred to me that I might be wise to have that printed on a T-shirt, for future use.

"Peter'll be glad of that," he said. "He sent me in to find out how you were; thought he might have overworked you on your first day out."

I assured him it took quite a lot to tire me. "I come from hardy stock, you know."

"Oh, aye?" The blue eyes didn't look convinced. "I thought you came from London."

"Very funny," I replied.

Jeannie smiled. "What part of London?"

"West London. Chiswick. But I live in Covent Garden

now, I have my own flat. The first Grey to leave Chiswick in two generations," I told them, proudly. "My parents thought it terribly brave of me, moving all that way. You'd have thought I'd gone to darkest Africa."

David's eyebrow arched. "And what do they think of you coming to Scotland?"

"Oh, well, after Covent Garden, nothing shocks them. And they got rather used to me gadding about when I worked for the British Museum."

"Aye, I ken how it is." Jeannie nodded, straight-faced. "The Eyemouth Museum is always sending me off to exotic places, like."

I grinned. "Is your museum in an old building, or a modern one?"

"The Auld Kirk," she replied. "Down by the harbor. But the museum itself is just new—they opened it to mark the hundredth anniversary of the Disaster."

"What disaster?" I asked, then watched while the two of them shared a look that seemed a sort of silent conversation.

"Maybe," David advised Jeannie, "you'd best take her through when Mum is there, after all. She tells the tale better than anyone."

Jeannie agreed. "You'll just have to wait," she told me, "and let Granny Nan tell you about the Disaster. I'd not want to spoil the story."

"I hate waiting," I complained.

David smiled. "Aye, so does Peter. And unless you want your headache to come back, you'd do well to stay clear of the sitting room. The rain," he said, "does not improve his temper."

Jeannie studied him with knowing eyes. "Is that why you're hiding in here, then?"

"I'm not hiding, I'm running errands. I was to see how Verity was feeling, first, and then go down and check on Fabia's photographs."

I looked at him, curious. "Is Fabia a good photographer, really?"

"Bloody good." His nod held conviction. "I had my

doubts when Peter gave her the position, but he kent what he was doing. He usually does.''

"It's only that she seems so young.''

"Aye, she'll be twenty this summer. But she's been practically raised in a darkroom, that lass. It's what her father did,'' he explained. "Photography. He could have made quite a name for himself, if he'd bothered to put in the effort.''

"I gather,'' Jeannie said, "that he was something of a . . . well, a . . .''

"Sod,'' supplied David, rocking back in his chair. "Aye, that he was. He and Fabia's mother, they made quite a pair. All their parties and flash cars and Paris weekends. Peter finally had to cut them off—they were spending his money right, left and center.''

Jeannie frowned. "She was a fashion model, wasn't she, Fabia's mother?''

"Aye.''

"And where is she now?''

"America, I think.'' He shrugged. "When the money stopped, she lost all interest in living with Philip. Fabia was only a wee thing when she left, I don't suppose she even remembers.''

I felt a twinge of pity for the girl. "Still,'' I said, "it can't have been easy.''

"No,'' agreed David. "It's amazing she's turned out as sane as she has, being brought up by Philip. He wasn't all there, if you ken what I mean.''

Giving in to my curiosity, I asked how Peter Quinnell's son had died.

"A bottle of tablets washed down with a wee bit of brandy,'' was David's blunt reply.

"Oh.''

"Not that it really surprised anyone—we'd all seen it coming a long time ago. And at least some good's come out of it. Peter's got his granddaughter back.''

I frowned. "I'm sorry . . . what do you mean, he's got her back?''

"Well, Philip wouldn't let him see the lass for years.

Never sent so much as a photograph, or a card at Christmas. Like I said, he was a sod. To Peter,'' he informed me, ''family is everything. Not seeing Fabia fair broke his heart.''

Jeannie made a sour face. ''He should have counted his blessings.''

''Now, don't be unkind.'' David grinned. ''She may be a wee bit difficult, at times, but she *is* doing a good job with the photography.''

''Speaking of which,'' said Jeannie, in her motherly tone, ''were you not going downstairs to check on the lass, Davy?''

''Aye, so I was. One more shortie,'' he promised, reaching for the nearly empty tin, ''and I'm away.''

He strolled out of the kitchen whistling, and Jeannie rose to salvage what remained of her shortbread, tucking the tin safely away behind a stack of plates in the cupboard. Draining my teacup thoughtfully, I leaned back in my chair.

''He seemed in a good mood,'' I remarked. ''Very chatty.''

''Who, Davy? He's always like that.''

''Not with me.'' I spoke the words half to myself, and turned my gaze to the window. The wind had risen again outside, throwing spatters of rain against the glass and drawing a faint half-human moan from the empty field. Outside, against a corner of the peeling window ledge, a large gray spider brooded, curled beneath its web, long legs drawn up in petulant ill-temper while it waited for the rain to stop. It reminded me of Quinnell, that spider—impatient to get on with things, but thwarted by the one thing neither spiders nor archaeologists could control: the weather.

The wind had played havoc with my hair, as well. Against my face I felt the strands that had been tugged free of their plait, and when I vainly tried to coax them back my fingers found a bit of twig tangled behind my ear. I drew it out with a rueful smile. ''I don't feel much like a stoater now,'' I confessed, ''no matter what your son might think.''

''You look just fine,'' said Jeannie firmly. ''And anyway, I don't think Robbie's alone in his opinion.''

''I'm sorry?''

"That's Davy's jacket you're wearing, isn't it?"

To be perfectly honest, I'd forgotten all about the wind-cheater. I looked down now at the dark green folds of it that swallowed me and smelled of him, a clean elusive scent, quite different from the men's colognes to which I'd grown accustomed. I was all but hugging it, like a schoolgirl proudly wearing her boyfriend's football jersey.

I hadn't been aware of the fact before, but now I found myself wondering whether David Fortune had noticed it, too. Frowning slightly, I cleared my throat. "He let me have the loan of it because I was cold."

Jeannie said nothing, but I caught the simmering laughter in her eyes as she bent to clear away the teapot and our empty cups. I sighed again, and let the matter drop, shrugging my arms out of the oversized jacket as though my wearing it was unimportant.

But I did feel cold, without it.

X

The rain fell steadily through the night and when the morning came there was no sun at all, only a dull gray light and a dull gray sky and the dreary rhythm of the raindrops beating ceaselessly upon the roof above. The only variation came from rain blown hard against my bedroom window—it spattered there and trickled down in crooked lines and struck the ground below with deep plop-plunks that formed a bass line for the uninspired melody.

I'd never learned the knack of leaping out of bed on dismal mornings. A quick look through unfocused eyes, a mental groan of protest, and I'd pull the blankets back up around my ears and wriggle purposefully into them, trying to reclaim the drifting realm of sleep. It never worked, of course. Once wakened, I could never quite drop off again, but still there was something gloriously sinful about stealing an extra quarter of an hour in bed on a Sunday morning. Besides, I reasoned, with the weather outside so bleak and the whole house shuddering with every blast of wind, there was little incentive to wake up.

The air outside the covers bit my nose, but my bed was warm, made all the warmer by the fact that both cats had chosen to join me some time in the night. The black tom

Murphy lay sprawled full across my feet, while little Charlie snuggled underneath my elbow, breathing shallow, even breaths that stirred her fur. Shame to disturb them, I thought . . . so I didn't. Instead I closed my eyes and sifted idly through the strange events of yesterday.

We'd found a potsherd, I reminded myself. And a ditch. Well, what appeared to be a ditch, my logical mind corrected me. My logical mind was, to be honest, still finding it difficult to absorb the fact that we'd found anything at all, let alone the ditch and rampart of a Roman marching camp. Not that the rampart—if it was a rampart—was necessarily Roman. In a childish way I almost wished it wasn't. I could forget, then, about psychic children and long-dead Roman sentinels and unseen people breathing down my neck.

As it stood, I hadn't a hope of forgetting. I felt like one of those poor blighters plucked from a magician's audience to play assistant onstage, forced to stand there dazzled by the mirrors and tempted at each sleight of hand to ask "How did you *do* that?"

The trick, when revealed, was usually dead simple, but that didn't make it any less impressive. And it was no small trick to make me believe, however briefly, in ghosts.

Even now, the morning after the fact, I still felt an irrational touch of panic when a floorboard creaked outside my bedroom. For the space of a heartbeat I held myself motionless, screwed my eyes shut tighter, turned away from it . . . and then I heard a thinly stifled yawn and knew that it was only Fabia, passing by on her way downstairs. Relaxing into the pillows, I breathed and reached an automatic hand to switch off my alarm before it sounded.

Murphy, disturbed by the small movement, raised his head to glare at me a moment before leaping neatly from the foot of my bed to the windowsill. "And don't you start," I warned him, as his tail began to twitch. "If you see anything through that mess you can bloody well keep it to yourself." As though he understood my words the black cat settled himself at the window and stared in stony silence at the pouring rain outside.

There was to be no digging today, not just because of the

wet weather but because Quinnell held Sunday to be a day of rest. "If the good Lord had wanted us to work on Sundays," he'd told me last night, sounding for the first time like an Irishman, "he'd not have allowed the pubs to stay open."

Which explained why, when I finally extricated myself from my blankets and made my way downstairs in search of coffee, I was surprised to learn that Quinnell had ignored his own decree.

"He's gone up to the Principia," said Fabia, uninterested. The *Sunday Telegraph* lay sprawled across the kitchen table in disordered sections, and she'd drawn up a second chair so she could prop her feet up, ankles crossed, and read in comfort. Picking up the Review section, she shook it out and looked at me over the spread pages. "He'll have coffee on up there, if you want some. I don't drink the stuff."

The kettle sat cold on the stove and the air felt cold in the kitchen. Deciding that Quinnell's company would be more cheering than his granddaughter's, I borrowed a bright yellow mac from a peg in the front entry and made a dash for it, up the hill.

I found Quinnell sitting at David's desk, tapping at the keys of the computer with one finger, aimlessly. He raised his head as I came in, and smiled at the picture I made.

"My dear girl, could you have found a larger raincoat, do you think?"

"It was the closest thing to hand," I told him, pushing back the hood. "My sister conveniently forgot to pack my own, you see . . ."

"Conveniently?"

"It's a Barbour raincoat," I explained. "Almost new."

"Ah." He looked me up and down, assessingly. "Well, I'm sure we can find something more your size. I can barely see you, in that one. You look like a large rubber duck."

At least I was dry, I consoled myself, shaking out the dripping folds while Peter returned his attention to the computer. "I thought Sunday was supposed to be a day of rest," I reminded him.

"What? Oh, yes . . . yes, it is." He typed something out

and frowned. "It's only that this system is still giving us some problems. Eating my reports, you know, and spewing out all kinds of unintelligible symbols—that sort of thing."

"That sounds rather like you might have a virus," I offered, moving closer to look.

"Yes, well, that's what we thought, too, at first. But we've had it all checked out and serviced since, and our consultant couldn't find a problem."

"How odd."

"Not to worry, I'm sure we'll get it sorted out." Switching off the machine, he stood and smiled warmly. "If all else fails, I can always hit it with my cricket bat. Would you like a cup of coffee?"

"That would be brilliant, thanks."

He went through to the common room and came back with two mismatched mugs of steaming liquid—black for himself, and white for me. He'd only seen me drinking coffee once, last weekend, and I was surprised he'd remembered how I took it; but then Peter Quinnell, I had noticed, made a habit of remembering.

"You look as though you need this," he said, handing the mug over. "Did the rain keep you awake, last night?"

I assured him I'd slept very well. "I only woke up once, I think, and that was the fault of your neighbor's horses. He ought to be shot, really, keeping them out in this weather."

Quinnell's eyebrows drew together, vaguely. "Horses?"

"Yes, the ones in the field behind here. Does he race them, or something?"

"There are no horses here, my dear. A few cows, maybe, but . . ."

"I've heard them twice now," I said firmly. "Galloping."

"Ah." He nodded, smiling faintly, a parent amused by an obstinate child. "Perhaps you've been hearing the shadowy horses."

"The what?"

"That's Yeats," he explained kindly, naming the great Irish poet. " 'I hear the Shadowy Horses . . .' Púcas, I suppose he meant—evil spirits in the shape of horses, though it's quite the wrong season for púcas, just now. November's their month." He tilted his head to one side, thinking. "Of course, Yeats might have been writing of Manannan's horses. In Ireland, our sea-god, Manannan Mac Lir, is also the god of the otherworld, riding his chariot over the waves in the wake of his magical horses. They carry men off, do those horses—over the water and into the mist, to the land where the living can't go. When I was small," he said, his eyes warming, "my father would show me the waves rolling in, with their curling white foam, and say: 'Look now, boy, look at the horses of Manannan, see their white manes . . . he'll be coming behind in his chariot.' "

Small wonder the Irish were poets, I thought, when their gods were as close as the waves on the sea. "And did you ever see him?" I asked.

"Manannan? Oh, no." The long eyes softened, turning inward. "But I shall, my dear, one day. No doubt sooner than I'd like."

His voice was gentle and resigned, but it bothered me to think of him as old, to think of the sea-god's horses coming to carry him off to the country of the dead. And anyway, the horses that I heard at night were either real or dreamed, not phantom creatures born of Irish folklore.

"I've been taking another look at that sherd you found, yesterday," he went on, changing the subject. "Gave it a bit of a cleaning. It came up rather nicely . . . would you like to see?"

Unlocking the door to the finds room, he switched on the light to show me where the gleaming bloodred fragment, freshly scrubbed, lay drying on a bit of newspaper beside the sink.

"The edges, you see," he pointed out, "aren't abraded, they're sharp, so it's possible that fragment was buried soon after deposit. In fact, I wouldn't be at all surprised if we didn't find a few more sherds, nearby—parts of the same shattered pot." Bending over the three buckets of excavated soil that David had brought indoors yesterday, when the rain began, Quinnell poked about in one, experimentally.

"Would you like me to help you look?" I offered.

But before I could lift a finger, a firmly feminine voice

spoke out in no uncertain terms from the open doorway of
the finds room, telling me that I'd do no such thing. "It's
your day off," said Jeannie McMorran, turning her mater-
nally reproachful gaze on Quinnell. "Peter, I'm that surprised at you."

He held his ground admirably. "My dear, she *offered*."

"Aye. Well, whatever she was going to help you with,
I'm afraid you'll have to manage on your own. I've something more exciting planned for Verity. You ken that Robbie's got his piano lesson in half an hour . . ."

Quinnell arched one eyebrow in an elegantly dismissive
gesture. "Yes," he said, "I can see how she would be just
fascinated . . ."

". . . and I thought she might want to come into town with
us. Granny Nan's minding the museum today. We could
show Verity the tapestry."

Quinnell paused, then put about like a ship changing
course with a shift in the wind. "Oh, right. Yes, that's a
capital idea," he endorsed the plan, smiling encouragement
at me. "Do go, by all means. No, I shall be quite all right
without you . . . have you got your raincoat? There."

And seeing that my hood was up and all my snaps properly fastened, he sent me on my way, the mention of David's
mother's name having clearly settled the matter.

Jeannie turned up her own hood and ran through the rain,
and I followed her, down the long drive to Rose Cottage,
where Robbie sat waiting for us in the kitchen, holding a
red-handled screwdriver.

Jeannie laughed. "What's that for?"

"Granny Nan wants one."

"All right then, give it here, and go and get your music,
or else we'll be late."

The prospect of arriving late for his piano lesson didn't
seem to trouble Robbie greatly. He took a while to fetch his
sheets of music from the front room. Jeannie looked across
at me and shook her head. "It's the same every Sunday."

"Do you play the piano, yourself?"

"Och, no. I've not much talent. My mother played,
though, and we've kept her piano."

It was a shame, I thought, that Robbie's grandmother could not have lived to teach him how to play the lovely instrument. I'd learned so many things, from my two grandmothers. But Robbie didn't seem to feel the deprivation.

As he bounced through the puddles beside me on our short walk to the shed where Jeannie's car was garaged, Robbie happily noticed that our coats looked the same. "Look, Mum, look . . . mine looks just like Miss Grey's."

"Aye, I see that. Don't splash, now."

"Did you mind the screwdriver?"

Jeannie reassured him that she had indeed remembered. "Have they not got a screwdriver at the museum?"

"Not a red-handled one." Robbie leapt with both feet into one final puddle, and sloshed his way into the shed.

It took scarcely any time to drive to Eyemouth. I rubbed the condensation from my window and peered with interest at the maze of narrow, one-way streets hemmed in by rough-cast square stone houses. Unlike the big posh homes that lined the main road into town, their large front gardens bursting with cascades of bright spring flowers, the houses here crowded right against the pavement, leaving little room for anything green. But they were cheerful houses all the same, solid and dependable, with bold names painted in the transom windows over gaily painted doors.

Ivy Cottage and Lily Cottage I could understand, but some of the names baffled me, rather, until I asked Jeannie.

She smiled. "They're named for boats, some of them. We passed a house a wee while back called Fleetwing—that belonged to my grandad, ken, and the *Fleetwing* was his fishing boat."

"It's the name of Dad's boat, too," Robbie put in.

"Aye." Jeannie's voice was dry. "My Brian's one attempt to honor the family tradition. Went over big with my dad, that did."

From which I gathered Wally Tyler wasn't pleased his son-in-law had used the *Fleetwing* name.

"Did your father fish, as well?"

"My dad? No, he's never been one for the sea. He hates boats, so he trained as a gardener. It was old Mrs. Finlay

herself hired him onto take care of things up at Rosehill, and
that was afore she was old Mrs. Finlay.'' Jeannie glanced
across and smiled. ''He's rooted there, now.''

''Like the Sentinel,'' said Robbie.

Jeannie nodded. ''Aye.'' Negotiating a final downhill bend
and crossing another road that looked very much like the
road I'd first come in on, she swung the car neatly into a
large car park. ''Right,'' she said to me, ''won't be a minute.
I'll just take Robbie in, then you and I can walk along to the
museum. It's not far.''

After waiting a few minutes, I pushed open my door and
stepped outside to stretch, pulling my hood tight against the
soggy weather. The rain had lightened to a spatter, but the
sea, just steps away, kicked up a lively spray to wet the wind
and make it taste of salt. Drawn by the thunder of the waves,
I turned and tried to see, through the flat gray mist, if the
foam on the crest of the waves really did look like white
manes on Manannan's horses, as Peter had said, but I only
caught a glimpse of them before Jeannie's footsteps sounded
briskly on the pavement behind me.

''Not too cold?'' she asked, close by my shoulder. ''Because we could take the car, if you want. I just thought, with
it being Bank Holiday weekend, the parking might not be so
simple.''

I'd forgotten about the Bank Holiday. In spite of the less
than perfect weather, there were a fair number of people
cluttering the pavement, determined not to waste their holiday indoors. Jeannie, more sensibly, headed straight for shelter, and as I followed her along the road I felt the smug
self-satisfaction of a stranger who has managed to orient herself.

Surely, I thought, this was the road I'd come in on, that
first day, when the bus had brought me down from Dunbar.
Which meant that the harbor lay just over there, and to reach
the Ship Hotel, where Adrian and David lodged, one had
only to go down that little road, and . . .

''This way.'' Jeannie steered me past a curving sweep of
shops and across the street into a small square edged on two
sides by an odd array of buildings. One, with its distinctive

symbol set above the wooden door, was obviously the Masonic Lodge, and beside it a white-plastered house in the old style proclaimed itself to be a fish merchant's. Set on the diagonal at the corner of the square, a towering redbrick marvel of modern architecture boasting bright green window frames and a landscaped courtyard proved more difficult to identify. But the smaller structure, dead ahead, was clearly the museum.

"The Auld Kirk," said Jeannie, and indeed it could be nothing else. The golden walls and arching windows and beautiful bell-tower could only have belonged to an old church, no longer sanctified but still demanding reverence. Below the graceful dome and weather vane that capped the hexagonal tower, a working clock declared the time to be 11:30.

Jeannie, looking at the clock, informed me we'd be lucky to be out again by three. "She likes to talk, does Granny Nan."

"But what about Robbie?" I asked.

"Och, he'll be fine. My dad collects him from his piano lesson, see, and they have a wee walk around the harbor, look in on Dad's friends. Robbie loves it. Besides," she added, "he'd be bored, here with us. He's been through the exhibits a hundred times, and Granny Nan will be wanting to show you everything, especially since she kens you're a museum person, too."

"Has she worked here a long time, then?"

"Aye, since it opened. The doctor tried to make her give up working after her heart attack, but she'd not hear of it. Might as well try to make the sun set in the east."

As we walked the final few steps, heads bent low into the blowing rain, Jeannie glanced sideways and shot me a mischievous smile. "You'll want to be taking your raincoat off, though, afore we go in."

I looked down. "Is it really so awful?"

"No, but it belongs to Davy," she informed me, smug at having twice caught me wearing the big Scotsman's clothes. "And Granny Nan's a noticing sort of woman."

XI

The wind slammed the door at our backs as we came in through the vestibule, but no one in the lobby took much notice. Two couples stood pressed close against the long L-shaped reception desk—young couples, smartly dressed and out of sorts. I couldn't see the woman who was helping them, but I could hear her talking on the telephone, asking someone if they had a room. Which seemed an odd question, until I remembered that David had told me the Eyemouth Museum was also the local tourist information center. Finding rooms for frazzled holidaymakers who hadn't had the sense to book ahead for the Bank Holiday weekend apparently went hand in hand with showing visitors around the exhibits.

A large part of the lobby had been set aside for wall displays and standing panels, spread with maps and scenic views and photographs of local B & Bs. Bus and train schedules jostled for rack space with a dizzying assortment of free pamphlets promoting everything from stately homes and gardens to a self-conducted walking tour along the rugged coast.

Folding the dripping yellow raincoat more tightly over my bent arm, I stepped aside to let a young man, loaded down with pamphlets, pass me by. He started up a flight of metal stairs that ran along the nearest wall, and I tipped my head up, curious. "Is there a floor above, then?"

"Aye," said Jeannie. "That's where the temporary exhibitions go. But the main displays are down here, through that door beyond the main desk, d'ye see?"

I looked, and saw an open doorway, double width, with swinging gates that marked the way in and the way out.

"We'd best wait for Granny Nan, though." Jeannie smiled. "She'll want to take you around herself."

My gaze moved once again to the reception desk, but the young couples were still tightly clustered around it and I only saw their backs. Denied a glimpse of David's mother, I pretended a keen interest in the shelves of souvenirs that lined the wall behind us.

One silly toy did catch my eye—a small around puffball of pale fur topped by a red tartan tam. Two beady eyes peered at me from between the tufts of fur as I picked the strange thing up and turned it over. "What is this supposed to be?"

"Och, have you never seen a haggis? Canny wee creatures, they are. You almost never see them, in the wild. This one sings, like." She pressed its little tam and was rewarded by a high-pitched rendition of "Scotland the Brave."

I laughed, I couldn't help it. It was so delightfully ridiculous. "A singing haggis?"

"Aye. The real ones aren't so friendly looking . . ."

"Oh, give it up," I said. "I may be English, but even I know a haggis is only a sheep-stomach sausage."

"Is it?" Jeannie made her dancing eyes deliberately mysterious, and moved away, to scan a nearby bookshelf. "Here you go," she said. "Here's what you're wanting."

Keeping hold of my haggis, I came across to join her, but before she could show me what she'd found we were forced to stand aside again to let the smart-dressed foursome leave, and in their wake I got my first good look at David Fortune's mother.

Having heard her called "Granny" so often I'd fully expected her to be like my own grandmother, a small saintly woman with withered cheeks and soft white hair pulled back in gentle wings. But Granny Nan, decidedly, was not my Granny Grey.

She put me in mind of those marvelous film stars of the thirties and forties, who'd flouted tradition by dressing in trousers and throwing off wittily crafted one-liners. She stood tall for a woman and ramrod straight, with the same strong, uncompromising angle of chin and jawline that she'd passed onto her son. Her eyes were wider apart than his, and the mouth was different, but her hair, like David's, had once been dark—there were traces of it in the short cropped steel-grey curls which framed a face that must have been pretty in youth, and in maturity was striking. Although her ailing heart had flushed her face with color her complexion remained clear, with hardly a wrinkle to mar the mobile features, and her blue eyes held a warm blend of intelligence and humor that I recognized.

"Tourists," she said, with a broad smile, and dusted her hands on her corduroy trousers. "How would you not book a room on Bank Holiday weekend? They're lucky that Margaret and Jimmy could take them."

"They're just sent to test you," said Jeannie. She paused, sniffing the air suspiciously. "You've not been—"

"Certainly not."

"Aye, you have so, I can smell it on you." Jeannie sniffed again, to prove her point, and this time even I caught the faint smell of tobacco smoke, but Granny Nan stood firm.

"You can blame that on your father," she said. "He was around here not an hour ago, stealing my biscuits and telling me about the ongoings up at Rosehill. He told me a lot about this lass," she added with a wink. "I hear our Robbie thinks she's a stoater."

"Aye, well, I don't think he's the only one."

"No, old Wally's fair taken with her. Even my Davy let dab she had bonny long hair, and he rarely notices a lass unless she's three hundred years dead."

After which comment it took all my effort to hold back a blush while I stood through our proper introduction. My one relief was learning that she had a real name—Nancy Fortune. I'd have felt dead silly calling her Granny Nan.

Over our handshake she nodded at my singing haggis, openly amused. "Found a wee friend, have you?"

"Yes, well . . ."

Jeannie cut in, grinning. "She's fair taken with it. And you'll want to sell her one of these as well."

This time I saw the book she was pointing to, and reaching out, I took a copy from the shelf. "Oh right," I said. "My Scottish dictionary."

"Scots," Nancy Fortune corrected me firmly. "A Scots dictionary, that's what you've got there. Scottish means anything having to do with Scotland, ken, but Scots is the name of the language. Most Scots speak Scots." She smiled broadly. "Except in the Highlands, it's Gaelic up there. And the way we talk here in the Borders is different again from what you'd hear in Aberdeen."

"Oh." I flipped a page of the pocket-sized paperback, scanning the strange-looking words. *Stoater. Fantoosh. Oose.* Where *did* one come up with a word like that, I wondered?

"Oh aye, oose," Jeannie said, when I read the word aloud to them. Lounging against the reception desk she sent me a rueful smile. "Fluffy dust, like. I've plenty of that under my beds. What d'ye call it in England?"

I shrugged rather helplessly. "Dust."

"Such an uninspired language, English," David's mother said. "Though northern English sounds a bit like Scots; we use some words the same. And then there's Ulster Scots as well, in Northern Ireland. Peter always said he had no trouble at all understanding us, when he first came over—it sounded just like home."

I smiled. "He's lived in Scotland a long time, I gather."

"Aye, since the early fifties. He was searching in the west of Scotland then, like all the other Roman experts. When I first went to work for him he'd up and bought a grand old house near Glasgow, to spend his summers in. Ah, those were good days," she said, eyes softening at the memory. "We must have walked every inch of Dumfries and Galloway, the two of us, looking for likely battlefields."

Looking for battlefields along the Scottish-English border,

I thought, must be rather like looking for paving stones in the heart of London. They'd be everywhere. Trying to find one specific battlefield among the many—*that* would be the difficulty. "Did you never get discouraged?"

She shook her head. "We were young then, lass, we didn't ken the meaning of the word. Peter still doesn't. He's a driven man, is Peter—he'll not die afore he's tracked down his *Hispana*."

I tried to imagine the two of them young. Peter Quinnell, handsome now, would have been irresistible in his thirties, I thought—tall and lean and full of charm. I found myself wondering what sort of man David's father had been, by comparison. "Did your husband work for Peter, as well?" I asked.

"Och, no. My Billy was a fisherman, a lad I'd grown up with. Peter had a right canary," she admitted, "when I left him to get married onto Billy. But I was thirty-five then, and a woman wants a bairn."

Jeannie raised an eyebrow. "He'd have understood that, surely. He was married himself, after all."

"It's different for men," David's mother maintained. "And besides, that was no kind of marriage the two of them had, with Elizabeth biding in Ireland. She never came out of the Castle."

Ordinarily I didn't pry, but Quinnell's life intrigued me. "The Castle?"

"That's what Peter called his family's home," said David's mother, fondly, "in the north of Ireland, near the Giant's Causeway. One of his forefathers made a fair fortune in sugar and slaves in the West Indies, ken, then came back and had someone design him the Castle. Peter never liked it, much. Built with blood money, he said. But Elizabeth—Peter's wife—loved a grand mansion. And Philip used to love that house, as well." I saw a shadow darken Nancy Fortune's eyes. "Poor wee Philip. Such a shame, that was."

I commented that it must have been hard on Quinnell, losing his son.

"Aye, well, he's not lost all his family."

Jeannie's mouth quirked. "Not yet," she said. "I can't

say I'm not tempted to stir a few things into Fabia's porridge, some mornings.''

''Jings! I hope you've not told Peter that. The problem is,'' said Nancy Fortune, her eyes twinkling, ''there's too much of her father in her. Philip never would take a telling from anyone.''

''Peter must have been wild himself,'' Jeannie speculated, ''when he was younger. He has that look about him.''

The older woman merely shrugged. ''I'll not tell tales.''

''So he owns three houses, then?'' I frowned, still trying to sort out the various properties. ''The one in Northern Ireland, and the one near Glasgow, and . . .''

She shook her head. ''He sold the Glasgow house, last autumn. He had no need of it, ken, once he'd bought Rosehill. This is where he needs to be.'' Her voice was very certain. ''He'll find his Romans here, like Robbie says.''

''Och,'' Jeannie said, ''that minds me. Robbie made us bring you something.'' Digging in her pocket, she produced the red-handled screwdriver.

Nancy Fortune laughed. ''The devil! I've been wanting one of these all morning. The one gate's sagging on its hinges, and it takes a red-handled screwdriver. I went all through our tool cupboard, but no joy.''

''Aye, well, he said you needed one, and you ken what he's like.''

I looked from Jeannie's face to Nancy Fortune's, frowning. ''Did he just *know*? I mean, you didn't ring him up, or anything?''

Her smile was warmly forgiving. ''You don't believe, I take it, in the second sight.''

''Well . . .''

''You will, in time. The bairn's fair gifted,'' she informed me. ''I used to have an aunt like that, who had the second sight. She always kent when I'd been smoking out behind the shed. Kent when I was going to be up to something, too . . . afore I did myself, sometimes.''

''And was she always right?'' I asked.

''Oh, aye.'' She glanced at me, noting my doubtful expression. ''It's all dead simple, second sight. My auntie said we're all made up of energy, and energy can't be destroyed. It changes. When a body dies, some energy goes off in heat and movement, but the rest of it remains, and so you get a ghost, like. My auntie said that folk who have the second sight, their brains are more receptive to the energy that's out there—not just to ghosts," she said, "but to the living. A living brain's electric, after all . . . electric impulses. Our thoughts go out the whole time just like television waves, and the gifted person acts like an antenna."

Reasonable enough, I admitted, although it didn't explain everything. "So how can someone see the future?" I asked. "Did your aunt have a theory for that as well?"

"That I can't tell you. She saw things, but how she saw them . . ." She shrugged. "My mother, bless her heart, who was a fair religious woman, thought that premonitions were a gift from God."

"Some gift." Jeannie wrinkled her nose. "Robbie almost never gets them, but when he does they drive him mad. He has nightmares, poor wee soul."

"Has he always been . . ." I stumbled over the word "psychic," and opted instead for the euphemism, "gifted?"

Jeannie nodded. "I used to find him standing in his cot and talking to the wall. Talking to a lady, he said. I thought it was just imagination, like, until he pointed out his lady in my wedding picture, and I saw that he'd been talking to my mother." Her smile was soft. "She died the year I married, afore Robbie was born, so she must have wished to see her grandson. She still does, sometimes, although now he's getting older he'll not always tell me when she comes. He's like that since he started school—he keeps his secrets now. Except," she added, grinning, "when he's out with a good-looking woman."

"Aye," Granny Nan agreed solemnly. " 'Tis why he tells me *everything*."

I laughed. "And when did he tell you about his Roman Sentinel?"

"Last summer." Granny Nan tipped her head back and thought. "Aye, in June. The lad was helping me go through my bookshelves, to sort them out, like, and he took to this old battered book on the Roman military. Full of illustrations, that book was. Robbie came to me all excited and showed me one of the legionaries and said, 'He lives in our field.' Just like that. So I picked up a pen and wrote Peter.''

''You were that sure?''

''Oh, aye.'' She suddenly seemed ageless, and very wise. ''Robbie's never wrong, lass. If he sees something in that field, it's there. It's the rest of us who are blind.''

And then, remembering the red-handled screwdriver, she tightened her grip on the tool and sent us a purposeful nod. ''Right, I'll just fix that wee hinge and then we're away. You two can leave that haggis and the dictionary in behind the desk, there, and I'm sure Verity won't want to drag Davy's wet raincoat around with her . . .''

Jeannie's dark eyes caught mine, laughing, and their message was a silent *See? I told you so.*

Ignoring her, I dumped my things behind the desk and, gathering my dignity, began my proper tour of the museum.

XII

Touring a museum was, for me, a busman's holiday.

My idle mind took note of every detail of design: did the gallery flow nicely from one section to another? Was the flooring easy on the feet, or did one's knees begin to ache before the tour was over? Were the labels written clearly, plainly, cleanly, and with care? And the artifacts themselves, were they displayed with thought, and properly protected? This final point was my obsessive passion.

In Paris my one and only visit to the Louvre had been spoiled by windows—rows of lovely windows pouring deadly direct sunlight on the priceless paintings opposite. And I'd never quite recovered from the horror of the flash-bulbs popping around the *Mona Lisa*, when the guard whose job it was to drone out "pas de flash" was off on tea break. All those tourists, all those flashbulbs, all that stupid, stupid ignorance, destroying the painting as surely as if they'd slashed it with a knife, and all for a snapshot that wouldn't hold a candle to the postcards one could buy for next to nothing in the gift shop.

I tended to avoid museums, when I wasn't working.

But this, I reasoned, was a special case. I would be living out at Rosehill for the digging season anyway—it followed

I should do my best to learn the local history. And to my relief, I found that there was nothing here to set my teeth on edge. Someone had done a professional job of presenting the town's past in a well-defined sequence of information panels and displays.

Border lords and Jacobean conspirators, boatbuilders and smugglers, the men who fished the North Sea for herring and the "fisher lassies" whose job it was to clean and salt the catch—all of them had their place in the Eyemouth Museum. And room had been made for the odd outsider.

David's mother paused before one panel. "And this, of course, commemorates the day the bard himself came here, to be made a Royal Arch-Mason."

My eyebrows rose. "What, Shakespeare came here?"

"Robbie Burns, you heathen," she corrected me, rolling her eyes good-naturedly in response to my English ignorance. "Our national poet, no less."

Jeannie thought it was a wonder Robert Burns had lived to tell the tale. "Coming to a smuggling town like Eyemouth, and him an exciseman."

I fancied even smugglers harbored some respect for genius. The poet's image kept proud company with nets and the herring barrels and the whopping great cannonball Jeannie showed off with a smile. "That came from the Fort."

"And where is the Fort?"

"Over there," she said, pointing in the general direction of the sea. "On the top of the cliffs at the end of the beach. You can see it from where we parked the car."

"Not a Roman fort, I take it?"

"Tudor," Nancy Fortune told me. "Built in the days of the boy king Edward of England, and torn down under Elizabeth. The French and the English kept fighting us for it. There's no telling whose cannon that came from."

Jeannie looked down at the heavy cannonball. "The two cannon still up there aren't Tudor, are they?"

"No, folk set those up on Fort Point in the French invasion scare, we think—the middle of last century."

Invasion, I reflected, was a constant theme along this stretch of coast. Invasion and slaughter and swift retribution, an unending cycle of fire and sword. Small wonder the soil here was red.

"The Fort," said Nancy Fortune, "was my Davy's favorite place, when he was younger. He did all his thinking there. It's peaceful, like—just grass and mounds and those two cannon looking on the sea."

Jeannie nodded, straight-faced. "And it's a rare fine spot to see the haggis."

"Oh, aye," agreed the older woman. "Wild haggis everywhere. They like to dig their burrows in the mounds."

Refusing to rise to the bait, I drifted on toward the next display.

It was dead clever, this display. In all the local history museums I had visited I'd never seen its match. Instead of relying on pictures alone to give one the feel of a fishing boat, they'd brought the boat itself inside. The front half of a boat, at any rate.

Stepping onto the bridge, I played like a child with the polished wheel and gazed in admiration through the glass window, at the ropes and nets and fish boxes piled on "deck," and the real stuffed herring gull riding the jutting bow into an imaginary wind. I thought the whole thing brilliant, and said so.

"Aye, it's fair impressive," David's mother said. "But ye've not yet seen our greatest achievement. That we save for last."

With great expectations I followed her around the remaining few displays until we arrived at the end of the loop, within sight of the lobby.

"There." She stopped dramatically before the final wall. "*That's* the treasure of our museum."

I saw only a tapestry, and a modern one at that. Attractive, yes, but hardly what one thought of as . . .

"The Eyemouth Tapestry," my guide's voice sliced evenly into my thoughts. "It took twenty-four ladies two years to make this, for the one hundredth anniversary of the Disaster." Her sideways glance was self-assured. "You'll have heard about the Disaster?"

"Heard it mentioned, yes, but—"

Jeannie interrupted me as Nancy Fortune's eyebrows rose. "We thought we'd let you tell her, since you tell the story best."

"Och, it's not so difficult. Any bairn here in Eyemouth could tell you about the Disaster. That's the Great East Coast Fishing Disaster," she explained for my benefit, speaking in obvious capitals. "Black Friday, they called it. And though it's been more than a hundred years since, you'll still hear folk talk like it was yesterday." She folded her arms and gave a small sigh before smoothly beginning the story. "It happened in October. A stretch of bad weather had kept all the boats in the harbor a few days, but the morn of Black Friday was fair bright and sunny, with never a breath of wind. The fishermen's wives set to baiting the lines, and their menfolk prepared for a fine day of fishing, though the old public weather-glass, down by the pier-end, was lower than any had seen." She shook her head. "It made some of the fishermen wary, that glass being low. Still, the day looked so grand and the sea looked so calm that the younger lads started on out." A practiced storyteller, she paused and let the sentence dangle until I gave her the prompt.

"What happened?"

"Well, it's a point of honor, like, that if the one boat goes out all the rest go, too. So at eight in the morning they sailed from the harbor and made their way out to the fishing grounds. Four hours they fished, then at midday the sea changed. It was the stillness that warned them . . . a horrible stillness . . . but afore they could move the whole sky turned to black and the wind rose up screaming and wild."

She pointed to the first panel of the tapestry. Against the vivid blue background of the sea, two terror-stricken fishermen clung desperately to the lines of their sinking vessel, struggling to guide it into shore. "Whole boats were tossed up from the water, their masts torn away, and their sails ripped to shreds, and the sea took the ones who were heading for harbor and dashed them apart on the rocks. Those on the shore tried everything—tossed out lines and made human chains, reaching out hands for the struggling men, but the waves took them anyway."

I stared, transfixed, at the tapestry's second panel, a more symbolic rendering of the tragedy, with seven childlike figures scattered around the outline of a boat, watched by a wailing line of human-faced cliffs. "How terrible."

"Aye. One hundred and eighty-nine men were taken in the Disaster, from all four local harbors—Burnmouth, Cove, St. Abbs and Eyemouth. That's what the four maps show, in this third section. And the sea wall, just here, has one stone for each Eyemouth man lost. One hundred and twenty-nine stones," she gave me the tragic count. "Half the men of the town gone, and all in one day. That was the toll of the Eyemouth Disaster . . . October the fourteenth, eighteen-hundred-and-eighty-one."

Embroidered with painstaking care on the tapestry were the names of all the fishermen who died in the Disaster, along with the names of their boats. It made a chilling record.

I stood a moment, deeply moved, reflecting on the ironies of history. Nearly two thousand years ago, if Quinnell's theories were right, another group of men had faced their own Disaster day in this same place—men who spoke a different language, served a different god, but who had dreams and wives and mothers, like the fishermen of Eyemouth.

And the shadowy horses had come for them, too, to carry them off to the land of the dead. I had a sudden and disturbing sense of something evil, undefined . . . some dark and vengeful entity that lay in wait to ambush all who passed this way, whether they travelled by land or by sea, chasing men down through the centuries.

The silence clutched at me and held a moment, and then Jeannie nudged me forward to the light, and shaking off the foolish vision I turned my back to the Eyemouth Tapestry and the terrified stares of its drowning men.

The weather had cleared a little by the time Jeannie and I finally left the museum. In the car park, we found Wally Tyler waiting for us.

He pitched his cigarette away when he saw us coming, and Kip, at his heels, jumped up joyfully. Behind them, through the thinning mist, I saw the long dark promontory where the Fort had stood, jutting out into the waves, and below that the waves themselves, white-capped and swirled by salt-sprayed wind that carried still the bone-chilling dampness of rain.

"Heyah," Jeannie greeted her father. "Where's Robbie?"

"Asleep in the car."

"Wore him out, did you? Where did you go?"

"Round aboot. Had a few pints, like, wi' Deid-Banes."

"Oh, aye? Well, we'd best get the two of you home, then."

The collie, soaking wet, brought an indefinable odor into the car, and Jeannie wrinkled her nose. "Och, Kip, you're mingin."

I sniffed myself, and decided that "mingin" was one word I needn't look up in my dictionary. "Deid-Banes," though, was something different. I flipped the pages casually, eventually translating the term into the equally unhelpful English "Dead-bones."

Jeannie, glancing in the rearview mirror, fixed her father with a stern accusing eye. "Granny Nan smoked a cigarette this morn."

"Oh, aye?"

"You gave it to her, didn't you?"

The old man shrugged, all innocence. "I might have left yin lying aboot, where she could find it."

"But Dad, the doctor said—"

"I mind whit the doctor said," he cut her off, his gray eyes unimpressed. "But Nancy Fortune's always done as Nancy Fortune pleases, and she wasna in the grave last time I looked."

Two hours later, sipping tea with Peter in the cozy red-walled sitting room, I learned that his opinion took a slightly different twist.

"A difficult woman," he mused, with a shake of his head. "Most difficult. She simply will not listen to advice, you know. She never has. Her doctor says she must slow down, but Nancy . . . Nancy never listens."

He'd been drinking, from the looks of it. The glass beside his teacup held a half-inch of clear liquid that I guessed would not be water. But his sigh implied his own health habits were above reproach, a pure example to be followed, if only David's mother would be reasonable . . .

"Well, she looked perfectly healthy to me," I said. "I quite liked her. And I liked the museum, it's very well organized."

"You saw the tapestry, of course? The Disaster tapestry?"

"Yes."

"They do remember their Disaster, here in Eyemouth." Scooping Murphy from the arm of the leather chair, he repositioned the creature so it draped across his knees. "Not that I've a problem with people living in the past," he went on, stroking the black cat absently. "I'm all for it, actually. My Irish blood, perhaps." He smiled. "I've always liked what that one writer said—that chap who wrote *Trinity*—"

"Leon Uris."

"Is that his name? He said there was no future in Ireland, only the past happening over and over. I get that feeling here, as well. The past is never far away, at Rosehill. Never far away."

Beneath his hand the cat yawned, turned staring eyes upon me for a moment, then shifted its gaze to the window. It didn't hiss, or make a sound, but the dark hair lifted all along its spine.

"You see?" said Quinnell, lightly. "Look, our Sentinel is passing."

I believe he meant it as a joke, but through the moaning of the wind I fancied that I heard the footsteps walking, walking, steadily, along the gravel drive.

XIII

David was already hard at it when I went up to the Principia on Wednesday, before breakfast. He swivelled in his chair as I came in, and his face, bathed in the hard blue light of the computer screen, looked beastly tired. "Morning," he greeted me, his jaw stiffening as he held back a yawn. He reached for the mug of coffee on the desk before him. "You're up early."

"Look who's talking." I took my own seat in the stall-cubicle opposite and hitched my chair sideways to face him. "Are you actually doing work at this ungodly hour?"

"Well, I'm not playing computer games." He seemed in good spirits this morning, relaxed. "Those are all on Adrian's machine, ken. He's got the golf and everything. Me, I'm just entering my field notes from Saturday, afore I forget what I was thinking." The blue eyes flicked me with a friendly challenge. "So what's your excuse?"

"Couldn't sleep." I thought of asking him if he had ever heard the horses running in the fields beyond, but after one more quick look at those sensible eyes, I decided against it. "Do you not teach on Wednesdays?"

He shook his dark head. "We have meetings and such, in the afternoon, but I do feel a wee cough coming on." He winked. "Anyway, Peter's been wanting to show me the things that he found when he widened the trench."

"Oh, yes. Potsherds." I fetched them from the finds room, to show him. "We found four, yesterday. I've not had much of a chance to look at them, myself, really. I'd have worked a little longer on them last night, only Peter wouldn't hear of it."

"Aye, well, he has a thing about us working late. It's like his Sunday holiday, you'll find—meant to be strictly observed by everyone but Peter himself."

"Yes, I noticed that. He was puddling around up here on Sunday morning, but he sent me off with Jeannie. We went down to the museum."

"So I heard." He raised his coffee mug to hide the slanting smile. "Behaved herself, did she?"

His smile had distracted me. "Who, Jeannie?"

"My mother. She didn't try to bully you into helping out at the next coffee morning, or anything? No? Eh well, it's early days yet. Give her time."

I looked at him with interest. "Do they have coffee mornings?"

"Aye, on a Saturday. All the local clubs and groups hold coffee mornings turn about, in the Masonic Hall. This next one coming's for the heart fund, and my mother's sure to be involved with that. You ken she had a heart attack?"

I nodded. "Jeannie told me. Very recently, was it?"

"Last July. Scared me more than it did her, I think."

"She seems to have made a full recovery," I commented. "I could barely keep up with her yesterday; she moves at a fearful pace."

"Aye, she does that." The big Scotsman's eyes held affection. "It'd take being struck by lightning to slow my mother down." The sound of an engine speeding up the long drive seemed to emphasize his statement. "That'll be Adrian," he told me, as I heard a car door closing. "Either that, or Nigel Mansell's come for breakfast."

I glanced at my wristwatch, surprised. "Adrian's normally still half asleep, at this hour."

"Well, we'll be starting to map out the ramparts today,

and Peter was keen on an early start. It's a time-consuming process, but it shouldn't be too difficult, assuming that we really have a marching camp. We ken the shape a camp would be—we only have to find the corners.''

I nodded understanding. Roman marching camps, and forts, and fortresses, tended to follow a playing-card kind of design—square or rectangular, with rounded corners. The Romans, being Romans, had imposed their rigid structure on whatever land they passed through, instead of letting nature dictate what design they ought to use. And so, as David said, once any section of the rampart had been found, one only had to follow the predicted shape around to plot the whole site's boundaries.

There were several methods they could use, to do this. Adrian, I thought, could take his ground-penetrating radar equipment and run it along inside the line of the southern ditch that we'd already found. Eventually, by taking measurements, his readings should show two marked anomalies, one at either end—two parallel blips on the computer map, to tell us where the eastern and western ditches had been. And then, by heading northwards along either one of those, he should be able to locate the fourth and final ditch, revealing the marching camp's outline.

David, when I asked him, confirmed that this would be their main approach. ''But we'll probe as well, just to be sure.''

Probing, I knew, was the tried and tested method—I'd seen a hollow probe used many times, to good effect. Though it sometimes could do damage to a fragile buried feature, most archaeologists relied on it to confirm the often ambiguous results of modern geophysical surveys.

The probe itself was nothing more elaborate than a narrow tube of hard steel with a sharp bottom edge and a cutaway gap down one side, topped by a T-shaped handle that helped the user force it downwards, deep into the earth. Withdrawn, the gap in the probe's side displayed a core sample of the layered soil deposits. In our case, the dark silt that filled a ditch would show up very clearly against the surrounding soil.

It was tedious work, though, and ramming the probe down again and again through tangled turf and heavy subsoil demanded a fair bit of strength.

David flexed his broad shoulders and stifled a yawn, linking his hands behind his head. "It's a shame that Robbie can't go around and mark the ramparts for us. It'd save a lot of bother."

It was the first time I'd heard anybody tell me something Robbie couldn't do. "Why can't he?"

"Because he's not so accurate, with things like that. He has his hits and misses. Most of what he tells you he just gets at random, walking over things. If you ask him the right questions, he can tell you quite a lot. But if you push him, and he tries too hard . . ." David shrugged, dropping his hands again to reach for his coffee mug. "He's only a lad, not some kind of machine."

I studied him a moment, weighing my next question. Since coming to Rosehill, I'd grown used to David keeping his distance, polite and professional, his manner not inviting any personal intrusion. But Saturday in the kitchen with Jeannie, and now again this morning, he'd been so easy to talk to that I thought he might not mind if I just asked for his opinion.

"David . . ." I found I liked the feel of his name, familiar on my tongue.

He drained his coffee, pulling a face at the taste. "Aye?"

"You're a scientist."

"Aye?"

"Well . . ." I steepled my fingers, and frowned. "How do you explain what psychics do?"

"I can't."

"But you believe in them."

He swiveled slowly in his chair, considering the matter. "That depends what you mean by belief. If you mean, do I accept the concept without question . . . no, I don't. But questioning things is the root of all science. Something happens we don't understand, so we test it, experiment, study the evidence."

"And is there evidence?"

"Oh, aye. You want to have a chat with a friend of mine who lectures in our psychology department, at the university. Did his Ph.D. mainly on parapsychology—he's been studying psychics for years." David's eyes touched mine, smiling. "He'll take you right back to the Oracle of Delphi, if you've the patience to listen. Thousands of years of reported occurrences. Mind you, it's only been since the last century that anybody took a scientific interest. The Society for Psychical Research, and all that. Flash cards in the laboratories."

I frowned harder. "But I still don't understand how Robbie—"

"Robbie sees things that the rest of us can't. You can test him any way you want to, laboratory or no, and you'll get the same result." He lifted one shoulder, dismissively. "It's uncomfortable, aye, when a thing won't fit into our orderly world, but then Western society's always been skeptical. And not very bright," he reminded me, wryly. "It took us till the sixteenth century to figure out the earth went around the sun."

He had a point, I thought. "So you're saying I should just accept the fact that Robbie's psychic."

"Christ, no. If we didn't have doubts we'd have no science at all, no reason to experiment. I'm only saying you should keep an open mind."

I promised to do my best. "And does the head of your department . . . what's his name? The one who's coming to lunch at the end of the month."

"Dr. Connelly."

"Right. Does he also have an open mind?"

"What d'ye mean?"

"Well, if we told him Robbie saw a Roman walking on the hill . . ."

"He'd have us all committed." David grinned. "No, we'll have to find some harder evidence, before Connelly will give his approval."

"I do wish we had more time."

"We've got two full weeks yet, lots of time. Besides, we're very close to something. I can feel it in my bones."

"You sound like Peter."

"Aye, well, it rubs off on you, after a while. And I was howking with Peter afore I could walk."

"Howking?"

He shot me a mischievous glance. "D'ye not have your dictionary with you? My mother said you were fair having fun with it on Sunday."

I couldn't help smiling back. "Sorry, no, it's back at the house. What's 'howking'?"

"Digging. To howk something means to dig it up out of the ground." He lifted his coffee mug again and grimaced. "God, that's awful stuff. I'll make another pot. Did you want a cup, as well?"

"Yes, please, if you don't mind. Cream and sugar."

"Right." David rose and stretched to his full height before disappearing in the direction of the common room, and while I waited for him to return I carefully arranged the four new potsherds on my desk and bent over them, thoughtfully.

The furtive pad of footsteps broke my concentration.

I felt the hair rise prickling on the back of my neck, and glanced up sharply, seeing nothing. "Hello?"

No one answered. The silence stretched my nerves to breaking point, and when I felt the brush of cold against my hand I nearly shot straight up into the rafters. Recovering, I looked down at my hand and the thing that had touched me. A pair of liquid brown eyes stared back in mild inquisition, and Kip's long feathered tail gave a tentative wag. Collies, I thought, always looked so damned intelligent, and this one appeared to be weighing the wisdom of making friends with someone this jumpy and unpredictable.

Since I'd always liked the company of dogs, I settled the matter by scratching his ears. "Hello, Kip. God, you didn't half give me a scare. Where's your master, then?"

I could have sworn the collie shrugged, as if to say he didn't know. At any rate, I saw no sign of either Robbie or Wally, and when I went on stroking him the dog collapsed like a spent balloon on my feet, rolling over slightly to make his tummy more accessible.

"You'll want to watch him," David warned me, returning

along the aisle. "He'll stay like that for hours if you let him."

Adrian, coming through the main door, heard the warning and laughed. "Oh, Verity won't mind. She's a right pushover, when it comes to animals."

And crossing to my desk he set a covered plate in front of me. "Your breakfast," he announced, whisking off the cover with a flourish. "Jeannie said I was to be sure you ate it, seeing as you sneaked off without eating this morning."

Sighing heavily, I looked down at the heaping great mound of square sausage and fried eggs, rimmed with strips of toast and rounds of tomato. "But I never eat breakfast, you know that. A little toast, maybe, but . . ."

"I have my orders," Adrian said, setting down a knife and fork.

David grinned, and handed me my mug. "Here's your coffee."

"I'll give you five pounds if you eat this for me." I made the offer hopefully, but he refused to play.

"I've had mine, thanks. So, what did you make of the sherds, then?"

I moved the plate to one side, temporarily, out of the way of the four small jagged fragments of bloodred pottery. "Well, they're definitely Samian ware—a small pot, I'd think, from the degree of curve. Maybe two pots. This one," I said, touching one end piece lightly, "doesn't seem to match the others."

"And what date would you estimate?"

I chewed my lip. "Offhand, I'd say they're earlier than what we're looking for. But then again . . ." Without the support of laboratory analysis, dating pottery could be a rather imperfect science. If the piece wasn't actually stamped by a known maker, one had to rely on comparisons to other bits of pottery dug up at other sites.

In the case of Samian ware my task was made somewhat simpler by the fact that German archaeologists had spent most of the last century studying and classifying artifacts found on Roman sites in that country, and had managed to work out a very useful and detailed typology of Roman era pottery. The advance and decline of the Roman frontier in Germany had been so well documented by historians like Tacitus that archaeologists could say with reasonable certainty when each site had been occupied, making it easy to fix a date upon the bits of pottery found there. All that remained for me to do was to try to match my own sherds to a documented German find.

Again I touched the suspect sherd. It was a rim fragment, broken from the top edge of a pot or bowl. "This one . . . I don't know, it strikes me as a later piece. I ought to ask Howard. A friend of mine," I explained, "at the British Museum. He's absolutely mad about Samian ware—knows the name of every potter. He could give these sherds a glance at fifty paces and tell us exactly what they were part of and when it was made. I could send him some sketches, and ask his opinion. And perhaps, if Fabia would take a few photographs . . . ?"

Adrian, rummaging at his desk, glanced around in midyawn. "What a good idea. Why don't I go and get her now, for you—no point in letting it wait."

"We can tell her on the way," said David. "Peter will be thinking we've forgotten all about him."

"Oh, right." Adrian looked disappointed.

His survey equipment was stored safe behind the locked door of the finds room, and while he went to retrieve it I took a thoughtful sip of coffee, touching the sherds again, feeling the raised impression of what appeared to be a flower petal. I'd seen a pattern similar to this one when I'd worked on Dr. Lazenby's excavations in the south of England, but that site had been Agricolan, dating from the seven-year period during which Gnaeus Julius Agricola had served as governor of Britain. And Agricola had been recalled in AD 84—forty years or so before the disappearance of the Ninth.

"Well, that's us away, then," said David, shouldering his probe. "We'll leave you in peace to eat your breakfast. And it's no good trying to give it away to the dog—he can't eat eggs. Bloats up like a balloon, he does."

His pale eyes were teasing, and I toyed with the idea of pitching a sausage at him, but instead, I took a bite of toast and chased it down with coffee, smiling my most amenable smile. "Right then. Have a good time."

I waited until I couldn't hear his cheerful whistling anymore before I glanced down at the dog sprawled beneath my chair. Kip's one visible eye met mine hopefully, and his tail thumped once against the floor. "Look love," I offered, "here's the deal. I'll eat the eggs, if you'll eat everything else. How does that suit you?"

Evidently, it suited the collie fine. The empty plate was positively shining when I set it on the corner of my desk.

Well satisfied, I washed my hands and settled down to start my labored drawings of the sherds.

XIV

I sent the drawings and photographs off by the afternoon post, then sat back and waited for Howard's reply. He'd always been frightfully efficient. I half expected him to ring me the following day, when the envelope hit his desk, but it wasn't until Friday morning that I got my call from the British Museum.

"Before I give you my opinion on these sherds," he said, "I simply have to ask: What the devil are you *doing* up there? We had to look Eyemouth up on the map, for heaven's sake. Pondered it all through tea break yesterday, but no one could recall an excavation going on in your area."

I smiled against the receiver, feeling in my pocket for a pen while balancing my notepad on the narrow front-hall table. "Well," I told him, "as I'm constantly being reminded by people here, you don't know everything down there in London."

"So it is an excavation? Led by whom?"

I told him, and waited while he paused for thought. Howard's memory was slow, but encyclopedic. It took him less than a minute to place the name. "Good God, not *the* Peter Quinnell? Don't tell me he's still on the trail of the Ninth Legion?"

"Well . . ."

Howard groaned, with feeling. "My dear girl, no one's taken Quinnell seriously since I was in short pants. And he must be ancient, surely?"

"Oh, don't be such a snob," I replied, picking a barb that I knew would hit home. "He's only in his seventies, that's hardly doddering these days. And I find him rather fascinating."

"Well, so long as he pays you heaps of money . . ."

"The sherds?" I prompted, patiently.

"Ah. Yes, well, your initial hunch was quite correct."

"They're Agricolan." I felt a twinge of disappointment even as I spoke the words.

"Yes."

"All of them?"

"All pieces of the same bowl, I should think."

"Oh." So much, I thought, for my suspicions that the rim sherd didn't match. Howard's knowledge of Samian ware was indisputable.

"Quite a lovely small bowl," he went on. "A perfect match to one dug up in Germany by—"

I cut him off. "So what date are we looking at, exactly?"

"Oh, somewhere between AD 80 and 82, I should think. Not much help to you in finding the Ninth Legion, I'm afraid."

"You never know. At least it's an earlier date, and not a later one. For all we know the pot might have been forty years old when it was broken," I reasoned stubbornly. "And anyway, we've only just begun to map the boundaries of the site. I'm sure we'll find more pottery when we start the proper digging."

"What you want to find," he coached me, "is a sherd that's been hammered down a post hole, or something, so you know for certain that it dates from the time of the . . . what is it, exactly, that you're excavating?"

"A marching camp."

"Ah," he said again, without enthusiasm. "Not much chance of finding post holes there, unfortunately. Not ones of any real size."

He was, as always, right. Marching camps, constructed for the one night only, had no permanent structures, and even the stakes used on top of the ramparts were smaller than those used in forts. They often left no trace at all.

"And anyway," Howard reminded me, "it's long odds that you'll even find a marching camp. Not if you're working for Peter Quinnell."

"I'll bet you a fiver."

"I'm sorry?"

"That this is a marching camp."

"Make it a bottle of Bell's and you're on."

"A fiver," I repeated firmly.

"Fair enough. Oh, by the way," he said, remembering, "you do know Lazenby is looking for you?"

"Dr. Lazenby? Whatever for?"

"He's taking a team out to Alexandria in September. Quite a high-profile venture, from what I've been hearing. The Beeb's sending a film crew along, and everything."

"And?"

"And he wants you as part of his team," Howard explained, speaking as if to a child.

"You're joking."

"Darling," he chastised me. "I never joke."

"Alexandria . . ."

"Mmm. Shall I give him your number?"

I thought of Quinnell, and shook my head. "No, not just yet. I'll . . . I'll give him a ring in a few days, all right? And Howard?"

"Yes?"

"Thanks. For the expert opinion, I mean."

"Any time." The smile in his voice almost made me miss my days at the museum, and I rang off with a small sigh.

The little gray cat, Charlie, neatly leapt onto the hall table to investigate my notebook, and I stroked her dainty chin, forcing the nostalgic mist from my eyes. I had made the right decision, after all, in leaving the museum, leaving Lazenby.

Charlie made a small sound like the squeak of a closing door, as though approving my desire for independence. A cat, I thought, was the very model of an independent animal, so long as someone remembered to scratch around its chin, just there . . .

Charlie's eyes snapped open and she raised her head, alarmed. Ears flattening, she arched her back and gave a sharp, high-pitched meow.

"For heaven's sake!" I burst out, when my lunging heartbeat paused for breath, "*Will* you stop that? I'll be a mass of nerves if you cats keep—" And then I too broke off and cocked my head, listening.

Someone was climbing the cellar stairs.

The footsteps were heavy—a man's footsteps—only all the men were down at the far end of the field. I knew that because I'd left them there, a quarter of an hour ago. Not just the men, but Fabia as well . . . and even Jeannie, who'd come down to fetch me for my telephone call, had stayed behind to watch the crew in progress. I ought to have been alone in the house.

But still the footsteps came on, climbing, bold and clearly audible.

My mind raced swiftly through the possibilities. The ghost . . . oh, God, don't let it be the ghost. A burglar . . . there, that was more probable, and in my muddled state of mind seemed much less frightening. My brain found reason, told my feet to move, but the message took a moment to reach its mark and in that moment the man came up the final stair and into the entrance hall.

He seemed, to his credit, more shocked by my presence than I was by his. "Jesus!" he said, then recovered and came forward, wiping one hand on the back of his denim jeans before holding it out in a friendly greeting. "Sorry," he apologized, with a self-deprecating grin, "I thought you were all down in the field. You must be Miss Grey, am I right? My son's not stopped talking about you."

So this, I thought, was Brian McMorran. I studied him with interest over the handshake.

He was nothing like I had expected. He was older, for one thing—nearing forty, I judged, with silvered brown hair and rather an appealing sort of face. Not a tall man either, though his body had the hardness of a lifetime of labor and I wouldn't have wanted to take sides against him in a fight. He wore an earring, which looked somewhat out of place; a small gold hoop that glinted dashingly against his graying hair, and below the rolled sleeves of his flannel work shirt his forearms were a fascinating canvas of dark tattoos.

Releasing his grip, he raised a hand to rake it through his hair, his brown eyes crinkling with surprising charm. He didn't look a drunkard or a bully, and I found it hard to reconcile the image I had formed with the reality.

"I expect," he said, "that I gave you a fright as well. You'd not have known I'd come home."

"No," I admitted. "No, I didn't."

"Eh, well. I don't imagine anybody's noticed, yet. I just got in. Is Jeannie anywhere about? I've looked, but—"

"She's down with Quinnell."

"Is she? Heading back yourself, then, are you? Good, I'll tag along."

He didn't talk much, while we walked. A brief exchange of comments on the warming of the weather was the closest that we came to conversation.

David saw us coming first. Leaning full on the handle of the hollow probe, he glanced up briefly, stopped and looked again. "Heyah, Brian," he said, coolly. "When did you get back?"

"About an hour ago. Stealing my wife again, are you?"

"Of course he isn't." Jeannie moved from David's side to give her husband a welcoming kiss in spite of her father's scowl. "Don't be daft. How did it go?"

Brian shrugged. "Not bad. We netted a fair haul, this trip."

"Any fish?" Wally asked sourly. I didn't understand the barb behind the comment but it glanced off Brian harmlessly, and he whistled a snatch of a tune through his teeth, ignoring the old man completely.

"You've been busy," he noted, looking back at the trail of brightly colored golf tees that marked our progress along the buried ditch.

From the trial trench in the southwest corner, the western ditch ran roughly parallel to the long drive, traveling up at a slight diagonal for some three hundred yards before it turned a rounded, playing-card-shaped corner, just below the ridge, and started back across the field.

Quinnell followed Brian McMorran's gaze proudly, not appearing to mind the man's presence. "Yes, we're making good progress."

"Looks like it. Is that where the walls were, then—where you've stuck all them tees? Bloody big camp, wasn't it?"

"About twenty acres," Quinnell estimated. "It's not like a fort, you understand. Forts were built smaller. They only had to house an auxiliary force, but a marching camp was meant to hold the whole legion, on campaign. It had to be huge."

"I see." Brian's eyes swung back across the field to the southwest corner, where the green thorn hedge blocked the noise of the road, and the russet walls of Rose Cottage showed plainly through the frieze of trees edging the drive. "And what's our Mr. Sutton-Clarke up to, over there?"

Fabia tossed the short fall of hair from her face. "Doing a survey, what else?"

I hadn't even noticed, to be honest, that Adrian wasn't with us. I'd been too absorbed in watching David, admiring the unholy force with which he rammed the steel probe home.

It was easy to see why the act of probing held little appeal for Adrian. His interest lay in the larger picture of what lay beneath the landscape, not in the soil itself. And he'd never liked getting his hands dirty. For a man who'd spent so many hours on archaeological sites, patiently mapping and measuring, he had a surprising lack of patience with the actual work of excavation. Give him good clean technology every time.

Indeed, when I wandered down to join him a few minutes later, I found him preparing the section of field for another pass with the ground-penetrating radar unit, happily laying out neat lines of nonmagnetic tape for guidance, and humming to himself.

"Guilty conscience?" I asked him.

"What?"

"You've already done this bit of the field, remember? Produced a smashing image."

"Sarcasm," he informed me, "doesn't suit you. And if
you must know, Peter asked me to repeat the survey. It seems
he's misplaced the initial results, and he wants to have a
record for his files."

"And how did he come to misplace them?" I asked, suspiciously.

"I had nothing to do with it." He raised a hand in Boy
Scout fashion, as proof of his sincerity. "I'm rather pleased
the damn thing's gone, mind you, but I had nothing to do
with it."

After scrutinizing his face a moment I decided he was
telling the truth. More likely, I thought, Peter had pitched
the fake survey results on the fire himself, thus solving a
prickly problem. Having "lost" the results, and being unable
to obtain a duplicate printout from Adrian's computer—I
was sure Adrian would have thought of some suitable tech-
nical excuse for *that*—Peter would be wholly justified in
asking for another survey of the southwest corner. Not only
would that erase all traces of the false record; it also gave
Adrian a chance to redeem himself professionally.

As a solution it was, I thought, decidedly Peter's style,
and endearingly gallant.

Adrian, who didn't know that Quinnell knew, and
therefore didn't fully appreciate the subtleties of his mission,
cast a vaguely impatient look at my knees. "Does that
blasted animal have to follow you everywhere?"

I looked down in mild surprise, and Kip looked back at
me, one ear flopped softly forward. During the hours when
Robbie was at school, the collie had taken to keeping me
company, trailing at my heels so quietly that I frequently
forgot he was even there. Wally had joked that the dog, like
its young master, was faintly besotted with me. Personally,
I put it down to the sausage.

"It's like you have six legs, these days," said Adrian. He
paused, his eyes flicking past my shoulder toward Rose Cottage. "Do me a favor, Verity love, and measure how far it
is from where I'm standing to that bit of wall over there."

"What, with this?" I bent to pick up his yard measure with a sinking heart. "Where's your little wheel thing? You know, the one you just push around?"

"Oh, don't be such a baby. You know how to use a yard measure, I've seen you do it." He nodded firmly in the direction I was meant to go. "Just to the wall, please."

"I thought you had this corner all mapped out."

"Verity . . ."

I measured. At the crumbling stretch of dry-stone wall, I stood up and called back, "Fifty-six feet, two inches."

He cupped a hand to his ear. "What?"

"Oh, for heaven's sake." With Kip trotting at my heels, I patiently retraced my steps. Across the field, I could see David and Quinnell, heads bent in contemplation of the rough turf at their feet, while Wally stood to one side, frowning, and Brian leaned close over Fabia's shoulder as though offering an expert opinion.

Jeannie, I noticed, had disappeared. Gone back to the house, no doubt, as it was now less than an hour till lunchtime and she probably had some culinary masterpiece to pop into the oven. My stomach gave a small anticipatory rumble as I drew level with Adrian.

"Fifty-six feet, two inches," I repeated.

"Thanks." He jotted the number down, tossing a quick glance over his shoulder at the others. A few minutes later he repeated this motion, and grinned. "Well, well," he said slowly, "I do believe the old man's jealous."

"What, Peter? Who would he be jealous of?"

Adrian's eyes came back to mine, vaguely pitying. "God, you are thick, aren't you? No, my love, not Quinnell. The other one. He's looking daggers at me."

I turned in time to catch the blunt edge of David's scowl before his head angled down again. Staunchly ignoring the tiny, unnamed thrill that coursed through me, I advised Adrian not to be an idiot. "It's nothing personal. He's been looking daggers at everyone since Jeannie's husband arrived."

"Ah, yes. The inimitable Brian." Adrian's tone was dry. "And what did you think of him?"

"I thought he seemed rather nice."

"You always did have rotten taste in men."

I shot him a sidelong glance. "Doesn't say much for you, that, does it?"

"Yes, well, I meant myself excepted. Although," he mused, "you did throw me over, didn't you, which only goes to prove my point. Was that a drop of rain, or did I imagine it?"

"I didn't feel anything."

"Good." Another pause, while he stretched a length of tape between two surveyed points. "You've noticed, of course, that our Fabia shares your high opinion of Brian McMorran?"

"Meaning what, exactly?"

"Meaning just what you think I mean." He slanted me a faintly superior look and jerked his head in the direction of the small group down the hill. "Look for yourself, if you don't believe me. It doesn't take a rocket scientist." He broke off, squinting skywards. "Damn, that *was* a drop of rain. I knew it."

Beyond his shoulder, Fabia threw back her head and laughed, her artfully tousled mop of hair whipped backwards by the wind to brush against Brian McMorran's jaw. He, too, was laughing, leaning closer, not touching her, but . . .

"She's very pretty," I commented, slowly.

"Yes, she is. If you like that type." Adrian had developed an intense interest in his preparations, hurrying his pace along to beat the darkening clouds, but though his voice sounded offhand, I wasn't in the least fooled.

"What type would that be?" I teased him. "The sexy-as-hell blond type? All legs and eyes and perfect teeth?"

He grinned. "That would be the one, yes."

"Ah."

"Mind you, I've gone head over heels on at least one occasion for the dark-haired, smart-talking type as well," he said lightly.

I knew him far too well to fall for the intimacy of that smile, those dark eyes levelled warmly on my own. He was rather like one of those snakes, I mused—those giant snakes that tried to mesmerize you, held you captive, unresisting, with the force of their gaze alone. I looked away with ease, and held my hand palm upwards to catch the light but unmistakable scattering of raindrops.

"Blast!" Adrian fastened off the final guiding line of tape as the rain began in earnest, a steady soaking shower that made spikes of my eyelashes and tasted sweet on my tongue.

"Come on," he said, turning to make a dash for it. But I lingered one more minute in the cool and cleansing rain, eyes closed, my face tipped upwards like a child's, wondering why the thought of David Fortune's frowning face, jealous or otherwise, made me so damnably happy.

XV

Jeannie promptly banished me upstairs, to take a bath. "You'll catch your death, with that wet hair," she told me firmly, "and you've half an hour till lunch."

There never seemed much point, I thought, in arguing with Jeannie. And it wasn't altogether unpleasant to strip off my soaked clothing and sink into the hot bath, scented with exotic hints of sandalwood and spice, courtesy of Peter's own expensive bath salts. Even the Romans, I was sure, could not have known luxury like this.

Although, to be fair, one had to admit that the Romans had been experts on the gentle art of bathing.

I'd visited the graceful arched chambers at Bath, with their great echoing colonnaded aisles and the water as pale as an aquamarine, water that had once closed around the shoulders of some tired Roman woman of my own age, who'd sought comfort in the heated pools from all the aches and chills that plagued her young but weary bones.

I closed my eyes, as she might have done, slipping down until the water touched my chin. The steam curled up deliciously against my face, as my hair sagged limply down from its loose pile atop my head.

I wondered if the Roman woman in her bath had dreamed

of men, as I did. If she'd thought on some old lover, some smooth merchant with a charming smile, or conjured up the wistful image of some strong and stoic legionary, dark-haired with eyes of blue, and a body that no mortal had a right to.

My sigh rippled the surface of the bathwater. I opened my eyes. Give it up, I told myself good-naturedly.

The woman who peered back at me from the foggy depths of the mirror, when I finally emerged from my bath, looked nothing like a Roman. The face was too scrubbed, and the hair too straggly. That was my one complaint with long hair, I reflected. I'd undone my plait and toweled dry the dripping strands as best I could, but a quick check of my watch told me I didn't have time to do a proper job. Leaving my hair loose and hanging damply down my back, I shivered into a dry pair of jeans and a clean shirt before scooting downstairs to join the others.

Peter Quinnell, I had learned, liked to take his meals on schedule.

Breakfasts were a bit of an exception. All of us woke at different times, and our morning routines made any sort of synchronization difficult. Adrian and David usually breakfasted at their hotel, before they came to work, while Peter, Fabia and I ate sometimes together and sometimes by turns in the bright narrow kitchen, with Jeannie standing over us, stirring her ever-present pot of porridge on the stove. Sometimes Wally was there as well, or Robbie . . . it all depended on the earliness of the hour.

But lunch was a different matter. Lunch at Rosehill House was a strictly observed ritual that, while not exactly formal, still carried a faint echo of the grand old days of the country house, when people dressed for dinner and the servants ate below stairs. The impression was made all the stronger by the fact that Jeannie, when she wasn't serving food or clearing plates, kept to her kitchen and left us alone. And the dining room itself seemed to demand a certain degree of gentility, of respect for the rules of etiquette.

It was a most impressive room, tucked discreetly away in the rear corner of the ground floor, just beyond the kitchen and directly behind the "posh" sitting room. The walls were paneled in palest oak, the window gleamed wide and uncurtained, a gas fire hissed in the elegant fireplace on the end wall, and beneath the long polished table, which could easily have seated twelve, a thickly cushioned carpet of rich Cambridge blue ran the length of the room, from skirting-board to hearth.

"It was originally a bedroom," Peter had told me earlier that week, when I'd remarked on the beauty of the room, "but a lady who owned Rosehill in the late eighteenth century had the bad fortune to be murdered in here by her butler. He cut her throat, I'm told. So they changed this to a dining room. For, after all," he'd said, buttering a slice of bread with admirable nonchalance, "no one would want to sleep in a room where there'd been a murder."

When Adrian had pointed out that some might not exactly relish the thought of *eating* in a murder room, either, Peter had dismissed the notion with a casual wave of his hand, maintaining that it wasn't at all the same thing. That was one of the marvelous things about Peter, I thought. He had a way of saying something, in that beautifully theatrical voice of his, that made the illogical sound entirely reasonable. It was a gift. Already this week he'd used that gift to win three lunchtime debates with Adrian.

But today, no one seemed inclined to begin a debate. Because it was Friday, with David not up in Edinburgh giving lectures, we were five, seated boy-girl-boy-girl in a half-circle around one end of the long table. Peter sat at the head, with his back to the fireplace and Fabia and I to his left and right, respectively. Adrian, being left-handed, had been assigned the seat beside Fabia, which not only gave his left arm a free range of motion, but also allowed him to keep an eye on me.

Adrian was an only child; he didn't like to share.

If David, at my shoulder, leaned too close or made me smile, it was a safe bet Adrian would smoothly intervene, like a child jealously guarding a discarded plaything. As he was past reforming, I generally ignored him, counting mentally backwards from one hundred while I turned my eyes to the window opposite and its peaceful view of garden, field and sky. Today I found myself admiring that view more than usual, not just because of Adrian but because I simply didn't know where else to look.

Jeannie had outdone herself, as usual, with plates of ham, and carrots done in mustard sauce, and parsnips and potatoes roasted golden, sweet and crisp. But not even Jeannie's cooking could dispel the curious tension that had settled around the lunch table, a tension so palpable that one inhaled it like a cloud of ash with every breath and coughed it out again in awkward, small, throat-clearing sounds that served as substitutes for conversation. Clearly, the change in atmosphere had something to do with Brian McMorran's coming home, although no one so much as mentioned his name. And the man himself was nowhere to be seen. I guessed he would be eating in the kitchen with his wife, and when I next looked out the dining room window I knew I'd guessed correctly. Wally Tyler normally lingered long over the kitchen teapot at lunchtime, but today his cap was pacing grumpily back and forth on the far side of the garden wall, spouting sharp rapid puffs of cigarette smoke that twisted in the rain-dampened air.

The rain shower had been a brief one—a "plump," as David called it—and already the sun was beginning to scatter the clouds. The group of us scattered as well, while our teacups were still warm. Peter walked into town to collect the post; David and Wally went back to the ditch, and Adrian, having lured Fabia into assisting with his survey, strolled whistling down to the southwest corner, radar unit in tow.

I suppose I could have lent a hand to any one of them, but since I wasn't really needed anywhere at the moment I chose instead to spend an hour throwing sticks for Kip, behind the Principia.

Here, at least, I could feel truly useful. And Kip was a brilliant fetcher of sticks. Not like my parents' dog, who clamped his teeth around whatever you threw to him and staunchly refused to bring it back. Kip not only brought the stick back, he actually *dropped* it at my feet and waited with a wide grin until I threw it again, then he wheeled like a dancer and bounded off happily to hunt the stick down in the tangle of swaying weeds and wild flowers.

He was bringing it back for what seemed the thousandth time when he suddenly stopped, planted his feet, and sniffed the warming air. After a second sniff he gently laid the stick down on the grass and looked expectantly toward the drive, his plumed tail waving as he gave a soft, impatient whine. I'd seen him go through this routine a dozen times since I'd been at Rosehill—he did it whenever a car he knew came up the drive, or when one of us came back from an outing. Only this time the drive was empty, and it was much too early for Robbie to be home from school.

He whined again, and I shook my head. "You're out of luck, love," I informed him. "False alarm."

The collie only wagged his tail harder, insistently, and raised his head to give a happy little woof of welcome. Picking up his stick again, he bounced past me and began to trot away along the ridge, performing an odd little dance that seemed to demand he turn full circle every several steps, followed by a joyful leap with stick in mouth until his head reached a specified level in the empty air. The same level every time, I noticed, hugging myself to ward off the crawling chill of recognition . . .

The same level at which a grown man's hand might hang, as he walked beside the dancing dog.

I'd seen him do the same thing when he walked at Wally's side, or David's, or my own. Kip loved to have his head patted. Of course, this time, there was nobody walking beside him. Nobody, I told myself firmly. Certainly not a ghost.

But when the collie turned and started back again, still bouncing and wagging, I didn't feel nearly so brave. I turned, too, half in panic, and bolted around the corner of the Principia, to get clear of the Sentinel's path.

"Darling, when I said I'd gone head over heels for you, I didn't mean it quite this literally." Adrian winced as he picked himself up and brushed grass off his leg. "Aren't you supposed to yell 'fore' or 'heads up' or something, before you come barrelling blind around a corner?"

"Sorry." I dusted the dirt from his sleeve, solicitously. "Are you all right?"

"I'll have my lawyers get in touch."

"Idiot. Have you finished with your survey?"

"Mmm." His eyes narrowed thoughtfully as he flexed his right arm, testing the action of his elbow. "If you promise not to make any sudden movements, I might even let you help me plot the readings on my computer. Or are you busy?"

"No, I'm not busy." I was glad to have a reason to go indoors, out of sight of whatever was walking the ridge. Relieved, I followed Adrian in through the gaping front doors of the Principia. The air was cooler here, and calmer, with a pleasantly sawdusty smell that defied the efforts of the quietly humming filters fixed to the beams overhead.

I wheeled my padded chair into Adrian's cubicle and watched him without really paying attention, content to let the drone of his computer soothe my superstitious fears, like a giant cross held up against a vampire. In the midst of all this gleaming bright technology, it was difficult to think of things like ghosts.

"I never did ask you," said Adrian, in a mildly curious tone, "what did Howard have to say this morning, about your sherds?"

"Howard?" I glanced up blankly, before remembering my telephone call from the British Museum. It seemed an age ago. "Oh, nothing helpful, I'm afraid. He says they're Agricolan."

"Well, that's what you thought yourself, wasn't it?"

"Yes." I ran an absent finger along the seam of my faded jeans. "Which only means the pot was made in that time period, really. It doesn't tell us when the thing was used."

His eyes touched mine with skepticism. "A forty-year-old pot, in military service? It's a bit of a stretch, don't you think?"

"It might have been broken years earlier," I argued, "by somebody else."

"Oh, right. I'm sure the wild Caledonians, when they weren't busy painting themselves blue and attacking people, served all their meals in Samian ware."

Refusing to concede the point, I changed the subject.

"Howard also said that Dr. Lazenby was looking for me."

Adrian always had been quick at putting two and two together. Swinging round, he raised an eyebrow. "Not to offer you a place on the Alexandria dig?"

"Apparently, yes . . ."

"Right. That's you gone, then, isn't it?"

"I don't know."

"Verity." Adrian's tone was superior. "This *is* me, remember? I know quite well what the merest mention of the word 'Alexandria' can do to you."

"Yes, well, I haven't actually spoken to Lazenby, yet," I defended my indecision. "And there isn't any rush—he doesn't leave until September."

Adrian smiled briefly before swinging his gaze back to the monitor. "D'you know, if I'd known you were going to get this attached to Quinnell, I'd have left you down in London."

"Hindsight," I reminded him, "is everything. Anyway, it's too late. If I wasn't committed to Peter before, I certainly am after talking to Howard."

"Why? What else did Howard say?"

"Only that Peter Quinnell was a flaming crackpot who oughtn't to be counted among the ranks of real archaeologists."

Adrian slanted a patient look sideways at me. "Well, darling . . ."

"Oh, it isn't *what* he said, Adrian, as much as how he said it. You should have heard him, he was so bloody patronizing. It needled me, a bit," I confessed.

"And?"

"What do you mean, 'and'?"

"If I know you, you'd not let Howard get away with being patronizing."

In response to his obvious amusement, I lifted my chin a fraction and let an edge of defiance cut into my own voice. "Well, as a matter of fact, I bet him a fiver we'd find a marching camp of the right period."

"That's my girl. Blind faith was always your best quality."

"It's not blind faith, it's—"

He cut me off. "Bloody hell," he said, without violence. He was staring at the screen of his computer, and something in his expression made me sit up smartly, instantly alert.

"What is it?"

"Look at this." He moved aside to make room as I rolled my chair closer and peered at the jagged black-and-white bands. At first glance, the radar profile bore a striking similarity to the image he and Fabia had faked, the boundary ditch and rampart marked at nearly the same spot by a sharp dip in the lines. But Adrian was pointing to a different, smaller feature. "There, do you see that?"

"What is it?"

"Hang on a minute." A few clicks on the computer keyboard replaced the single image with six smaller ones, while Adrian explained. "I made several runs across that area, this afternoon, and this is what the chart recorder printed off. You see? There's one blip, there. And that's another."

I scrutinized the profiles. "I count three."

"Right. Now," he told me, keying in another series of commands, "let me show you what they'd look like, on our site map."

The image on the screen changed shape again, becoming a topographical map section of the southwest corner, on which the three mysterious blips now showed as small black dots.

I shook my head. "They could be anything."

Ignoring me, Adrian drew in the known line of ditch and rampart, and positioned one more dot on the screen. "Look again," he advised.

I looked. He was speculating, of course—adding the fourth dot to create a perfect square, set at an angle to the rampart's corner curve. Still, the image *was* suggestive. On any other site, I would have said those dots were post holes, hinting at some buried structure underneath the level turf. And on any other site, I'd have been tempted to identify that structure as a guard tower, only . . . only . . .

"I'm afraid you've lost your fiver, darling," Adrian said slowly. He sounded nearly as stunned as I felt, and he turned his head to lock his eyes with mine. "This is no marching camp."

THIRD HORSE

And hear at times a sentinel
  Who moves about from place to place,
  And whispers to the worlds of space,
In the deep night, that all is well.

Tennyson, "In Memoriam", CXXV

XVI

Quinnell rejected the evidence. "Your equipment must be off, my boy," he told Adrian, leaning forward to tap the computer screen with an accusing finger. "Blips on the landscape, that's all. Or the remnants of a garden shed."

It was obvious to me why Peter didn't think that what we'd found could be a guard tower. Roman marching camps didn't have any permanent structures—only forts and fortresses had guard towers.

And our site could not have been either.

Roman forts were much too small. Built to defend and supply the spreading imperial forces, they were occupied by auxiliary troops, not legionaries. The famous fort at Housesteads on Hadrian's Wall could have barely held a quarter of a legion, and that only if the men stood cheek to jowl.

At the other end of the scale, a legionary fortress would have been enormous—fifty acres or more. And we knew from our surveys and excavations that our ditch and rampart had enclosed an area of roughly twenty acres. Which left us somewhere in between—too large to be a fort, too small to be a fortress. Marching-camp size, as a matter of fact.

But one couldn't deny that the survey had found something, down in the southwest corner. And that something *did* look like a guard tower.

The three of us frowned at the computer screen until David joined us, took one look, rubbed his jaw, and offered another solution.

"Might be a vexillation fortress," he said.

Which was, I thought, entirely plausible. A *vexillatio* was a detachment of a legion, so a vexillation fortress didn't need to be as large as a full legionary fortress—it didn't need to hold as many buildings. I'd seen a vexillation fortress myself, at Clyro in Wales, that was roughly the size of our own site. And since they were only built as temporary campaign bases, they left very little evidence behind, much like a marching camp.

But Quinnell rejected *that* suggestion out of hand, refusing to admit the possibility. He wanted a site from the early second century, after all, and vexillation fortresses were remnants of the century before—the conquest years.

"No, no," he said, and tapped the screen again, accusingly. "A garden shed, or some old fence. That's what we'll find down there."

But as the week wore on, a careful expansion of the trial trench exposed clear evidence of post molds, and by the following Saturday Peter's optimism had evaporated. "A guard tower," he identified it, sadly. "It can be nothing else."

And marching camps, whatever else they had, did not have guard towers. Which meant that what we'd found could not have been the marching camp that sheltered the Ninth Legion on the eve of its last battle.

Peter sighed and poked the soil despondently with his trowel. "No, this really is the worst thing that could have happened."

It was the first time I had known Peter Quinnell to be wrong. Because the *worst* thing turned up half an hour later, on the end of his own trowel.

"The terrible part," I told Jeannie the next morning, as we sat together in the tiny, homely kitchen of Rose Cottage, "is that the head of David's department comes to lunch on Tuesday, the day after tomorrow, and Peter seems to have completely given up.''

I'd never seen a man so unutterably depressed, so devoid of any interest in the goings-on around him. Since yesterday at noon I'd hardly seen him, and when I did he looked a shadow of his normal cheerful self, sitting wrapped in morose silence with one or both of the cats to comfort him, and his vodka bottle close at hand.

He didn't want company. And so, after breakfast, feeling utterly helpless, I'd come down to Rose Cottage and Jeannie.

She was a most relaxing woman. For all her energy and bubbly nature she seemed somehow to radiate an inner calm. Motherly, I thought, putting my finger on the quality. She was very motherly. Already she had filled my teacup twice and urged half a plate of her chocolate biscuits upon me.

''Aye, well, naturally he's disappointed,'' she said, stirring a second lump of sugar into her teacup and settling back. ''It was coins that you found, was it?''

I nodded. ''Three Roman *asses*—copper coins—from the reign of the Emperor Domitian. He was Emperor during Agricola's campaigns.''

''And who was Agricola?''

''Oh, sorry. Governor of Britain, for a time. Agricola,'' I explained, ''built forts and things all over Scotland, trying to push back the native tribes. Only then Domitian called him back to Rome, and the army withdrew again. They didn't really have enough men, anyway, to keep a proper occupying force up here. Our own fortress, or whatever it is, was probably abandoned within a year or so of AD 86—long before the disappearance of the Ninth.''

''Why AD 86?''

''That's when the coins we found were minted.''

Her expression was doubting. ''But the coins could have been old when they were dropped here, couldn't they?''

''No.'' I shook my head, positive. ''No, they were all three in splendid condition, unworn. And that kind of coin, once it's in circulation, tends to show wear very quickly. So they had to have been buried just a short time after they were struck. It gives us a very tight *terminus post quem*.''

"Oh, aye, that's just what I was thinking." Jeannie's mouth curved. "You're worse than Davy, you are, for explaining things."

"Sorry," I apologized, again. "It's just a term we use, for dating sites. In translation, it would mean the time after which something happened."

"Like, the Romans left *after* those coins were made?"

"That's right. We use a *terminus post quem* to help set a date range for the site, to say when it was occupied. Here at Rosehill, with the pottery we've found, and now these coins, we're looking at a rather tight date range of only a few years . . ."

"Terminus post quem," she murmured slowly, testing the sound of the words. "That's Latin, isn't it? D'ye ken Latin very well?"

"Well enough. It comes in handy, in my work."

"Aye." Her smile surprised me. "Robbie said you kent it. He was wanting to ask you what a word meant, I think, only yesterday wasn't the best day for it. I guess he decided to wait."

"He could always ask David," I said. "Archaeologists study Latin and Greek as a matter of course."

"Aye, so they do," agreed Jeannie. "But I think my son prefers your opinion to Davy's. You've prettier eyes."

Which was, I thought, a debatable fact, but I knew what she was saying. Robbie, like his collie dog, had rather taken to following me around while I did my work, and though the boy was much too young to have a true romantic crush on me, he evidently thought I was, as my father would say, "a bit of all right."

Neither Robbie nor Kip was around at the moment. Out for a late morning ramble with Wally, I expected. And Brian McMorran was away on his boat again, fishing. Which left just the two of us, Jeannie and me.

"Have another biscuit," she invited, nudging the plate closer.

I did as I was told. "I am glad you're here. I'd have gone mad this morning, with no one to talk to."

"What, is Fabia not around?" she teased.

"Oh, very funny. And no, since you mention it—Fabia isn't around. She went roaring off in her Range Rover, after breakfast. Seemed quite cheerful, actually. I don't think she has any clue how disappointing all of this is for Peter."

Jeannie shrugged. "No, well, she wouldn't. Fabia can't be bothered, ken, with other people's feelings." The words were spoken lightly, but I didn't miss their sharpness and I found myself wondering whether Fabia really had made a play for Jeannie's husband.

Still, I thought, it wasn't altogether fair to Fabia to suggest she didn't care how Peter felt. After all, by her own admission, the plan she'd hatched with Adrian to fake the radar survey—misguided though it was—had been in aid of keeping Peter happy. And everyone, surely, had some redeeming feature.

But before I could voice my opinion to Jeannie, the peace of the kitchen was shattered by the boisterous return of Robbie and Kip. The collie, muddied from his long walk, greeted me energetically, distracting me while Robbie made a grab for the last biscuit.

"Not till you've washed your hands," Jeannie told him with a firm shake of her head. "You'll be carrying germs, you will."

I held back a smile as I watched him trudge reluctantly to the kitchen sink, showing the same enthusiasm for soap and water as I'd felt myself at his age. Not that I knew exactly what his age was, mind, but . . .

"Nearly eight and three-quarters," he told me, turning as though I'd spoken the words out loud. "I'll be nine in September."

I sighed. "*Must* you do that?"

"Do what?"

"Answer my questions before I've asked them. It puts me at a disadvantage."

Jeannie smiled. "Aye, well, we're all at a disadvantage, with this wee laddie around. All of us except his dad, that is," she corrected herself. "He can't read Brian, very well. Can you?" she asked her son, who simply shook his head.

"Dad's fuzzy."

"He is that," Jeannie agreed, her smile widening. "Och, I'm forgetting now, what was that word that you wanted to ask Miss Grey about? The Latin word?"

"Solway," came the answer, through a mumbly mouthful of biscuit. "I looked in Mr. Quinnell's dictionary, but I couldn't find it."

Jeannie frowned. "Solway?"

The dark curls bobbed affirmatively. "Aye, that's what he said. At first I thought he meant the Firth, like, but Granny Nan says it would have had a different name, back then, and anyways he wouldn't speak English."

Thoroughly confused, I gave my own head a faint shake, to clear it. "Who wouldn't?"

"The Sentinel."

My teacup clattered in its saucer. "The Sentinel *talks*?"

"Aye. Granny Nan says he's probably talking Latin, like, only I don't ken Latin."

"He talks." I repeated the words to myself, surprised that anything still had the power to surprise me. Rosehill had forced me to suspend my natural skepticism. There were no horses in the field behind the house, yet horses ran there every night. There were no ghosts, yet one had walked right past me. And there could be no psychics, yet I knew whatever Robbie spoke was certain truth.

I cleared my throat. "Does the Sentinel talk to you often?"

Robbie raised one thin shoulder in a cavalier shrug. "He just says 'solway'. And then I don't ken what to say back, so he goes away again."

"Oh."

"What does 'solway' mean, then?"

"Well, I think he's saying *salve*, Robbie," I said, and spelled the word out for him. "The Latin 'v' is pronounced rather like our 'w'. And *salve* means good day, how are you doing, all of that."

"So he's just saying hello, like."

"That right." It was pointless to tell the boy to say *salve* in return, since he wouldn't understand anything else the Sentinel said to him. Pity I couldn't see the ghost myself, I thought—it would be quite an experience, conversing with a Roman legionary . . .

"What?" asked Jeannie, watching my face.

I glanced up. "Oh, nothing. I was just thinking, that's all."

Kip yawned beneath my chair, and Jeannie looked down at her watch to check the time. "Och, it's nearly eleven already. Robbie, finish up now and get ready, you don't want to be late for your piano lesson."

He pulled a telling face, slid down from his chair, and went scuffing along the back corridor to his bedroom, while I drained my cooling cup of tea. "I might just beg a lift, if you don't mind."

"What, into Eyemouth? Of course."

"Just as far as the Ship Hotel, if that's no bother."

"Oh, aye?"

I nodded, too deep in thought to notice her sudden interest. "I want to catch David, if I can, before he goes out anywhere. I've got a proposal for him."

"He'll be pleased," said Jeannie, straight-faced, but her dark eyes danced with humor as she stood to clear the tea things.

"Yes," I murmured absently, still thinking. "Yes, he just might be, at that."

XVII

It was difficult to tell, from his expression, what he thought. He had that damned impassive Scottish face that could mask almost anything.

Taking a long drink from his newly poured pint he settled back and stretched one arm along the top of the padded bench, looking rather too large and too powerful for this small corner of the pink and pale wood dining lounge. He'd have been more in his element, I wagered, in the public bar, but the conversation drifting through the dividing glass door sounded decidedly rough, and David Fortune was nothing if not chivalrous.

He'd been in the public bar when I'd arrived, as a matter of fact, but a word from the cheerful waitress had brought him through with a half-finished plate of sausage casserole in one hand and a pint of dark beer in the other. He'd seemed almost pleased to see me. But that, of course, had been before I'd started talking.

Now his features showed nothing save a vague air of thoughtfulness. I shifted in my chair and sent him a smile that felt a little stiff.

"You think it's a silly idea," I guessed.

"No sillier than some." His voice was slow and measured.

"No, I'm just surprised you'd think of it, that's all. I thought you didn't put much faith in ghosts."

"I didn't . . . don't." I frowned. "Not all ghosts, anyway. Just this one."

"Robbie's Sentinel."

"Yes."

"Because it's Robbie's?"

"Yes."

"I see." He took a long draft of his beer and eyed me keenly. "And so what you're saying is, you think we ought to ask him questions."

"Well, we know he talks," I reasoned, "and we know that Robbie hears him. I assume the ghost hears Robbie, too, though of course since they're speaking different languages there's no real proof of that. But I do think," I said, setting down my glass for emphasis, "I do think it's worth a try."

"And why is that?"

"Because of Peter. He's already talking about chucking the entire excavation, did you know that?"

"Aye." He spoke the single word without surprise. "It'd not be the first time, for him. He's been chasing the Ninth Legion since afore I was born, and he doesn't waste time on a trail that's gone cold."

"But is it cold?" I challenged him. "I mean, don't you think we owe it to Peter to examine every possibility?"

His eyes met mine with patience. "We've got the coins, lass. And the potsherds. Textbook evidence, for dating . . ."

"Yes, I know. But just because the Romans came—and presumably went—in Domitian's day, that doesn't mean they didn't come back later, does it?"

It was David's turn to frown. "I'm not sure I follow."

"All right." Leaning forward, I tried to explain. "Suppose you're the commander of the Ninth Legion, and you've been ordered to march north to fight the Scottish tribes."

"I'd have had more sense."

"Be serious. So anyway, you march your legion north, along the road. If there had been a vexillation fortress here," I reasoned, "then there would have been a road. The Devil's

Causeway, even—it heads up this way from York, and we don't know *really* how far north it went."

He conceded the point. "Go on."

"Well, you have to pitch camp somewhere, don't you? And if you chanced upon an old abandoned fortress . . ."

"A vexillation fortress," he reminded me, "was not designed to hold a legion."

True, I thought. Only a part of the fortress held barrack blocks—the rest was given over to administrative buildings, workshops . . . "But suppose the buildings were all gone. The Romans had a habit of destroying their camps, when they withdrew. That would leave you a nice level bit of ground, large enough for your legion to pitch its tents on, and protected by a lovely ditch and rampart."

"We've found no sign of later occupation."

"We've only been digging a couple of weeks," I said, defiantly. "It's a bloody big site. And a marching camp won't leave much in the way of evidence."

David settled back a moment, considering my theory. As he drained his pint he studied me above the upraised glass, as though I were a tiny item on his trowel, that defied classification.

"You're fair determined, aren't you?"

I set my jaw. "I just think we ought to make absolutely certain, before Peter packs it in."

"And we all find ourselves out of a job." His tone was lightly mocking, and I bristled.

"It's nothing to do with the job."

"Aye, in your case," he said, "I ken fine that it's not. Adrian, now, he'd miss the money, and I'd miss working where I can keep an eye on my mother, but you . . ." He shook his head. "You've no such vested interest, have you, lass? I reckon it's the work itself you'd miss. And Peter."

Actually, I longed to say, *it's you I'd miss.* These past two weeks I'd grown to like the sight of David walking down the field to meet me; the low pleasant roll of his voice; the strong, sure movements of his big square hands. But admitting my attraction wouldn't help. If Adrian had taught me nothing else, he'd taught me that it wasn't wise to get involved with co-workers. Doomed to failure, those affairs were . . . not to mention unprofessional.

Mind you, I thought—curing myself with a dose of reality—there was no real danger of any involvement with David. The clear blue eyes that watched me now held no expression save a mild curiosity.

Pretending a fierce interest in my barely touched glass of dry white wine, I lifted my shoulders in a deliberate shrug. "Certainly I'd miss Peter. I'm very fond of him. That's why I don't like seeing him like this."

"He climbs out of his depressions," David promised me, "eventually."

"Yes, well, I'd climb out of my own rather more quickly if I could do something constructive."

"Like interview the Sentinel?" He smiled faintly. "Seems to me that you and Robbie can take care of that yourselves. You'd not need me."

I disagreed. Courage in daylight was one thing, but wandering through that field at night and looking for a ghost was not my idea of fun. I'd feel quite a bit better with David's reassuring bulk beside me, shielding me from danger. But I didn't tell him that. Instead, I said: "My Latin's rusty. I'd like somebody around who speaks it better than I do, and asking Peter is a non-starter, isn't it? I mean, if the Sentinel is a soldier of the Ninth, that's well and good, but if he isn't, I don't imagine Peter wants to know."

"No," David agreed, "it wouldn't help matters."

"Besides," I said, "I think there ought to be a few of us present, if we do this. So there isn't any question of a hoax."

"Och, you needn't worry there. I don't imagine Peter would suspect you of twisting the truth."

"No," I said, not thinking, "but you might."

Which was, I realized with a mental wince, admitting rather more than I'd have liked. After all, it shouldn't much matter to me what David thought . . .

He arched an eyebrow, as though surprised. But even as his eyes began to look at me more closely, I was rescued, unexpectedly and rather disappointingly, by a smooth familiar voice that spoke behind me, from the door.

"Now there's a sight one never sees," said Adrian, laconically. "A Scotsman with an empty glass."

David took the jibe without offense. "You'd best buy me another, then."

Fabia, who'd blown into the lounge at Adrian's side, shrugged her coat off carelessly. "And you can order me a coffee, while you're at it."

David shifted over on the bench to make room for her, his eyebrow lifting higher. "Only a coffee?"

"I'm driving," she explained. Sliding into the seat, she combed her fingers through her bright hair, to tidy it, and glanced across at David, half-accusingly. "Does the wind always blow like this? It nearly knocked the Rover off the road."

David assured her the wind wasn't permanent. "Sometimes," he said solemnly, "it changes and blows from the east, like."

"Oh, wonderful," said Adrian. "Something to look forward to." He joined our little group at the corner table, his hands wrapped around two dripping pints of beer. "The coffee's on its way," he said, to Fabia. "And Verity, love, I'm ashamed to have forgotten you. Are you all right with that?" He nodded at my still full glass of wine, and I nodded.

David raised his pint philosophically. "She's been too busy talking to drink it," he said.

"Ah," said Adrian, in a knowing tone. Having fetched Fabia's coffee from the bar, he took the seat beside me, stretching an arm along my chair back in an attitude of casual possession. "So, what have the two of you been talking about?"

He voiced the question lightly, but that didn't fool me for a second. *Oh hell*, I thought, *he's jealous*. Adrian, I knew from experience, could be an absolute pain when he was jealous.

"Oh, this and that," said David, who either hadn't registered the tone of voice or didn't care. He swept a shrewd eye over Fabia. "How's your Latin, lass?"

She looked up blankly. "My what?"

Adrian lowered his glass and grinned. "I didn't do well

with Latin, myself, at school. I'm lost with any language where the words are given genders. Why should *legio* be feminine, for heaven's sake? A legion is made up of men, there's nothing feminine about it. No logic, that's the problem. And I never could make sense of the declensions. Verity's rather proficient though, aren't you, darling? At least," he qualified, "she *reads* with real authority. One can only assume she understands it."

Fabia frowned prettily, still looking at David. "What difference would it make if I spoke Latin?"

"None. It's only that Verity and I," he said, glancing at me for consent before continuing, "are thinking of having a go at Robbie's Sentinel, to see if he'll talk to us."

Adrian snorted in open disbelief. "You're joking." His gaze flashed from David to me and back again. "Verity doesn't even believe in ghosts."

"Does she not." The bland Scottish voice wasn't asking a question, but Adrian answered it anyway.

"No, she doesn't. Practical from head to toe, she is. I ought to know," he reminded David, in a voice as smooth as polished steel. His smile implied he knew me head to toe in other ways as well, but if he'd hoped to produce an effect he was disappointed.

David merely shrugged. "Ask her yourself, then."

Adrian shifted his dark eyes to my face and read my expression with the ease of long practice. "My God," he said, "you really do believe in our little Roman friend, don't you?"

"Yes." Lifting my wineglass, I braced myself for the inevitable arguments, backed up by stories of false hauntings and invented ghosts. Fortunately, Fabia was the first to speak.

"Well, Peter certainly believes in him," she said. "Peter thinks that all our troubles with the computer system are somehow the fault of the ghost."

"Give over," said Adrian.

"No, really—he does. After all, the technician couldn't find any mechanical reason . . ."

Adrian rolled his eyes heavenwards. "I'm bloody surrounded."

David smiled quietly. "Since you've no belief in ghosts, then, I assume you'd not be wanting to take part in our wee séance?"

"You assume correctly."

But the idea clearly intrigued Fabia. "Do you think you *could* talk to him?"

I nodded. "He's already tried to talk to Robbie, only Robbie didn't understand the words, you see."

Adrian's eyes sought the ceiling a second time. "Oh, please."

"Be a skeptic if you like," I invited him stoutly. "But I'm willing to give it a go."

Fabia frowned slightly, working through the logistics. "So you'd take Robbie with you then, and have him speak to the ghost, is that right?"

I nodded. "With David and me providing the Latin."

"And Peter, of course."

I glanced at David, and he stirred in his seat, adopting the voice of reason. "I don't think," he said, "that we should take Peter with us, lass. Not yet."

She considered this, then nodded, comprehending. "In case it doesn't work, you mean."

I bit my lip. "Or in case the ghost says something Peter wouldn't want to hear. Our Sentinel might be from the wrong legion, after all . . ."

Adrian slid incredulous eyes to mine and made a sound between a chuckle and a groan. "The ghost," he assured me, "isn't going to say a bloody thing. You *do* realize this?"

He looked across at David. "Surely you must know how asinine—"

"We'll not lose anything by trying," David calmly cut him off. "Peter will probably scrap the excavation anyway, but . . ."

"What?" Adrian snapped to attention.

"Aye, unless we turn up something that gives evidence of later occupation . . ."

"You mean he'd just shut down completely? Sell the house?"

"Aye," repeated David, as if talking to an idiot. I thought

I caught the barest glimmer of a smile behind his blue eyes as he watched Adrian's reaction, but the rest of his face stayed exactly the same and I might have been mistaken.

"Well then." Adrian tossed his beer back quickly, as though he needed it. "Well then, I don't suppose that talking to this ghost would do us any harm."

"We're all decided? Right." David levered away from the back of the bench and leaned his elbows on the table, fixing us all with a satisfied, purposeful eye. "Then here's what we'll need to do."

XVIII

We must have looked a motley little crew, assembling on the hill behind the stables in the still watch of the night. Eleven o'clock had been the hour fixed as our gathering-time, but it was very nearly half-past before we were properly organized. Fabia was the last to arrive.

"That's it, then," she said, breathless after hurrying up the gentle grassy slope from the darkened house. "He's asleep, I checked. We should be in the clear."

"Good." David cast a quick, assessing eye around the group of us. "Now where the devil's Adrian?"

"I'm right here," Adrian replied, emerging from the shadowy cluster of trees that screened the farther field from view. Kip came with him, padding lightly over the soft thick grass and fallen branches, dark eyes gleaming with reflected moonlight.

The end of Wally's cigarette glowed red against the stable wall. "Best get on with it," the old man advised, "and let the laddie hie hisself to bed."

Robbie, with the legs of his pajamas tucked deep into his wellies and one of his father's jackets drooping to his knees, cheerfully assured his grandfather there was no need to hurry. "I don't have to go to school tomorrow."

"Oh, aye?" Wally raised an eyebrow. "Whae's telt ye that?"

"Mum said."

"He'll be wanting a long lie, the morn," Jeannie defended her decision, "and it's only the one day."

Fabia shifted, impatient. "Are we ready to do this, then? Davy?"

"Aye." David flashed a torch upon his wristwatch, sent a final, searching glance in the direction of the slumbering, square-walled house, and motioned to Robbie. "We can't stay here," he said, "we might wake Peter with our talking. Can you lead us on a little further, just where the Sentinel walks?"

Robbie nodded. "He goes this way."

It was easy to follow the small bouncing figure in the oversized coat as he headed east along the narrow line of ridge that marked the boundary of the great deserted field. The moon hanging bright in the midnight sky lit everything plainly, and I could see the patchwork spread of other fields falling off to my left and fading in a ragged fringe of trees that stood up blackly in the distance.

The wind had died to a whispering kiss and the clouds had dissolved to the odd floating wisp of dark gray that passed over the nearly full moon, sending furtive shadows scurrying across the empty fields in search of cover.

A larger shadow scuttled past and I caught my breath, but it was only Kip.

"Boo," said Adrian, by my shoulder.

I called him something rather rude. Beside me, Fabia stopped walking.

"Look, this is far enough, surely," she said, hunching into her jacket. "Davy, isn't this far enough?"

He agreed that it probably was. We'd come roughly a quarter of the way across the field, fully one hundred yards from the house. There was little chance of Peter hearing us from here, unless we shouted.

"Perfect night for ghost-spotting," said Adrian, as he flung himself full length upon the grass. "Pass me my flask, will you, Verity love? Or have you drained it already?"

"I only had a taste." I rummaged for the leather-covered bottle. "Vile stuff, that."

"Yes, well, Russian wine is not exactly noted for its subtlety," he told me, taking a healthy swig.

Jeannie smiled. "A gift from Brian, was it?"

"Not exactly a gift. I paid him ten pounds for the case, I think." He rolled his head sideways to grin at her. "Not that I recall the deal too clearly. We'd already downed a bottle between us by then." He offered the flask around, but Fabia was the only one brave enough to accept. She gave a little choking cough and passed it back.

"God." She grimaced. "That is terrible." Pushing the tumbled hair out of her eyes, she drew her knees up and rested her chin on her hands. "I was just thinking, we don't really know that this ghost is roaming about at night, do we? I mean, Robbie's only seen him in the daytime."

"That's true," said Jeannie, sagely. "But it does seem rather a safe bet . . ."

"Ghosts always prowl at midnight," Adrian cut in, with smooth authority. "Didn't you watch films at all, when you were growing up?"

"He'll be here," Wally said. His voice was simple, calmly knowing. "He walks by night as well as by day. Just ye ask yon dog."

I looked to where the collie lay sprawled out upon the grass, head up, ears perked, and I remembered it would probably be Wally who took Kip out late at night, when Robbie was in bed. Perhaps Wally had seen what I had seen—the collie dancing at the heels of an invisible companion, begging to be patted, broad tail waving. It was a sight one didn't soon forget.

Something, some animal, scuttled through the rough grass and Kip gave an eager whine, but Wally's hand reached out to keep the collie still. My own gaze moved from the waiting dog to the old man's moonlit profile, and I rubbed my leg with a thoughtful hand. "Do you believe in ghosts, Wally?"

His shrug was noncommittal. "Depends."

"You're all daft," Adrian pronounced his judgment lazily,

leaning back on his elbows. "A ghost is merely a projection of a less than stable mind."

David's voice came quietly. "Is that a fact?"

"It is. Christ, I've been working here two months now, puttering about this field with my equipment, and I think I would have noticed anything out of the ordi—"

"Salve," Robbie said.

He was sitting close beside me, near my feet, and the sudden sound of his small voice made me jump. Just as suddenly, he turned around and showed me a brilliant grin. "Hey, it works!"

My throat worked for a moment before the words found their way out. "That's wonderful, Robbie. Where is he?"

I wouldn't have believed my voice could sound so calm, when I was anything but calm inside. My nerves were thrashing wildly, like a netted bird, and my heartbeat pulsed a hard and rapid rhythm in my throat. It was one thing to come up with the idea of talking to the Sentinel, I thought, but my bravado shriveled with the knowledge that our ghost was standing right in front of us.

"Right there," said Robbie, pointing to the vacant air.

David slid the few feet down the slope to join us, coming to an abrupt stop directly behind me and steadying himself with a hand on my shoulder. I could feel the warmth of him through the thick folds of my jumper, but I don't believe he even noticed the touch. Above my head, he watched the darkness steadily. "Say *'salve custos,'* Robbie," he instructed.

"What's *custos*?"

"Sentinel."

We were all silent now, leaning slightly forward in anticipation as Robbie dutifully repeated the words. I counted my heartbeats . . . one . . . two . . . before the boy turned around a second time, his eyes going over my head, seeking David's. "He's not saying anything, but he's smiling. He's looking at you, now."

"Is he, by God?" David frowned a moment at the nothingness, then raising his voice he explained in perfect Latin

that we couldn't see or hear our long-dead visitor; he would
have to talk through Robbie.

"Now, Robbie," David murmured, "if he says anything,
if he makes a sound, you repeat it, all right? Like a parrot."

"All right."

David nudged my shoulder. "Go on, then," he invited me.
"It's your party. You ask the first question."

Fabia, who'd been holding her breath all this time, let it
out again in a swift, expectant rush. "Ask him," she hissed,
"if he knows he's a ghost."

Adrian ventured dryly that, after walking the same field
for several hundred years, a person must surely begin to suspect . . .

Turning, I sent him a withering look. "*Will* you be serious?"

Adrian rolled his eyes. "Oh, right. You're talking to thin
air, and I'm meant to be serious."

I opened my mouth to respond but the big hand on my
shoulder tightened warningly, cutting me off, at the same
moment Jeannie breathed an urgent whisper: "Verity!"

"What?" I brought my head back round, and saw what
had alarmed them.

The Sentinel had moved.

Robbie, beside me, was watching the air not two feet from
my face. I drew a sharp breath and then found that I couldn't
breathe out again, so I swallowed instead. "Robbie," I said
cautiously, afraid to move a muscle, "what is he doing?"

"He's kind of crouched down," came the reply, "to see
you better, like. Now he's reaching out his hand, I think he
wants to touch your hair."

David swore softly, the word brushing warm down the
back of my neck. I might have imagined the ghost's gentle
touch and the sweeping thrill of cold—I'd always had a
rather wild imagination. But it didn't stop me shivering.

Adrian, unconvinced, raised the wine flask for another
drink. "Go on, then, Verity, my love. Here's your chance to
clear up one of history's little mysteries. Ask your friend
what legion he belonged to."

He meant it in jest, of course, but I found my voice and asked the question anyway.

The night gave no reply. And Robbie, if he heard an answer, didn't pass it on. Instead he scrambled to his feet, staring uncertainly into the darkness. Behind him, Kip whined sharply, struggling to break free of Wally's hold, but Robbie didn't seem to hear that, either. Slowly, as though following another's gaze, he turned his head and looked toward the house.

The windows were no longer dark. Lights blazed in both the kitchen and the upstairs hall, and even as I registered the fact a small familiar sound came echoing across the field— the sound of someone starting up a car. The motor coughed, and caught, and purred; was pushed till it became a roar, and two clear yellow headlights plunged between the trees that fringed the drive.

The headlights struck the red walls of Rose Cottage and sharply wheeled away again as the car spun out into the road with a panicked shriek of brakes.

"He's going," said Robbie, urgently. "Davy, he's going. He's . . ."

He didn't finish. His large eyes swung toward us, suddenly anguished, and even as Jeannie leapt forward to catch him, he crumpled like a broken doll and fell face-down upon the grass.

"It's all right," said Jeannie, lifting him gently. "He's only had a vision, he'll be fine." But her face, in the cold moonlight, didn't look so self-assured.

Adrian, in his typically selfish fashion, had noticed only one thing. "That was my car," he burst out, indignantly. "The bloody bastard took my car!" And then he turned and sprinted for the house, and the rest of us, after an exchange of glances, followed.

On the level sweep of gravel at the top of the drive, we found Brian McMorran brushing off his trousers. "Crazy bugger," he said sourly. "Nearly ran me over."

Fabia stared at him, disbelieving. "It wasn't Peter, surely?"

"He took my car," Adrian repeated, bleakly, his eyes

fixed on the empty square of gravel where the bright red
Jaguar should have been.

Wally eyed his son-in-law suspiciously. "What d'ye think
yer doing, then, coming home at this hour?"

Straightening, Brian raked a hand through his silver hair
and laughed lightly, without humor. "If I'd known this was
the welcome I'd get, I'd have stopped the night in town,"
he told us. He fished in his pocket for his cigarettes and lit
one, lifting an eyebrow at Jeannie above the brief flame of
the match. "I might ask the same of you, at any rate—the
cottage was empty when I got here."

"We were out in the field," she answered.

"In the—?" He broke off, seeming for the first time to
notice Robbie's condition, and his lips compressed impatiently. "Aw, bloody hell, you've not been after the ghost?
Where's your head, woman? Give him here." The tattooed
arms closed protectively around the little boy. "You've been
putting a strain on him, can't you see?"

Jeannie set her jaw in self-defence. "He wanted to help
Peter," she explained. "And it wasn't the ghost that made
him faint. He saw something else, something . . ."

Robbie stirred at the sound of his mother's voice. "Granny
Nan," he mumbled, weakly. "Davy, Granny Nan . . . you
have to go."

In the sudden silence, David leaned in closer, his jaw tight-
ening. "Go where, lad?"

"Hospital . . ."

"Oh, Jesus." David straightened and wheeled, his eyes
darkening. "Fabia, get me the keys to the Range Rover."

"But Davy . . ."

"Just do it," he snapped.

Robbie, in his father's arms, slipped back into delirium.
Even after David had gone, when the taillights of the Range
Rover were faint receding points of red, the boy kept calling
out to him. "Davy . . . Davy . . . Granny Nan. Must help,
must . . . nona . . ."

"What was that?" Startled, I turned. "Robbie, what did
you—"

"Leave the boy be." Brian gathered his son closer, staring

me down with contempt. "He didn't say nothing, just leave him alone."

But I knew what I'd heard.

"Nona"—that's what Robbie had said. It was, I fancied, a belated answer to the question I had asked the Sentinel, before the boy collapsed. *Which is your legion?* I had asked.

And *nona* was the Latin word for "Ninth."

XIX

Somewhere in a shadowed recess of the dining room a mantel clock whirred softly and began to chime the hour: four o'clock. I shifted on my window seat and sighed. The house felt very lonely, with everyone asleep.

Fabia, having sensibly decided there was nothing she could do, had long since said goodnight and gone to bed. I'd expected Adrian, still worrying about his precious car, to wait up longer with me, but after comforting himself with a well-aged brandy from Peter's drinks cabinet, he had drifted off as well. I'd left him snoring in the sitting room, stretched out full length on the old sofa. Even Wally, who'd displayed no great desire to hurry home with the McMorrans, had eventually taken his leave, and the little cottage slumbered now in darkness at the bottom of the drive.

Which left me on my own, fretful and sleepless, wandering from room to room with only the cats for company.

And even the cats lacked a certain enthusiasm, I thought. Murphy had given up following me in favor of a warm seat in the kitchen, where he patiently waited for me to reappear as I made my restless rounds. Charlie, more persistent, had begun to gently protest my constant movement by simply flopping onto my lap whenever I sat. This time, as I prepared

to leave the window seat, the little gray cat tested her claws
on my knee and let out a plaintive meow.

"Sorry, love." I scooped her up and held her while I
stood, turning away from my reflection in the tall glittering
window.

In the kitchen, I set Charlie down on the chair beside the
big black tom, and put the kettle on for yet another pot of
tea. The two cats exchanged a rather long-suffering glance,
and I rather fancied Murphy sighed before he began to clean
himself. I was disrupting their nightly schedule, and I knew
it. Ordinarily at this hour they would be peacefully asleep
on my bed, or on Peter's.

But Peter wasn't here, and after what I'd experienced out
in the field, I knew that I wouldn't be able to sleep. To go
upstairs to bed would prove a total waste of time. Even with
the light left on, I'd be aware of every tiny seeping draft
within the room, of every creaking floorboard, and of every
slanting shadow.

A month ago, I reminded myself, I hadn't believed in
ghosts. Now I heard them breathing in the silent air behind
me, and felt the cold slow crawl of fear along my neck.

It wasn't the Sentinel himself that made me jumpy. It was
the *idea* of the Sentinel—the knowledge that beyond the
window, in the blackness, something walked, and watched,
and waited . . .

The kettle boiled. I turned from the window and forced
my trembling hands to make the tea. *Don't be such a coward*,
I reproved myself. *Fabia's upstairs, and Adrian's only a
couple of rooms away, and Peter will be back soon.*

The thought of Peter was a welcome distraction. Frowning, I glanced up at the kitchen clock to check the time again.
Four-twenty. More than three hours now since Peter and David had roared away from Rosehill, and still no word from
either of them.

"I'm sure she'll be all right," I told the cats out loud, in
an attempt to reassure myself. "She seemed like such a
strong woman."

But my brave thoughts failed to convince me, and worrying about David's mother only led to worrying about Da-

vid, which was rather worse than thinking about the ghost.
I sat heavily at the table and Charlie slipped onto my lap
with a weary yawn, rolling and stretching in an effort to find
comfort.

The cats, at least, were quiet. They hadn't once looked out
toward the field, or arched their backs, or hissed, so I felt
fairly sure the Sentinel was not pressed up against the window, peering in. But far off, fading in and out between the
mournful moanings of the wind, I swore I heard the hoofbeats of a lone horse, galloping.

I'd searched the fields around Rosehill for horses, and
found Peter had been quite right—there were none. Only a
small herd of mild-eyed cows, grazing drowsily down by the
river, and a disgruntled-looking black pig in a fenced yard
further up the road. But the horses came anyway, out of the
darkness, galloping over the high waving grass.

I listened again, straining my ears to catch the rhythm of
the running hooves. More than one, now, surely. *I hear the
Shadowy Horses* . . . I summoned the line of the Yeats poem
that Peter had quoted, wishing my imagination wasn't working overtime. After all that had happened tonight, I could
almost believe in those Irish sea-horses, the horses of Manannan, coming to carry the living away. It gave me the
creeps, sitting there in the old house and hearing that sound
drawing steadily nearer.

By the time I'd finished my second cup of tea, my nerves
were so completely frayed I chose a desperate remedy—I
dragged the kitchen telephone off its stand and dialed the
number of my London flat.

My sister Alison answered on the third ring, her voice
clear and coherent despite the fact that she had, I knew, just
woken from a sound sleep.

"How can you do that?" I asked her, skipping the prelim-
inaries.

"Do what?"

"Sound so bloody alert when you've just woken up?"

"It's a gift. Are you all right?"

"Just having trouble sleeping."

"Ah. Wanted to share it, did you?"

"Brat." Feeling better already, I settled back and poured another cup of tea. "How are you getting on down there?"

"Marvellously, thanks. Your flat's brilliant. I'm never going to leave."

I smiled. "Well, it won't want me back, after you. I'm sure the place has never been cleaner."

"Dusting things," my sister told me loftily, "does make a difference, Verity. Oh, and your African violet's in bloom. Remember how you said you couldn't ever . . ."

"How on earth did you get it to bloom?"

"I watered it."

"Ah." I smiled again, feeling much less lonely. "That's the secret, is it? And how is school?"

"Less brilliant," Alison admitted, "but not bad. Oh, by the way, I meant to ask you—what is the name of the man you're working for?"

"Peter Quinnell."

"Oh right. That was my mistake, then."

"What was?"

"Well, I knew it was Quinnell, but I couldn't remember the first name, and last week in Waterstones I saw this book by a man named Quinnell, so I bought it, thinking it might be your boss, you see." She paused for breath. "But anyway, once I got it home and took a proper look, I saw it couldn't have been *your* Quinnell, because the man who wrote the book is dead, according to the dust jacket."

"Ah." I digested the information. "It was thoughtful of you to buy it, at any rate."

"Yes, well, I ought to have known that it wasn't the sort of thing an archaeologist would publish. It's just a lot of photographs . . . you know, a coffee-table book. But Quinnell's not a common name, and I thought—"

"Photographs?" I cut her off. "The author wouldn't be a Philip Quinnell, by any chance?"

"Hang on, let me check, I've got the thing right here. Yes, that's it . . . Philip. Who is he, then?"

"He was Peter's son."

"Really? Well, his photographs are deeply weird," was her pronouncement. "They're those awful computer-enhanced things, all distorted. But the man himself looks gorgeous, in his photograph. Does his father look like that?''

"Peter? Yes, he's very handsome.''

"Is he nice to work for?''

"Wonderful.''

"Then it must be Adrian.''

I frowned, uncomprehending. "What?''

"Making you unhappy. And don't tell me you're not, because you never ring me at five in the morning unless you're unhappy. You're not involved with him again, are you?''

"With *Adrian*? Don't be absurd.''

"Then who—?'' She broke off, paused, and shifted gears subtly. "Who else is in your field crew, did you say?''

The Spanish Inquisition, I thought, could have used someone like Alison. Once she hit on something she was like a terrier with a rat; she never let go.

"You're way off beam,'' I told her, trying to sound convincing. "It's nothing to do with a man. It's just . . . well, we had rather a crisis here, tonight. Someone's mother had a heart attack, and we don't know yet how she is, and I'm just on edge, that's all. Waiting.''

"Oh,'' said my sister.

"Honestly.''

"I believe you,'' she said.

"Look, I probably ought to go, come to think of it. Keep the line clear, in case someone's trying to ring.''

"Right. Shall I keep this book, then? The one by Philip Quinnell?''

"Please. I'd rather like to see it.''

Something was nagging at me as I rang off—some minor point that I'd just heard, but couldn't quite remember. Closing my eyes, I replayed the conversation, trying to recall what Alison had said . . .

No, it was gone. Whatever it was, it was gone.

I sighed again, with feeling. Charlie the cat showed me a weary eye as I gently lifted her for the umpteenth time. "Sorry, darling,'' I apologized. "It's time to move.''

Peter's sitting room was out, I thought, since Adrian was still asleep in there. But across the hall, the posh sitting room offered warmth and light and a glowing gas fire. I drew an armchair up to the hearth and stretched my legs out, coaxing the cat to settle down once more. With a less than trusting look at my face, Charlie lay down and fell instantly asleep, her small sharp claws hooked neatly through the fabric of my jeans.

Time crawled.

I leaned my head back, counting off the minutes on the mantel clock, a great gilt clock with a soporific tick. Another half-hour had passed before I saw the gleam of headlights curving up the drive, and heard a car door slam above the unrelenting wind. The front door opened and closed. Soft, measured footsteps crossed the entrance hall; paused in the doorway behind me.

"My dear girl," Peter Quinnell said, his low voice mingling faint surprise and weariness. "You ought to be in bed."

I twisted around in my chair, gently so as not to disturb the slumbering cat. "I couldn't sleep." He looked gray, I thought, and frightfully old, and I asked my next question with some hesitation. "How is she?"

"Nancy? Resting comfortably, the doctors say, but doctors always say that, don't they?" Rubbing the worry from his forehead with a tired hand, he crossed to the drinks cabinet. "Can I get you something? Brandy? It's good medicine, for sleepless nights."

He poured one for himself as well, and lowered his long frame into the chair next to mine, staring at the hearth. "You've got the fire on," he said, after a long moment.

"Yes. I was cold."

"Were you? It's the house, I expect. Old houses," he informed me, "feel the cold more. Like old bodies." He sat back, eyes half closed, and let the silence stretch until I killed it with a cough.

"David found you all right, then, did he?"

"What?" His eyes slid sideways, not really seeing me at first, and then he seemed to pull himself together. "Oh, yes. Yes, he did. He's a great help, that lad. A good son. He'll stay all night with her, I shouldn't wonder."

"It must have been a frightful scare for him." I looked at his face and amended my statement. "For both of you."

"Yes, well, it's not the first time." Quinnell swirled his brandy, turning back to the fire. "This is her third attack, you know. She never did like listening to doctors. For years now they've been telling her she ought to be more careful, have some help around the house; but she's a bloody-minded woman, Nancy Fortune. She still thinks she can do it all herself." He smiled faintly, shook his head. "We used to call her Henny, in the old days, after the Little Red Hen in the fairy story. 'I'll do it myself', that's what she'd say. And she'd do a damned fine job of it, too. Always mastered anything she put her mind to."

I heard the ring of pride in his voice, and glanced at him with interest. "It must have been a great loss, when she left you."

"A terrible loss," he agreed. "Terrible. But of course, she had her reasons."

"David's father."

"Yes." He smiled again, a little sadly. "I'm afraid I was rather ungracious about the whole affair. I never quite forgave her for leaving, but in time I understood. Time," he told me, "gives us all the gift of perspective."

Of course, I thought, he'd lost much more since then. His wife, presumably . . . she must be dead, since Peter never mentioned her. His son. He'd lost them both. How tragic.

I tried to think of something suitable to say, but nothing came to mind.

Behind us, in the hall, the floorboards creaked. My shoulders tensed in sudden, foolish fear, and then relaxed again when Adrian said sleepily: "Ah, here you are. I thought I heard voices."

He shuffled over to the drinks cabinet, smoothing back his rumpled hair. The gesture didn't help. He looked like he'd been romping through the sheets with someone, barefoot and bare-chested, his shirt slung on loosely as an afterthought, his jeans unbuttoned.

Quinnell arched an elegant eyebrow in my direction and I hastened to explain, not wanting him to get the wrong idea.

"He stayed to keep me company, and fell asleep on the sofa."

Adrian grinned. "What she means to say," he told Quinnell, "is that I've been behaving myself, in spite of appearances. But if you will insist on leaving me stranded . . ."

The eyebrow lowered again. "Ah yes, your car. I do apologize, my boy. Couldn't find the keys to the Range Rover, I'm afraid. Fabia puts them in the damnedest places. And when I went to look in the Rover itself, I found your car beside it, with the keys in the ignition, so . . ." He spread his hands and smiled an apology. "I wasn't thinking very clearly, at the time."

Adrian sloshed a measure of gin into a glass, and shrugged magnanimously. "No harm done. Not to me, anyway. Poor Brian McMorran's a bit shaken up, though. You nearly ran him over."

"Did I?" Quinnell frowned faintly, trying to remember. "I do seem to recall something leaping into the bushes . . . that was Brian? Did I do him any damage?"

Adrian shook his head. "Just rattled him a little."

"Ah." The charming voice sounded rather disappointed, to my ears. "Pour me another brandy, would you, there's a good chap." He passed his empty glass to Adrian, and turned to me expectantly. "And now, since I have you both here, perhaps you'll be good enough to tell me what all of you were up to tonight, out in the field."

Adrian turned.

The black cat Murphy, drawn by our voices, materialized in the doorway. After a moment's pause he came padding across the carpet and leapt lightly to the arm of Quinnell's chair. Nothing else moved.

My eyes met Adrian's uncertainly. He lounged back against the drinks cabinet, his expression deliberately blank. "I'm sorry?"

"Come now," said Quinnell, taking the brandy from Adrian's outstretched hand. "I may be an old man, but I'm not a complete fool." His eyes slid from one to the other of us, waiting. "Now, what did the Sentinel say?"

XX

"Ye've telt him." Wally Tyler wasn't asking a question. He slowly lit a cigarette and nodded like some ancient sage pronouncing judgment. 'Tis well ye did. It'll take his mind off Nancy, some."

I took a seat beside him on the low stone wall that ran around the small neglected garden at the side of the house, and watched while he threw a stick for Kip.

Already it was early afternoon, and the betraying shadow on the sundial at the center of the garden shamed me for sleeping away half the day. Not that I could have helped it. When sleep had finally found me in the hours after dawn, it had claimed me with a sure and final vengeance. But I was sorry to have missed what must have been a lovely morning.

Without the wind, the sun would have felt exceedingly hot; even as it was, my plain outfit of jeans and T-shirt seemed too warm. Spring had nearly faded into summer. Come Saturday week, it would be June. Which left us three full months still, in the digging season. Time enough to prove our theory. Our theory . . . I smiled faintly, raising a hand to rub my tired eyes. When I'd begun this, I had thought it Peter's theory, and his alone.

"Actually," I confessed to Wally, "he wasn't much surprised to learn what we'd been up to. He'd figured most of it out already, on his own.''

"Aye." Wally nodded. "Thought he might. I had a feeling, ken.''

"God." I sighed in mock exasperation. "Don't tell me you're psychic, as well.''

The wizened features smoothed into a smile. "No, lass. There's only Robbie has the sight, and he didna get it fae my side o' the family.''

Kip trotted back toward us, stick in mouth, and Wally patiently tossed it out again across the garden.

Another voice intruded unexpectedly. "You'll make the dog boak, if you keep that up.'' A smooth voice, not unpleasant, but not the one I'd been hoping to hear. Brian McMorran's hair shone silver in the sunlight as he sauntered over to join us.

"Away wi' ye," said Wally, flatly. "And mind your language.''

"Aw, she doesn't know what boak means, do you?'' Brian looked to me for confirmation. "See? Of course she doesn't know. She wants to come out on the *Fleetwing* with me and the lads, when the sea's a bloody roller coaster, then she'd know what boaking is.''

"That's enough." Wally's eyebrows lowered, and Brian grinned, exposing a line of wolfish teeth.

"All right, all right. Sorry if I've shocked you." But he didn't look the least bit sorry as he settled himself on the garden wall beside me. "I am," he confessed, "a rotten bastard, as Wally will no doubt have warned you. Cigarette?'' He drew a battered packet from his rolled-up shirtsleeve, and I shook my head.

"No thanks. I don't smoke.''

"Bloody filthy things," said Wally. Since he himself was smoking, I deduced that he was talking, not of cigarettes in general, but of Brian's in particular. They were a foreign brand—I didn't recognize the writing on the packet—and the smoke stank to sweet heaven as it drifted past my face.

Tucking the cigarettes back in his sleeve, Brian folded his

tattooed arms across his chest and tipped back his head to look at the glorious sky.

"Grand weather," he remarked. "I'm surprised you're not out digging in the fields, the lot of you, especially after that little panto you staged last night."

"No work today," said Wally shortly. "Peter needs his sleep."

"Up all night with Granny Nan, was he?"

"Most of it."

"Silly old sod." Brian shook his head. "It'd take more than a heart attack to level that woman. She's a tough old bird."

I had no doubt that Wally privately agreed with Brian's opinion, but of course he would never have admitted as much, and so he said nothing; he simply went on tossing out the stick for Kip and smoking, and it was left to me to pick up the dropped stitch of conversation.

"How's Robbie?" I asked Brian, then saw from his expression that I'd picked a touchy subject.

"I reckon there's no damage done, no thanks to all of you." Balancing the cigarette between his lips, he squinted through the haze of smoke. "He was rabbiting onto Jeannie just now, when I left them. Wanting to go into Berwick to visit Granny Nan in hospital, though I don't imagine she'll be having any visitors today."

I murmured something vague, thinking back. "Was it her heart attack he saw, last night?" I asked. "Was that what made him faint?"

Brian nodded. "He didn't get it when it happened, on account of he was already tuned in to your Roman ghost, but once the ghost was gone I guess the signal came in loud and clear. Bit too much for the lad, having all that happen in the one night. His mind's like a fuse box, see. You overload the circuits and the lights go out."

It was, I thought, an apt analogy.

"Anyhow," said Brian, "it won't be happening again. I've told Jeannie." His face relaxed a little. "She's having a soft time of it today as well, with all of you having a late lie. No breakfast to make, and she can't even hoover the sitting room till Sutton-Clarke shifts himself. Still sleeping, is he?''

"Adrian? Yes, I think so." Kip nudged my leg and I took the damply chewed stick from him absently, tossing it out again toward the sundial. "At least, I've not seen any movement from the house."

"Fabia must be up, though. The Range Rover's gone."

"What? Oh, no," I corrected him, turning, "David's got it."

"Still?" He raised his eyebrows in surprise, and I found myself wondering whether Brian McMorran had a mother. Poor woman, I thought to myself. *Her* son would never sit up all night at her bedside, that much was obvious. "Bloody inconvenient, that," he commented. "I hope he brings it back by teatime."

"Why?" Wally speared his son-in-law with a narrowed glance. "What d'ye want with the Range Rover?"

"Got some boxes to unload, off the boat. Our car's too small," he explained. "I told Jeannie we shouldn't buy an import—not enough room in the boot, I said, but she thought it'd save us a few pounds in petrol."

I rose to Jeannie's defense. "And did it?"

"Oh, aye." He smiled a boyish smile that made me understand in part why Jeannie found him attractive. "But I'd rather have a Rover, wouldn't you?"

Wally calmly pointed out we couldn't all have Fabia's money.

Brian laughed. "Speak for yourself, old man. I've not given up trying."

Kip, having carried the stick back to Wally, drew back a pace, panting, then suddenly brought his lovely head up and around to stare past our shoulders at the front door of the house. When he gave his now-familiar whine of recognition and the feathered tail began to wave, my heart lurched downwards to my stomach.

But it wasn't the Sentinel, this time.

The figure coming around the house toward us, dressed in a loose shirt and trousers, blond hair swinging wildly in the warm wind, was very definitely not a ghost.

Fabia tossed us a surprisingly cheerful greeting and swung herself over the low garden wall, saving herself the bother of walking the few steps further onto the gate. She looked disgustingly vibrant and full of life. The privilege of youth, I supposed. On top of which, she'd slept a good twelve hours against my six, and she hadn't stayed up all night drinking brandy and discussing whether a child's mumbled "*nona*" was enough to base an excavation on.

"What have you done to Adrian?" she asked me, curious. "He's dead to the world in there. Didn't so much as bat an eyelash when the phone rang; I had to get up and answer it myself."

I moved to make room for her on the wall, between myself and Brian. "We were up rather late last night," I explained, through a yawn. "Talking to your grandfather."

"Ah." Swinging her legs, she met my eyes candidly. "Did you tell him, then? About our ghost?"

"Sort of. He's awfully pleased about it, really."

"Yes, I expect he would be." Fabia's satisfied eyes swept away from me and out across the wide green field that stretched beyond the garden wall to meet the rolling horizon. Returning her attention to the rest of us, she looked Brian up and down, assessingly. "You seem to have recovered from your hit-and-run."

"Oh, aye." His golden earring caught the sunlight as he tossed his head back, grinning. "It'd take more than an old man in a sports car to finish me off."

Wally puffed a smoke ring skywards and observed, in a dry voice, that it might depend entirely on which old man was doing the driving.

"Ha ha," said Brian. "Anyhow, my darling, I promise I'll not sue your grandad for damages, if you'll just do me one small favor."

Fabia leaned forward expectantly. "Name it."

"Let me use the Range Rover."

"Sure. When do you need it?"

"Well, as soon as it comes back . . ."

"It's back," Fabia interjected. Then, as we all turned to look toward the empty stretch of gravel where the vehicle should have been, she shook her head and set us straight. "No, not *here*, but Davy's finished with it. That was him ringing a moment ago, to say that his mum was all right and he's back at the Ship Hotel, and did I need the Range Rover before this evening? I told him no," she confessed, to Brian, "because I didn't know you needed it. But we could walk in now and get it, if you like."

"Walk, hell," was Brian's reply. "We'll take my car. There's two of us, two vehicles. We can each of us drive one back." He chucked his spent cigarette into the tangle of weeds at his feet, and stood up away from the wall. "Anyone else want to help unload boxes?"

I stood too, and stretched, brushing the dust from my jeans with an idle hand. "No, thanks. But I think I could do with a bit of a walk."

Wally angled his head to look up at me, and I caught the faintest glimmer of amusement in his crinkled gray eyes. He doused it soberly, and nodded. "Away ye go, then, lass. I'm fine the now."

The three of us left the garden together, which presented Kip with something of a dilemma. As much as the collie loved following me about, he wasn't too keen on Brian, and even my mention of the word "walk" failed to ease the dog's misgivings. As I went through the gate Kip stepped forward, hesitated, then turned again and, settling with a thump at Wally's feet, began to gnaw at his stick with a disgruntled fervour.

I rather missed him, on my walk.

Because I didn't want Wally, with his knowing eyes, to think that I was going where he thought I was going, I purposely struck out in the opposite direction, following the road down through the small ravine where the narrow river sang in the green coolness and the trees stretched out protective arms above the primroses and wilting daffodils; then on a half-mile or so beside low walls and thorn hedge and the lush, verdant, nondescript growth of the verge. But having got safely out of sight of Rosehill, my purpose reasserted itself and I turned back, abandoning the road in favor of a narrow footpath that ran along the riverbank.

It was lovely and quiet, here. Above the calming sound of the water, gurgling over the stones in its shallower places, the only noises I could hear were a whisper of wind high above in the trees and the chirping calls of small sparrows and chaffinches. The thick, sweet smell of wild garlic swirled around me, and I brushed against a hawthorn bush that scattered small white petals at my feet.

The footpath itself proved a bit of a challenge. Every now and then it snaked off in several directions, here climbing the steep wall of the ravine, there hugging the murmuring water, in other spots losing itself completely in a clump of gorse and greenery. A railway bridge had spanned the stream at one time, and the soaring brick supports still bore mute testimony to the fact, lending a rather eerie and deserted quality to that stretch of the river, but I was much too busy scrambling over fallen trees and trying not to slip on the wet red clay of the path to take much notice.

In time, the footpath led me upwards, past an old and creaking wooden mill that shivered with ivy, and I found myself back on the road again. And the road, after ten minutes' effortless walk, led me straight to the center of Eyemouth.

I didn't see the Range Rover in the car park of the Ship Hotel—Fabia and Brian must already have been and gone. But I did find David, sitting in the public bar.

He looked rougher than his usual self, his eyes red-rimmed and dull above the day's dark growth of beard. Seeing him like that, I felt a pang of sharp emotion that I put down to concern.

"You ought to be in bed," I told him, hoisting myself onto a neighboring stool.

It took him a long moment to register my presence, but eventually he turned and slanted me an unreadable look, and meeting his eyes I was forced to admit that concern wasn't all I was feeling.

After what seemed an age, he looked away and shrugged. "Can't sleep."

"Well, *that's* not going to help much, is it?" I nodded at

the untouched mug of coffee that he cradled in one hand. "You need a Scotch, or something."

The blue eyes lost a little of their dullness. "I've had two," he said. "This is meant to be the chaser."

"Oh."

"Would you like one?"

"Well, I wouldn't mind," I admitted. "I didn't get much sleep last night myself."

"Got to you, did it?"

"The ghost? Yes, it did." I waited while he ordered my coffee, then showed him a rueful smile. "I haven't been that frightened of the dark since I was a kid, and it was vampires then, not ghosts. Hammer Films," I explained, to his curious face.

"Ah. Well, I don't think that our Sentinel bears any great resemblance to Christopher Lee, so you've nothing to worry about."

"It isn't the ghost that frightens me," I rationalized, "so much as the idea."

"Aye, and I'm sure I'll be leaving the lights on as well, when I've had a chance to think about it." He sounded weary when he said that, reminding me that he'd had other things to frighten him, these past twelve hours.

My coffee came, and I sipped it, studying his face above the rim of my mug. "How is your mother doing, really?"

"She's over the worst of it; that's what they tell me. They'll be keeping her in for a while, yet, though. Not that they want to," he told me, with an unexpected grin. "She's not so bad when she's tranquillized, but my mother's aye crabbit in hospital."

"Aye crabbit?"

"Always in a bad temper," he translated. "Have you not got your dictionary with you the day?"

"No, I haven't . . ." Frowning suddenly, I looked down. "I haven't even brought my handbag, I'm afraid."

David assured me his means were sufficient to cover the cost of my coffee. But he arched a quizzical eyebrow, all the same. "What were you planning on doing in town without your handbag, may I ask?"

"Oh, I don't know." I attempted a nonchalant shrug that fell short of the mark. "Just out for a bit of a walk, that's all."

He watched me for a moment, thinking. "Adrian's not here."

"No, I know he's not. He spent the night at Rosehill."

"Oh, aye?" The eyebrow lowered, and I cursed myself.

"On the sitting room sofa," I said clearly. "Peter took his car, you see, and he didn't fancy walking back."

"All that way." David's face relaxed into a smile that held a hint of mockery.

"Yes, well. Adrian's not the walking type."

"I had noticed."

I watched while he took a drink of coffee, curious in my turn. "You don't like Adrian much, do you?"

"He's all right," David conceded, with a small dismissive lift of his shoulders. "But he's sleekit. And you can look *that* up in your dictionary, when you've a mind to." After a moment's silence he set the coffee mug down again and swung his gaze back to mine. "So if Adrian's up at the house, and you've not brought your wallet with you, what the devil are you doing at the Ship?"

It was a blunt question, and a reasonable one, and it left me with no graceful way of escaping an honest answer. I shifted on my stool and cleared my throat. "Well, if you must know, I was rather worried about you. We all were."

The blue eyes softened. "Were you, now?"

"Yes. And I thought you might need somebody to . . . well, to cheer you up."

He stroked a thoughtful hand along his unshaven jaw. "It's not a job for the faint-hearted, cheering me up."

"No?"

"No." He looked at me, hard, for another long moment, until I felt certain I'd never be able to breathe again. And then he smiled. "But get that down you," he said, pointing to my coffee, "and we'll see what we can do."

XXI

What we did, in the end, was go outside in search of fresher air.

On the quayside, in front of the Ship Hotel, David bent for a moment to tie a shoelace while I dug my hands in my pockets and looked around.

I'd never seen the harbor when the fishing fleet was out. It didn't look at all forlorn, as I'd expected. Instead it had the peaceful and serene demeanor of a housewife who, having finished her day's labors, had found an hour of freedom in the absence of her family, and had settled down happily to enjoy herself.

Not that the "family" was entirely absent. Three boats, at least, had stayed behind, and from the far end of the harbor came the strong persistent throbbing of an engine, competing with the shrill cries of the herring gulls that dipped and wheeled above our heads.

"Which boat is Brian's?" I asked David, and he raised his head from his crouching position, scanning along the narrow length of the harbor.

"That one," he identified it. "Second up along the middle pier."

The middle pier, I gathered from the direction of his nod,

was the long bit running parallel to us, on the far side of the harbor, though why it should be called the middle pier escaped me, as it didn't appear to be in the middle of anything. Of the three boats moored there, Brian's was the biggest—a bright red monster of a fishing boat with *Fleetwing* freshly painted on its prow.

Still, it looked frightfully small when one thought of the sea that it had to battle, for all those days on end. I shrugged off an involuntary shudder, glad that I wasn't a fisherman.

David stood and flexed his shoulders. "Want to walk around and take a look? I don't ken whether any of the lads are working on the boat the day, but . . ."

"Brian might be there himself," I told him. "He and Fabia were coming down to unload some things from the boat, I think."

"Is that why she wanted the Range Rover, then? She came and got the keys a while back, but she didn't tell me what for." Whistling a snatch of some unrecognizable tune, he shortened his stride to match mine, and put out a hand to steer me around a thick black cable coiled like a snake upon the quayside. I shot him a questioning glance.

"He smuggles, I take it?"

The whistling died as David grinned. "D'ye work for the Customs and Excise?"

"No."

"Well, then, it's best to keep your head tucked down, lass, in a place like this." But he yielded to my curiosity, nonetheless. "He has a friend of sorts, does Brian, in one of the Baltic ports. Poland, maybe. I'm not sure. Since the Berlin Wall came down it's not so hard to get things from that corner of the world."

"Like Peter's vodka," I suggested.

"Aye. It's what our Brian carries, mostly. Peter lets him use the cellars at Rosehill for storage, till Brian's mate comes through with his lorry. So Peter gets a bottle or two every month, in return."

"It doesn't bother Peter?" I asked. "That it's illegal, I mean."

"Och, no, a wee bit of free trading never bothered him,

so long as it's not in drugs or guns. Vodka," David said, "is hardly something Peter would turn out of his house."

I looked with interest at the little harbor, peaceful in the sunshine with the water lapping smooth and innocent against its walls. "Is there much smuggling goes on here, now?"

David shook his dark head. "Only Brian, that I ken about. In the old days, though—and I do mean the old days, back afore my grandad's time—nearly everyone had a hand in the business. That's why they built the old town like they did, all wynds and vennels, twisting lanes. It's fair impossible to chase a smuggler when the streets don't run straight. And that house over there," he told me, warming to his subject, "Gunsgreen, that was a smuggler's paradise. It's got tunnels and storage dens built underneath, and every room has two doors—one to the corridor, and one leading into the next room along. So you could leave an exciseman standing in the hallway, pounding at the one door, while you took off through the other rooms, and made a clean escape. It's magic."

I'd noticed Gunsgreen House, earlier. It was a landmark, difficult to miss, set just above the harbor opposite the Ship Hotel. It reminded me of the houses I used to build with my blocks, when I was young—a tall square solid structure with no softness anywhere, its yellow walls and gray roof outwardly respectable.

"Mind how you go," David warned, putting out a hand to stop me tripping on another cable. "You'll not cheer me up if you land in the water."

I cast a dubious eye at the cold gray surface that, in spite of the fact that the tide was in, still shimmered some distance below us. Stepping cautiously over the cable, I let David shepherd me the few yards across the harbor road and onto the pavement, where walking was safer. A little further on, I paused for a better view of the long fish market building that hugged the harbor's edge. It was open to the air, most of it, paved like a car park and sheltered by a sturdy roof that rested on squared wooden posts. Open markets never had looked finished to me—as a child, I'd always assumed that the builders had simply forgotten the walls—but at the nearest end of this one, painted metal sheeting closed off one large section. Outside the market, a lorry blocked most of the road, and the driver, leaning up against his cab and smoking a cigarette, nodded politely and said, "Heyah" as we passed.

"He's waiting for the auction," David told me, when I asked. "It doesn't start till four o'clock."

"What sort of auction?"

He sent me a patient look, such as a teacher might send a rather thick student. "A fish auction, lass."

"Oh." I twisted my wrist to check the time on my watch. "But it's nearly a quarter-past three."

"So?"

"Well, there aren't any boats around, are there? And I don't see any fish."

In truth, the fish market was completely empty; so empty I could see clean through it, between the posts and across the harbor to where Brian's boat was moored. But David refused to tell me how the miracle of the fishes was to be achieved. Instead he led me past the market, close against the buildings to our right, which opened up from time to time in narrow arching alleyways that offered glimpses of deserted packing yards of brick and concrete, slick with moisture.

"Right," he said, "now we can cross back over, here . . . hang on, you might want to wait for this lorry." One strong arm held me back when I would have stepped into the street. "You're an accident waiting to happen, you are. Did your mother not teach you to look both ways?" Another lorry rattled past us, squeezing through the street, and David relaxed his hold on my shoulder. "All right, come on."

The throbbing of the unseen engine was loudest here, at the bottom edge of the harbor. "The ice plant," David told me, as we turned our backs to the sound and started up along the middle pier.

I was forced to admit that, in spite of my former skepticism, the term "middle pier" was, in fact, wholly appropriate. It was indeed a true pier, with water on both sides. To the left of us, the harbor lay serene and almost empty, while on my right a mud-walled channel carried what David assured me was the same river that I'd walked along from Rosehill. I didn't believe him, at first. Down here, within the confines of the narrow channel, the water looked different, its current faintly sluggish, more sedate.

"I wouldn't tell you lies," said David. "That's the Eye Water. The town takes its name from that wee trickle, ken. Our harbor was built around the mouth of the Eye. Mind the nets," he added, as we drew level with Brian's boat.

I smiled. "You sound just like my mother." But I was careful, all the same, to step around the green and orange mass of netting stretched like some great sleeping beast at the edge of the pier.

At first glance the *Fleetwing* seemed deserted, but in response to David's call a small, wire-limbed man wearing bright yellow brace-and-bib overalls came out on deck and raised a hand in greeting.

"Heyah, Deid-Banes." He leaned over the aft end to look at us. "Heard about yer mither. Bloody shame. She still in Berwick?"

"Aye. And don't you go thinking of burgling the cottage while she's in hospital, neither."

The other man laughed. "Ye've no faith, lad. I'm no sae tarry-fingert. And I'd no steal fae yer mither."

"You'd steal from yours."

"Aye, but I like yer mither better. Were ye wanting something?"

"Looking for Brian. Is he about?"

"Nah." Still chuckling, the wizened man in the overalls lit a cigarette and shook his head. "He's away the now, the skipper is."

"Left you in charge, then, did he? Trusting man."

"Aye, well, he cannae trust Mick, so that only leaves me." David tilted his head. "Do I ken Mick?"

"The new lad, fae Liverpool. Ye dinna wish tae ken that one, Deid-Banes. He's a nasty wee bugger."

"Christ, Billy, coming from you—"

"Ah'm dead serious." The older man pulled sharply on his cigarette and the wind caught the smoke, whipping it past his squinting eyes. "The lad's been up the gaol half his life, and it wasna fer thieving. I'll no turn my back tae the bastard." And then, remembering my presence, he shot me a crooked smile. "Sorry, lass. Ah'm no minding my manners."

David folded his arms and looked at him. "Well, now you've switched on the charm, you might offer the lass a wee tour around the *Fleetwing*, show her how a fishing boat works."

The other man shrugged helplessly, his teeth clamped around the cigarette. "I canna do it the day, Deid-Banes. I'm painting the day, and the paint's no dry yet."

I couldn't see any paint cans on deck, nor smell the faintest whiff of fumes, but David didn't press the point. He did permit himself a smile, though, as we turned and walked on, up the middle pier. "I kent he'd say no," he confessed, "but I wanted to see what excuse he'd come up with. He's a brilliant liar, is Billy."

I tipped my chin up, curious. "What does the 'Deid-Banes' mean, exactly? I mean, I know Wally calls you that, sometimes, but . . ."

"It's my byname," he supplied. "A kind of community nickname, if you like. A lot of folk have bynames, here in Eyemouth."

"Why?"

"Helps to tell us apart, for one thing. When you've more than one David Fortune running about, things get a bit confusing."

I was openly intrigued. "*Is* there more than one David Fortune?"

"Oh, aye, there'd be four of us, I think. Or was it five?" He narrowed his eyes, thinking. "No, just the four. My uncle David, and my cousin—he's a few years younger, ken—and then there was another David Fortune at school with me. If I traced the family history back I'd no doubt find he's a cousin as well. But we're nothing compared to the Dougals," he added. "You can't spit in town without hitting a Dougal."

"So how does one get a nickname, then?"

"Different ways. I was always digging things up as a lad,

playing at being an archaeologist, so my grandad called me 'Deid-Banes'—dead bones—and it stuck. He'd have called me plain 'Bones' if he'd had his way, but there's a Bones already in Eyemouth, and a Young Bones.''

"Ah," I said.

"Some of the bynames are more obscure, ken. There was Deddy; don't know where that came from. And Pamfy and Racker and Duffs. Now Duffs,'' he explained, with a broad smile, "*that* came down from a lad who worked as a cook on a fishing boat. All he knew how to make was plum duff, so Duffs he became. His daughter got the byname, too, and I think her son still gets it sometimes.''

Wrinkling my nose, I hopped over another coiled fishing net. "So women get bynames as well?''

"Oh, aye. If you'd been married onto Duffs, you'd have been Verity Duffs.''

"No, I wouldn't,'' I assured him.

David smiled. "That's not nearly as bad as my mother's byname.''

"What, Granny Nan?''

He shook his head. "Granny Nan's not her byname, lass. That's just what Robbie calls her—Robbie and a few others. No, she hates her byname. Call her by it and you're asking to get your teeth knocked down your throat.'' He glanced down at me, his smile broadening. "And you can stop looking at me like that, because I'm not going to tell you what it is. It'd be more than my life is worth.''

"She's fierce, is she, your mother?''

"You have no idea.''

Encouraged by his openness, and the growing ease of our companionship, I chanced another question. "Your dad was a fisherman, wasn't he?''

"Aye, so they tell me. I can't really mind him. I have this memory of a big man in a gansey—a guernsey, you call it in England—that always smelled of fish; but that might not have been my dad. Everyone smelled of fish, in our house. My grandad was a cadger.''

"Oh,'' I nodded sagely. "Sort of a traveling fish-salesman, you mean.''

We'd come to the end of the middle pier. A sharp right turn would have taken us over the Eye Water by a small metal drawbridge, then on around the lifeboat station to the looming bulk of Gunsgreen House. But David chose instead to lean his elbows on the bright red railing at the pier's end, and study my innocent face.

"Been sleeping with that dictionary, have you?" he asked, in a tone laced thick with amusement. "How d'ye ken what a cadger is?"

"Well, I had to look up 'ca' canny' the other day, and 'cadger' is right on the same page, so I thought I might as well memorize it, too."

He quirked an eyebrow. "'Ca' canny'?"

"Yes. It means to take care, or be cautious."

"Aye, I ken fine what it means. Why'd you need to look it up?"

I shrugged, and leaned in my turn on the railing. "Wally said it, last week. When Jeannie went out in the car. I don't know where she was going, but Wally told her to 'ca' canny along that road.' And I just wondered what it meant."

"You could have asked."

"I don't like asking all the time. Besides," I pointed out, "my dictionary works just fine. I *did* know what a cadger was."

"Aye, so you did." He smiled a little and turned his face forward again, looking across to the harbor's shielded entrance. Every now and then a stiff gust of wind caught the swirl of the sea and tossed a mist of white spray over the barrier wall. I could faintly taste the salt from where I stood, and smell the cleanly biting scent of the cold North Sea. The smell of fish was fainter still, but for David, at least, it stirred memories. "He had a small business, my grandad did, selling fish up north, around Edinburgh. Mostly miners up there, in those days, with large families. Two pieces of fish to the pound was no use to them—they wanted ten pieces, to feed all those mouths. And that meant whiting. Ever clean a whiting?" he asked me.

"No."

"Bloody awful things." He grinned. "My grandad used

to come to auction every day, to get his boxes of whiting, and every day when I got home from school I'd have to help to fillet them. Got a bit of a break at the weekend. There were no fish taken over the weekend, ken, so we didn't have to face the whiting till Monday teatime. But then the shed would be full of boxes again.''

"Even in winter?''

"Oh, aye. Only in winter it got so cold we'd be standing on an old filleting board to keep off the floor, with rags soaked in boiling water laid across our wellies to keep our toes from freezing, and bowls of boiling water to dip our fingers in to keep them working. Christ,'' he shuddered at the recollection. "I hated working at the fish. We'd all get so cheesed off that we'd stop talking, after the first hour or so. Nothing to do but count the fish. Used to be two hundred and thirty-seven whiting,'' he informed me, "in a six-stone box. They've changed the weights now, but that's what it used to be.''

I propped one foot on the red-painted railing and followed his gaze out to sea. "Is that what put you off being a fisherman?''

"Not really. You're either born to the sea or you're not, and I'm not. My mother kent that, early on. She always tells the story of how Peter caught me digging up the garden, and said that I was born to be an archaeologist.''

"And he was right.''

"He usually is.''

It was a simple statement of fact, and I stayed silent a moment, thinking about the excavation at Rosehill. About the disappearance of the Ninth Legion, all those years ago, and about a ghostly presence that last night might have said *nona* . . .

A white shape glided silently beneath us, and I looked down, startled. No ghost, I reassured myself, but something just as strange. "David, look!''

"Oh, aye, the swan. I wondered where he'd got to.''

"Do you mean he actually lives here? Here, in the harbor?''

The bird cocked its head at the sound of my voice, and

having surveyed me with one round uncertain eye, turned smoothly and floated back underneath the little red drawbridge, seeking the relative security of the channel.

"He's magnificent," I said.

"Aye." David watched the bird's sleek figure disappearing underneath the bridge.

"Does he have a mate?"

"Not yet. There was a female here, a few years back, but she only stayed a fortnight. She couldn't seem to settle down to life inside the harbor." He turned his head and met my gaze unhurriedly. "And he's well stuck here now, that lad. Too old to change his ways."

He'd only moved his head, I thought, and yet I felt as though the space between us had grown smaller. I felt suddenly aware of just how near he was, of how little effort it would take to move toward him, feel his warmth . . . to raise my hand and touch the hard unshaven contours of his face . . .

His eyes flicked down toward my lips, and back again, a smile in their depths. "Ca' canny along that road," he told me gently.

But he wasn't warning me off. No, I decided with growing amazement, watching the smile spread slowly from his blue eyes to his mouth; he wasn't giving me a warning. He was issuing a challenge.

And I was already beginning to respond to it, leaning forward, my pulse increasing crazily, when an unexpected shadow fell between us.

"Hello," said Adrian. "I thought I'd find you here."

XXII

I wasn't thrilled to see him. It must have shown plainly on my face when I glanced round, but Adrian took no notice. He was doing his dog-in-the-manger again, and his eyes were not on me, but on David.

"God, you look awful," he said, with typical tact. "You ought to be in bed."

I caught the uncharacteristic gleam of mischief deep in David's eyes as his gaze swung meaningfully to me. Leaning back against the red painted railing, he folded his arms across his wide chest and turned to Adrian. "Plenty of time for that, yet."

One could almost hear the slap of a gauntlet thrown down upon the pier. Adrian smiled smoothly and raised his chin a fraction, measuring the challenge.

I frowned at him. "You don't look very wonderful yourself, you know. Or haven't you seen a mirror recently?"

Adrian, being somewhat more appearance-conscious than David, had showered and shaved, and his clothes and hair were as sleekly neat as ever, but his face looked rather ravaged. It was the wrong color, and his bloodshot eyes had pouches underneath. "My dear girl," he said smoothly, "if you will insist on keeping me up until all hours of the night . . ."

Oh, no you don't, my lad, I thought. Tipping my head up, I showed him a smile that was dangerously sweet. "I'm surprised you're up and walking, after all that drink. Peter was rather concerned about you."

"Was he indeed?" Adrian grinned and let my dart glance off him harmlessly. "Well, he didn't look at all concerned an hour ago, when he came downstairs and turfed me out of the sitting room. In fact," he added, rubbing the back of his neck with a rueful hand, "I can't prove anything, but I believe the old boy kicked me."

I thought it unlikely, and said so. "You've probably just got a hangover."

"I never get hangovers."

"Fancy a few raw eggs then, do you?"

He sent me a withering glance. "I don't know why you're picking on me, my love. I look a damned sight better than he does," he said, with a nod toward David, "and Peter looks a damned sight worse."

"Peter," I reminded him, "is twice your age. And David's had rather a stressful night."

Adrian stopped rubbing his neck and turned to David, suddenly remembering. "Oh, right. Of course you have. She's all right, though, your mother, isn't she? Peter said . . ."

"She's doing fine the now," said David. He fixed his eyes on Adrian's face, as though trying to focus. "Did you say Peter's not looking so well?"

"Just exhaustion, I expect. Nothing too serious. He seemed to be in good spirits, when he woke me up. Said he wanted the sitting room all to himself, to write his report for the university . . ."

"Oh, Christ, that's tomorrow, isn't it?" David levered himself upright, away from the support of the railing, and winced at the effort. "Connelly comes tomorrow. I clean forgot. Peter'll be needing my notes . . ."

"Peter," I said firmly, "is not an idiot. He knows where to find your notes, if he wants them."

"Aye, but—"

"But nothing. The man's been doing this for fifty years, you know. I'm sure he'll manage. You'd hardly be a help to him, anyway, the state you're in."

He raised his eyebrows. "Would I not?"

"Well, look at you—you're falling asleep on your feet. I'll bet if I gave you a nudge you'd go straight over into the harbor."

A warm glint of amusement lit the weary blueness of his eyes. "Come on, then. Give it a try."

Adrian, always suspicious of bantering that didn't include him, smoothly put his oar in. "I wouldn't dare the girl, if I were you. It's like waving a red flag in front of a bull. You're liable to find yourself treading water."

"Och, I'd not be budged so easily," David promised. With a fleeting wink at me he bent his head to check his watch. "But if you've a mind to push me in, lass, you'd best do it from the far side of the harbor, or we'll be late for the auction."

Adrian greened a little. "The fish auction, do you mean?"

"Aye. She's never seen one."

"Fancy that." The smile he summoned up was rather sickly, and I couldn't help but laugh.

"You don't have to come, you know."

"No, no," said Adrian, with a deceptively languid glance at the big man standing close behind my shoulder. "No, the auction's open-air, I'll be all right."

"And you're absolutely sure," I checked, "that it's *not* a hangover?"

"Absolutely. The smell of fish can turn my stomach any day, drink or no drink. You know that." His tone had grown intimate again, purposeful, and as the three of us moved to walk along the middle pier he briefly slung his arm across my shoulders, not in his normal friendly way but with a touch that implied possession.

I stiffened—I never had liked being anyone's possession—but then it wasn't my reaction that interested Adrian. The male of the species, I thought with a sigh, could be so bloody maddening. As we passed through the shadow of Brian's fishing boat, its nets rolled up alongside the pier, I pretended to lose my footing and ducked neatly out of Adrian's embrace.

He scarcely seemed to notice. Flashing a thoughtful look at the bright red hull of the boat, he raised a hand to rub his jaw. "Anyone seen Brian today?"

"He was up at the house, earlier," I said, straightening. "He and Fabia were going to move some boxes up from here, I think he said."

"Move them where? Up to Rosehill?"

"Well, yes, I believe so," I told him. "Why?"

"No reason." He shrugged and walked on, nonchalant. "It's just that neither of them was around, when I woke up, and I wondered where they'd got to."

The problem with Adrian, I thought wryly, watching as he kicked another tangle of nets out of his path, was that he hated competition. He reminded me of an old Wild West gunslinger, puffing out his chest and drawling, in menacing tones, "This town ain't big enough for the two of us." Certainly Rosehill was not quite big enough for Adrian and Brian, philanderers both, and when only one blond was available . . . well, I decided with another faint sigh, it was going to be a very long summer.

Adrian turned at the sound of my sigh. "What is the matter with you, Verity? You sound like the bloody Mock Turtle."

Fortunately, we were just then rounding the narrow bottom of the U-shaped harbor, past boatyard and ice plant, where the throbbing of engines drowned out any attempt at speech, and by the time we'd reached the covered fish market Adrian had quite forgotten his question.

"What time," he asked David, "did you say the auction starts at?"

"Four o'clock."

"Ah." Adrian cast a doubtful eye along the open length of the building, at the empty shadows and the idle waiting lorries. "In twenty minutes."

David checked the clock face on the tower of the Auld Kirk, and nodded agreement. "Aye, that's right."

"There is," said Adrian, "a noticeable lack of fish."

"Ye've no faith, that's your problem." David gave the Auld Kirk's clock a second glance, then looked across the road at what appeared to be a tea room. "Does anyone fancy a coffee, or—"

"God, I could murder a pint," Adrian cut him off, setting his sights on the beckoning white walls of the Ship Hotel, further up the harbor road.

The red Jaguar gleamed conspicuously in the car park, and David stroked one hand along the bonnet. "Got it back, I see," he said, to Adrian. "And in one piece, too. That's magic."

"Why, is Quinnell a rotten driver, or something?"

David shrugged. "I've never seen him drive."

Come to think of it, neither had I, until last night. Suddenly curious, I stole a sidelong look at David's face. He was still studying the sports car and whistling a careless little ditty through his teeth. "Why doesn't Peter drive?" I asked him.

"Well," said David simply, "he'd need a license to do that, wouldn't he?"

"What?" Adrian, blanching, spun around in horror to stare at his precious car.

I caught the satisfaction in David's smile, before he, too, turned away, narrowing his gaze on the sea that surged and plunged beyond the harbor wall.

"Here they come, now," he announced, and crossed the road to the quay, for a better look.

Adrian's face fell. "What about my pint?"

"Go and have it, if you like," I told him. "I'd like to watch the boats come in."

He wavered for a moment, but his less than trusting nature won out in the end. He was standing on the quayside, square between myself and David, when the first returning fishing boat came nosing through the narrow channel. It hit the harbor like a bullet, that first boat, kicking up an arc of spray and bringing behind it a great wheeling halo of gulls that screamed and dived and screamed again in search of scraps from the deck.

The boat was a small one, just two men on board, both

wearing slick yellow overalls. Even with the tide full in, the boat still bobbed a fair distance beneath the quayside, and the man standing on deck had to tip his head a long way up to see us. He looked frozen through, his face lashed red by the wind and salt waves, but he grinned when he noticed David. "Heyah, Deid-Banes," he called out, tossing up the mooring rope, "gie us a hand, will ye?"

David obligingly tied the line off, then stood back as the fisherman came scrambling up one of the metal ladders set into the harbor wall. He was not a young man, but his arms and shoulders bulged with sturdy muscle, and his smiling eyes were keen and very clear. They looked me up and down, passed briefly over Adrian, and shifted back to David's face.

"How's yer mither the day?"

David dropped into broad Scots as he gave yet another update on his mother's medical condition, so I missed a good deal of what he said, but his explanation seemed to satisfy the older man, who nodded twice and switched his attention to Adrian and me.

David introduced us. "My cousin Danny," he explained, as the fisherman's ice-cold hand closed firmly around mine.

"The better man o' the family." The shrewd eyes slid accusingly to David. "Is this how ye impress a lass, these days? By hanging around the quayside?"

David smiled. "She's never seen the auction."

"Aye, well, it's high excitement, that is," the older man agreed. He turned to me with a wink. "Ye'll no be getting roses and sweeties wi' this miserable lad, ken."

Before I could so much as smile in answer, Adrian draped an arm across my shoulders to drag me backwards and three paces right. It was, on the surface, a purely protective movement, pulling me out of the path of a rattling forklift that, after sprinting up the harbor road, had wheeled now to a halt just inches from David's feet. But when the danger had passed and the forklift driver cut his engine, Adrian didn't let go. His arm still held me firm against his side.

A wasted gesture, really, since both David and his cousin had by this time turned their backs to us, and were busy lowering chains over the edge of the quay. A moment later they hauled the chains back up again, in practiced unison, and I saw the hooks on the ends of the chains that had been fastened into either side of a blue plastic box, the size of a shallow laundry basket. The box, brim-full of steel-colored fish, was rapidly unhooked and loaded on the forklift, and the chains were lowered once again.

I couldn't see much, thanks to Adrian, but as one boat after another came into the harbor and the process was repeated all along the quayside, I was able to appreciate the mechanics in greater detail—the speed and rhythm with which the men on the boats slid and sorted and hooked the fish boxes onto the dangling chains, the smooth rattle and pull of the chains sliding over wet concrete, and the final thump and shuffle of the blue and white boxes as they landed on the forklifts.

In all it took David and his cousin less than ten minutes to unload the day's catch. Stacked high, the forklift rattled off again, toward the market, and I heard the spray of a hosepipe below us as the fisherman still on the boat began to clean the empty deck.

The gulls whirled thick as thieves above our heads, crying incessantly, their bright eyes hard and predatory.

"Damn and blast!" said Adrian suddenly, letting go of me to clap a hand around the back of his neck. It came away smeared with white. "Bloody birds!"

David's cousin turned round, grinning. "Got ye, did they? Aye, well, ye can gie yer hand a dicht wi' that," he said, passing over a dampish rag from his pocket. Adrian obediently wiped both his hand and the back of his neck, wrinkling his nose at the fishy smell of the cloth.

"It's a fish auction you're going to," David told him, laughing at Adrian's expression. "No one will care if you smell like a codling."

Behind me, someone called out David's name and all of us looked around to see a woman standing in the open doorway of the Ship Hotel's public bar. It was the barmaid who had served us earlier, a young woman, looking worried. "Telephone," she told him, raising her voice above the rattle and hum of chains and machinery.

My own first pessimistic thought was that it must be someone ringing from the hospital, and from David's face I knew
he was thinking the same thing.

His laughter had died, and the blue eyes, meeting mine,
were soberly apprehensive. "Look," he said, rubbing his
hands clean on his jeans, "it's nearly four o'clock. Why
don't the two of you go on ahead? I'll meet you down there,
at the market."

He was gone before I could reply, and Adrian nudged me
from behind.

"You heard the man," he told me. "Nearly four o'clock."

David's cousin Danny had also vanished, and short of
standing alone like a fool on the quayside I had little option
but to follow Adrian back down the harbor road.

The fish market fairly bustled now with activity. Young
men in wellies and stained jumpers jostled past in purposeful
confusion while the lorry drivers hovered close with keen
expectant eyes, watching the red-faced auctioneer while he
rummaged through the stacks of fish boxes, the bright orange
flash of his rubber gloves poking and prodding with knowl-
edgeable speed. A younger man hung at his shoulder, awaiting instructions. "The lemon sole, first," the auctioneer
decided, then jerked his head up as the Auld Kirk's bell
pealed out four times. "Right, lads, let's go!" he ordered.
"Four o'clock!"

The buyers funneled through into the metal-walled enclosed part of the market. It put me in mind of a giant garage,
with one long open side facing out on the harbor. The auction
was all very interesting, I thought, once one got used to the
smell, and if I hadn't been so worried about David and his
damned phone call I would probably have enjoyed myself.
As it was, I stood like a stick to one side of the crowd,
frowning faintly as I tried to concentrate on what was being
said and done. Even Adrian, not known for his powers of
observation, eventually noticed I wasn't really there.

His glance was rather hopeful. "Look, if you're bored
with this, we needn't hang about. I really *could* do with a
pint . . ."

"I'm not bored."

"Well, that makes one of us."

"Besides," I said, "we promised to wait for David."

"Oh, right." He said the words quite lightly, thrusting his hands in his pockets and squaring his shoulders as he always did when he was about to pick an argument. "It wouldn't do to disappoint old David, would it?"

Imploring the ceiling to give me strength, I held my tongue and began to count backwards from one hundred. Silence in the face of nonsense, that's what my father always said. Sound advice, really, except it didn't often work with Adrian. My silence only gave him more space to sound off.

"Of course," he went on, "disappointing *me* is quite another matter, isn't it? No one seems to care a damn what *I* think."

Stoically, I kept on counting: Eighty-five . . . eighty-four . . . eighty-three . . .

"At least with Fabia, one can understand the appeal. McMorran is a charming devil, and she's little more than a child. But you, my dear," said Adrian, in a patronizing tone, "you do surprise me. After all your high-minded lectures on professional behavior, to find you all but bonking our Mr. Fortune on the middle pier . . ."

That hit the mark. I lost my count. "Hyperbole."

"And what is that supposed to mean?"

"It means a gross exaggeration. You're a master," I informed him, "of hyperbole. And bonking in broad daylight on the middle pier, or any pier, is really not my style."

"Well, you were definitely lusting. Don't bother to deny it."

"And if I was?"

He looked wounded. "Well, you might have considered my feelings. We do have a history, you and I."

"We were only together three months."

"Three wonderful months."

My sidelong glance was skeptical. "Yes, well, I'm sure they were wonderful for you, considering you were also seeing Sally Jackson at the time."

He closed his mouth.

"And anyway," I continued, "that was years ago, Adrian.

How many women have you had since then? Thirty? Fifty? Refresh my memory.''

"I'm only saying . . ."

"You're only being a covetous brat," I told him, bluntly. "And a flaming hypocrite. Now, back off."

"Hey," he coaxed me, in his best persuasive voice, but even as he raised his arm I turned and froze him where he stood.

"And if you put that arm around me one more time," I told him, calmly, "I will not be held responsible."

"OK, OK." He pulled back, lifting both hands in a self-defensive gesture. "Christ, I only meant . . ."

The auctioneer's voice cut him off, and looking round, I noticed that all eyes had turned in our direction. Adrian paused, lowering his own hands with dawning comprehension. "Dammit, I think I just bought something."

"Come on, laddie," the auctioneer called out, "don't be playing yourself all day, we've a muckle fish to get through yet."

Delighted, I watched Adrian shuffle forward to collect his unexpected purchase.

Close by my ear, a deep voice said, "He'll not do that again."

Twisting my head round, I looked up in some surprise at David's face. "I wouldn't count on it. He doesn't always learn from his mistakes." I studied David's expression. "Was it the hospital that rang you?"

"Aye. My mother's being difficult," he reported, looking pleased. Someone bumped him from the side and he shifted to stand directly behind me, his chin clearing the top of my head by a few inches. His breath stirred my hair while he watched Adrian poking reluctantly through a fish box packed with ice. "Gave him a ticking off, did you?"

I followed his gaze, a little embarrassed. "Sort of."

"Well, I reckon he deserved it," David said, approvingly. "Bonking on the bloody pier, indeed!"

I tipped my head back sharply and my face flamed. "You heard!"

"Only a few words, like," he promised me. "I didn't hear the part about the lusting."

Growing several shades redder, I hastily lowered my chin again and found myself face to face with Adrian, who'd returned with two great ugly flatfish. He had, if nothing else, recovered his sense of humor. Shifting his burden, he solemnly passed me the keys to the Jaguar.

"And what are these for?"

"I seem to be having a run of bad luck," he replied. "You'll have to do the driving, I'm afraid. No point in tempting fate."

"But you're not superstitious," I reminded him.

"Better safe than sorry. In the past hour I've been shat on by a seagull and done *this*." He held the two fish up, to prove his point. "And bad luck, as you've always been so fond of telling me, does tend to come in threes."

XXIII

Jeannie must have heard the car come up the drive. She met us in the hallway and placed a warning finger across her lips, jerking her head dramatically toward the closed door of Peter's sitting room. "It's genius at work in there," she told us, low, "and we're not to interrupt him. Pain of death, he said. Come on into the kitchen."

The four of us moved across the front hall like a band of burglars, wary of every squeaking floorboard, and it wasn't until we were safely ensconced in the warm narrow kitchen that anyone dared to breathe.

David let his breath out in a long sigh that became a yawn as he dropped into a chair at the kitchen table. Bracing his feet on the floor, he tilted the chair back to rest his head against the wall while he watched Jeannie filling the kettle.

"The genius," he said, stiffening his jaw against another yawn, "is probably asleep."

"He's more awake than you," Jeannie defended our absent employer. "Up to his neck in papers he was, when I took his tea in, and he didn't show signs of stopping. He's wanting to get that report of his finished, before Dr. Connelly comes . . ." Her voice stopped as she lost her train of thought, sniffing the air experimentally. "What *is* that smell?"

Adrian, in the act of hitching a chair forward, glanced up smoothly. "That would be me," he informed her. Tossing his newspaper-wrapped parcel onto the table, he sent her a generous smile. "Don't say I never bring you anything."

Curious, she unfolded the paper and stared at the fish. "Lemon sole!" she exclaimed. "Well, aren't you wonderful? I can do them for lunch, tomorrow—they'll be nicer than chops, for our company." She glanced around at the three of us. "Been to the fish auction, have you?"

"Aye." David rubbed a hand across his eyes and nodded. A third yawn gripped him, but he tried to get the words out anyway. "Verity hadn't . . . ever . . . seen . . ."

"God, Davy," Jeannie cut him off, shaking her head, "you've not stopped ganting since you came in. You'll be making me tired, if you don't stop."

"Sorry." He closed his mouth and eyed her mildly. "Can't help it."

"He hasn't slept," I explained.

"Has he not?" Jeannie's bright head whipped around and David cringed, his bloodshot eyes seeking mine a shade reproachfully.

"Aye, well," he said cautiously, "I think I'll just go up to the Principia, and do a bit of playing with my own notes. There are one or two things on the computer that Peter will be wanting . . ."

"Don't be so bloody stupid." Jeannie, hands on hips, surveyed him with a stern eye. "You're as bad as your mother, you are. You keep pushing yourself till you fall on your face, and what use would you be then to Peter?"

"I'm really not . . ."

"Away upstairs," she instructed him firmly, "and have an hour's sleep afore supper. You can use the spare bed in Verity's room, she'll not mind—will you, Verity?"

Enjoying the sight of the big Scotsman being firmly ordered about, I solemnly assured Jeannie that I wouldn't mind in the least.

David's dark head rolled against the wall in a negative

motion. "I've not got time, lass. My notes . . ."

"Adrian can take care of all that." Jeannie waved the excuse aside. "If you're just wanting to print them off the computer . . ."

"Ah." Adrian, settled in comfort against the wall, interrupted archly. "Well, you see, I wouldn't know exactly *what* files to print, would I? There's the problem."

"So print them all," Jeannie advised him, with unarguable logic. "Peter will ken what he wants when he sees it." She turned to David. "There's nothing secret in these notes of yours, is there? Nothing Peter couldn't read?"

"No, but . . ."

"Well, then." Satisfied, she looked from one to the other of them, expectantly. The clock on the wall ticked loudly while she waited.

With a sigh of resignation David let his chair drop forward and stood rather creakily. Even Adrian, who didn't ordinarily submit to being bossed about, rose to his feet without rebuttal, and headed for the hall in David's wake. They looked so exactly like two small boys being sent to their rooms as punishment, that I couldn't keep from smiling, just a little. I tried to hide the smile but David caught me anyway, and his eyes, as he looked back from the doorway, promised retribution.

"Now," said Jeannie, when the two of them had left us and we'd heard the sullen thud of David's footsteps fading up the stairs, "let me just move these fish out of the way, and I'll make the tea."

Taking a seat in Adrian's still-warm chair, I watched her with open admiration. "I am impressed. I don't believe I've ever seen Adrian go quite that willingly without being bribed."

She grinned at me over her shoulder. "Well, I've had plenty of practice, living in a house full of men. Not that my dad ever listens. And Brian just does as he pleases."

"I saw his boat, this afternoon."

"Oh, aye? Did you get him to give you a tour?"

I shook my head. "Brian wasn't actually there—it was some older man, with white hair."

"Billy." She nodded, setting the teapot to brew on the counter while she started scrubbing vegetables for our evening meal. "He's all right, is Billy. It's that sleekit lad from Liverpool that I can't bide. Brian thought he'd give the kid a chance, like. Help him straighten out. But some folk," Jeannie said, with emphasis, "won't go straight. They're born fair twisted."

Something she'd said struck a chord in my memory. "Jeannie?"

"Aye?"

"What does 'sleekit' mean?" It was the word, I remembered, that David had used earlier, to describe Adrian. The word he'd advised me to look up in my dictionary.

"Sleekit?" Jeannie checked, with half-raised eyebrows. "Well, it means . . . when you call a man sleekit, you're saying he's sort of all charm on the outside, like, but inside he's a sly lying devil."

"Like Adrian."

Her laugh was a lovely thing. "Aye, he's a perfect example. My dad still can't believe you used to go with Adrian. He thinks you're far too clever."

"Yes, well, it's surprising what a handsome face will blind you to."

Peter poked his head in from the hallway. "Do I dare hope that you're speaking of me?"

"Well, naturally." Jeannie's smile held mischief. "There's not a man so handsome in the house."

"My dear girl," Peter said, "how very kind. Remind me to give you a raise."

"D'ye fancy some tea?"

He politely declined the offer, and turned instead to me. "I was wondering, Verity, whether you'd seen my red notebook?"

"Is it not on your desk?"

"No." He shook his head, frowning faintly. "No, I've looked everywhere that it *ought* to be, but I'm afraid the blasted thing's gone missing."

"Perhaps someone moved it, and forgot to tell you." But even as I suggested that, I knew it wasn't likely. Quinnell's desk was his domain, and no one in the field crew would be fool enough to touch the red notebook containing his field notes.

"Perhaps." Peter wasn't convinced. "Only it's something of a problem, you see, because without that notebook I can't finish my report for Connelly."

Jeannie brought her knife to rest against the cutting board. "I thought you put everything in the computer, like."

"Well, yes, we do." He rubbed his neck, ruefully. "But I'm afraid I hadn't quite got around to entering my notes from Friday last, or Saturday."

Forgetting about the tea, I stood. "I'll go and take a look, if you like. A fresh pair of eyes can work wonders."

Up at the Principia, having searched through Quinnell's desk and come up empty-handed, I shunted Adrian aside to check the floor beneath David's chair. "Are you *sure* you haven't seen it?"

"I'm positive." Patiently, he moved his feet to let me finish searching underneath the desk. "Shall I strip off, to prove I haven't got the thing stuffed down my trousers? Would that help?"

"It might." I banged my head on the desk, backing out, and straightened, massaging my scalp. "Honestly, Adrian, I can't think where that bloody notebook's got to."

"Maybe your friend took it."

"Sorry?"

"The Sentinel." He wasn't serious. I saw the smirk as he bent to key a command into David's computer, sending the nearby laser printer into action with a half-protesting whine. "If Peter thinks him capable of crashing our computers, I don't see why our ghost should balk at stealing Peter's field notes. Come to think of it," he said, clapping a hand to his cheek in mock horror, "my coffee cup's gone missing, too . . ." And he whistled the theme of *The Twilight Zone*.

"Yes, that's very helpful, thank you," I dismissed his comments, looking around with hands on hips. "I'm glad you're taking this so seriously."

He leaned back, rather smugly. "Well, I warned you, didn't I? I told you something else was bound to happen.

Bad luck, my darling, comes in threes—remember?'' When I ignored him, starting on my search again with even greater vigor, he sighed and turned his chair from the computer. ''Right, I'll help you hunt,'' he said. ''Just let me get another cup of coffee, first. Want one?''

''No thanks.'' Returning to the tall steel filing cabinet on the end wall, I yanked the top drawer open for another look, even though I knew the odds of Peter's field notes being filed by mistake were slim. At any rate, the drawer was nearly empty. I was closing it again when I heard Adrian come back. ''God, that was quick,'' I told him. ''Look, I don't suppose that you could—''

I didn't manage to finish the sentence. Without warning, the drawer handle was wrenched from my hand as the filing cabinet slid a good foot sideways, scraping heavily along the hard clay floor. Startled, I spun around to look at Adrian, and found he wasn't there.

Nobody was.

And yet I knew, as I struggled to speak, to move a finger, *anything* . . . I knew that I wasn't alone. I screwed my eyes tight shut and pressed my back to the unyielding bulk of the filing cabinet, drawing reassurance from its cold solidity while phantom footsteps, faint but certain, slowly moved toward me . . . paused . . . and finally passed me by. Only when the sound had died completely did I dare to even breathe.

The clink of a spoon in a coffee mug brought my eyes open. ''You'll put your back out, doing that,'' said Adrian, not noticing that anything was wrong.

I licked my lips, to make them move. ''Doing what?''

''Shifting furniture.'' He nodded at the filing cabinet. ''That's too heavy for you.''

''Yes, well, I didn't . . .''

''Still, I see you managed to find it,'' he said, cheerfully. ''Well done.''

Still rather numb, I peered around at the blank wall where the cabinet had been, and stared, transfixed, at the large red notebook lying there.

Adrian bent to pick it up, flipping through the dog-eared pages. ''Quinnell must have left this on the cabinet, and

somehow it got joggled and fell down behind. You see?"
Handing me the notebook, he hid his superior smile behind
the coffee mug. "Not everything," said Adrian, "can be the
work of ghosts."

I could have told the truth to Peter—*he* would have believed
me. But when I handed him his notebook he was so delighted
I could barely get a word in edgeways, so I let the matter
drop. Instead I sat with Peter in the comfort of his sitting
room and had a gin-and-it to calm my shakes.

And if the ghost *was* on the prowl in the Principia, he
didn't seem to interfere with Adrian, who, in an unexpected
show of diligence, stayed up there working straight through
until dinnertime. He didn't simply print off David's notes,
as I had thought he would—he also took the time to sum-
marize them, creating an impressive brief report, illustrated
at appropriate intervals with sections of his own surveys and
my drawings of our Roman-era finds.

Peter, scanning through the pages as we lingered over
after-dinner coffee, was ecstatic. "Brilliant!" he pronounced
it. "Marvellous, my boy. I knew those damned computers
would be useful. Now, we just have to combine your report
with *this*," he said, waving his own thick sheaf of hand-
written jottings, "and we're all set."

Adrian's face sagged a little, but I had no doubt he'd manage the revisions. He did his best work when he stood to
profit by it, and he had a vested interest in our learned lunch
guest's final judgment of our site. If Dr. Connelly agreed to
approve the Rosehill excavation, to let students from Edinburgh do their vacation work here, then our jobs would be
safe for the season. But if Connelly refused . . . well, Peter
was a proud man. I didn't know, myself, how he'd react.

Which left me feeling rather like poor Damocles beneath
the hanging sword, expecting any moment that the slender
thread might snap.

We all of us felt it, I think. David, freshly showered but
still unshaved, sat silently across from me, head lowered,
deep in thought. And even Fabia, who'd arrived home in a

relatively good mood just as we sat down to eat, showed signs of growing restlessness.

"I'll give him a hand," she said, suddenly, and Peter glanced up distractedly from his papers.

"Give who a hand?"

"Adrian. With the report. I'm much quicker on the keyboard than he is, it'll take him an age to type all that into the computer."

"Oh, right." Her grandfather nodded his assent. "A good idea."

That opinion was shared, predictably, by Adrian himself, who wasted no time in finishing his own coffee. His face, as he guided Fabia from the room, put me in mind of an indolent cat who'd just been handed the keys to the canary cage.

David leaned back in his chair and folded his arms across his chest, awaiting instructions. "And what can I do?"

"You, my boy," said Peter, glancing at his watch, "can drive me into Berwick, if you'd be so kind. I promised your mother I'd look in on her this evening. We can take the Range Rover, if Fabia's left any petrol in it."

"Aye, all right." David pushed his chair back, looked at me. "You're welcome to come, if you like, but be warned. My mother hates being in hospital, especially Berwick hospital."

Peter commented that Berwick hospital was, in his opinion, rather nice.

"Aye, but if you die there," David said, "you die in England. That's a terrible fate for a Scot. So my mother's been giving them hell, all the nurses and doctors, in hopes they'll send her home. And unless they've shot her with a tranquillizer dart," he told me, "I'm not sure that she'll be fit for you to meet."

I smiled. "That's all right. I should probably stay here, anyway. I've plenty of work to do myself, before tomorrow."

But when everyone had gone, I couldn't find a single bit of really useful work that needed to be done. I had no desire to wander up to the Principia, not in the dark, and anyway,

I knew it was more than my life was worth to spoil Adrian's seduction scene. I would have cleared the dishes from the dining room and done the washing up, only Jeannie wouldn't hear of it.

So, thwarted in my efforts to be useful, I retreated to the red-walled sitting room, where Peter kept his television.

The cats, at least, were glad of my company. They'd been ignored for most of the day, while Peter worked on his report, and as usual they'd been banned from the dining room during our evening meal. I found them sulking on the sofa, curled like serpents around each other with their eyes shut tight, deliberately shunning humanity. But when I sat beside them, Murphy strolled over to settle himself on my lap, and Charlie stretched her graceful form out full length, purring like a motorboat, while I searched the television channels for something watchable.

My best bet seemed to be the nine o'clock news, followed by a supposedly suspenseful film that proved a disappointment. It was an American film, with a murky plot and a pace that dragged intolerably. Pure tosh, about some man who'd programmed his computer to commit the perfect murder . . .

Computers . . .

I sat upright. *That* was it. That's what had niggled at my brain last night, when I'd rung off from talking with my sister Alison. She'd mentioned Philip Quinnell, and the fact that, in the book she'd bought, he'd used computers to enhance his photographs. And since he'd passed his photographic skills onto Fabia, presumably she'd also learned a bit about computers. But had she learned enough, I wondered, to tamper with the system here at Rosehill?

The credits of the film began to roll, and Murphy yawned. "I know," I said, and switched the television off. "I'm only being paranoid." Practically everyone used computers in their work these days—it wasn't any crime. And just because somebody had the knowledge, didn't mean that they would use it. I might not *like* Fabia, I told myself, but that hardly gave me reason to believe she'd want to sabotage the dig.

Puttering through to the kitchen, I made myself a cup of tea, and then, since there was still no sign of anyone returning, I went upstairs to bed. At least one of us, I reasoned, ought to have a good night's sleep, so as to be alert for Dr. Connelly tomorrow.

My bed looked different, sheets and coverlet pulled up unevenly, as though someone had turned it down and made it up again. And then I realized that was exactly what had happened. David hadn't used the spare bed, by the window, to take his nap. He'd used mine. Not that he'd have any way of knowing which bed was which, I reasoned—they looked identical. And not that I really minded, come to that.

There was a certain sinful pleasure in knowing he'd been sleeping in my bed; in sliding between sheets that his body had recently warmed, and pressing my face to the pillow that still smelled faintly of his hair, his aftershave. I tugged the blankets up and rolled to switch the light off, feeling drowsy and at peace.

The cats, curled at my feet, slept soundly, deeply, silently. And if the horses came that night, I didn't hear them.

XXIV

It was the birdsong that woke me, as the first pale rays of sunlight crept across my windowsill and spread their gentle shadows through my room. Smiling, I nudged aside the sleeping cats and rose and stretched and went to greet the day. Through my window I could see a cloudless sky arched wide above a world of brilliant green; the distant edge of blue that was the sea; the scattering of primroses beneath the dancing branches of the chestnut tree; and Peter, leaning on the stone fence with his back toward me, watching the empty field.

He looked old, suddenly, seen from a distance. Old and tired, and very much alone.

It didn't take me long to dress. My feet made very little noise as I crossed the dew-sprinkled garden to join Peter at the fence, but he heard me nonetheless. He half turned, showing me an absent smile of welcome.

"You'll catch your death of cold, my dear, coming out without your jumper."

"Nonsense. It's a warm shirt." I lifted a thick cotton fold to show him. "Besides, it's nearly June. One shouldn't have to wear a jumper, this late in the spring."

Peter accepted my statement with tolerant eyes that slid away from mine again to gaze across the field. I leaned my elbows on the crumbling bit of wall beside him and looked out, too. Long shadows feathered the far edge of the field, where another broad hill rose beneath a tiny, neat white farmhouse, but everywhere else the sun played softly upon the rippling grass. The field appeared serenely innocent, deserted.

Only both of us knew that it wasn't deserted. The Sentinel, I thought, might be standing on the other side of the wall this very minute, watching us . . .

Hunching deeper into my sleeves, I quickly glanced at Peter. "Are you worried?"

"Hmm?"

"About this lunch with Dr. Connelly."

His smile was so faint I almost missed it. "He thinks the Ninth went onto Palestine."

"I see. Well . . ."

"Fragments of it, possibly. That's what I told him. Fragments of the legion, units, those who didn't perish. But the Ninth itself?" He shook his head. "They're here. I know they're here." Pushing himself away from the wall, he straightened with a sigh. "I only wish we'd found some scrap of evidence. Besides the ghost, I mean. Some concrete bit of evidence to put before old Connelly. I'd have dearly loved to knock the bottom out of his beliefs, smug bastard."

He spoke lightly, without violence, but I heard the bitter current in his voice. And suddenly I felt very sure that, whatever Connelly decided after today's meeting, Peter would have his excavation notwithstanding. It wasn't just the dream that he was grasping for, it was the more elusive garland that he'd worn when young, and lost along the way. Respect, I thought—that's what he wants. Respect and recognition.

I looked away again, and rested my chin on my hands. "We're bound to find something before the season's done. And anyway," I added, my tone brightening, "at least you'll have the satisfaction of telling Connelly we've probably found a vexillation fortress, where nobody knew there was one."

"Yes," he agreed, "I will have that. And Robbie did tell me, a long time ago, that our field would be full of people."

"There you are, then." My nod was happily certain. "It must have been the students he was seeing. So you've nothing to worry about. Robbie," I reminded him, "is always right."

"Yes." Peter's languid gaze was drawn outward once again, to the silent green expanse beyond the wall. "But with Robbie, one is never sure," he said slowly, "whether what he sees are shadows of the future, or the past."

"Remarkable." Dr. Connelly excavated a small trench in the middle of his creamed potatoes and pushed in a pat of butter, neatly sealing up the mound again with surgical precision. He was a tidy man, with spectacles, his thinning hair kept closely trimmed to match his still-dark beard. "It's quite remarkable," he said again, "that you've found anything at all. A vexillation fortress, do you say?"

Peter eyed him like a gladiator sizing up a lion. Or was it, I wondered, taking a closer look at Peter's face, the other way around? Still, when he replied his voice was smooth and cultured with no hint of condescension. "We have come to that conclusion, yes."

Connelly savored a mouthful of sole, and thought for a moment. "And is it then your theory that the Ninth *Hispana* came upon this fortress on their northward march, and made their camp here, and were then engaged in battle?"

"Yes."

"Interesting," Connelly admitted. "Unorthodox, but interesting."

Across the table from me, David shifted forward and assumed the role of spokesman. "We're fairly sure the fortress is Agricolan, and Agricola did bring the Ninth north during his campaigns. It's not so great a leap of logic to suppose that, forty years later, when the Ninth was ordered north again, it chose to camp where it had built before. The land is good here, near a river, and the ramparts and ditch would probably still have been standing."

Connelly's eyes were sharp behind the spectacles. "And have you proof, that this is what the legion did?"

I looked at Adrian, who looked at Fabia, and for a moment

silence hung between us all; a curiously apprehensive silence, as though each of us expected the other to blurt out: "Well, there's this ghost, you see, who might just be a soldier of the Ninth *Hispana* . . ." Hardly proof, I thought, for someone as meticulous as Dr. Connelly. Any man who cut his carrots into cubes before he ate them was unlikely to put faith in walking ghosts.

Fabia began to point out, rather huffily, that we had only been working on site a short time, but Peter cut across her in a ringing voice that sounded not the slightest bit ashamed. "We have no proof."

"None whatsoever?"

"None."

"I see."

Adrian's smile had lost some of its certainty. "We *have* prepared a brief report," he said, "that summarizes what we've found, in this initial survey. Perhaps, if you would care to look through that . . ."

"Yes, yes, of course. I'll give it a read after lunch. You do realize," he said, peering over his spectacles at Peter, "that your finding of the fortress might create a difficulty for you, even with your permits. The site might be scheduled."

He meant that Rosehill might be designated an ancient monument, and that might in turn stop our dig cold. Preservation of a site was, after all, the prime concern of archaeology, and digging, by its nature, was destructive. We kept notes, of course, and scrupulously published what we found, but still, a site once excavated could not be restored. Schliemann, in his search for Troy, had shattered several layers of the ancient town above.

So now there were rules, to protect important monuments—like Roman fortresses—from being unnecessarily disturbed.

"Because it's not only me that you need to impress," Dr. Connelly explained. "You'll want to get Historic Scotland on your side as well, and the regional archaeologist over at Newtown St. Boswells. And unless the site is being threatened by development or road-building, they might well not approve of your digging."

Peter refused to blink. "Did I mention," he said, in his elegant voice, "that I'm thinking of having a swimming pool built? In the field, as it happens."

It was his way of saying that, if he couldn't dig unless the site was in imminent danger of being damaged, he was willing to invent an urgent threat.

Dr. Connelly shook his head, and sighed. "You can't always have things your own way, you know."

But he did read the report. We gave him Peter's sitting room, for privacy, while the rest of us waited across the hall. It was, I think, the most unnerving hour I'd spent since my first interview at the British Museum. Fabia paced ceaselessly, like something in a cage, while Adrian straightened picture frames and rearranged the objects on the mantelpiece. David, slightly more relaxed, put Chopin's *Etudes* on the hifi, and leaned back, eyes closed, to listen. And Peter simply waited patiently, his hand quite still upon the black cat stretched across his knees.

At length the door to our sitting room creaked open, and Connelly's head came around it. His expression, I thought, was preoccupied—carefully bland. "Right," he said. "I'd like to see the site now, if I may. Just Miss Grey and myself," he added, as everyone made to rise, "if that's all right."

Surprised, I looked at Peter, and he nodded.

This must be how an Olympic torch-bearer feels, I thought uncomfortably, as I led Dr. Connelly up the grassy slope to the Principia. I tried hard not to stumble over any of my explanations, but it was difficult to keep my nervousness from showing, and when we finally stepped outside again and a figure leapt from the building's shadow, I nearly jumped a mile.

"Sod it! Sorry," I apologized, remembering too late to mind my language. "It's only Kip, our . . . well, not *our* collie, exactly. He belongs to the cottage, down the bottom of the drive."

"Fine fellow," Connelly praised the dog, giving the

cocked ears a friendly scratch before turning to me with an expectant expression. "Now, shall we have a look at your trial trench?"

Kip's presence made me braver, less self-conscious. After twenty minutes of touring the field, I frowned and looked at my companion. "Why did you want me?"

"I'm sorry?"

"To show you around. Why me, specifically?"

"Ah." His mouth curved into a smile that was not unpleasant. "Because I reasoned you were the only person likely to be truthful, my dear."

"But why?"

"Well, Peter has a rather deep investment here, now doesn't he? His granddaughter, I'd imagine, doesn't want to see him disappointed. That surveyor—Sutton-Clarke—his kind say anything to keep their jobs secure. No point killing the goose that lays the golden eggs. And young Fortune," he concluded, "would swear black was white, if Peter asked him to. Which left only you."

"Oh."

"Besides," he said, confidingly, "I know old Lazenby, and he speaks very highly of the work you did on his Suffolk excavations. I gather that he wants to take you out to Alexandria."

"So I'm told." Only I didn't want to think of Alexandria, or Lazenby, or the decision I would have to make before the summer's end. I kicked over a stick in the grass and threw it out for Kip to chase.

Dr. Connelly stopped walking. "There are people," he said slowly, "who'd call Peter Quinnell mad. And you must admit he acts the madman, sometimes. I have been told he sits out in this field at night, and talks to ghosts."

I looked up sharply, trying to read his inscrutable face. "Who told you that?"

"It's true, then?"

"No, it's not. I've never known Peter to come out here after dark," I answered truthfully. "You must be misinformed."

Connelly accepted this with a philosophical nod. "So tell

me, Miss Grey, in your professional opinion, is there anything behind all this Ninth Legion nonsense?'' His eyes
peered at me through the spectacles like hard, glittering
stones. "Do you believe—honestly believe—that we are
standing, right this moment, on something more than a vexillation fortress?''

They seemed too bright, those eyes. Too penetrating. I
looked away.

Kip had stopped chasing the stick and was loping happily
up the hill, tail wagging a welcome to the empty air. He gave
a small woof and stopped suddenly, tipping his head up and
wagging more violently, as though someone were bending
down to stroke him.

Slowly, I brought my gaze back to Dr. Connelly's. "I've
never been so sure of anything in all my life.''

He studied my face for a long moment, and what he saw
there must have satisfied him because at last he gave a fatalistic nod. "Then I must bow to your conviction,'' he said
grandly. "You shall have my students for this digging season. And God help both our reputations, if you find there's
nothing here.''

XXV

The next three weeks sped past me like a whirlwind, in one long connected blur of motion and emotion and that tingling raw excitement that one feels when starting any voyage.

Bank Holiday weekend came and went, and no one really noticed. David's mother came out of hospital and surprised everyone by checking herself into Saltgreens, the local home for the aged, for a few months' convalescence. That is, she surprised everyone except Jeannie.

"Have you seen Saltgreens?" Jeannie'd asked me, grinning.

"Isn't it that modern building, the brick and glass one, beside the museum?"

"Aye, with its front end facing onto the harbor, across from the Ship Hotel's car park. You'd think it was luxury flats, to look at it. She'll not be suffering in there, I expect," Jeannie had added, turning away to chop an onion, "she's only doing it to get a bit of peace."

"What do you mean?"

"Well, she's got Davy on the one hand, saying he'll hire someone to live in at the cottage, so she'll not be on her own; and Peter on the other hand, saying that she ought to sell the cottage, and let him buy her something in the town."

Jeannie smiled. "But she's an independent woman, Davy's mother, and she'll not be a burden to anyone."

A woman cut from my own cloth, I'd thought approvingly. "*Will* she sell her cottage, do you think?"

"Oh, I have my doubts. She'll probably stay on at Saltgreens for the summer, like, then go back home and get a wee companion in. But not with Davy's money. She's an independent woman," Jeannie had repeated, as though it bore repeating, like the bold refrain of some old Scottish ballad. "Whatever she does, it'll be Nancy Fortune's choice and Nancy Fortune's money paying for it."

Robbie, I was sure, already knew what David's mother would decide, but he was much too excited by all the preparations for the arrival of the university students to waste time telling fortunes on demand. This morning he and Kip had been my shadows, dancing up and down and up again between the house and the Principia. Now, as we came into the offices for the third time, with Robbie's constant chatter ringing cheerfully behind me, Adrian looked up from his computer and sighed, with feeling.

"Robbie."

"Aye, Mr. Sutton-Clarke?"

"Do you know what a filibuster is?"

"No, Mr. Sutton-Clarke."

"Well, when you grow up," Adrian suggested darkly, "you must really stand for parliament. You'd make a cracking good MP."

Robbie replied that he'd rather join the lifeboat brigade. "I really like the lifeboat. Ours doesn't go wheeching down a ramp, like some of them do, but *I* think it's magic."

"Marvelous." Adrian looked at his watch. "Shouldn't you be in school?"

"It's Saturday."

"Ah."

"The people come tomorrow."

"Do they, really?"

But all attempts at sarcasm were wasted breath with Robbie. "Aye," the boy said, sagely. "Grandad and Davy are putting up the tents. Will you be living in a tent, Mr. Sutton-Clarke?''

"No," said Adrian.

"Wouldn't you like to live in a tent?"

"No," said Adrian.

I smiled, moving past them to my desk. "Mr. Sutton-Clarke would miss his nice room at the Ship Hotel, Robbie."

"Mmm." Adrian swivelled in his chair and leaned back, hands linked comfortably behind his head. "Not to mention the bar. D'you know, my love, if you cleared your desk once in a while, you'd not have to shift a mountain of papers every time you needed something. What have you lost this time?"

I frowned. "The list of the students. Have you seen it?"

"No, but it's a simple thing to print you off another one." Clicking into his database, he punched a key and set the printer humming. "What do you want it for? Counting numbers again? Because I think there were seventeen . . ."

"Eighteen," I corrected him. "And it's not for that. Peter asked me if I'd go through all the names and group them into threes, for sharing tents."

"Oh, well, I can do that . . ."

"Give it up." I tore the paper from his hand and grinned. "You'd have them all mixed in together, boys among the girls—I know you."

"It is meant to be an educational experience."

"How they choose to educate themselves is their business. But when they sleep," I said, with matronly firmness, "it's boys with boys and girls with girls, and good strong canvas in between them."

"*I'd* like to live in a tent," said Robbie, essentially picking up his train of thought where he'd left off. "Davy's got his own tent, did you see it? It's a barrie big tent, with a window and all."

"Yes, well, Davy is an idiot," Adrian replied, rocking back in his soft padded chair.

"Mr. Sutton-Clarke is only joking, Robbie," I assured the boy, not looking up.

"Mr. Sutton-Clarke," said Adrian, "is wholly serious. Any man who throws over a nice wide bed in a warm room—with private toilet, I might add—in favor of a leaky tent on soggy ground, with students for neighbors, is indisputably an idiot."

I cocked an eyebrow. "Even if half those students are nubile young women?"

"My dear girl, what *can* one do with a nubile young woman in a leaky tent? Besides, I don't think that was the deciding factor where our Mr. Fortune was concerned."

I ignored the meaningful look. "No, you're right. He just thought one of us should be there, close at hand, in case the students needed anything."

"And the location of the camp," said Adrian slyly, "is so very convenient. You can see it from your bedroom window, can't you? And vice versa."

Robbie came to my rescue. Clasping the post that divided two of the box-stall offices, he swung himself from side to side and looked at Adrian. "Why don't they put the tents up here?"

Adrian knew as well as I did why the camp was where it was, but after a quick glance at me he proceeded to give Robbie a more complex explanation. "Well, the ground is much more level over across the road, and the stream runs right along there, and it's very important to keep tent pegs and open fires away from the digging site, and . . ."

"Is it because the Sentinel doesn't go over there?" Robbie wanted to know.

Adrian paused, looking to me for assistance.

"Some people," I put in, "don't like ghosts, Robbie. Peter thought it might be better if we put the students where the Sentinel wasn't likely to bother them."

He thought about this. "He wouldn't hurt them. He just watches, like."

Resisting the sudden urge to look over my own shoulder, I gathered up a stack of notes and shoved them into a drawer. "Some people," I said evenly, "might not want to be watched."

He pondered this as well, then seemed to dismiss the idea as one of those queer conundrums of the adult world. Still swinging back and forth around his post, he watched me working at my desk. "I'm going to be a finds supervisor, when I grow up," he announced.

Adrian, in a dry voice, reminded Robbie he'd already promised himself to the Royal National Lifeboat Institution.

"I can do both," said Robbie, confidently. "Lifeboat men are volunteers, like, so I can work on the lifeboat, and be a finds supervisor, *and* live in a tent."

"I don't suppose," ventured Adrian, "you'd also want to learn computer maintenance?"

"What?"

"Because my computer's going to need repair, if you keep banging around my wall like that."

"Oh. Sorry."

"Come on, then," I invited, shifting my chair to make room for Robbie in my cubicle. Taking a few of the less impressive potsherds from the shelf beside me, I set them neatly on my desk and gave the boy a drawing tablet. "If you're going to do my job, I'd best start training you. Draw me some pictures of those, all right?"

He happily complied. Adrian, across the aisle, threw me a grateful glance and in the blissful silence gave his concentration back to the computer.

It took me less than half an hour to sort the students into threesomes for their tents. To my relief the twelve young women and six young men divided evenly, not leaving any stragglers to clutter up my chart. As I finished jotting down the tent numbers beside the names, Robbie proudly thrust his drawings in front of me.

"There," he said.

"Well done." I studied the papers solemnly. "And what do you make of our finds, then, Mr. McMorran?"

"They're OK."

"Come now, dear boy," I said, in a fair imitation of Dr. Connelly, "that's not very scientific."

Robbie giggled.

Continuing my gruff impersonation, I chose a sherd and handed it to him, peering closely at him through imaginary spectacles. "Now, what would your impressions be of this piece, for example?"

Playing along with the game, Robbie frowned in a way that made his small face, for an instant, look like David's. Rubbing his jaw as he'd seen David do a hundred times, he turned the broken bit of pottery over twice, and frowned still harder. "It's from a pot, like."

"Brilliant!" I applauded him.

"And it's red."

"Well spotted! Anything else?"

"He didn't like it here."

Across the aisle the steady clacking sound of Adrian's computer keyboard stopped abruptly, and in the small, surprised silence I dropped my Dr. Connelly impersonation. "Come again?"

"The man who used this pot," said Robbie, handing back the tiny Samian-ware fragment, "he didn't like it here. He was always cold, ken, and his tooth hurt."

"Psychometry."

Peter rolled the word out in his glorious voice, balancing the heavy dictionary in one hand as he ran his finger down the definition. The daylight had grown flatter, which meant clouds were moving in, and the red walls of the sitting room looked cheerless until Peter put the light on, to read by. "Yes, psychometry. I thought that was it. 'The divination of facts about an object from the touching of that object.' "

"Well, whatever it's called, Robbie can do it." I tossed a little ball of paper onto the carpet for the cats to chase, and tucked my feet beneath me on the sofa, leaning back against the leather with a tired sigh. "Mind you, he didn't rattle off the chap's name, rank and regiment, and of course we have no way of knowing just how accurate his observations are, but I just thought you'd like to know."

"Yes, quite." He closed the dictionary and hefted it back into place on the shelves. "I'm sure it will be very useful, when we're sifting through our finds."

I knew what he was thinking—I'd been thinking it myself, these past few hours. Through methods of pure science we could learn an awful lot about an artifact. Dating methods, simple or sophisticated, helped us fix an object in its place in time. We could learn where it was made, and what culture or group had made it, and identify the tools they'd used to make it with. Quite often, objects spoke to us about their owners. A pair of shoes, for example, when examined for signs of wear, might tell us that someone had walked with a limp. A shattered helmet might reveal, in gruesome detail, how the man who'd worn it had died. But how the man who'd worn it had *felt* . . . that was a mystery quite beyond the reach of science.

I envied Robbie terribly. I'd spent years holding bits and pieces of the past, poking them and prodding them and willing them to tell me things. And now this child, this little child, just touched a potsherd and was instantly connected to the person who had held it several centuries before. How wonderful, I thought wistfully.

Aloud, I said: "I did think I might keep a separate notebook, to record what Robbie says about the things we find. A sort of unofficial record, if you like, to complement the finds register. I know the pundits frown on things like this, but . . ."

"Pundits," Peter told me, "frown on everything. I think your notebook is a very sound idea. Would you like another drink?"

"No thanks." My half-closed eyes drifted guiltily past the empty glass on the coffee table. "One whisky's quite enough for me, this time of day. I think you'll have to wake me up for teatime, as it is."

"Whisky does have that effect," Peter agreed, with an amiable nod. "I can't abide the stuff myself. A traitorous thing for an Irishman to admit, I know, but there it is. I switched to vodka in my Cambridge days. The chap I roomed with fancied himself a Marxist, very strange lad, always talking revolution. He'd have gone to Russia himself, I imagine, only he couldn't bear the cold. *Das Kapital* and vodka was the closest he could get." Peter smiled to himself, remembering, as he poured himself another measure. "Symbols," he said, "do intrigue me." Lowering himself into his customary chair, he casually crossed his legs and sent me a rather naughty look. "For instance, I can't help noticing you've traded in your English gin for good stout Scottish whiskey.''

I closed my eyes and opted not to respond to that, blaming the good stout Scottish whiskey for the growing flame of heat along my cheekbones.

"Rather suggestive, that," he went on, and from the tone of his voice I knew that he was now speaking to the cats, as if I were invisible. "Don't you think so, Murphy my boy? I wonder what—"

His words were interrupted by the rhythmic crunch of footsteps coming up the gravel drive. Not Adrian, I thought. I'd left him up at the Principia, and these footsteps were coming from the opposite direction. At any rate, they were too quick to be Adrian's, just as they were too heavy to be Robbie's and too even to belong to Wally, who walked with a distinctive scuffing sound.

The front door banged and I opened my eyes, careful not to look at Peter as David materialized in the doorway of the sitting room.

"Heyah," the deep voice greeted us briskly. "Getting drunk again, are you?"

Peter smiled archly. "Would you like one?"

"Wouldn't mind." Crossing the worn carpet, David helped himself at the drinks cabinet and came to sit beside me, sagging into the sofa and stretching out his legs. The little cat, Charlie, attacked his bootlaces. David tasted his whiskey with a satisfied air, and turned his attention to Peter. "Well, the tents are up, if you'd like to have a look."

"Splendid. Six tents, were there?"

The dark head nodded. "Six, plus mine, plus the big dining tent. We've some fair puzzled cows in the pasture next door."

"Good, good. When you've finished your whiskey, then . . ."

"Christ," David said, with a roll of his eyes, "I've been up to my ears these past two weeks with exams, ken. Three invigilations and heaps of papers to mark. And today, between the marking, I've been pounding bloody tent pegs. I'm fair jiggered," he concluded. "Can you not get Wally to show you? He's down there the now."

Peter looked from David's weary face to mine and back again, then smiled secretively, lifting his own glass to drain it. "Of course, my dear boy. You stay here and relax. I'll go and have a good look around myself."

The room seemed smaller, somehow, with only David and myself and the two cats in it. Or perhaps it was only the sofa that seemed smaller, or David who seemed larger, or . . .

"Just my luck," he said, in a mild voice. "I finally get you alone in this house and I'm too bloody tired to do anything about it."

A sharply pleasant thrill coursed down my spine and lodged in the pit of my stomach. There was no reason for it, really—only that I hadn't known he *wanted* to get me alone in the house, in the first place. Since the day of the fish auction we'd both been so busy I'd barely seen him, and though he hadn't exactly retreated behind his polite wall, neither had he given me much cause to hope he shared my own attraction. Until now.

Sinking lower in the sofa, he rolled his head sideways against the leather, to look at me. "You've been drinking as well, haven't you? Damn."

This time the thrill of pleasure was so strong I couldn't keep from smiling. "I'm not any easier when I've been drinking," I assured him. "Just more likely to fall asleep."

"No use trying to cheer me up." He turned his face away again and sighed, raising his glass. "Ah well, maybe I'll have a rally once I get this down me."

I was truly in bad shape, I thought. I couldn't even concentrate, with him this close. Just watching the man take a simple drink, my senses went on overload. The clean soap smell of him that blended with the pungent tang of whiskey, the way the fabric of his work shirt strained against the muscles of his arm, the one dark curl that never stayed in place— I noticed all of these. And I felt the most appalling need to touch him. *Deeply unprofessional, my girl*, I reprimanded myself. *Doesn't do to get involved with colleagues.*

Still, when David shifted around to stretch full length upon

the sofa, the last shreds of my judgement went completely
out the window. He lay on his back with his head in my lap,
quite as if it belonged there, and balanced his glass with both
hands on his chest.

"Is this a rally?" I asked, looking down.

His eyes drifted closed. "I'm afraid not."

I watched him for a long while, aware of the exact moment
when his heartbeat slowed, the lines of strain smoothed gently from his forehead as his breathing shifted subtly to the
rhythm of a deep contented sleep.

Then, reaching down, I carefully pried what was left of
the whiskey from his unresisting fingers. "Damn," I said,
and drained the glass myself.

FOURTH HORSE

Something it is which thou hast lost,
  Some pleasure from thine early years.

Tennyson, "In Memoriam," IV

XXVI

"Men," said David's mother, two weeks later, "are impossible creatures. They ought to be shot."

She meant Peter, of course. It had been Peter's idea that I should stop in at Saltgreens to deliver the long bulky package wrapped up in brown paper. "It's nothing breakable," he told me. "Only a few old photograph albums that Nancy was wanting."

There were four albums, actually. The old-fashioned type, with plain black paper pages bound between long covers heavily embossed and whorled with peeling imitation leather. They looked out of place here, in the modern common lounge of Saltgreens Home, the sleek pine coffee table seeming to disdain their age and well-loved shabbiness.

I put one hand out now, straightening the edges of the albums so they made a tidy stack. "Peter said you wanted them," I offered as an explanation, and heard David's mother sigh hard in the kitchenette behind me.

"Out of the cottage, I said. I just wanted them out of the cottage in case it burned down or was burgled, that's all. He didn't need to send you all this way."

"Oh, I don't mind. I had to come into town, at any rate. We're nearly out of soap."

"Soap?"

I nodded brightly. "Our eighteen students take eighteen showers a day, sometimes more if the work's very dirty. Peter's hired a service to supply the towels, but we can't quite keep up with the soap."

"I'd have thought they'd have brought their own."

"Well, some of them did," I replied with a shrug, "only Peter feels he ought to be taking care of little things like that. You know what he's like. He'd be doing their laundry as well, I believe, only Jeannie told him our machine wouldn't stand the strain."

"Aye, he always did like taking care of people, Peter did." I heard the reminiscent smile in her voice. "Are you sure you'll not have a biscuit? They've got nice ones this week . . . chocolate cream."

"No, thanks." I turned in my armchair to watch her bustling around the narrow kitchenette.

It was a lovely place, Saltgreens—nothing at all like one expected from a council-run home for the aged. The building itself was modern and smartly designed, all fresh red brick and clever angles and gleaming polished windows. The windows here, on the second floor, showed a lovely slice of sky and sea and harbor, and the sunlight, slanting in between great hanging baskets filled with plants, danced on the gaily covered sofa backs and spilled along to warm the tiled floors.

David's mother looked completely in her element, bustling around the cupboards while she made our instant coffee.

"Is there anything I can help you with?" I asked.

"Och, it's just Nescafé, lass. I can manage that yet. The doctors," she said, as she brought the cups through to the lounge, "haven't warned me off lifting a kettle."

I did think they'd have warned her off cigarettes, though, and I couldn't help casting a questioning glance at the packet set out on the coffee table.

"They're not mine," she said, taking a seat on the over-stuffed sofa opposite. "They belong to old Harry in room number three. Can't smoke in the rooms, so he leaves them out here. But he does let me help myself to the odd one, when the mood strikes." She lit one now, to demonstrate, and settled back against the cushions with an ease that denied any hint of ill health. "If I'm still on my feet, then I'm meant to be living. I'll not give up all of my pleasures."

She was a stubborn woman, I conceded with a smile. And incredibly attractive, for all she must be over seventy. In fawn-colored trousers and twin-set, she once again put me in mind of a film star who, having played the headstrong female lead in films of the forties, was aging now with equal flair and class. Small wonder that Harry in room number three didn't mind if she pilfered his cigarettes.

"It's only the one a day," she assured me, with a confiding smile. "I always did enjoy one with my coffee. Is the instant all right for you?"

"Fine, thanks." I took a sip of the steaming sweet Nescafé to prove it. "Did you want me to take these albums back again to Rosehill, then?"

"Oh, no, I'll find space. I've a dressing table in my room, and a lockable cabinet. I'm sure these will fit somewhere." She touched one battered cover fondly. "It's mad the things we worry about, isn't it? My cottage is jammed to the rafters, and all I could think was that someone might break in and steal my old snapshots."

I told her I didn't think her worries were the least bit odd. "After all, you can't replace photographs, most of the time. And they're memories, aren't they? Worth keeping."

"Worth keeping," she echoed. Leaning forward to tap the ash from her cigarette, she glanced across at me with a conspirator's eyes. "Would you like to see what Peter looked like, when he was a younger man?"

I had known he would be handsome. To see him in his seventies was to know that much. And yet I was still unprepared for the reality of Peter Quinnell, thirty-something, leaning jauntily against a gatepost, with a spaniel at his knee.

His hair had been blond, as I'd known it would be. And he'd been riding, from the looks of things. Wearing a thick-knit jumper over breeches and boots, he stood hatless, laughing at the camera, his long, lean frame propped casually against the five-barred gate behind. It was the same sort of lazy and effortless pose he still struck, out of habit, yet here in this snapshot one had a strong sense of the energy burning behind it, a restless and magnetic energy like that of some great lion poised upon a windswept plain. The edges of the photograph seemed much too small to keep him in. At any moment, I thought wonderingly, he will leap out of this image altogether, and shake his golden hair and laugh, and lead us all off on some glorious adventure.

"He was a handsome devil," Nancy Fortune said.

"Yes, he was." I touched a corner of the photograph with one finger, as if to make absolutely certain it wasn't alive. I'd always found it fascinating, especially with faces that I'd only ever known as being old, to see how people looked when they were young. When I was very small myself, my parents had for some occasion held a fancy-dress ball, and I could vividly recall the moment when the pirate I'd been so sure was my father let his mask slip unexpectedly, to show a stranger's features underneath. Magic, I had thought it at the time. Looking at old photographs was like that. Magic.

I slowly flipped to the next page in the album, and saw Peter crouched in a field, taking notes; Peter sitting on a drystone wall; Peter sleeping on a garden bench, hat tipped down to cover his eyes, a book propped open on his chest. It was as well, I thought, that I had only come to work for him when he was old. If I had known him in those days, when he looked like that, I would have fallen hopelessly in love with him.

I wondered how David's mother had managed to avoid it, and then she said: "That's me," and pointed to a photograph, and I saw that she hadn't avoided it at all. The vibrant, dark-haired woman standing next to Peter in the garden of a big house was looking at him in a way I recognized at once. *That could be me*, I thought, feeling an instant sympathy for Nancy Fortune. *That could be me standing there, looking at David.*

"And that," she said, her finger moving on the page, "is Peter's wife, Elizabeth."

An unstable woman, I decided, my eyes already prejudiced. "Is this their son, then?"

"Aye. Young Philip. He'd have been about Robbie's age,

I think, when I took that. Very proud of that pony, he was. Whenever he came for a visit, the first place he went was the stables."

My brow creased in mild confusion. "When he came to visit? Did he not live at home?"

"Oh, aye, but not in Scotland. Not with Peter. Philip stayed in Ireland, with his mother. Elizabeth," she said, "wasn't well. You kent that?"

"No, I didn't."

"Manic depressive, is what the doctors called her. She'd had a breakdown, ken. She didn't like to travel. Philip came to us like clockwork every August and at Easter, but Elizabeth always worsened with him gone, and Peter didn't like to keep the laddie from his mother. Bit of a mistake, that," she reflected. "If he'd grown up with Peter, Philip might have turned out differently. Less wild, like."

I thought of Fabia, and was rather inclined to disagree. Some things, I reasoned, simply ran in a person's blood. Like Jeannie said, some folk were just born twisted. Keeping my opinion to myself, I turned another page of the photograph album. "So this is Philip as a baby?"

She looked. "Och, no. That's Davy."

"Really?" I peered with greater interest at the wrinkled bundle sleeping in its pram. The problem with babies, I thought, was that one looked very much like another. It took a few more photographs before I could distinguish David's features, roughly formed in miniature—the slanting fall of eyelashes, the broad and sloping smile, the little jaw already growing stubborn. And the hair, of course. One could hardly mistake all those tumbled dark curls.

He looked more like his mother than his father, I decided—assuming that the cheerful-looking chap in fisherman's clothing who held David in several of the snapshots was his father. I didn't like to ask. I remembered David telling me his father had died young, and I had no desire to rake up painful memories.

Instead, I opted for the somewhat safer comment that David had been a beautiful baby.

"Aye," his mother agreed, "he was a bonny wee thing. And he's not lost his looks, has he?"

I caught the keen, amused edge to her voice and glanced up swiftly, feeling my cheeks begin to redden. "No, he hasn't."

"An honest lass." Her eyes were warmly approving. "That's rare, these days. No wonder Davy fancies you."

Radish-red now, I broke free of her gaze and looked down, pretending concentration on the photographs. "And who is this?" I pointed to a snapshot showing Peter with one arm slung around the shoulders of a long-legged younger woman, her dark hair caught back neatly in a brightly patterned scarf.

"That's Pamela," said Nancy Fortune, watching my expression. "She was married onto Davy."

Making a convincing show of nonchalance, I nodded. "Oh, right. Jeannie told me he'd been married."

"Pamela came from London, too." The shrewd blue eyes stayed firmly on my face. "Not a bad lass, but she wasn't keen on Eyemouth—didn't like the quiet life. It bored her, so she took it out on Davy. Broke his heart, she did, in leaving."

I took a closer look at the young woman in the photograph, remembering what David had said that day on the middle pier, when I'd asked him if the lone swan had a mate. She'd left—that's what he'd told me. *She couldn't seem to settle down to life inside the harbor.*

David's mother read my thoughts, and smiled. "He'll have been fighting demons since the day you first arrived."

"Yes, well, it rather feels as though he's fighting *me*," I said.

"Aye, I believe he said you were a difficult woman." The smile in her voice was more pronounced. "Though when a man says that, you ken he only means you have an independent mind. I'm a difficult woman myself," she confessed, stubbing out her cigarette and settling back against the sofa cushions with the air of one well satisfied. "So tell me, now—I've been fair curious, and Peter never tells me anything for fear I'll drop down dead from the excitement— how is the excavation coming on?"

• • •

The excavation was, in fact, coming along rather well. In the beginning, I'd found it strange to have so many bodies working around me in the field, but now that nearly a fortnight had passed I could come around the bend in the road by the thorn hedge and not be surprised by the sight of an army in T-shirts and denims, digging away with true militant vigor.

Two of the students had been assigned to me, as finds assistants, and another two were helping Adrian continue his electromagnetic survey of the site. The remaining fourteen wielded trowels under Peter's watchful eye, like loyal troops that moved according to their general's wishes. And if Peter was a general, I thought, my mind still playing at the military parallel, then David was his field officer, always on patrol among the rank and file.

Even from a distance, as I walked toward the house, my eyes could find him easily amid his scattered charges. I'd grown accustomed to the little tug I felt inside my chest each time I saw him as I saw him now—a tall familiar figure with a sure, unhurried stride that commanded attention. He was threading his way through the maze of activity down in the southwest corner, but when he saw me turn up the drive by Rose Cottage he altered his course, and came across to meet me at the low stone wall, beneath the rustling canopy of trees.

"You've averted the crisis, I see," he said, nodding at my bulging carrier bags. "We'll not have to plunder Jeannie's washing powder for our showers."

I smiled, hoisting the bags of soap up to rest them for a moment on the wall, giving my arms some relief from the strain. "You look as if you've had a shower already."

"If the breeze was blowing the other way, you'd ken otherwise." Grinning, he turned his back to the wall and leaned his elbows on it, so that we were both facing in the same direction with our shoulders barely a foot apart. "It's this bloody heat. I ken it's the fourth of July, but Christ! It feels like the Costa del Sol."

It *was* a warm day. I'd been rather enjoying the weather, myself, but then I hadn't been slaving away in an open field, under the sun. David's dark hair curled wet around his temples, and the effort of working had wilted his shirt to the muscled contours of his chest and back.

"How's it going?" I asked him, looking at the partly excavated corner of the field.

"We're making slow progress, I'm afraid."

"Because of the heat, do you think?"

"Indirectly." His eyes held amusement. "Fabia turned up after lunch, wearing shorts."

"Ah." Slow laughter simmered in my own gaze, as I watched the students working. It was generally accepted that every young man working on the dig found Fabia decidedly distracting. She had only to walk across the field to produce a rather comical effect. "It's a good thing I'm back with the soap, then," I said. "Your boys will be needing those showers."

The deep blue eyes, no less amused, came around to rest on me. "Did you buy the soap in Eyemouth?"

"Yes, of course I did. Where else?"

"I thought," he told me dryly, "that you might have walked to Berwick. You were gone a bloody age."

"Yes, well, I can explain that." I leaned more comfortably forward on the wall, confidingly. "I was looking at pictures of you in your pram."

The quick sideways glance only showed surprise for a second, then a dawning comprehension. "You've been visiting my mother."

"Mmm." I nodded. "Peter asked me to call around and give her some photograph albums he'd fetched from her cottage. She wouldn't let me leave the things and run—you know your mum. I had to stay for coffee."

"Oh, aye?" He shifted against the wall, folding his arms across his chest. "And how is she behaving?"

I sidestepped the question by saying she'd appeared to be in good health. "We had quite a lovely visit, looking at old snapshots of Peter and your mother, and of you."

"Showing off all of my shortcomings, was she?"

A provocative smile tickled the corners of my mouth.

"Well, we didn't actually get as far as the pictures of you in your bath, but perhaps next time . . ."

He laughed. "Bloody cheek! You'll be paying for that."

Happily scoring a point, I looked at him, satisfied. "I do like your mother."

"She's a likeable woman," he agreed, "when she's not being a pain in the—"

"Your mother says," I cut in, "that when a man accuses a woman of being difficult, he really means she has an independent mind."

"Is that a fact?" David's mouth curved, and his gaze grew warmly intimate. "What else does my mother say?"

Tipping my head down, I traced the creases between the stones with one finger. "She seems to think," I said, "that you might fancy me."

"Aye, well," he replied, with a shrug, "that'll teach me to tell her my secrets." He looked toward the field again. "Damn."

"What is it?"

"They've found something."

I smiled. "A fine attitude, for an archaeologist."

"I'd best go see what it is," he said heavily, and pushing himself away from the solid comfort of the stone wall, he slowly walked back out into the full heat of the afternoon. I watched him go, still smiling, and was turning from the wall myself when a sudden sound against the silence made me stop.

Beyond the wall, not three feet from where I was standing, a low clump of gorse crackled sharply, and the long grass bent and shivered as a set of measured footsteps followed David from the shadows, heading out into the wide and waiting field.

XXVII

It really was a most impressive sprint, considering the day's heat and the weight of my carrier bags. No one waited at the top of the hill, stopwatch in hand, to clock me as I came flying up the gravel drive, but I doubted Linford Christie could have bettered my time.

I must have looked a sight when I stumbled into the Principia, face burning, breathing hard, but my two student assistants were too deeply absorbed in their work to take notice. And I, for my part, was so hugely relieved to see them that I quite forgot to be embarrassed. The simple primal instinct to seek comfort and security in numbers was surprisingly effective, really. Just knowing I wasn't alone was enough to dissolve nearly all of my fears. The ghost might still walk, but I wasn't alone.

I breathed, a deep breath. My pulse calmed.

The students, hunched over their desks like monks transcribing the gospels, still hadn't looked up. With a smile I set down my carrier bags and walked over to lend a hand with sorting through the day's finds. It took a certain twist of mind to do this work. Jeannie, after watching me labor for twenty minutes, had pronounced my job "fykie," and when I'd later looked the word up in my trusty Scots dictionary I'd thought it awfully appropriate. Like cleaning whorled silver or painting in miniature, dealing with finds was indeed a fykie task.

I'd always felt a wistful sense of envy for my colleagues who broke open long-sealed tombs, or for film heroes who scraped about in the dirt for twenty seconds before pulling out some rare bejewelled and golden statue, carefully preserved, intact.

Almost everything I'd ever touched—with the notable exception of one small military dagger—had come to me in pieces, dull with dirt and worn with age.

The Rosehill dig, so far, was no exception. Every new day brought more bits of animal bone and shattered pottery and broken metalwork. And every scrap and fragment, no matter how unimpressive it might appear, had to be cleaned, sorted and labeled with an identifying number.

I hated labeling artifacts. My hands were never steady and my numbers came out crooked, and the work itself was mind-numbingly tedious. It was enough of a challenge sometimes just to find a small spot on the artifact where a number could be visibly written without being glaringly obvious. Then, having applied a thin film of clear nail varnish on that spot, to seal the surface, I had to take an old-fashioned straight pen and liquid ink and, ever so carefully, write the number along that varnished strip, in tiny neat digits of white or black ink according to the color of the artifact, finishing off with a second coat of varnish, for protection.

This fussy method had its purpose, I admitted. Because of the sealing coats of nail varnish, the whole number could be easily removed without damaging the artifact, and since my penmanship left much to be desired I tended to remove as many numbers as I painted on.

And then, of course, the number had to be written down again, in the finds register, along with the particulars of the artifact itself—where and when it had been found, in what condition, what its dimensions were, and any other details we could think to add. Before, I'd always kept such notes by hand, in a series of ring-binders, but here at Rosehill the "finds register" was all on computer, in a uniform, fill-in-the-blank style that kept the format consistent whether an assistant or myself entered the information. Much more efficient, I thought, than the old methods.

But that didn't stop me from making odd notes and sketches of the artifacts, in my old-fashioned notebook, and from time to time I called Fabia in to take photographs.

And every evening, while the students were having their meal in the long tent, I trundled the day's finds down to Rose Cottage, for Robbie to read.

Tonight, I'd chosen to vary our game a little, without his knowledge. Taking my seat at the now familiar kitchen table, with the smell of baking biscuits drifting comfortingly around me and the collie sleeping underneath my chair, I watched with special interest while Robbie felt through the things I'd brought. It wasn't really fair to test him, I knew, but his abilities intrigued me. It was already clear to me that certain pieces "spoke" to him, transmitting some impression of their former shape and usefulness, and of the people they'd belonged to. But did they also speak to him of time?

Robbie was, after all, only a very small boy. He had a small boy's sense of time. He knew the Sentinel was Roman, and that the Romans came from a long time ago, but then so did Napoleon. So, to a child, did Churchill. At Robbie's age, I had been confused about chronology too—it had taken my father several days to explain why Cleopatra and the first Elizabeth could not have taken tea together.

And yet, on this dig, time was so important. The fortress we were excavating dated from the late first century, but what we really hoped to find, evidence of the site's occupation by the Ninth Legion, would date from the early second century. A potsherd left behind by the Ninth would be some forty years younger than the ones we'd found so far. Would Robbie, I wondered, be able to tell the difference?

Curious to know the answer, I'd set up a little experiment. Mixed in with the Roman-era sherds was a piece of a Victorian flowerpot that Wally had found broken in the garden. The glaze was red, almost the same color as Samian ware, and to the untrained eye the pieces looked very much the same, but Robbie picked the impostor out with ease, his fingers closing around it and then opening again abruptly.

"Hey, Grandad, feel this one—it's hot!"

Wally, at the far end of the table, looked up from his paper and took the sherd obligingly, weighing it in his hand for a moment before passing it back to the boy. "Aye," he agreed, "so it is."

Jeannie, making use of her Thursday night off to catch up on her baking, turned from the counter, a smudge of flour clinging to her dimpled cheek. "You lying old devil," she accused her father. "You don't feel anything."

"Do I not?" Wally raised his chin belligerently. "For a' ye ken, the lad might hae got his gift fae me." With a quick sideways wink in my direction, he shook his paper out and, lighting yet another cigarette, resumed his reading.

"You feel it, don't you, Miss Grey?" Robbie turned his trusting eyes on me, but after dutifully holding the sherd in my hand for a moment, I had to admit that I didn't.

"Is it very hot?" I asked him.

The small dark head tipped to one side as he considered the question. "Like a teacup," he decided. He leaned forward and chose another sherd, to illustrate. "See, this one's cold. That means it's right, like. It belongs to the Roman part."

"The fortress."

"Aye. But the hot one belongs to the house."

I puzzled over this statement for a minute, then realized that Robbie was making a judgment of time. When the Romans had come here, the hill and the field had been empty, but by the Victorian age the hill had been crowned with a house. A sherd that belonged to the house must be younger than one that belonged to the fortress. At least, I assumed that's what he meant. I shifted in my chair, wanting to be sure. "Do you mean it comes from a later time? After the Romans were gone?"

He looked at me in silence, his face perplexed. "Gone?"

"Yes, after the Roman soldiers left Rosehill . . ."

"But they didn't leave."

I'd learned, with Robbie, not to alter my expression when he dropped a bombshell in my lap. If I looked at all excited it just made him want to please me more, and the strain of trying seemed to block up all his faculties. I kept my gaze trained now on the grain of the table, and asked him very lightly what he meant.

"They didn't leave," he said again. "They're still here."

God, I thought, if he could point us toward the bodies . . . "Where exactly are they, Robbie? Do you know?"

His shrug implied that the answer was obvious. "Everywhere."

Wally's paper crackled as he set it aside to peer across at his grandson. "Whit d'ye mean, they're everywhere? Are ye sayin yon field's stappit fu wi' deid bodies?"

Jeannie turned and met my eyes knowingly. "Stappit fu," she said, as I reached automatically for my pocket dictionary. "That's s-t-a-p-p . . ."

Filled with as many of something as possible, was the dictionary's definition, and satisfied, I snapped the pages shut and gave my attention back to the conversation.

Robbie was shaking his head. "Not with bodies."

"Ye ken whit I mean," said Wally, who knew as well as I did that Robbie sometimes took things rather literally. "They'll no' be bodies like ours efter sae lang i' the ground—they'll be banes. Dry banes."

Robbie tipped his head, rethinking his position. "No," he said at last, "I don't think there are any bones. Not people bones."

I cut in, to clarify. "So the soldiers, the Roman soldiers, they're still here, but their bodies aren't."

The dark head nodded. "Aye."

"What happened to the bodies, Robbie?"

He didn't know the answer to that one, but he had a clear idea who might. "I could ask the Sentinel for you," he offered, eagerly. "He'd ken all about it."

Wally and Jeannie and I exchanged impassive glances and I sank back in my chair. "Yes, well," I said to Robbie, "I don't think that would be such a good idea."

"Dad doesn't have to know."

I blinked at that, surprised. We'd all been so careful not to mention Brian's opposition to our using Robbie in the field again. Whatever I thought of Brian McMorran, I couldn't bring myself to make him look a villain in the eyes of his own son. I'd simply forgotten that Robbie, while he couldn't tap his father's thoughts, could read the rest of us with ease. We had no hope of keeping secrets.

"Well now," Jeannie said, "it'd not be very nice, to do a thing your father didn't approve. And to do it without telling him would be the same as lying."

Robbie didn't appear overly concerned by the ethical implications. Suppressing my smile, I tried to bolster Jeannie's argument. "Besides," I reasoned, "it made you ill the last time, remember? We don't want that to happen again."

"But he wants to talk to you."

My eyebrows lifted. "To me?"

"Aye. He tries sometimes, but you can't hear him so he takes himself away again."

My fingers curved in reflex around my teacup. "He tries to talk to me?" I echoed Robbie's words, unable to form ones of my own.

"He likes you," was the boy's explanation. "I think . . . I think you mind him of someone, Miss Grey. He sort of looks at you sometimes, and . . . well, he likes to look at you."

"I see."

"Follows after you, he does," Robbie added, helpfully. "So you're always safe."

Safety, I thought, was a relative term. My fingers were still clamped tightly around the empty teacup and I quietly willed them open, flexing them to ease the painful tension.

Jeannie was watching my face. "It must be the hair," she decided.

"I'm sorry?"

"Men do have a weakness for bonny long hair."

I smoothed my plait back with a self-conscious hand and Wally shot me an appraising look, eyes twinkling.

"That's three ye've got noo," he observed. "Three wee shadows. Our Robbie, the dug, and an auld Roman bogle."

"I'm not a shadow," Robbie defended himself, his chin

jutting out in a stubborn expression. "I'm a finds assistant, aren't I, Miss Grey?"

"Yes, Robbie, you're a very good assistant."

"And Kip's not a shadow, neither."

Under the table the collie stirred and shifted at the mention of his name. Yawning widely, he twisted his head around to look at me, giving a few hopeful thumps of his tail. Wally rose to his feet with a whistle. "Gaun yersel, then," he urged the dog, and Kip flipped eagerly onto his feet, padding across to the door. Pausing to stub his cigarette, Wally squinted through the rising haze of smoke and studied me. "Did ye want tae come wi' us, back up tae the hoose? I can carry thon thingies for ye," he added, nodding at my shallow box of potsherds.

It was, I thought, rather gallant of him—not his offer to carry the sherds, which weren't the least bit heavy, but his thinking I might not want to walk home alone this evening. Not up that long drive, with the trees telling things to each other in whispers. Not in the fading light, with darkness coming on.

"Thanks," I said, "that would be a great help."

"Let me, Grandad," said Robbie, scooting forward to grab the tub. But as he climbed down from his chair, Jeannie intercepted him.

"You," she said firmly, "are taking a bath, my wee man, and then going to bed. Say goodnight to Miss Grey."

The stubborn chin came out again, but he knew better than to argue. Handing the sherds to Wally, he trailed over to give me a hug. As he drew back, he looked at me hopefully. "Am *I* a great help to you, too?"

"A very great help."

I meant it sincerely.

But that didn't stop me wishing, as I walked with Wally up the hill, with the warm evening air pressing close all around us . . . it didn't stop me wishing Robbie wouldn't tell me *everything*.

"Bad dreams, last night?" Fabia steadied the camera against her eye and snapped the row of potsherds from a different angle.

I glanced up rather vaguely from my desk. "No, why?"

"You left the light on."

"Ah." She would know, I thought. Fabia was always the last in at night, these days. She had cooled a little toward Brian, and I might have suspected she'd found herself a boyfriend among the students if it hadn't been for David's careful supervision of the camp. He hadn't gone so far as to set an official curfew, but after one or two incidents early on he'd made it quite clear that anyone who wasn't fit to work would have to answer to him, and since no one seemed willing to test that threat, the students were usually out of the pubs and tucked into their sleeping bags well before midnight. If some young man was keeping Fabia out late at night, I could safely say he wasn't one of ours.

At any rate, the late nights didn't seem to be doing her any great harm. She looked lovely this morning, eyes glowing with vigor and youthful good health, her movements quick and fluid. I felt dreadfully pallid by comparison.

"Well, I didn't mean to leave the light on," I lied. "I was reading, you see, and—"

"Where did Peter want me to go next?" she asked, losing interest, replacing the cap on her lens.

I tried to recall exactly what Quinnell's instructions had been, at breakfast. "Well, I think he said they were going to start a new trench where the *principia* ought to be, and he wanted you to take a photograph before they stripped away the sod and topsoil."

Fabia frowned. "But we're *in* the Principia."

"No, he means the real one." When she still looked blank, I stared in open disbelief. "Don't tell me you're Peter Quinnell's granddaughter and you've never learned the layout of a basic Roman fortress?"

"Well, I—"

"Oh, Fabia!"

"It's like I said. My father hated all this stuff, and Peter just assumes I ought to know."

"Then for heaven's sake, come here," I said, "and let me sketch it out for you." Pencil in hand, I tugged an unimportant letter from one of the stacks on my desk and turned

it over to its blank side. "Here, the average fortress looks
like this—you see? A bit rectangular, with rounded corners,
like a playing card. A ditch, sometimes a double ditch, outside, and then the ramparts, with a guard tower at each corner. Now . . ." I took my pencil and drew a square, bang in
the center. "The *principia*, or headquarters building, is here.
And running right along in front of it is the *via principalis*,
that's the road that links the fortress's two side gates." I
sketched in the gates, too, to keep things absolutely clear.
"From the front gate to the headquarters is another road, the
via praetoria. And from the headquarters to the back gate,
there's the *via decumana*. Now, here," I said, drawing in
another square to the left of the *principia*, "you'd have the
granaries, and maybe a workshop. And on the other side of
the headquarters building would be the *praetorium*."

"What's that?" Fabia asked, showing a faint spark of interest that made me think she might not yet be past all hope.

"The commander's house. And then the hospital is usually
sort of in this spot right here, and most of the rest would be
barrack blocks, and stables for horses." I filled in the hollow
spaces above and below the *principia* with neat rectangles,
to show her.

She leaned over to study my drawing. "So it's really just
barracks, and then this row of important buildings, and then
more barracks, with a few criss-crossed streets."

"Pretty much," I agreed, smiling at her dismissal of the
brilliant efficiency of Roman military planning.

"And this is where we started digging, isn't it? Down
here, at this guard tower?"

"Indeed it is."

"So . . ." Her finger trailed up the makeshift map, toward
the center. "Peter's going to start his new trench up in here,
somewhere."

"It shouldn't be too hard to find," I assured her. "Just
look for a big bunch of people with spades."

She took my drawing anyway, tucking it into one pocket
of her shorts while she gathered up her camera and equipment. When she'd gone, I put my pencil down and stretched,
trying to ease the knot between my shoulders.

My two young assistants were outside, manning the water
flotation tank that Peter had installed behind the building. An
upright, barrel-shaped device with hoses attached for fresh
water and drainage, it sifted excavated soil through screens
so fine that we could then recover tiny seeds and insect parts,
as well as bits of pottery or bone. Bone, I thought, would
have been useful. A nice full skeleton, clad in legionary armor, with an ancient Scottish sword still buried in its
skull . . .

But Robbie had said that there weren't any bones in our
field. That struck me as odd. If the Sentinel was, as he
claimed to be, a soldier of the Ninth, and if the Ninth had
truly perished here, then there ought to be bones, and plenty
of them.

A high-pitched snatch of laughter floated in through the
long back wall, from where my two students were working.
I sighed, and pushed back my chair. As finds supervisor, I
reminded myself, I ought properly to be out there with them,
supervising, instead of hiding in here like a coward.

The outdoors looked harmless enough, the field an anthill
of activity beneath a sky of rolling cloud and brilliant bursts
of blue. David was down by the road, by the thorn hedge,
crouched over a bit of newly exposed earth that a few of the
students were clearing with brushes. More post holes, I speculated. They'd found the edge of what appeared to be one
of the barrack blocks yesterday.

Peter, hoping to find some evidence of the Ninth's presence in the fortress's *principia*, stood now like stout Cortez
upon a subtle rise of ground near the center of our carefully
staked site, directing Fabia's photography.

Surely any ghost would find activity like that far more
interesting than my own boring little scribbles in the finds
register. Bolstered by that thought, I turned my back to the
field and took a tentative step away from the stable door.

I stopped. Paused. Listened.

Nothing followed but the breeze, and even that was
brightly cheerful, not the least bit cold or threatening. The
laughter drifted out again from the far side of the building,
and I set my shoulders, walking on more bravely now along

the long front wall of our Principia. Just around that corner,
I promised myself, hating my sudden nervousness. Just
around that corner, and up the deeply shaded side wall, and
around another corner, and I'd be with people again.

Still, before I left the sunlight and the full sight of the
field, I stopped again and listened for the fall of ghostly footsteps. And only when I was satisfied that there was no sound
but the distant voices of the dig and the trilling warble of a
songbird in the trees ahead of me . . . only then did I turn the
first corner.

XXVIII

I reacted like a cat. Spinning blindly around I brought my own hands up to knock away the ones that held my arms, then bristling, backed against the wall, preparing for a fight.

When I saw who it was, my terrified posture collapsed into swift indignation. "God, Brian," I accused him, "you nearly gave me a heart attack."

And then, because he didn't say anything immediately, I folded my arms defensively across my chest and took a stab at normal conversation. "When did you get back?"

Ignoring the question, he fixed me with an unimpassioned gaze, making no attempt to be charming. "You've been using my boy again, haven't you?"

"I'm sorry?" My forehead wrinkled in faint confusion.

"Making him do your work for you. D'you think I'm that bloody stupid I wouldn't find out?"

He'd been drinking. Now that my senses had returned to normal I could smell the lightly mingled scents of beer and sweat that rose from his T-shirt and denims, and hear the slurred edge to his speech. The dashing pirate with the quick smile and a gold hoop earring glinting through the silver of his hair was definitely out this morning. The man before me looked a hardened cutthroat, tattoos snaking up his muscled arms, his dark scowl seeking to intimidate.

It had the opposite effect, with me. "Well, actually," I challenged him, "I didn't think you were that bloody stupid you'd raise a fuss over something so harmless."

His eyebrows lowered. "Look, I told you—"

"Robbie wanted to help me." I cut him off, curtly. "So I let him. I've not taken him out in the field or had him speaking with the dead, or anything, I've only let him play with a handful of potsherds and tell me his impressions. It's a game for him, Brian. There's no risk involved."

Brian McMorran's brown eyes narrowed oddly on mine. With remarkably steady fingers, he placed a cigarette between his lips and touched a match to it, inhaling tersely. "And how would you know," he asked coldly, "just what risks there might be?"

Unable to respond to that, I spread my hands in mild frustration. "Why are you so against Robbie *using* his abilities to—"

"I'm not," snapped Brian. "But he'll use them for his own self, not for anybody else. It's his gift; no one else has got a right to it."

"But he wants to help."

"It's taking advantage."

"I am not," I said carefully, "taking advantage. I'm only letting Robbie do what Robbie wants to do."

"Is that a fact?" He lifted the cigarette, staring at me hard, but when he spoke again his voice, still slurred, sounded less angry. "Aye, well, you can keep on with the sherds, then, if he likes it so much, but that's all, d'you hear? If I find you've been making him do more than that—and I'll know if you do—"

Oh, great, I thought, trying to squelch my uneasiness with humor. *Don't tell me Brian is psychic as well.*

He stopped talking suddenly, still watching me. And, unbelievably, I saw his mouth curve in a knowing smile.

"Did it only just occur to you?" he asked. Pitching the cigarette away, he came toward me, his smile growing predatory as my instinctive step backwards brought me up against the cold boards of the stable wall. "Afraid, Miss Grey? Of what? Of me?"

"Of course not."

"Oh, I think you are." He stopped mere inches from my body, leaning his hands on the wall to either side of my shoulders, effectively pinning me in place. And with a prickling rush of irritation, I realized I was very much afraid. Not afraid of him physically—for all he was deliberately trying to make me uncomfortable I didn't for a moment think he'd lay a finger on me. But knowing that he, like his son, could invade my private thoughts . . . I'd grown used to it, with Robbie, but with Brian the very idea seemed a violation.

"Brian, get off," I told him.

He laughed quietly, leaning in closer, breathing stale beer, enjoying the feeling of power. "That an invitation?"

My mouth tightened. I could have kneed him one, but given that it was Brian, and a very drunk Brian at that, it did seem a little excessive. Besides, I'd have had a devil of a time explaining it to Jeannie. And calling for help from my students was out as well—by the time they'd turned the corner Brian would have backed away and left me looking like a bloody spineless fool.

I was holding my ground, trying to decide what to do, when I heard someone approaching from the far side of the building, to my right. Someone walking heavily. A man. David, I decided, with a surge of sheer relief.

But even as I formed the thought, David himself proved me wrong as he came whistling around the corner to my left. He stopped short, looking at the scene in front of him. "What the devil's going on?"

Brian shrugged, not bothering to turn his head. "Just having a bit of fun, Deid-Banes."

"Aye, well, fun's over. Let her go."

"Why should I?"

"Because I'll belt you one if you don't."

I couldn't see David for Brian's shoulder, but although he clearly wasn't pleased he didn't sound particularly violent. So it stunned me when Brian jerked backwards, spun round, and then fell at my feet like a puppet whose strings had been cut.

I stared down in dismay. "You didn't have to do that, David. I can take care of . . ." But I never did finish the sentence. Because by then I had lifted my head to look at David, and I'd seen that he was standing fully ten feet from where Brian lay, his face as surprised as my own.

Across the empty shadows his gaze met mine and he arched an inscrutable eyebrow. "Bloody hell," he said.

"Oh no, I'm sure he'll be quite all right," said Peter, who had come in search of me and stood now looking down at Brian's spreadeagled form with the cheerfully disinterested air of a botanist confronted with a common garden weed. "No, he's breathing very normally. I'm sure there's nothing to worry about." He smiled encouragement at David. "What did you hit him with?"

"I didn't touch him."

"No? Then who . . . ?" The long eyes shifted, curious, to me. "Verity, my dear, you do amaze me. I had no idea . . ."

"It wasn't me," I said, with a shake of my head. "I know this is going to sound awfully foolish, Peter, but I think"—I looked to David for support—"I think the Sentinel did this."

Peter looked inestimably pleased. "*My* Sentinel? My soldier of the Ninth?"

"Yes."

"Good man." Peter looked down at Brian again and nodded, highly satisfied. "Well done. Still doing his job, as a good soldier should. Being a pain, was he?"

I frowned faintly. "The Sentinel?"

"Brian. I expect he was making an ass of himself?"

David stepped in, diplomatically. "He'd been drinking."

"Ah." Peter nodded again, looking very pious and righteous for a man who was himself more often soused than sober. "Yes, well, I suspected as much. Never mind," he said happily, turning to me, "you must come and see what we've been up to. I've a rather good feeling about this new spot where we're starting to dig."

Incredulous, I looked from his face to the man on the ground and back again. "But . . . I mean, we can't just leave him here . . ."

"Whyever not? I'm sure he's been laid flat in much rougher places than this."

"We ought to tell Jeannie, at least."

Peter paused for a moment, measuring the resolution in my face, then sighed and lifted his shoulders in a shrug that plainly said I was being unreasonable. "All right, if you insist, I shall inform Jeannie that her husband is lying up here, and let her decide what she wants to have done about it. But then," he said firmly, "you really must come and see what we've done."

David came across to stand beside me as we watched Peter sauntering down to the house. "He truly is a character."

I made some vague response and David's head dipped, his eyes keenly searching my face. "Are you sure you're OK?"

"I'm fine. Only . . ." I rubbed my arms to warm them, nodding toward the man at my feet. "He has second sight as well, did you know that?"

"What?"

"Like father, like son, I suppose." The shock had left me feeling a little hysterical, and even I could hear it plainly in my voice.

David studied me solemnly for a moment, then opted for a logical response. "Pull the other one."

"It's true. He even said . . ."

"If our lad Brian had the second sight," was David reasoning, "he'd have more luck in choosing his lottery numbers. And I'm sure he'd not have let himself get flattened by a ghost."

Still looking down, I hugged myself a little tighter, considering this. "*Can* a ghost really hit someone, do you think?"

David laughed. "What the devil are you asking me for? I'm no expert."

"I just didn't think a ghost could touch a human being, that's all."

"Well, apparently . . ." He let the sentence hang, self-evident. "I do mind a program I saw on the telly—about a ghost in some stately home down south, and supposedly *it* slapped a woman on the face. Left a great bloody welt, if that eases your mind."

My mind had already moved on, to other thoughts. In an absent voice, I said: "He follows me."

David frowned. "Who, Brian?"

"The Sentinel. Robbie says he follows me around sometimes, and tries to talk to me."

After another briefly searching look, David smiled and took my shoulders in his warm hands, reassuring. "Well, I'd not be worried. He's just taken with your bonny face, that's all."

"Jeannie," I informed him, "seemed to think it was my bonny hair he liked."

"It's possible." The blue eyes crinkled, warm on mine. "Either way, I doubt you'll come to any harm. Poor Brian's proof of that."

His expression altered slightly as a sudden thought struck him, and before I had time to gauge his intentions the hands on my shoulders tightened and his head dipped swiftly down.

If first kisses were a harbinger of things to come, I told myself, then I was in serious trouble. I couldn't remember a first kiss like this one. There was nothing searching or tentative about it; it was certain and deep and it brought the blood pounding to my ears. Strangely enough, it also seemed to drain all the energy out of my body, so that when he pulled away again, I found it took great effort to stand upright. But then focusing my eyes, too, took great effort, as did breathing, and though I tried to look quite natural my shaking voice betrayed me. "David, honestly . . ."

"What?"

"Well, you do choose your moments, don't you? I mean, we're practically *standing* on a drunken man, and my students are just around the corner, and Peter could be back at any minute . . ."

"Just experimenting."

"Oh, really?"

"Aye. Your Sentinel's protective, but he's not a jealous fool."

"And how do you figure that?"

"He's left me standing." His grin was very cocksure.

"So he's a rotten judge of character," I said, drawing a deep breath to calm my still-racing heartbeat. "And anyway, I wouldn't look so smug if I were you . . . for all you know the Sentinel wasn't even paying attention."

"Give me some credit, lass. I am a scientist."

I paused, mid-breath. "And what does that mean?"

"It means that when you're testing a hypothesis, you'd be a fool to trust just one experiment." As he lowered his head a second time, I glimpsed self-satisfaction in his eyes, those laughing blue eyes that were suddenly all I could see, and then even those eyes disappeared and for several long minutes I found myself unable to think at all.

"That's the third time you've stopped listening," Adrian accused me, wheeling his chair around to face me in amused exasperation.

I glanced up, my pencil frozen in mid-doodle. "I am listening."

"No you're not."

"I am, too." I took a brave shot in the dark. "You were saying you've been having some success . . ."

"I was saying," he contradicted me, "that we're being attacked by an army of six-foot-tall killer penguins, and since you didn't bat an eye at *that*, I can only conclude you weren't listening."

"Ah."

"Ah, indeed." Settling back in his chair, he hooked the dustbin from under his desk and propped his feet up on it. "Still, I'll not take it too personally. I expect you're feeling the effects of your morning's adventures."

It was clearly a probing sort of comment, not at all random or casual, and I sighed when I saw his expression. "How did you find out about that?"

"I know all kinds of things."

"Adrian . . ."

"Well, if you must know," he said, smiling, "I had the whole story from one of your own finds assistants."

My head drooped forward, into my hands. "Oh, God."

"No, the redhead, actually. The one with the enormous—"

"And what, exactly, did she tell you?" I wanted to know.

"Only that you'd knocked our Brian senseless."

"That *I'd* . . . ?"

"I didn't think you had it in you, darling," he admitted, lacing his fingers together. "But your young assistant claims you've got a cracking good left hook."

"But surely she can't actually have seen . . ."

"Oh, yes. Apparently she heard your voices, and had just popped her head around to investigate when you sent Brian sailing."

It might have looked like that, I conceded, from a certain angle. "But I didn't see anyone."

"No . . . well, she is a rather polite young thing, and seeing that you had everything so well in hand, you and Fortune, I assume she didn't want to poke her nose in where she wasn't needed."

I massaged my forehead, closing my eyes. "And how many people did she mention this to, do you suppose?"

"Only to me, as far as I know. Of course," he went on, before the news could cheer me, "I myself could not resist sharing the tale with a few of my own lads."

"Oh, Adrian."

"Don't 'oh Adrian' me. One doesn't just *sit* on a story like that."

"But now everyone will know."

"And why not? It can only raise your stock among the students, darling. My lot already thought you rather smashing—now they're in absolute awe."

I counted backwards from ten. "I'm very flattered. But it wasn't me that hit Brian."

Adrian raised his eyebrows. "It was never our Mr. Fortune?"

"No, of course not, don't be stupid."

"Who, then?"

"You won't believe me," I warned him.

"Yes I will. Who was it?"

"Robbie's Sentinel."

Adrian stared at me. "Bollocks."

"See, what did I tell you?"

"Ghosts can't hit people."

"How do you know?"

"Because there are no such things as ghosts."

"Brilliant logic, that," I commended him. "And anyway, if you keep on arguing, you might find out otherwise. The Sentinel's become a bit protective of me, as it happens. That's why he went for Brian."

"Oh right." Adrian assumed a completely accepting expression, then rolled his eyes heavenwards. "Am I the only person on this dig who hasn't gone completely mad?"

Before any higher being could answer him, Peter came striding through the doorway like an actor who'd received his cue.

"Horses!" he announced, in his richly melodious voice.

Adrian looked at me. "As I was saying . . ."

Coming to a halt beside my desk, Peter reached for one of my hands and, turning it palm up, pressed into it a flat, around lump of metal, flaking with corrosion.

His eyes shone with the exhilaration of discovery, and for an instant I saw, not the old man standing there, but the Peter Quinnell of those fading photographs, his blond hair falling on his unlined face as he pointed again to the roughened bit of metal and smiled beatifically.

"*There*, my dear," he told me, "are your horses."

XXIX

After two months of handling nothing but rough ware and Samian ware and scattered old coins, cleaning that single scrap of Roman horse harness was like polishing Priam's treasure.

I could barely wait for the evening meal to finish so I could make my retreat to the kitchen, spread some old newspapers over the table, and set to work again, carefully removing the ugly disfiguring crust of age to reveal the underlying glint of silvered bronze.

Conservation work always made me rather single-minded. I took very little notice of Jeannie's leaving, or of Peter popping in to say goodnight, and when Fabia came home a few hours later she found me still sitting there, deeply absorbed.

"You're mad," she said. "It's half-past one."

"Is it?" I looked up, blinking like a shortsighted watchmaker, and she shook her head.

"Mad," she repeated, moving across to open a cupboard. "Want some cocoa? I always have to have my cocoa, every night. My mother's fault. She was forever bringing me cups in my nursery, and now I can't sleep without the blasted stuff."

Fabia almost never mentioned her mother, and when she

did I'd found she tended to keep to a pattern—one brief reminiscence and then nothing more, as though a door slammed instantly to keep her mind from following after the small random memory. It scuttled like a leaf along an empty street and swirled off into silence.

I said, "yes please" to her offer of cocoa and bent again to my work.

After several minutes Fabia brought both mugs of steaming cocoa over to the table and sat down across from me, frankly curious.

"Is that what Peter found, this afternoon?"

"Mm. A *phalera*," I named it, shifting the partly cleaned disc safely out of range while I sipped my cocoa.

"What does it do?"

"Well, it's sort of a connector, if you like, for the straps of a horse's harness. You see these little rings, here, on the back? The leather straps went through there."

"Oh right." She peered more closely, pointing. "What's that little slot thing for?"

"To hang a pendant on. When this was on a harness, there'd have been a pendant hanging from it, a flat metal piece shaped like a wolf's head, or something like that. For decoration."

Fabia, with a dubious look at the corroded lump of metal at my elbow, remarked that she couldn't imagine anything so ugly being in the least bit decorative. "But then I've no imagination anyway. If I saw it in a drawing, maybe . . ."

"I could do better than a drawing. I could take you down south this summer," I told her, "to watch a display of the Ermine Street Guard."

"The who?"

"A Roman re-enactment group. Their cavalrymen are brilliant, fully kitted out and everything, with replica saddles and harnesses. When those chaps come charging at you with the sun blazing off all those silver *phalerae*, you know how the ancient Britons must have felt."

"I'll take your word for it," she promised. "Being run down by Romans is *not* my idea of fun."

"It's tremendous fun, really."

"Didn't the Britons have horses, to fight back with?"

"Chariots."

Her eyebrows arched over the rim of her cocoa mug. "Chariots? What, like in *Ben-Hur*?"

"Didn't they teach you about Boudicca, when you were at school?"

"Very probably."

"Queen of the Iceni," I elaborated, with a smile. "A rather fierce woman, who stomped all over our Ninth Legion, as it happens."

"Oh right. Peter's mentioned her, I'm sure."

"Well, the next time you're in London you should take a small detour to Westminster Bridge, right across from the Houses of Parliament. There's a whopping great statue of Queen Boudicca on that corner, charging about in her chariot."

Fabia clearly didn't think it a very practical mode of transport for the British terrain. "Must have rattled one's teeth a bit, running a chariot over this ground."

I agreed that it must have. "But they managed it somehow. The Caledonii—that's the tribe that lived north of here, up in the Highlands—even they had chariots, according to the Roman writer Tacitus."

She frowned. "Were there tribes here in Scotland, then? I didn't know that. I thought they were all one big group."

"No, they were rather divided. The tribe that lived here, in the eastern Borders, would have been the . . . God, don't tell me I've forgotten it, I used to know them all . . ." Pressing a hand to my forehead, I struggled to sift the fact from my overcrowded memory. "The Votadini, I think. I'm afraid I don't know much about them, though. No one does. The Romans didn't bother much with this part of Scotland—most historians take that to mean the Votadini were a peaceful lot, no real trouble."

Fabia shrugged. "Or dead vicious." She took a sip of cocoa and rolled it around in her mouth. "Mind you, the Romans probably deserved it."

"How do you mean?"

"Well, they were the invaders, weren't they? You can't

just go around as you please, making a mess of other people's lives, and not expect some kind of retribution."

Only a twenty-year-old, I thought, could so neatly dissect history into black and white, heroes and villains. It was true that, to the Votadini, the Romans were invaders, foreigners, who had no right to be here. But on the other hand, those "Romans" had been settled here in Britain eighty years or so by then—at least two generations had been raised to feel that this was now their home.

I started to explain to Fabia that history could sometimes be more complicated than it first appeared, but she was in no mood to hear my argument.

"Nothing complicated about it," she cut me off, her tone definite. "It's only justice, pure and simple. An eye for an eye. Take Robbie's Sentinel, for instance," she said. "He came up here to kill the Votadini, right? So they had every right to kill him back."

One simply couldn't argue with youthful logic, I thought wryly. "Well, they didn't make a very thorough job of it," I commented, "if he's still wandering about in the field."

I'd meant it as a joke, but Fabia, still in her righteous attitude, appeared to be weighing the matter. "Yes, but then that's the ultimate punishment, isn't it?" she said, finally. "To take your enemy's life away, to see him lose the people and the things that he most loves, but not to let him die."

Watching her, I had the feeling she was speaking of herself, of her own loneliness and devastation, having lost her father and the life that they had shared. Certainly her eyes had grown distant, deeply thoughtful.

I tried to bring her out of it, by lightening the mood. "I see I'll have to watch my step," I teased her, "and keep in your good favor, if that's your idea of the perfect punishment. I don't much fancy being made a ghost."

She glanced up, shaking off her reverie. "What? Oh right. I wouldn't worry," she said, smiling. "Anyway, I'd be afraid to tangle with you, after what you did to Brian."

I sighed. "I didn't hit . . ."

"It was a little over the top, though, don't you think? He's rather harmless, really."

"But I didn't—"

"It's just a good thing," Fabia said sagely, "it was you that did it, and not Davy. A man's punch does more damage."

When I repeated that to Jeannie the next morning over breakfast, she doubled over laughing. "Just you try and tell that to my Brian," she said. "Being hit by a woman's the worst form of insult. He went off down the pub last night and didn't rest until he'd got himself into a good manly fight— he came home with a keeker. A black eye," she translated, saving me the trouble of looking up the word. "And all on account of you."

"But I didn't hit him," I said, for what seemed like the hundredth time.

"Aye, you and I both ken that, but Brian was too guttered to mind anything too clearly. Here now, have your porridge while I put your eggs on."

I took the bowl obediently, yawning as I forced my eyes fully open. I'd stayed up well past three cleaning the little *phalera* and Peter must have known because he let me sleep late, undisturbed. Jeannie had very nearly finished with the washing-up when I finally came down. I would have gone straight out into the field, but she was not about to let me pass without a proper breakfast. Like the Sphinx, I thought. It was impossible to get by her, only instead of having to answer riddles one was forced to eat two eggs with toast and sausages.

"Jeannie," I said, "can I ask you something?"

"Certainly."

"Does Brian . . . I mean, has Brian ever . . ." This was difficult. "Is Brian like Robbie?"

She set my plate of eggs down cautiously, clearing away the empty porridge bowl. "Like Robbie how?"

"Does he see things? Is he . . ."

"Gifted?" Her eyes met mine in mild surprise.

"He said something to me yesterday," I told her, hesitantly. "That is, he sort of told me that he was. And David said he wasn't, but I thought . . . I thought I'd ask.''

She turned away, but not before I saw the smile. "Davy doesn't ken everything."

"So Brian really *is*—"

"Not like Robbie," she broke in, correcting me. "He's not as good as that. He only gets impressions sometimes, hunches; nothing sure. But I reckon that's why Robbie never kens what Brian's up to. And I reckon that's why your old Roman ghost could do his trick."

I frowned. "What do you mean?"

"Well, I doubt if he could have knocked anyone flat but Brian—ghosts don't go around hitting anybody, really, do they? But a person with the second sight, that's different. Vulnerable, they are. You saw what happened to Robbie, out there in that field. He just had too much flowing through his wee brain."

"So you think the Sentinel did what he did just by thinking."

"Aye, thinking or wishing it. Still," she added, smiling openly this time, "I'd not be too quick to suggest that to Brian. He's fair respectful of you now, I'd try and keep it that way." She turned away again and started chopping vegetables for lunch. After a moment's thought she added: "Verity?"

"Yes?"

"You're the only one who kens, apart from me. You'll keep it secret?"

"If you want me to."

"I mean, I'd not be cross if you told Davy . . ."

A floorboard creaked in the passageway. "If she told Davy what?" asked David, crossing to check the shortbread tin and frowning when he found it empty. Stealing a piece of toast from my plate instead, he looked from one to the other of us expectantly, waiting for an answer.

I glanced at Jeannie for approval before I gave him one. "That Brian really does have second sight, like I said yesterday. Not as accurate as Robbie, but even so—"

"Away!" said David, cutting me off as he, too, turned to Jeannie. "Why did you never tell me?"

"It's meant to be a secret," I explained, then told him what Jeannie thought had happened yesterday, with the Sentinel.

"Aye," agreed David, reaching forward to dip his piece of toast in one of my uneaten eggs. "It's possible."

A heavy, muffled thump sounded from the vicinity of the cellar stairs, and Jeannie turned her head sharply. "What the devil's that?"

"Your husband," said David. "His mate's finally come with the lorry, so they're shifting the vodka."

"I'd not say it so loudly," Jeannie chided him, with eyes that disapproved of the whole affair. "We've got students running around the now, and it'd not do Peter any good if anyone found out what's going on."

David, grinning, shrugged off the warning. "It's only a wee bit of free trading. Don't be so difficult. Och, that minds me," he said, looking down at me. "My mother said I was to ask you if you'd do her a wee obligement?"

"A favor, you mean?" I checked, showing off my growing Scots vocabulary. "What sort of a favor?"

"The museum's setting up a new exhibition, and my mother was hoping you'd provide a bit of expert advice, seeing how you've been with the British Museum and everything."

"Of course," I said, "I'd love to help. When are they wanting to open this new exhibition?"

"Not this weekend coming, but the next one. My birthday weekend, as it happens. Are you going to eat that sausage?"

I pushed the plate nearer to him. "Is it really your birthday in two weeks' time?"

"Aye. I'll be fully twenty-two this year."

Jeannie laughed. "Liar! You're thirty-seven, same as Brian."

"I am not," said David loftily, "the same as Brian."

"No, you're much more trouble. D'ye never stop eating? That's Verity's breakfast."

"Verity's not so keen on breakfast," he defended himself. "If I don't eat this for her she'll be here all day, when she's meant to be working."

I had to admit, an hour later, that a large and cowardly part of me would have preferred staying down in the kitchen with Jeannie, eating cold eggs, to sitting up here on my own scrubbing down shelves in the finds room. Well, not entirely on my own . . . my two student assistants were hard at work out in my stall-cum-office, typing madly away at the computer with a diligence that quite escaped me. I could hear the steady tap-tap of the keys and now and then a snatch of conversation, but for all intents and purposes I felt as if I were alone.

It was the fault of the room, as much as anything. It was a quiet room, close walled and stale for want of windows. No amount of cleaning could remove the air of mustiness, like old books growing moldy in their bindings. There were pleasant smells, as well. In the days when these stables had sheltered horses, this room had been the tack room, and now and then a whiff of leather from some long-discarded saddle drifted past me, hauntingly, and died again in silence. One could almost hear the dust settling in the corners.

Still, I cheered myself, working in here was preferable, today, to being out of doors. Our summer sun had taken temporary leave and in its place the sky was gray and melancholy, with the hard relentless wind I'd come to think of as a feature of the Borders. I didn't envy David and Peter, scraping away in that merciless wind, and poor Adrian had stormed in several times already, swearing bloody murder at the weather, which had twice knocked over his equipment.

The students, uncomplaining, soldiered on. They looked like little limpets, clinging bravely to the sloping field, their heads bent low as they worked in groups at the patches of excavated ground.

Here in the finds room, at least, I was warm and dry and only had to contend with one draft that struck like a pillar of cold near the open door—the fault of the wind, no doubt. At any rate, it was easy enough to avoid.

I was down on my knees with bucket and sponge, starting in on the bottom shelves, when one of my assistants poked her head in. "Thought you might fancy a cup of tea," she told me, kindly holding up a steaming mug.

"Brilliant. Thanks very much."

"I'll just leave it here, then, shall I?" She set it down at one end of the long work table and hovered in the doorway a moment, watching me. "Are you sure you don't want *us* to do that, Miss Grey?"

"And why should you have all the fun?" I asked her, smiling over my shoulder. "Besides, you're both much faster on the computer than I am, it makes more sense for you to be doing what you're doing."

"Yes, well . . ."

"Aren't you freezing to death in that draft?" I asked, sounding disturbingly like my own mother.

The young woman frowned. "What draft?"

"The one that you're standing in."

"I don't feel anything."

"Well, they do breed you hardier, up here in Scotland."

"I'm from Yorkshire, Miss Grey."

"Even better," I told her. "And I'm quite all right, really—you needn't keep looking so guilty. I *like* cleaning things." Which was a colossal lie, of course, but it did succeed in shifting her out of the doorway.

As her footsteps retreated, I slopped the sponge into the pail at my feet and stood, humming tunelessly as I turned to walk across to where she'd left my tea.

The pillar of cold had moved.

I walked through it and out the other side before my mind had time to register its presence; before I remembered that, scarcely ten minutes ago, the same spot had been perfectly warm.

Silly, I chided myself. Drafts don't follow a person around . . .

"Jesus," I breathed, as the sudden realization hit me. My heart surged painfully upwards and lodged beneath my collarbone as I spun to stare behind me at the innocently empty air. I put out a shaking hand, not really wanting to, but unable to stop myself . . . and touched nothing but warmth. With the back of my neck prickling, I wheeled and stretched my hand out searchingly. Into the cold, and back again.

I took a hasty backwards step, then thought how foolishly

futile that was, and hugging my ribcage defensively I stopped and held my ground. Three months ago, if someone had tried to convince me I was facing down a ghost I would have laughed out loud at the very idea; now I had no doubt at all that he was there, directly in front of me, trying to touch me, perhaps; trying to talk to me . . .

This has to stop, my mind cried silently. *I can't keep on with this, it has to stop.*

"I can't," I said aloud, in a raspy voice I hardly recognized as mine. Closing my eyes for a moment, I struggled to concentrate, and stammered out the words again in Latin. "I can't hear you. I'm sorry. I can't hear you or see you—the boy's the only one who can do that, and I can't use him because it does him harm. Do you understand?"

Only the silence answered me. I hugged myself tighter to ward off the shivers, my voice dwindling to a pleading sort of whisper. "Look, I know you want to tell me something, but you'll have to find another way . . . this just won't work. Do you understand? You'll have to find another way . . ."

"Miss Grey?" The living voice, close outside the doorway, made me jump.

I turned my head. "Yes?"

"You all right?" My student's head appeared around the corner for the second time, her expression wary. "We heard you talking, but we weren't sure whether you were saying something to us, or—"

"No," I told her, "sorry. I was talking to myself."

"Oh right." She paused a minute. "It's just that you sounded different, you know . . ."

"Yes, I imagine I would have." I forced a smile. "I was speaking Latin."

Her look made it clear she considered me strange—a fussy old bluestocking, maybe, or a plain raving idiot. But she withdrew again politely, saying nothing.

I drew a deep breath, took up my mug of tea with a trembling hand and dived with purpose through the doorway, out of the finds room, out of the Principia, crossing the field with swift steps that were just this side of an actual run.

David didn't notice anything amiss when I appeared at the

edge of his barracks trench—but then he wouldn't have noticed, anyway. He was deeply, happily absorbed in the dirt, like a small boy with bucket and spade at the beach. "Heyah," he greeted me, his eyes crinkling against the wind. "You didn't have to do that."

"Do what?"

"Bring me tea."

"Oh. I didn't," I assured him, wrapping my hands more closely around the warmth. "It's my tea. But you're welcome to share it, if you like."

"I do like. Thanks." He prised the mug out of my fingers and drank, crouching back on his heels. "Wicked weather."

I nodded. "Having any luck?"

"Aye. We've cleared the outline of one of the barracks blocks—I've got the lads putting golf tees in all of the post molds so that Fabia can take a photograph before it rains."

"Yes, I see that. So what are you doing down here, with your trowel?"

He grinned. "Mucking about. I thought this looked interesting, this darker bit here, so I'm checking it out. You never ken what you'll find, on this blasted site. You can have this back now," he added, handing over the half-empty mug. "Thanks."

The dark head bent again and for a while I watched him work in silence, drawing comfort from his company, his quiet calming strength. I'm safe here with David, I thought, and the words became a lulling litany as I sipped the warm tea and relaxed: Safe, safe, perfectly safe . . .

The cold passed through me like a knife blade, and I jerked upright. "David."

"It's all right," he said, in an excited tone, not looking up. "I see it."

I stared down at him, watching his motions without really seeing them, trying to focus on what he was doing. He had tossed his trowel aside and was brushing the dirt away now with his fingers, trying to free something small from the soil. And then he raised his head to whistle sharply across the trench, catching the attention of one of his students. "Go get Mr. Quinnell, lad."

"David, what is it?" I leaned closer, trying to stop shaking. "What have you found?"

For an answer he held out his hand, and I saw the small medallion, the shred of a chain and the glitter of gold, and the tiny stamped figure of a woman, holding what looked like a ship's rudder.

"It's Fortuna," David told me.

"Yes, I know."

I'd come across her image countless times in my career—one of the first things I'd been asked to draw for Dr. Lazenby, on the Suffolk dig, had been an altar erected by some unnamed Roman soldier, inscribed "To Fortune, Who Brings Men Home." Those few words had moved me, and I'd wished that I could meet the man who'd had them carved in stone.

Be careful what you wish for, that's what my father always said. I ought to have listened to him. Because standing now and looking at the image of Fortuna, goddess of good luck and destiny, steering her ship of fate over the waters, I felt certain I'd already met the man to whom the golden pendant once belonged.

XXX

Brian wasn't pleased to see me coming down the drive. He'd been making a savage attack on the weeds that grew to either side of the cottage path, his head bent low into the wind that carried away the small regular puffs of white smoke from the cigarette clamped at the corner of his mouth, but when he saw me he switched off the strimmer and straightened his back, belligerent.

Jeannie hadn't been lying about the black eye. It stood out angrily against the tan of his cheekbone, seared along its bottom edge by a nasty-looking scrape on which the blood had dried. Still, I thought, he wore it like a badge of honor; even raised a hand to rake the silver hair back from his face, so I could have a clear view of that eye.

I was meant to make some comment, I felt sure. Halting my steps a few feet away, I searched for an appropriate compliment. "That looks painful."

"Not your handiwork," he shot back, shortly. Lifting one hand he plucked the cigarette from his lips and narrowed his eyes. "Got it down the pub, last night. Had to put a couple of buggers from Burnmouth in their place."

"Ah." I looked again at the set jaw and the hardened

muscles of his arms, and said honestly: "I imagine they look rather worse than you, then."

"Bloody right." His gaze moved down, to my hands, to the notebook I carried and the tiny square packet of tissue paper. But he didn't say anything. He just went on standing there, smoking, waiting for me to explain why I'd come.

"I was wondering," I said, "if I could talk to Robbie, for a minute."

"Were you?"

"Yes. We found something this morning, in one of the trenches, and it might be something quite important, so—"

He cut across my speech, impassive. "The lad's just home from school," he said. "He's not yet had his tea."

"Well yes, I know, but Jeannie said . . ." I stopped myself, seeing from his expression that it made little difference what Jeannie had said. "I won't stop long, Brian, I promise. It's just that . . . well, it *could* be important, and everyone's curious to hear what Robbie has to say, and nobody wanted to wait till this evening."

Jeannie had actually put my chances of getting past Brian at slim to none, and looking at him now I was inclined to agree with her odds.

He stared at me, stony-faced, for a long moment, then glanced at the small wrapped packet. "That it?"

"Yes."

"Let's have a look."

I unwrapped the paper and let him examine the tiny pendant. "Gold, is it?" he asked, not touching it.

"Yes."

He frowned, and shifted his gaze to study the air past my shoulder. "When I was Robbie's age . . . younger than Robbie, even, I used to be a wizard with the horses. My dad and his mates, they'd show me a betting slip and I could pick the winners, every time. They must have made a bloody fortune," he said, sourly. "Never showed me a penny of it, nor my mum. Dad left us both when I was ten." He paused, drawing deep on the cigarette, and brought his hard eyes back to mine. "You can think what you like of me, of what I do for a living, but I've never used my boy to line my pockets. Never have, and never will. Nobody uses my boy.''

"Yes, I understand that. But I thought we agreed . . .''

"I was legless.''

"You said I could do this.'' My tone pleaded with him to be reasonable. "You said that if I came down on my own, I could—''

"I know what I said.'' He exhaled sharply, discontented. "All right, you can have ten minutes with the lad. But only ten minutes, and I'll be there counting them, d'you hear?''

"Thanks.''

Wading through an untidy pile of weeds, he leaned the strimmer upright against the cottage wall and walked around to open the door to the kitchen.

It seemed strange to be here when Jeannie was absent— the cozy little room looked less inviting, but that might have simply been the lack of sunlight. Brian kicked off his boots and called to Robbie.

"Wally's out, is he?'' I guessed, noticing the empty place under the table, where Kip usually lay.

Brian's mouth quirked briefly, the shade of a smile. "That's right. He makes himself scarce, when I'm home.''

Robbie came bouncing around the corner and gave me a buoyant greeting. "Heyah,'' he said. "Are you and Dad still fighting?''

I smiled. "No.''

"Good. Did you see Dad's black eye?''

I assured him I had.

"She was very impressed,'' Brian told his son. "Now, sit yourself down on that chair there and look what Miss Grey's got to show you.'' And with that mild instruction he moved past us to put the kettle on.

Robbie clambered obediently onto his chair, preparing himself for our game. "Did you find the necklace?''

I stopped in the act of unwrapping the packet, to stare at him. "The what?''

"The Sentinel's necklace.''

Brian, by the counter, lit a cigarette and smiled faintly, the proud parent, while I peeled away the final layers of tissue and wordlessly passed the golden scrap of pendant to Robbie.

"Aye, this is it," he said, nodding his head. "I thought so."

I cleared my throat, casually. "Are you sure it's the Sentinel's?"

Again the nod, quite certain. "He's always got it on."

"I see."

"He never takes it off, see, 'cause it belonged to her."

I opened my notebook, feeling a sudden need to have something to focus my attention on. "Belonged to who?"

Brian broke in. "Can you see her name, lad?" To me, he explained: "He can sometimes pick up names and all."

Robbie fingered the pendant, screwing up his face as he tried to come up with the answer. "It starts with a 'C', I think . . . C-1 . . . here, I can write it out." Taking my pencil he scrawled in large letters across the open page of my notebook.

I read the name. "Claudia?"

"Aye."

Brian flicked ash into the sink, where it fell with a whispering hiss. "And the name of the Sentinel, Robbie? D'you know that as well?"

"It's a long name," said Robbie. "Hold on." Closing his eyes, he stayed silent a full minute, thinking. "Three names. The middle one's the same as *her* name, like . . ."

"What, Claudius?" I asked, and he opened his eyes.

"Aye. And then Maxy . . . Maxy-moose . . ."

"Maximus." I jotted it down with remarkably steady fingers. "And the first name?"

"It starts with a 'C,' too. It's . . . no, I can't get it. It's gone. Sorry."

"Don't be sorry," I told him. "You're doing just fine. This is brilliant." I looked at the name in my notebook: *C. Claudius Maximus*. No longer a nebulous ghost, but a name. It gave me an odd feeling.

"Claudia and Claudius," Brian said dryly. "Devoted couple, were they?"

She wouldn't be his wife, I thought. Not his legal wife, at any rate. A legionary couldn't marry until he retired from the army. Still, common-law wives weren't unheard of—soldiers sometimes had whole families living in the towns outside their forts.

I was about to ask Robbie whether Claudia had been the Sentinel's girlfriend, when a new thought struck me. Claudia and Claudius. That was the Sentinel's *second* name, Robbie had said. His clan name. Romans named their children according to a fairly rigid custom: an individual first name, then the clan name, and finally the family name. Thus only the first names varied, in a family. C. Claudius Maximus— say his first name was Caius, or something like that—Caius Claudius Maximus might have a brother named Publius Claudius Maximus. And their sisters would most probably be called by just their clan name, in its female form. *Claudia*.

I looked across at Robbie. "Was this Claudia . . . was she related to the Sentinel?"

His brow creased. "Related?"

"From the same family."

"Oh. Aye, she was his sister."

The kettle screamed and Brian moved to make the tea, his eyes meeting mine with a grudging amusement. "Full points for you."

Robbie moved his fingers, held the pendant tighter. "She had long hair," he told me. "Long like yours, and the same color."

In the brief silence that followed, Brian voiced the question I was too afraid to ask. It must have crossed his own thoughts, after what had happened yesterday. "Does Miss Grey mind the Sentinel of his sister, then?"

"Aye." No hesitation there. "He loves her."

I kept my attention fixed on Robbie, my pencil resting on the page. "And she gave him that pend . . . that necklace?"

"Nah, she gave it to the other guy," said Robbie. "For luck, like. So he wouldn't be hurt."

"She gave it to the other . . . ?"

"Aye, the Sentinel's friend." Robbie looked at me as though the details were self-evident. "The one she was going to marry."

"Ah."

Brian raised his eyebrows. "Christ, it's better than *EastEnders*, this."

My ten minutes, I thought, must surely be up, but Brian appeared to be gaining interest in our little game, and made no move to stop it. He turned his back to the sink and waited for the tea to brew, watching while his son rolled the pendant and chain in his small hand, like dice.

"He was a soldier, too," said Robbie, finally.

"The Sentinel's friend?" I asked.

"Aye. He was older, and he kent a lot of things. *He* said the ship would come. He said . . ." He paused, his small face falling. "Only it didn't. And then the horses came, and the Sentinel had to put him on the fire."

Enthralled, I leaned forward. "Why, Robbie? Why did he put him on the fire?"

But the mists through which he viewed these things had swirled again, and Robbie shook his head. "Sorry," he said, looking up, and I was shocked to see his eyes were filled with tears. "He's so sorry. He promised her that he'd protect . . . but he couldn't. He couldn't stop it."

I watched, concerned, as a single tear traced a crooked path down one small freckled cheek. "Robbie, it's all right, you needn't—"

"Claudia," he whispered, quite as if I hadn't spoken, and his face collapsed in anguish. "So sorry, Claudia."

"Right." Brian pitched his spent cigarette into the sink and pushed himself away from the counter, his eyes wary. "That's enough, I think."

I nodded agreement. Stretching out my hand for the pendant, I sent the boy a bright smile. "That's wonderful, Robbie, you've been a great help. I'll just take this back up to the finds room, now . . ."

"No!" It was a violent, unexpected response, almost a shout, and even Brian looked startled.

"Now, lad . . ."

Robbie ignored him, fixing me with an imploring gaze. "This can't go in the finds room. It's for protection. You don't understand."

"Robbie—"

"No." Wincing, he shut his eyes tightly and shook his head once, as though trying to clear it. "Must keep my promise . . . must protect . . ."

"Now." Brian looked from his son's face to mine. "It stops now."

"Robbie," I said, "it's all right, love. I'm perfectly safe. Just give me the—"

The boy's head jerked backwards as if a string had pulled it, and his eyes rolled. *"Periculosa,"* he said, in a hollow voice that sounded nothing like his own. *"Via est periculosa."*

"No, you don't!" Brian surged forward, brimming with anger. "You let the lad be!"

Stunned, I was opening my mouth to argue my innocence when Brian turned and roared again into the empty air around us. "D'you hear me, you great bloody bastard? You let my son be!"

The emptiness blinked. A sharp gust of wind shook the glass in the windows, and Robbie, the tearstains drying now, forgotten, on his cheeks, turned to look up at his father. "Who are you yelling at, Dad?"

Brian drew in a steadying breath. "No one, Robbie. Just yelling."

"Oh."

"Give that back to Miss Grey now, there's a good lad."

Robbie handed the pendant back placidly, and I took it with trembling fingers. "Thank you." My hand closed for a moment around the small raised image of Fortuna, around the charm of good luck that a ghost had meant for me to find. For protection. And now he'd handed me a warning, too, through Robbie. In Latin, *periculosa* meant dangerous.

Nearby a match flared as Brian lit another cigarette, and his eyes found mine in silence over Robbie's head.

"Via est periculosa?" Peter rolled his tongue around the words, considering. "He actually said that, did he?"

"Yes." I leaned back into the sofa and stroked the gray cat's ears, grateful to be back in the sitting room at Rosehill with its cheerful clutter everywhere and Adrian and Fabia slumped in armchairs on either side of me, drinks in hand. My own dry sherry had been sorely needed. I was halfway down it already, and I hadn't been back a quarter of an hour.

"How curious," Peter said. He was sitting in his own chair with Murphy draped across his knees, as usual. "I wonder what he meant."

"Gosh," said Adrian, stretching his legs out and tipping his head back. "Let's think this one through. He arranges for you to find a medallion of Fortuna, or Fortune, then tells you, 'That way's dangerous.' Now who could he be warning you *about*, I wonder?"

I rolled my eyes sideways to look at him. "Must you always be annoying?"

Fabia frowned. "Davy's not dangerous."

Adrian, swirling his drink with great dignity, remarked that it depended entirely upon one's point of view.

Fabia made a great show of studying Adrian as she lifted her own glass. "Your eyes are awfully green, aren't they?"

"Frequently." Across the room their eyes met, and she looked away abruptly.

"*Via est periculosa*," Peter repeated, thoughtfully. "Of course, *via* has several meanings, doesn't it? The road, the way, the method."

" 'The road is dangerous'?" Fabia tried the translation. "That sounds more a warning against your driving, Adrian."

"Very funny."

She curled herself into her armchair, like one of the cats. "Where is Davy, anyway?"

Adrian shrugged. "Still playing scoutmaster, out in the field. He'll be in when he feels like it."

Out in the field . . .

I closed my eyes a moment, fighting the image that formed in my brain—the image of a solitary Roman soldier walking back and forth across the waving grass for all eternity, unheard and unseen, with no companions but the silent dead. How lonely that would be, I thought . . . how horribly lonely. I tried to clear my mind, but the soldier would not leave. He walked a little further, looked across the field and thought he saw his sister standing, waiting for him, only it wasn't her . . . not Claudia . . . a young woman with long hair, but not Claudia. Close enough, perhaps, to stir the coals of memory. Did ghosts have memories, I wondered? Did they love?

I opened my eyes, and knew from the dreamy expression on Peter's face that he was wondering the same thing. "Extraordinary," was his final pronouncement. "Quite extraordinary."

"Yes." Adrian looked at me, lazily. "So I suppose Brian's banned you from the premises now, has he?"

"Not at all. He handled the whole thing rather well, I thought. No recriminations."

Peter arched an eyebrow. "My dear girl, you do work miracles, don't you? First Connelly, and now Brian. You have a great facility for dealing with difficult men."

I couldn't help but smile at that. "I've had a lot of practice."

Adrian cast a sharp eye in my direction. "Watch it."

Fabia leaned forward. "Have you still got the pendant, Verity? I haven't had a chance to really look at it yet."

I shook my head. "I gave it to one of my students, to put in the finds room."

"Trusting soul," Adrian said.

"There's a lock on the finds room door," I defended my action.

"I meant giving it to a student. I'm surprised you gave it to anyone, actually, after what Robbie said." His tone was dry. "If it's supposed to be keeping you safe . . ."

"I feel safer," I said, "with it locked in the finds room, thanks all the same."

Peter stretched his hand out. "May I see your notes again, my dear? There's one point in there that makes me rather curious."

"Of course. They're on the table there, beside you."

"Ah." He flipped the page and frowned. "Yes, here it is. 'He said the ship would come' . . . that's the bit I'm after. 'The ship.' Now, I wonder . . . ?" And with that he lapsed into a sort of trance, unspeaking, drinking steadily and staring at the carpet.

Archaeologists, I thought, were a breed apart. There was David, still out in the field in a bone-chilling wind with the rain coming on, because he didn't want to stop what he was doing; and here sat Peter, completely oblivious to the world around him while he rebuilt the past in his mind.

Neither one of them sat down to supper.

David stayed out until it grew dark, then came and grabbed a plate of food to take up to his desk in the Principia. He took a plate in to Peter as well, but when I stopped by the sitting room later I found that plate untouched, the meat and vegetables turned cold and unappetizing. Peter, lost in his own world, didn't seem to mind. He still had Murphy on his lap, and the vodka bottle was very nearly empty. He surfaced at the sound of my voice.

"What's that?" he asked.

"Goodnight," I repeated.

"Not off to bed already, are you?"

"Well, it is"—I checked my watch—"nearly half-past eleven, and I was up rather late last night."

"Oh." He sounded disappointed, and I hesitated.

"I suppose . . . I suppose I *could* stay up a little longer, if you wanted company."

"No, no." One hand waved the offer aside, with a tragic air. "No, I'm quite all right, here by myself."

"In fact," I said, more firmly, looking at his face, "I rather fancy a cup of coffee."

"No need to trouble yourself . . ."

"Or perhaps a drink."

He beamed at me, delighted. "Well, if you're absolutely certain. Because I've just been sitting here thinking, you know, about the fate of the *Hispana*, and I've hit upon a most intriguing theory . . ."

XXXI

"Has Peter *always* drunk like that?" I asked David's mother, the following Wednesday.

"Like what?"

"Well, huge amounts."

Nancy Fortune smiled and stepped backwards, hammer in hand, to be sure that the picture she'd just hung was level. We'd been left to ourselves on the mezzanine floor of the Eyemouth Museum, in the large bright room used for temporary displays. "Aye, he does fair like his vodka," she admitted, "but he holds it well, he always has. You'll not see Peter act the fool. And you'll rarely see him take a drink alone. If he does *that*," she warned me, "it means deep thought, and that's when you want to watch out, because when he's done thinking he . . ."

"Talks," I supplied, rubbing my head at the memory. "Yes, I know. He kept me up till dawn, last week."

"Had a new theory, did he?" Her dancing eyes held sympathy. "He does like to talk them through. Used to be me that bore the brunt of it. He'd ring me up at all hours—still did, up until a few years back, but after the first heart attack he stopped all that. Never tells me anything now, for fear it might excite me. And Davy's just as bad." She hammered in another nail, with a vengeance. "If it wasn't for you and Robbie I'd not have a clue what was going on up at Rosehill."

I caught the frustration in her voice. I'd never been able to understand why she didn't visit, or why Peter and David didn't seem to want her at the house. David loved his mother, and Peter was terribly fond of her, and her interest in our work was undeniable. I fitted my back to the wall, contemplatively. "Why don't you come up and see for yourself? I'd be happy to show you just what we've been up to."

Her mouth pulled down at the corners. "Then Peter'd have a coronary, worrying I'd overdo the walking. No, until the damn fool doctor says I'm fit to run a mile, I'd not be welcome at Rosehill." She leveled the second picture and looked at me. "There, how's that looking?"

"Lovely."

It really was, which relieved me no end. I'd only met the head of the Eyemouth Museum briefly this morning, but she was clearly expecting great things from the "visiting expert" that David's mother had brought in to help, and I'd been trying my best to live up to her expectations. Attractive exhibits, unfortunately, had never been my forte. I was fine when it came to the actual artifacts—how to support them, what light levels to use, that sort of thing—but I fell all to pieces on proper design.

Still, I hadn't done too badly. The jumble of photographs and long formal gowns that we'd started with earlier had become a rather professional looking display that traced the history of Herring Queen Week.

And Herring Queen Week, David's mother had informed me, was *the* big event in Eyemouth's summer calendar.

From what I'd heard, the traditional choosing of a local girl to be the new year's Herring Queen sounded rather splendid—the girl and her attendant maids in gorgeous gowns and sashes, the careful ritual played out against a general air of festival. David's mother had done her best to explain what went on, but in the end she'd said I ought to ask Jeannie. "Jeannie was Herring Queen, she'll be able to tell you all about it. This was her frock, the purple one. I mind her mother making it.''

At the British Museum I'd handled some marvelous artifacts—ancient mosaics and old Roman glassware, rare things beyond price. But the feeling I'd had when I'd set them on display was nothing compared to the satisfaction it gave me to take that one Herring Queen gown—a hideous flounced thing in grape-colored taffeta—and carefully arrange it in its place in the exhibition.

Local history museums, I thought, did have advantages over their larger cousins. They were, if nothing else, a great deal friendlier. I didn't belong to Eyemouth, as the locals would say—but standing here in the fishing museum with Nancy Fortune's cheerful talk like a bracing breeze off the sea and Jeannie's gown on a stand in the corner and the whole past of the community pressing in around me, I did feel a curious sense of belonging.

It crept over me with the comfort of a woolly blanket, and I snuggled deep for a moment before practicality drove me to push it aside. *You're only here for the summer, really*, I reminded myself. When the digging season ended and the field crew had disbanded for the unworkable winter months, I'd have to go back home, and then . . . well, there was always Dr. Lazenby's new dig in Alexandria—I couldn't keep avoiding him forever. Sooner or later he would track me down, and I would have to give the man an answer. *Alexandria*. I sighed. But then, the whole point of my leaving the British Museum had been the quest for change, for new adventures, for . . .

". . . a breath of air," Nancy Fortune was saying.

I looked up. "Sorry?"

She smiled at my inattentiveness. "That's perfect proof, that. I just said we've been cruived in too long: four hours of this work is far too long. D'ye fancy a bit of a walk?"

I had grown accustomed to the wind and almost welcomed it as we stepped outside, lifting my face to the freshening scent of the sea and the sun that fell warm on my skin. Now, in midsummer, the streets seemed too crowded, and the harbor behind us bustled with the preparations for Saturday's crowning of the Herring Queen, and so instead of walking in that direction, we turned and went through the town's center, coming out at length onto the Bantry—the smooth paved promenade that ran from Eyemouth harbor to the beach, along the sea.

There were people here as well, but not so many, and the sound of their chatter was drowned by the roar of the surf. The tide, coming in, rode on high rolling waves that broke like thunder against the harbor mouth. It proved too much to resist for one young girl playing at the end of the sea wall. Laughing, she darted like a bullet back and forth through the narrow gap between the wall and the harbor's parade, testing her speed against the incoming waves and getting well soaked in the process.

Below us, the empty beach, growing narrower by the minute, curved away to meet the blood-red cliffs that rose immovable against the sea, supporting the ruins of Eyemouth Fort, the playground of David's childhood.

I sighed, a little happy sigh, and rested my hands on the smooth stone wall that ran waist-high along the Bantry. "What a beautiful day," I said.

David's mother smiled. "I take it you're not keen to get back?"

For an instant I thought she meant back to London, and fancied she had read my mind, but then I realized she was only speaking of Rosehill, and my work.

"Peter did say I should take the day," I told her. "He thinks I've been looking tired, lately."

"And small surprise, if he's been keeping you up nights expounding his theories."

Conscience and fondness made me come to Peter's defense. "It was a good theory, actually. Would you like to hear it?"

"If you think my heart can stand it," she said, leaning beside me on the sea wall.

"Right. Well, you know we found the gold medallion, with the image of Fortuna on it?"

"Aye, Robbie told me."

"There's a bit more story to the piece than even Robbie

knows," I said, and proceeded to fill her in on all the details, before moving on. "And so after I came back up from Rose Cottage, that's when Peter began to think deeply, as you put it." My lips twitched. "He thought himself right through a whole bottle of vodka."

"It's not uncommon. But I'll lay odds his mind touched on genius."

"Well, he does think that the reason why we haven't yet found any trace of bodies is because the men were cremated. You know, the fact that Rosehill used to be 'Rogue's Hill,' which could come from *rogus*, or funeral pyre."

"That would fit with Robbie saying that the Sentinel put his friend on the fire," she agreed. "But still, there were thousands of men."

"Yes, I know, but . . . maybe I should just run through it all, like Peter did, from the beginning. We're assuming that the Ninth came marching north and set up camp at Rosehill, within the ramparts of the old Agricolan vexillation fortress, which presumably had disappeared by then, right?"

"Aye."

"And one of the reasons Agricola probably built here in the first place was because of the harbor," I said. "The Roman navy had to be able to send in ships, to supply the legions on the northward march." The critical role that the navy had played in the conquest of Britain was all too often overlooked. Absorbed as I was in land based excavations, I'll admit I hadn't thought much about the naval connection myself until Peter had leapt on that statement of Robbie's.

"Robbie mentioned a ship that didn't come," I explained. "And Peter thinks it might have been a supply ship. Now, if the men depended on that ship, and if they were besieged or something, in their camp . . ."

She nodded. "Aye, they might have taken ill, or starved."

"Or even mutinied. The Ninth," I said, "did have a history of mutiny, as I recall. At any rate, they probably weren't in any shape to ward off their attackers, when the final battle happened."

She admitted that, as theories went, it wasn't bad. "So what became of the survivors?"

"That's a mystery, still. But we do know the Sentinel stayed." The sea cast up an arc of spray that spattered cold against my face. Like tears it clung, and tasted salt.

"Love and honor," Nancy Fortune told me, "are a complicated mixture. If he really did promise his sister that he'd keep her man from harm, then he might well have felt he could never go home, that she'd never forgive him for failing."

"Or he might have been mortally wounded, himself," I suggested. "Who knows?"

"He does, I'll wager."

We thought about that for a moment, both of us, in silence, and then she said: "It *is* a shame you can't use Robbie."

"Yes, I know, but after what happened . . ." I shook my head, slowly. "No, it's too risky, really. And I'm not sure even he could pin down evidence of mass cremation—bits of charred bone and ashes all over the field, they'd be murder to find. Still, if we're patient, and stick to our digging, I'm sure we'll come up with proof."

The restless wind tore at my hair, and I felt the warm touch of her eyes on my face. "You believe Peter's theories, then."

"Yes, I do. But then it's rather hard *not* to believe Peter, isn't it? I mean, he only has to look at you and give an explanation, and you can't imagine any other way it *could* have happened. You know?"

The faint smile gentled her expression. "Aye, that's what Davy says, too."

I stayed silent a moment longer, thinking, then bit my lip and said, rather tentatively: "They're very much alike, aren't they, Peter and David?"

"Very much," she agreed.

Our eyes met for the briefest instant, then I turned my face away again. It was nothing to do with me, I reminded myself. Whatever suspicions I might have, whatever questions I might want to ask, the answers were none of my business.

Instead I fixed my eyes on the incoming waves, watching the long curling crests of white foam that formed along their tops before they crashed themselves to death upon the sand. They did remind one of the manes of wild horses, I thought, just like Peter had said. The Irish horses of the sea, coming to gather their dead.

David's mother watched me in her turn, and after a long pause she said, very simply: "He doesn't ken."

My head turned. "I'm sorry?"

"Davy. He doesn't ken who his father is. That's what you're wondering, isn't it?" In the face of my guilty silence she smiled and went on. "It's no shame for me to tell you, lass. You've more right to the truth than anyone, and if you don't ken why," she said, cutting me off as I opened my mouth to protest, "then you're not near as clever as I had you pegged." Her gaze raked me rather fondly. "You're very much as I was, Verity Grey. And if you'd gone to work for Peter Quinnell, years ago . . ."

"If I had worked for Peter then," I told her, honestly, "I should have been in love with him."

"Aye. So you would. And so I was. Only of course, he was married at the time."

"Not happily."

"No, not happily. But there it was." She raised a shoulder dismissively and turned her face seaward.

"Could he not . . ." I paused to clear my throat. "Surely mental illness, even then, was just cause for divorce."

"Oh, aye," she said. "But there was Philip, too, you see."

"Well yes, but—"

"Philip saw us," she said, slowly. "One day, quite by accident. He had something of his mother's illness, Philip did, and seeing me with Peter made him crazy. It was an awful thing, for Peter—Philip never did forgive him. All his life, if anything went wrong, it was his father's fault. His mother's death, his own bad marriage, all his money problems, everything." She shook her head. "He had a talent, Philip did, for hating."

"All the more reason for Peter to leave," was my comment.

"Perhaps. But Peter loved the lad, I saw the pain it caused him. And I didn't want him torn in two. I kent, see, that he would divorce Elizabeth, if he'd kent I was carrying Davy."

I blinked at her. "If he'd . . . ?"

"He'd have wanted to marry me," she said. "To take care of me. It's his nature. And I'd have hated that."

"But you loved him."

Her eyes shifted, and I could see her trying to find the right words to explain. "Love and marriage, they were two different things to me, then. Marriage meant settling down, giving yourself over to a man . . . losing your independence, like. Much as I loved Peter—and I did love him terribly—I loved my own self more," she said. Again the flicker of a smile. "I was young."

A gull swooped in front of me, hanging in the wind, and I frowned at it. "And yet, you did get married."

"Aye, on paper. Billy Fortune was an old friend, and a good man. It was his idea, like—to save my reputation, and to give the bairn a name. We only meant to keep it up two years, and then divorce, but Billy died afore that." Her voice, I thought, was so amazingly calm. She might have been telling me someone else's story, and not her own. "Poor Billy," she said. "Peter never did care for him, much. Couldn't fathom why I'd married onto a fisherman."

I struggled to make sense of it all. "So Peter . . . Peter doesn't know?"

She shook her head. "After Billy died he took a hand in Davy's bringing up—he couldn't help himself. But Davy's Billy Fortune's son, so far as Peter kens."

"And David doesn't know."

"That's right."

"Then why . . . ?"

"Why tell you?" The clear blue eyes, so like her son's, touched mine knowingly. "Because, as you say, my Davy's a lot like his father. And you, lass, like me, are a difficult woman."

"Well, yes, but . . ."

"I took one road, that's all I'm saying. I went down the one road and, now that I'm old, I can see that it wasn't the best road to take."

The herring gull cried and she followed the flight of its shadow with thoughtful eyes, watched it pass over waves rolling in with such force that the sand beneath them boiled and the narrow strip of beach dissolved in foam.

"It's never too late, though, is it?" I ventured. "I mean, you and Peter, you're both single now, and living here, and surely if you wanted to . . ."

She shook her head, and for the first time since I'd met her she looked her full age. "You can't ever go back." Far out beyond the harbor mouth the sea-god's horses tossed their curling manes and rushed in on the inevitable tide, and Nancy Fortune stood and watched them come. "Life moves on," she said gently, "and you can't go back. You've only got one chance to get it right."

XXXII

The inside of the tent was much more comfortable than I'd imagined, high-ceilinged and spacious with a camp bed in one corner and even a small wooden desk, buried of course beneath papers. The flaps, tied back to catch the breeze, let in a spear of morning sun and when I breathed, the pungent scents of leather and warm canvas rose up to mingle pleasantly with fainter smells of soap and aftershave.

David, bent over his bootlace, flicked a glance upwards. "Have I grown an extra head?" he asked me.

"Sorry?"

"You've been staring at me strange since you came in." Straightening, he tucked his shirt-tails into the waistband of his khaki shorts and shot me a wicked grin. "Or is it just that I'm so irresistible?"

He was looking rather irresistible, actually, fresh from his morning shower with his hair still damp and rumpled like a boy's. I had a momentary urge to comb my fingers through the curls to tidy them, but instead I answered his question with a noncommittal smile and tipped my head back, admiring the canvas overhead.

"I do like your tent," I said.

"Aye. Pure Abercrombie & Fitch, don't you think? Like

being on safari. I wake up every morning with the feeling
that I ought to go and shoot something. Of course," he qualified the statement, "I'd be bound to feel like that anyway,
wouldn't I, working with Adrian. Tent or no."

I laughed. "Adrian's not so bad."

"Is he not?" He strapped on his wristwatch, considering.
"Well, maybe you're right. But his mouth's been making
my hand fair itch these past few days."

"He always turns sarcastic when he's foiled in love."

"Oh, aye?"

"And it isn't me he's pining for, whatever you might
think," I set him straight. "He's head over heels for Fabia."

David grinned again, more broadly. "Is he, poor sod? He
and Brian ought to form a club, then—cry into their beer
together. She's got a new lad in her snares. One of these sub-
aqua nutters come down for the diving."

I'd suspected as much myself, but I'd never seen her with
anyone. I wondered that David had—he almost never left the
site now, so absorbed was he in the dig. "You seem to know
an awful lot about it."

"Oh, I ken everyone's business," he said cheerfully. "Especially now that my mother's sitting up there at Saltgreens
looking out on the harbor all day. It's fair amazing, what she
sees."

"Too bad you're not still living at the Ship," I teased him.
"She might have kept an eye on you."

"Just as well I'm here, then." The light in his eyes was
decidedly sinful. "There are some things," he said, "I'd not
want to do, in full view of my mother."

"Such as?"

He laughed, and took my face in his hands, and showed
me.

"Oh," I said, when I could breathe again. "*Those*
things."

"And others. But I'll have to demonstrate another time.
We're running late as it is."

In the kitchen at Rosehill we found Robbie impatiently
swinging his legs. "I've been waiting and waiting," he told
us. "You said ten o'clock, and it's the back of eleven."

David apologized. "But we'll not be late, I promise you."

Jeannie turned smiling from the stove. "You're sure it's no bother, now? Brian said he'd meet you down there, when the boats all come back in."

The fleet had sailed this morning up to St. Abbs, near where David's mother had her cottage, to pick up the young Herring Queen and give her a royal escort back along the coast to Eyemouth. David had explained that it was always done this way—the Herring Queen being taken by car to St. Abbs, to be met by the full fishing fleet. Their return was timed for high tide, in the middle of the afternoon. And then there'd be the pomp and circumstance of the crowning ceremony, held on Gunsgreen, right beside the harbor.

Robbie wasn't keen on seeing the crowning ceremony, but he *was* keen on the children's races held beforehand. Jeannie would have taken him herself, only she'd been battling a headache since breakfast, and with Brian away up to St. Abbs, and Wally leaving at daybreak to help set things up in town, it was down to me and David.

"Of course it's no bother," said David. "And after the races, we'll take Robbie around to the museum, and show him that stunning gown *you* wore as Herring Queen."

"You do and I'll make you wear it," she threatened him. "All those purple petticoats . . . and the *flounces*!"

"Well, it was the fashion," I consoled her. "I used to have a bridesmaid's frock like that myself."

When she pointed out that my frock wasn't on display for everyone to see, I shrugged. "I wasn't a Herring Queen. How *do* they choose the Herring Queen, anyway?"

"Looks," she said, straight-faced, but David didn't let her get away with it.

"Wasn't it school grades, in your day?" he asked her.

"In my day? And what am I, a dinosaur? Which one of us is turning thirty-seven?"

David shook his head. "Not till tomorrow. I'm a young man yet, the day."

Robbie grabbed his sleeve and hauled him bodily toward the door. "Come *on*," he said. "We'll be missing everything."

Peter and most of the students had gone into town before us, drawn more by the lure of open pubs, I thought, than by any real desire to see the Herring Queen crowned. Fabia had promised several of the young men she would follow within the hour, but she was, as usual, running late. As we passed into the front hall she was talking on the telephone.

". . . in the cellar, yes. Tomorrow? But that's Sunday, are you . . . ? Oh right, yes, that's fine," she said, turning slightly at the sound of our footsteps. "OK, I will. Thanks very much."

She rang off with a faintly guilty air, and David grinned.

"You're never ordering more supplies?" he asked.

She opened her mouth, as if to deny the charge, then thought better of it. "Well, I need them. And anyway, Peter said that I could order anything I liked, for my darkroom." Tossing back her bright fair hair she gathered up the keys to the Range Rover. "Are you off to this Herring Queen thing, then?"

"Aye, any chance of a hurl into town? We were going to walk, but Robbie's in a wee bit of a hurry and I don't fancy jogging the mile."

"With thighs like that?" Her eyes dipped down and back again, flirting from habit. "I'll not believe it. But sure, I can give you a lift, if you want."

She dropped us by Market Place, in front of the museum, where a boisterous group of children appeared to have completely taken over the small paved square, laughing and jostling and chasing one another with alarming energy. David and I moved to one side, joining the ranks of the parents who stood around the edges of Market Place, keeping well clear of the rampage.

As I stood watching Robbie run wild with the rest of them, his dark curls tossed anyhow, eyes shining happily, it suddenly struck me that our child would look very much like that—David's and mine. And then the implications of that one stray thought sank home, and I felt my face grow warm.

"Wave to my mother," David said, his own hand raised toward the corner of the square, where the windows of Saltgreens reflected the brilliant blue sky.

"Where is she?" I asked him, shielding my eyes from the sun as I looked up. "I can't see her."

"Neither can I. But she'll be up there somewhere. She doesn't miss much."

Smiling, I sent a general wave to all the watching windows, and turned again, expectantly. "So, if the children's races are run on Gunsgreen," I asked David, "then what are we doing here?"

"Waiting for the pipe band."

My eyes shone. "What, bagpipes?"

"Like them, do you?" He laughed at my reaction. "Well, you'll not have long to wait. They come at noon, to gather up the children and pipe them over the water."

"A pipe band," I repeated, unable to hide my delight. "Do we get to follow them, too?"

"Oh, aye. You can run in the races and all, if you want to. And if you're a good wee lassie," he promised, "I'll buy you an ice lolly, afterwards." His indulgent smile warmed me as he took hold of my hand, lacing his fingers through mine.

I smiled back, indescribably happy, then turned away again as a rising drone of music heralded the arrival of the pipe band.

Released from work, with no worries to think of, no ghosts to dog my steps, and the sun shining bright in a perfect blue sky, I felt younger than Robbie as we followed the skirling pipes down to the harbor and over the middle pier onto the level sweep of lawn that spread toward the sea from Gunsgreen House.

There were people everywhere. They ebbed and flowed around us like a tidal stream, in colorful confusion. David, still holding my hand, steered me expertly through them and found a spot where we could stand and cheer the races. There was Highland dancing as well, with its bright swirl of tartan and toe-tapping music. I couldn't remember when I'd had so much fun.

David appeared to enjoy himself, too, though he did cast a critical eye over Robbie's free lunch. "Soggy pie and yucky apple tart it was, in my day," he complained. "These kids are spoiled, now."

It surprised me how quickly the time passed. When the first fishing boats nosed their way into the harbor, I had to check my watch to convince myself it was, in fact, the middle of the afternoon.

David took firm hold of Robbie with his other hand and the three of us shifted with the crowd, to watch the Herring Queen set down upon the small red bridge at the end of the middle pier. She was a lovely girl, fresh-faced and fair, and her gown, though purple, was a decided improvement on Jeannie's.

Robbie fidgeted through the crowning ceremony, bored by the speeches, and finally tugged at David's sleeve. "Davy, Dad's looking for me."

The blue eyes slanted downwards. "Oh, aye? And where's your dad the now?"

"Over there." Robbie pointed across the harbor, toward the fish market.

"Right, we'll go and find him." David looked at me, apologetic. "You can wait here, if you'd rather, I'll not be more than a few minutes."

"No, it's all right," I said. "I'll come, too."

Brian McMorran, waiting in the shade of the fish market, didn't appear to be actively looking for his son; but then again, I reasoned, perhaps when both father and son had second sight, finding one another was a simple thing to do.

"Heyah, Dad!" Robbie went bouncing over. "Did you see the Herring Queen?"

"I did."

"Was Mum that bonny, when she was Herring Queen?"

"Your mother was the bonniest Herring Queen ever," said Brian, firmly. He propped his shoulder against a post and looked from David to myself. "Been taking good care of my boy, then, have you?"

"It's no use asking Verity," David said. "She's ages with Robbie today, and just as much trouble. I've had to keep the both of them from wandering off."

Relaxing slightly, Brian smiled and lit a cigarette. "I'll take one of 'em off your hands. I've a few hours yet before my work starts."

David glanced across the harbor at the *Fleetwing*'s gleaming red-and-white hull. "Are you taking her out tonight?"

"Planning on it," Brian answered, pitching his spent match into the black water. "I'm a man short at the moment, but I'm working on it."

David frowned. "Who's gone, then?"

"Mick." The boy from Liverpool that no one liked, as I recalled. Brian's shrug held no regret. "He took a swing at our cook, this morning. It was either me give Mick the shove, or Billy would have killed him." He pulled at his cigarette, blowing out smoke. "But I've got a lad lined up to take his place, so we might get a few days' good fishing in, before the weather turns. That front brewing down to the south hasn't shifted—it's still only sitting there, doing no harm."

I looked at him. "There's a storm coming?"

"Maybe," said Brian. "Might come north, or go elsewhere. You never can tell. Why, are you worried the *Fleetwing*'ll roll belly-up?" His eyes surveyed me mockingly as he exhaled a drifting smoke ring. "We've come a long way since the days of the Disaster—we've got sonar, radar, everything, these days. If a storm cloud so much as burps I've got the weather service on the phone to warn me."

"And if you *did* get stuck," said Robbie, "I could come out with the lifeboat men, to rescue you. I've been watching them real careful, like."

"Have you, now?" Brian's hard eyes softened on his son's upturned face.

"So," David asked Brian, "which of them do you want?"

"Eh?"

"You said you'd take one of these two off my hands," David said, standing between Robbie and me, "but you never did tell me which one."

"Oh. This one," Brian said, claiming his son with a hand on the boy's narrow shoulder. "He's not so much trouble."

"Right then, we're away. We want to catch the last part of the crowning, ken." David took my hand again like a teenage lover and, whistling tunelessly, led me back onto the middle pier. "See your swan," he said, pointing. "I wonder what he thinks of all this activity."

I ignored the swan. "Do you know," I told him, putting my head to one side in a pretense of thought, "I'm not sure which was the more insulting—having you offer me to Brian, or having him refuse me."

"Aye, well, if I'd thought he'd choose you I'd never have asked him."

"I mean, it's not as though I'm difficult . . ."

The tuneless whistling became a chuckle. "Maybe I like a difficult woman."

"Well, keep it up," I dared him, "and you'll find out just how—"

"Careful," he cut me off, putting a hand out to hold me back as a young man came vaulting over the *Fleetwing*'s railing onto the pier, landing directly in our path.

He looked an ordinary young man, with cropped ginger hair and a long face that was neither handsome nor ugly, but his eyes made me uneasy, and I didn't need to hear the Liverpool accent to recognize him as the lad that Brian's mate Billy had wanted to kill. "Did I give you a scare?" he asked, adjusting the bulging daysack slung over one shoulder. "Sorry."

"No harm done," David told him. "Only look where you're going, lad, next time."

"I'll do that." There was something almost evil in the way he smiled at David, and I felt cold until the young man had moved past us, heading down the pier. I watched him out of sight.

"And *that*, I take it," I said, "would be Mick."

"Aye." David arched an eyebrow. "Clearing off with his things, from the look of it. Either that, or he's been robbing Brian blind."

I frowned. "Should we tell Brian, do you think?"

"There's not much point. Brian can hardly report a theft to the police, now, can he? One look below deck and they'd have the boat swarming with excisemen," David said, grinning. "Come on, we'll be missing the crowning."

The crowning ceremony had, in fact, ended by the time we made our way back to Gunsgreen, and the Herring Queen was being settled in a horse-drawn carriage while the pipe band started up again, preparing to lead her away on parade.

David's eyes teased me for jigging in place. "If I'd kent you liked the pipes so much, I'd have taken lessons."

"It's not the bagpipes, really," I confessed, "so much as the kilts."

"Oh, aye? My mother," he informed me, "doesn't think most men these days should wear the kilt. She says they've not got the behind for it." I could easily picture her saying that, though one could hardly accuse David of being inadequate in that department. He caught me looking and smiled more broadly. "I'll wear mine tonight, if you want, to the ceilidh."

"What does it look like, the Fortune tartan?"

"There isn't one. I wear the Hunting Stewart," he informed me. "Sort of an all-purpose tartan, for those whose families never claimed their own."

But then he wasn't a Fortune anyway, I reminded myself. Not really. What did the Anglo-Irish have, I wondered, in place of the Scottish tartan? What was the mark of the Quinnell family?

"You're doing it again," said David.

"What?"

"Staring."

"Ah." There was no trace of Peter in his features, I thought. None at all. Except, perhaps, in the sure, unhurried way his eyes slid sideways, angled down to lock with mine.

"Keep looking at me like that," he promised, "and we'll not make it to the ceilidh."

I smiled. "And you call poor Adrian vain."

"Nothing vain about it. It's simple fact. I'm no saint," he said, pulling me close with one arm around my waist.

"Careful," I warned, as his head began to lower. "Your mother might be looking out her window."

David said something decidedly rude about his mother, and kissed me anyway.

The voice that spoke behind us wasn't Nancy Fortune's, but it nonetheless brought us apart like a pair of guilty schoolchildren.

"Verity, my dear," said Peter, his richly theatrical tone cresting the music with ease, "you do have the most appalling taste in men."

XXXIII

"No, no," he went on, casting a critical eye over David, "I'm sure you can do better than this. I'll admit, a Scotsman *is* a marginal improvement on an Englishman, but my dear, what you really want now is a nice Irish chap."

David grinned. "Away with your Irishmen."

"Scoff if you will. But if I were some thirty years younger, my boy, I'd leave you at the post." His suave smile proved the point as he came to stand at my other shoulder, his hands clasped behind his back. "So," he said, rocking back on his heels, "how are you enjoying your day so far?"

I assured him I was enjoying it very well. "We've been all over. I'm surprised we haven't bumped into you, before now."

"I've been well hidden." Peter angled a confiding glance at me. "The young people quite wore me out, I'm afraid, so I gave them the slip and went up to see Nancy. Had a cup of coffee and a very jolly game of chess. And of course, one can see everything from her room, you know, without having to endure the crowds. She's got a lovely big window."

David winked at me. "What did I tell you? My mother's a regular spy."

"Well," I remarked, "she has to do something with her

time, since the two of you insist on keeping her in the dark about the dig.''

Both of them turned to stare at me. ''My dear girl . . .'' Peter began, but I didn't let him finish.

''She's longing to know what we're doing. And I must say I think that it's dreadful, your shutting her out.''

Peter tried again. ''But her doctors . . .''

''Are idiots,'' I told him bluntly. ''She's not made of glass. I would think the frustration of *not* knowing would do more harm than the ounce of excitement you're liable to give her.''

Smiling, David lifted his gaze over my head to meet Peter's. ''She may have a point, there.''

''Perhaps,'' Peter said, ''but she doesn't know your mother, my boy. One might begin by simply telling Nancy things, but it wouldn't end there. She would want to be out in the field, you see. Just to have a better view of things, that's what she'd say. And the minute I turned my back she'd be in there with trowel in hand . . .''

''She could work with me,'' I offered. ''Nothing strenuous about what I do. And it certainly wouldn't be anymore tiring than the work she does for the museum.''

''She works two afternoons a week at the museum,'' David informed me. ''If we had her up to Rosehill she'd be there from dawn to dusk.''

''I just think you're both being very unkind.'' I said nothing further, but even I could feel the rigid set of my jaw as I turned to watch the Herring Queen parade pass by. Above my head, David and Peter exchanged glances again.

''We've been told,'' Peter said.

''So we have.''

''Perhaps . . . perhaps we ought to pay your mother a visit, after *this*''—Peter nodded at the passing parade—''is over. She'll have had enough of my company for one day, but I'm sure she'd be pleased to see the two of you.''

But when we stopped in at Saltgreens half an hour later, Nancy Fortune was not in her room.

One of the nursing staff, bustling past, paused long enough to explain. ''Oh, she took herself off home, for the weekend.

Said she wasn't too keen on the crowds, and with the ceilidh tonight there was bound to be noise. And anyway, she wanted to collect some things from her cottage, like.''

"Oh, aye?" David's face settled into a resigned expression. "Took the car, did she? The white car from the car park of the Ship?''

"Aye, that's right. Coughing a bit, it was, but she reckoned it would run all right once it got going." The nurse smiled broadly. "She's wonderfully thrawn, your mother, isn't she?''

I had to look that one up. My dog-eared dictionary informed me that a "thrawn" person was one who delighted in being difficult and obstinate, and David agreed that the word was an apt summing up of his mother's disposition. "You'll want to put a star beside that word," he told me, stabbing the page with a finger. "It's a good one for you to learn.''

"And why is that?''

He grinned. "Because you'll probably be hearing it a lot from me, this summer. My mother's not the only woman I ken who's wonderfully thrawn.''

Peter took the news less lightly. He stayed the nurse with one hand on her arm, his forehead creased in anxious lines. "But surely . . . that is, will she be all right up there, do you think? Alone?''

"Och, she'll be fine." The nurse smiled again, confident. "There's a telephone at her cottage, isn't there? And she's got her medication. It'll do her a world of good, getting away for a wee while—she's not one to sit watching the television all day.''

I did my best not to look smug as the three of us came out of Saltgreens and stood blinking in the sunlight. Peter's eyes adjusted first, and settled on the brilliant white walls of the Ship Hotel.

"I say," he said, forgetting his concern for David's mother, "does anyone fancy a drink?''

I wouldn't have minded a half-pint myself, but a glance at my watch convinced me I didn't have time. "If I want to be ready for the ceilidh tonight, I really ought to head back now. I still need to bathe and wash my hair, and I thought I might ring my sister, since it's Saturday—see how she's getting on.''

"Ah yes, your sister Alison," said Peter, with an understanding nod. He had the most amazing faculty for names, I thought.

"That's right. But you two go ahead and—"

"She's of an age with Fabia, as I recall." Peter looked to me for confirmation. "Yes? Oh, dear. Very brave of you, letting her live in your flat."

"You haven't met Alison. She thinks cleaning is jolly good fun. I doubt I'll recognize my flat when I get back to it.''

And then suddenly the very idea of getting back to my flat seemed bleak and unappealing, and I didn't want to think about it, and with a mumbled parting word I turned and started back along the harbor road.

"Oh," said my sister, "I nearly forgot. Howard rang."

"Howard?"

"From the museum. He said you'd know who he was."

"Oh right, *Howard*." My old friend and colleague, the pottery expert—the one who'd given me his opinion on our first finds here. "What did he want?"

"Just your number in Scotland. He said you gave it to him once but he's mislaid the paper it was written on, and could I give it him again?"

"So did you?"

"Heavens, no." Alison's tone was crisply practical. "He might have been a psychopath. One never knows, these days. No, I took his number instead, and promised to pass it on. Have you a pencil handy?"

I cradled the handset against my shoulder and took the number down. "Got it. Thanks. Is there anything else? No? Because I really ought to go and run my bath . . ."

"Got a hot date, tonight?"

"Yes I do, actually."

She paused. "Not with Adrian?"

"No."

"Good. With who, then?"

"With whom."

"Don't dodge the question."

"A dark handsome Scotsman," I said, "in a kilt."

Again the pause. "You are joking?"

"I'm not. He's taking me to a ceilidh."

"A what?"

"A ceilidh. It's a dance."

"Yes, I know what it is," said Alison. "I'm just surprised you're going to one. You don't dance."

"I do, too."

"Well, you'd best have someone taking photographs," was her advice, "or else I won't believe it. And while you're at it, you might take a picture of your mystery man in the kilt."

"Don't you believe in him, either?"

"Of course. But I do have a thing about men wearing kilts," my sister admitted. She sighed. "I saw *Braveheart* five times."

I laughed and rang off, thought for a moment, then dialed Howard's number. He was out. Leaving the number for Rosehill on his answerphone, I put the receiver down again and, having done my duty by everyone, went up to have my bath.

The ceilidh was enormous fun. At least, that was my overall impression . . . I had a vague awareness of flushed faces and riotous laughter and wild, reeling music played so loudly that it rumbled in my breast like thunder. I danced until I couldn't breathe, until my head felt light and the room rolled and my legs could no longer support me.

And then it was David's arms supporting me, his shoulders warm beneath my hands, the walls and bright lights spinning past his dark head. I breathed again. The music slowed. People pressed in on all sides, but I saw no one else. Only David.

I might have blamed the kilt. He did look smashing in the blended green hues of the Hunting Stewart tartan, with his white cotton shirt clinging damp to his back and the sleeves rolled up over his biceps. Only a Scotsman, Highlander or no, could wear a kilt and look like he'd been born to it. It was as if, by trading in his trousers for a length of tartan, David somehow tapped the pride and wild passion of his ancestors. He seemed to drift in time, not altogether of this century, and his gaze now and then held the glint of a warrior.

Yes, I thought, I might have blamed the kilt; but that wouldn't have been entirely honest. It was the man, and not the clothes, that held me fascinated.

He stopped revolving, and the blue eyes smiled. Lifting one hand from my waist he brushed back a strand of my hair that had worked itself loose from its plait, and I saw his lips moving, soundlessly.

"What?"

This time I caught the words. "Too many people."

"What people?" I asked, and the smile touched his mouth.

"Come on," he said, turning me toward the door, "let's get some air."

Outside the night was clear and warm, and the wind, for once, was still. The harbor lay like glass beneath a moon that needed one small sliver yet to make it full. High tide had come and gone six hours ago, and the *Fleetwing* had slipped her moorings and gone with it. In her place, a small pale specter floated on the water. It might have been a mere reflection of the moon ... until it tilted up and turned and stretched a searching neck along the blackness. The swan.

"David." I stopped walking, and grabbed his arm. "Look at that." A second ghost had glided from the shadows, neck arched smoothly, wings at rest. It met the first and touched it and the two moved on together. "Oh David, look—he's finally found a mate."

David looked and said nothing. After a long moment he smiled faintly, and turned his face from the harbor, and started walking again, his arm settling warmly across my shoulders.

I didn't really notice which direction we were taking, but since David was going there, I went, too. After several long minutes the pavement ended and the ground became rougher. I sensed that the sea was below us now, the waves kicking spray on the rocks and the beach.

Clearing my mind with an effort, I took a proper look around. "Where are we?"

"Up on Eyemouth Fort."

Of course, I thought. That massive spear of land that jutted out into the sea; the red cliffs topped with long green grass. David's childhood thinking-place.

It didn't take genius to know there had once been buildings here—some of the ridges were rather steep. "Mind the haggis hole," warned David, as he helped me over a tufted hillock.

"A haggis," I told him, refusing to bite, "is a sausage in a sheep's stomach."

"Aye, well," he said, straight-faced, "you'll ken differently when you've stepped on one. Vicious wee things."

I sighed, and stepped around the hole of the imaginary haggis, and in the shelter of the second ridge he sat, and pulled me down beside him.

We were more lying than sitting, I suppose, our backs fitted to the angle of the grass-covered slope. I tipped my head back and watched the stars glittering into infinity.

David stayed silent, hands linked behind his head. And then he said simply: "Verity."

"Yes?"

"What are you going to do about Lazenby's job offer?"

I rolled my head sideways to look at him. "What?"

"You ken what I mean. Alexandria."

"How do you know about that?"

"Adrian told me."

Reminding myself to smack Adrian next time I saw him, I pointed out to David that I hadn't actually been offered *any* job, as yet. "Lazenby hasn't been in touch, he hasn't asked me—"

"When he does," said David calmly, interrupting. "What will you tell him?"

For a moment, in silence, I studied his profile.

Then I said: "If he'd asked me two months ago, I think I would have said yes."

"And now?"

"Now I'm not sure." I shrugged, and pulled a clump of grass with idle fingers.

"And why is that?"

I tossed the grass away and sighed. "Look, I'm never very brilliant at this sort of thing . . ."

He smiled faintly at my choice of words. "Happens a lot, does it?"

"No." The word came out of its own accord, and once out, it couldn't be taken back again, so I swallowed hard and repeated it. "No, it doesn't. In fact, it's never . . . well," I stumbled, as he slowly turned his head to look at me, "that is to say, I've never felt . . ." But that sentence faltered as well, so I gave up trying.

He held my gaze a long while, silently, his eyes turned silver by the moonlight. And then he stood, and held a hand out. "Time we were getting back," he said.

"David . . ."

"I've said I'm no saint. I can't stay here like this and not touch you," he told me, his tone carefully even. "And fond as I am of the Fort, I would rather our first time took place in a bed, if it's all the same to you."

I thought of his camp bed, and of my twin-bedded room at Rosehill, and of the other people who were constantly around us, and I shook my head in argument. "But David . . ."

"Some things," he said, "are worth waiting for."

The Fort path led out past the caravan park, and a snatch of music blaring from a radio gave way, as we walked, to the muted sound of a couple quarreling. David kept possession of my hand, whistling softly under his breath as though he were well pleased. As we passed the last row of caravans he slowed his step, and the whistling ceased. "There you are," he said quietly. "What did I tell you?"

Two figures were standing locked in an embrace alongside the furthest caravan. The man I couldn't see too well, but he was clearly kissing Fabia. One couldn't mistake her, even at this distance.

David nudged me along. "See? My mother is always right."

"Hard luck on poor Adrian."

"Aye." David smiled. "Still, I reckon he'll find some comfort in that redheaded lass he was trying to pull at the ceilidh."

"I missed that, actually. How was he doing?"

"Not bad. Did you really not notice?" He raised a dark eyebrow. "He was being dead obvious about it."

In all honesty, the entire Royal Family could have been dancing a reel beside us and I wouldn't have noticed, but I didn't tell him that.

He didn't take the road toward the harbor, but led me uphill instead, along a curve of darkened houses, and out again onto the road that would take us back to Rosehill.

I didn't pay too much attention to our walk home. One minute we were crossing the motorway at the edge of Eyemouth and the next we were turning up the long drive, in companionable silence. The windows of Rose Cottage were dark, and up at the house the only light still burning was the one over the front door. Peter, if he'd come home before us, had gone to bed.

David didn't kiss me goodnight at the door. He followed me into the entrance hall, and up the curve of smooth stone stairs, and when I turned in the middle of my bedroom he was still there behind me, putting the cat out.

"David," I asked him, low, "what are you doing?"

He glanced over his shoulder, as though it were plainly self-evident. "I'm locking the door."

I heard the key catch. And then he was coming toward me and I found myself suddenly at a loss for words, nervous in a way I hadn't been in years. I was trembling—actually trembling—when he touched my hair, his fingers working to undo the plait, arranging the long strands over my shoulders.

XXXIV

The horses woke me in the dark hour before dawn. Snorting and stamping, they thundered past beneath my window and were swallowed by the lonely field and the wind that wept through the chestnut tree like a wandering lament.

I shivered into wakefulness, and forced my leaden eyelids open, momentarily confused by the heavy weight of something warm across my waist, the quiet even breathing close beside me on the pillow. And then I remembered.

"David."

He shifted at the whispered word, his face against my hair. "Mmm?"

"Did you hear that?"

But it was obvious he hadn't. Still half asleep, he tightened his arm around my waist to gather me closer against him, his powerful body shielding me from harm. "Whatever it is," he murmured, soothingly, "it'll have to come through me, first. Go to sleep."

And closing my eyes, I turned my face against his shoulder and felt all my fears flow from me while his strong and steady heartbeat drowned the shrieking of the wind.

It might have been a minute or a lifetime later when I heard Jeannie's voice calling my name. She sounded close,

I thought drowsily. A good thing David locked the door, or else . . .

"Come on, Verity—waken up, now." Jeannie's hand jostled my arm and my eyes flew open with a guilty start to focus on her face. She shook her head, her expression neither shocked nor judgmental, and crossed to draw the curtains. "Jings! You do sleep like the dead."

The warm weight across my stomach shifted and stretched, and looking down I saw that it was Murphy, rolling over on his side to test his claws against the blankets. He had not quite recovered from the indignity of being chucked out of my room last night, and his level stare was icily aloof. Beside me, the mattress was empty and cold.

"It's nine o'clock," said Jeannie, briskly. "Peter said to knock you up at nine."

Closing my eyes again, I let my head drop back against the pillows. "On a Sunday?"

"He didn't want you missing all the excitement."

"Kind of him," I mumbled. Then, as her words began to penetrate: "What excitement?"

"D'ye never watch the news?" she asked me. "They were talking about it all yesterday, ken—that big storm out over the Channel."

"Oh right, Brian said something . . ." I frowned, trying to remember what he'd said, exactly. "It was just sitting there, wasn't it? Not moving."

"Aye, well, it's moved. Can you not hear the change in the wind? It'll be here by noon, I should think."

"The storm's coming here?" I opened my eyes as the realization struck, and levered myself onto my elbows. "God, the excavations . . . we'll have to cover—"

"It's already been done," she informed me. "Davy and Peter and Dad did all that, afore breakfast. And they're moving the students up into the stables, in case those wee tents don't stand up to the storm."

"Is there *room* in the stables?"

"Oh, aye. In the common room, like. Peter," she confided, "would have put them all downstairs in his own sitting room, I think, only Davy told him that was daft. It's only for one night, and they'll have more fun up there, without us old folks hanging round.''

"I've no doubt." Turning my head, I looked at the dappled sunlight dancing through my window, and the sliver of blue sky that glinted beside the great chestnut tree. "Will it be a bad storm, do you think?''

Jeannie nodded. "Brian brought the boat back in at half-past two this morning, and there's not much makes my Brian cautious. Oh," she said, as an afterthought, turning at the door, "you do mind that it's Davy's birthday, don't you?''

As if I needed reminding, I thought, stretching my weary limbs beneath the sheets. Hopeful that Jeannie wouldn't see the tiny flush that touched my cheeks, I nodded, feigning nonchalance. "He's thirty-seven, isn't he?''

"Aye. Not that you'd ken that from looking at him." She smiled indulgently. "He's been bouncing about like a lad Robbie's age, all the morning.''

Where he had found the energy to bounce, I didn't know. I felt rather deliciously lazy, myself. Simply rising and dressing and brushing my teeth took me all of twenty minutes, and my fingers were so clumsy with my plait that in the end I gave up the effort. The wind caught the loose strands as I stepped outside, and blew them stinging across my eyes.

I nearly walked straight into Adrian's red Jaguar, parked at a crazy angle just a few steps from the house, the keys still dangling in the ignition. Adrian had been quite cautious with his keys since the night we'd sat up in the field, and this was hardly his usual parking technique, but when I caught up with him in the Principia a few minutes later, I saw the reason for his carelessness. He put me in mind of a stylish corpse—deathly white and draped artistically across his desk, his arms outstretched.

"Late night?" I asked him.

"You have no idea.''

"What are you doing here, then?''

Raising his head, he propped it up with a hand and half opened one eye. "Herring Queen.''

"I'm sorry?''

"Bloody Herring Queen," he spelled it out more clearly. "Herds of people milling about, underneath my window. It's impossible to sleep."

No one else was around at the moment, so I filled my coffee cup and took my chair. "Where is everybody?"

Adrian shrugged. "I haven't the faintest idea, but I'm sure they'll be back. They've been in and out all bloody morning . . . every time I start to nod off."

"Very thoughtless of them," I agreed.

Hearing the smile in my voice, Adrian opened his eye wider, to stare at me suspiciously. "You're looking rather ragged yourself, my love."

"Am I?"

"Mmm. Almost as ragged as our Mr. Fortune. He's—"

"Adrian," I interrupted, not listening, "how long have you been sitting here?"

He consulted his watch. "About an hour and a half. Why?"

Frowning down into the drawer of my desk, I pushed aside a ballpen to get a better look at the tiny gold medallion gleaming in my pen tray. The Fortuna pendant. "You didn't see who put this in here, I suppose?"

He squinted as I held it up. "Let's see . . . it might have been that Roman chap. Big man . . . a bit transparent . . ."

"Don't."

My tone surprised him. "Darling, I'm only joking."

"Well, don't. Not about that."

"Then no, I didn't see anyone putting that thing in your desk," he said. "But that doesn't mean anything. Even I have difficulty seeing with my eyes shut, and a pack of burglars could have stripped the finds room bare without my noticing."

It must have been one of my students, I told myself. They both had keys to the finds room. Or it might have been Peter, or David. But still . . .

"Here's the watchdog," Adrian announced. "Ask him."

Kip came dancing through the arching door with energy to spare, half running down the aisle between the desks to check that I was really there, then bounding back to watch Wally and Peter maneuver a bundle of sleeping bags into the room.

"Dear, oh, dear," Peter said, when he caught sight of me. "You ought to be in bed, Verity."

When I reminded him that Jeannie had woken me on his own orders, Peter, as endearingly contradictory as ever, dismissed that as irrelevant.

"Yes, I know," he said patiently, "but I hadn't *seen* you then, had I? And you ought to have known that once I'd seen you I would send you back to bed."

"Well, I'm up now. So there." Smiling to soften the comment, I held up the golden pendant. "You didn't put this in my desk drawer, by any chance?"

"No, I'd imagine David did that."

"David?"

Peter nodded. "He found it on *his* desk, as I recall, but as none of us had our keys to the finds room handy he must have thought your desk was the safest option. Rather careless of the students," he remarked. "I really ought to have a word with them about security."

"Ye canna be too careful," Wally said. He'd finished stacking the sleeping bags in a temporary pile against the wall, and straightened now to light a cigarette. "I saw a bluidy thievin' Hielanman go creepin' past the hoose this very morn."

Peter's eyebrows arched. "Did you, by God? A Highlander? Wearing a kilt, was he?"

"Aye. Ye'd best count yer coos."

Peter, who had no cows to count, took the advice with a solemn nod, his face perfectly straight. If I hadn't looked at his eyes, I'd have thought him serious. But Wally had no such pretensions. He grinned broadly as he drew on the cigarette, and sent me a wink that made Adrian swivel his head, his gaze narrowing.

"Now," said Peter, turning his attention to the common room, "I'm wondering if we shouldn't bring the camp beds up, as well? Davy," he addressed the man just struggling through the doorway with another load of sleeping bags, "what do you think?"

"What do I think of what?"

"Camp beds."

"Christ, no," David said, with feeling. "They're students, Peter—they *like* sleeping on the floor." He dumped his armful of sleeping bags and turned to me, his smile warming the air between us. "Morning."

"Good morning."

Peter, looking the picture of innocence, was preparing to say something clever, and Adrian, aware that he was missing something, was glowering across at me, when I was suddenly saved by—of all people—Fabia. Waltzing through the stable door, her blond hair fetchingly ruffled by the fierce rising wind, she provided a welcome distraction. Adrian's eyes left my face like a compass needle swinging to magnetic north.

But she didn't appear to notice. She'd come looking for David. "Your mother just rang," she said. "She says she's having trouble with the car, and can you please go up and get her."

"What, now? Right this minute?"

Fabia nodded. "She didn't sound too keen on being stuck up there alone, with this storm coming."

"Nonsense," Peter said. "Nancy's rather fond of storms, as I recall. She likes the thunder."

David smiled. "All the same, I'd best not keep my mother waiting, not when I've been summoned."

"You can take the Range Rover, if you like," said Fabia.

"Aye, all right." Turning, he held out his hand. "Give us the keys, then, and I'm away."

Brian came through the doorway as David went out, and shuddered as a sudden gust of wind shook the building. "Jesus," he said, ducking his head to light a cigarette, "it's worse up here than it is at the harbor."

Peter arched a solicitous eyebrow. "How's the boat?"

"Oh, the boat's fine," said Brian. "But Billy's a wreck. We had the bloody Customs and Excise officer around this morning. Scared poor Billy half to death. Good job we'd only been out a few hours—the boat was clean. And the last shipment's safely up here, where nobody would think to . . ." He suddenly stopped, and his head came up.

I'd seen that expression before, I thought—that strange, fixed expression. I'd seen it on Robbie.

Fabia, beneath his stare, swallowed apprehensively. "What?"

"You stupid cow," he told her, slowly. "You bloody stupid cow."

Adrian stood up, protectively. "Brian . . ."

"I'd figured it was Mick who grassed," said Brian, heedless of the interruption, seeing only Fabia. "But it was you put the officer onto the *Fleetwing.*" His tone was certain of the fact, and I remembered what little I'd heard of Fabia's telephone conversation yesterday, in the front hall. *Tomorrow morning*, she'd said. Had she been ringing the Customs and Excise then, telling them to inspect Brian's boat? But why?

Brian had his own theory. "What, angry with me, were you, for giving your boyfriend the shove?"

"Her boyfriend . . ." Adrian frowned.

"Oh, aye. She and young Mick have been having it off for a month or more, now. You and I," he told Adrian, "outlived our usefulness."

The storm was drawing closer. I could feel the pricking heat of it, the dark oppressive heaviness that dulled the dead air around me. Peter, standing by the wall, shook his head slightly. "Brian, my dear boy, this hardly seems . . ."

"I didn't make that call because of Mick," said Fabia, rising to Brian's bait. "And I never wanted them to search your stupid boat. I wanted them to come *here.*" Her eyes freezing over, she turned to face Peter. "They will come, you know—they'll be on their way now. And they'll find what you're keeping down in the cellar. I can just see the headlines, can't you?" The tone of her voice was pure venom. "And what will Connelly say, do you think, when he finds you've been using the dig as a cover for smuggling?"

Peter's eyes held a terrible sadness, like a god who must witness the fall of an angel. "Fabia, why?"

"Because," she said, "I want to see you suffer."

Adrian, shocked, burst out: "Fabia!" and she wheeled on him in a temper.

"You don't know anything about it!" she accused him. "He killed my father, understand? He made my father's life a living hell, and then he killed him."

Peter seemed to age before my eyes, his features collapsing with the weight of painful memory. "Fabia," he tried to explain, "your father was ill . . ."

"He was not."

"He was ill but I loved him."

"Liar!" She hissed the word. "You never loved Daddy as much as you loved your precious work, your precious reputation. He told me." Her eyes, filled with hate, found her grandfather's stricken ones. "He told me everything."

The lights flickered briefly and I suddenly realized how dark it had grown outside—the shadows closed around us and vanished again as the warm glow hummed to life. And then the sky exploded, and the storm came down like vengeance.

XXXV

Jeannie, blown into the big room on a wet and swirling wind, seemed scarcely to notice the tension. She was too busy looking at Brian. "Where's Robbie?"

Forgetting the drama in progress, he turned. "Is he not with you?"

She shook her head. "I thought you had him down the harbor."

The thunder crashed directly overhead, and Kip cringed under my chair, whining. I'd forgotten him completely. I reached down to stroke his head, reassuring him softly.

"Right." Brian crushed the dead cigarette under his heel. "I'll go and have a look. Did you ring around his friends?"

"I couldn't," she said. "It's this wind, see. Our phone line's been out of order since breakfast."

"It can't be out," said Adrian. "Fortune's mother rang not long ago, from her cottage."

But Jeannie disputed the fact. "She couldn't have. I've been checking the line myself, every ten minutes, like."

"But Fabia said . . ."

"No one rang," Jeannie told him a second time, positive.

In the space of an instant my own mind sifted through a hundred things that Fabia had said, and fitted the statements together like the pieces of a jigsaw puzzle. I didn't like the picture that was forming.

Above all, I remembered her saying that the perfect revenge on one's enemy would be to take from him everything and everyone he loved, yet make him go on living. Everything Peter loved . . . well, that would be his work, his reputation. She'd already tried to take that. And as for the "everyone" . . . My mind balked, not wanting to follow that thought, but I forced it.

If Fabia knew what her father had known—if he had, as she said, told her everything—then she knew about Peter and Nancy. Was she trying to harm Nancy, somehow? And had she needed to get David out of the way, first, by inventing that telephone call; by sending David out alone on the road to St. Abbs?

The storm rose and wailed like a living thing, beating its fists on the shuddering walls, and I clenched my fist, convulsively. *The road.*

The road is dangerous.

"Oh, God," I breathed, as the shred of doubt grew and swelled to certainty.

My head jerked round, to stare at the tiny gold medallion sitting atop my disordered papers. The Fortuna pendant. It had been on David's desk, this morning—that's what Peter had told me. *David's* desk.

Oh, how could I have been so stupid? Stupid, stupid—thinking that the warning was for me. It was David that the Sentinel had tried to warn. David who had found the pendant in the first place, not by chance. What had Robbie said? *It's for protection. You don't understand.*

And now, too late, I understood.

I understood why Fabia had chosen the nasty, unlikeable Mick to be her latest boyfriend. As Brian had told Adrian, Fabia's interest only lasted so long as the men were useful. And Mick, at the moment, was terribly useful. She needed a violent, unprincipled man to help her destroy what her grandfather loved. She needed a man who could murder.

And now that same man, I felt sure, was somewhere near St. Abbs, where Nancy Fortune—an old woman with a weak heart—sat waiting out the storm in her cottage, alone and unprotected. And where David, unaware of the danger, would shortly walk into an ambush.

I was not aware of moving, but I heard my own voice saying "No" quite loudly, and somebody reached to take my arm, but I pushed them away and was through the great arched doorway before anyone could stop me. Kip howled after me, and I thought I heard Adrian shouting my name, but the sound of the wind swallowed both of them and I was running, running, the rain in my eyes and the bitter wind tearing the breath from my throat.

The Jaguar roared to life at the first twist of the dangling key. I hauled at the wheel, spinning gravel, and took the drive at twice the prudent speed.

The students had abandoned their tents in the downpour and were scurrying across the road toward the safety of Rosehill, holding their coats above their heads and screaming with laughter. I swerved to go around them and the bonnet kissed the big stone gatepost with an ugly grating sound, but I didn't slow the car at all and two of the students were forced to jump clear.

I barely noticed.

I was too busy praying. "Please," I whispered to the furies that were beating on the windscreen. "Please let me be wrong."

The rain was so thick I could scarcely see and the windows steamed, but I kept my foot to the floor through the village of Coldingham, taking the hills and the turnings blindly, letting the tires shriek their protest through a stunning arc of spray.

Biting my lip until I tasted blood, I tightened my grip on the steering wheel. "Please let me be wrong."

But as I came out onto the Coldingham Moor, the wiper blades swept cleanly through the pounding flood of water and I saw what I'd been fearing.

He had lost control of the Range Rover, and it had rolled, coming to rest on its battered roof. One metal door, bizarrely twisted, lay drowning in the river that had been the road. What remained of the windscreen was pure white with splinters, like smashed river ice. There was no sign of life.

The Jaguar spun out as I hit the brakes, and I covered my face with my hands. When I lowered them a minute later, they were wet. The car had come to rest against a rail fence at the far edge of the road, directly across from the battered Range Rover. I could see the empty seats. Fumbling with my door latch, I stumbled out, uncaring of the storm.

"David!" I screamed in panic, raising my hands in a futile defense against the lashing of the wind. He wasn't in the Range Rover. My hands scraped raw against the battered metal as I pulled the vehicle apart in search of him, but he wasn't there. Sobbing now, my body trembling with shock and pain, I turned away and staggered through the tangle of gorse and thorn at the side of the road. "David," I called again, but the storm stole my cry and I sank to the ground, defeated.

My hair was streaming water and I couldn't see before me and my hands made bloody marks upon my water-plastered clothes. The wind passed through me like a frozen blade. I shivered.

A deep voice called me, indistinct. I raised an anguished face. But it wasn't David. It wasn't David.

It wasn't anybody. A jagged spear of lightning showed the empty moor, the blowing thorn. But as the thunder rolled and died I heard the voice again, strangely hollow, as though straining to reach me across a great distance. "Claudia."

Struggling to resolve itself, the faint transparent outline of a man took form and faded in the slashing silver rain. And as I blinked against the stinging wetness, he made a supreme effort and his shadow reappeared. Dark eyes, not wholly human, met mine, softened.

He raised what might have been an arm, a hand, as if he meant to touch me, and I saw the effort this time, saw him fight to frame the words. *"Non lacrimas, Claudia."*

Don't cry.

I felt a gentle trail of ice across my cheek, as if he sought to brush the tears away, and then I half-believed the shadow smiled. *"Non lacrimas,"* he said again, and melted in the rain.

Afraid to move, I went on staring at the place where he had been, unmindful of the screaming wind, the dark and rolling sky. The lightning split the clouds again, and flashed across the roughened ground, and all at once I felt the breath tear from me in a sob of pure relief.

A man was coming across the moor.

He looked enormous to my eyes, a great dark giant moving over bracken and thorn with an effortless stride. It was as if the hourglass had tipped and the sands were spilling back and I was sitting on the bus again, and watching for the first time while he came to me across the wild moor.

He was carrying something, wrapped up in a bright yellow mac. Some animal, with legs that dangled.

I saw him stop, and standing square against the storm he stared at the Jaguar, its bright red bonnet buried at a crazy angle in the rail fence. Then his chin jerked upwards and I knew he'd seen me, crouched amid the wreckage of the Range Rover, and even as I raised my voice to call him he began to run.

I couldn't seem to let him go. We were safe inside the Jaguar, warm and safe and dripping on the leather, but my hands had fastened to his wet shirt and I couldn't let him go.

David, one-handed, had made use of Adrian's cellphone to check that his mother was safe, and now he rolled me sideways so he could replace the handset in its cradle. We were both of us wedged in the passenger seat, but he didn't seem to mind. Flipping a lever he slid the seat back to make room for his legs, and settled me against his chest, one arm wrapped warm around my shoulders.

The bundle he'd brought with him sat propped on the driver's seat, small head lolled sideways, and I reached my hand to smooth one darkly dripping curl away from Robbie's pallid face. He was unhurt, and breathing normally, and tucked within the folds of David's raincoat he slept soundly, deeply, unaware.

Which was just as well, I thought. The things I'd said to David as we'd clung to each other outside in the rain . . . such things were not intended to be overheard by anyone. Least of all an eight-year-old.

I frowned. "You're sure he's all right?"

"Aye. Though how a wee laddie like that got himself all the way out here . . ." David put his own hand out to pull the folds of the raincoat tighter around Robbie's shoulders, then closed his fingers around my own and drew my hand back, away from the child's face. "You'll wake him if you keep that up."

I stopped fussing, and snuggled against David's heartbeat. "It's only that he's so pale."

"I'm the one that should be pale. I nearly ran him over. The lad bolted clear across the road in front of me—fair scared me to death. I barely had time to see that it was Robbie afore I rolled the Rover, and after I got myself clear of that mess, I had to go chasing after him. I couldn't leave him out on the moor in this storm," he explained. I felt his chin turn against my hair as his gaze drifted back to the sleeping boy. "I wanted to take my hand off his face, to begin with. I might have been killed."

His voice trailed away and his chin shifted a fraction further, so he could look to where the moor stretched out toward St. Abbs, beyond the fogging window.

"I might have been killed," he repeated.

I held him tighter. I had explained, as best I could, what had happened, but I knew my explanation had left much to be desired. My words had tumbled out in no specific order, incoherent, a confusing narrative that leapt from Fabia to the Fortuna pendant, with yawning gaps between. I'd have to do a better job, I told myself, and sort things out more clearly, so that he could understand them.

But not now. Not now. There would be time enough for talking, when we all got back to Rosehill.

"David?"

"Aye?"

"I think I've lost the car keys."

He laughed. "Not to worry. They'd not be much use, from what I can see. We're well stuck in this fence."

I moved my head, to look out in dismay at the crumpled bonnet of the Jaguar, but David's hand in my hair drew me back again, holding me close while the gusting wind set the car rocking. "It's all right," he assured me. "If I ken my mother, we'll not have to wait long for the cavalry."

He barely got the sentence out before the blue lights flashed behind us and the storm itself was drowned beneath the stronger wail of sirens.

REQUIESCAT

> ...and trust
> With faith that comes of self-control,
> The truths that never can be proved
> Until we close with all we loved

Tennyson, "In Memoriam", CXXX

XXXVI

The storm had passed by teatime but the sullen sky, flat gray and dreary, pressed heavily upon the sodden fields and dripping walls of Rosehill.

"For God's sake," Peter said, "do put a light on, somebody." Stretching himself in his cracked leather armchair he took up his half-finished drink and settled his free hand on Murphy's black back. "I've had enough of shadows, for one day."

I reached to switch the lamp on, and the red walls warmed. The gray cat Charlie, on my lap, stirred and blinked in the sudden light, then burrowed her small face against my leg with a tiny sigh. She and I, I thought, were rather the odd ones out in this room—two females being suffered by a gathering of men. But then this was, essentially, a man's room. Wally, with his feet up in one corner, eyes half closed against the drifting haze of his cigarette, looked perfectly at home here, as did David, slouched beside me on the old worn leather sofa, one arm slung lazily along my shoulders while the other cradled Robbie close against his other side.

Robbie, wide awake now, showed no ill effects from his morning's adventure. He couldn't remember leaving Rosehill, or walking cross-country to Coldingham Moor—a trip that must surely have taken him two and a half hours, by David's estimate. Nor could he even clearly tell us why he'd done it. "The Sentinel needed me," was the only explanation he could give.

I suspected that the Sentinel, lacking human hands, had needed Robbie to fetch the Fortuna medallion from the finds room, as well, and leave it on David's desk. But Robbie couldn't recall being in the Principia, either. His memory of the day's events were blurred at best. "Was I really in Mr. Sutton-Clarke's car?"

"Indeed you were." Adrian, lounging in a corner chair beyond the reach of lamplight, chased down another headache tablet with a swallow of stiff gin. "I've got the waterstains on the seats to prove it."

Adrian, I thought, was bearing up remarkably well, all things considered. I'd expected histrionics when we'd arrived at Rosehill with the Jaguar in tow, but Adrian had merely looked in mournful silence at the dents and scratches, then he'd sighed and turned to David. "Well, at least *you're* in one piece. That's something, anyway." With which surprising speech he'd left us, and gone back inside the house.

David had raised his eyebrows. "What was that, d'ye think?"

"A beginning," I'd told him, linking my arm through his with a smile.

Adrian, I knew, had meant it as a peacemaking of sorts; a gesture of conciliation and acceptance. Not that he and David were ever likely to become firm friends, I admitted, as I looked from one face to the other now in the cozy redwalled sitting room, but still . . . I had seen stranger things today, and could no longer call anything impossible.

The comforting thing about the past, to me, had always been that it repeated itself in predictable patterns. One knew which result to expect from which circumstance. But today, here at Rosehill, the past had come loose like a runaway cart and the present ran on in confusion, a horse still in harness with nothing behind it and no one controlling the reins.

And so Adrian, who had always read me the riot act if I so much as slammed his car door, was now sitting across from me, holding his tongue. And Wally, who had always hated Brian, had spent the past hour praising what his son-in-law had done.

And what Brian had done, I decided, was in itself a fine example of how the patterns of the past had been disrupted. Brian, selfish and conceited, who lived at his own whims for pleasure and gain, had today risked his own neck to save Peter's. Once word had reached him that Robbie was safe, he had set about clearing the cellar of anything incriminating. At the height of the storm and in three separate carloads, he'd shuttled the crates of vodka and cigarettes from Rosehill House to their new hiding place, in the town. "And efter a' that," Wally'd told us, complaining, "the dampt exciseman didna even come."

But at least, if they did come, the house would be clean. There'd be no damage done, now, to Peter's credibility—no scandalous headlines, no ruinous charges. The only news would be that Peter Quinnell's granddaughter, still suffering from nerves after her father's suicide, had been admitted to an undisclosed private hospital, where she'd be receiving counseling and treatment.

"So it was Fabia," said David, "who did all that messing about with the computers."

"And mislaid Peter's notebook," I added. "And told Connelly about our ghost hunt in the field, that night, saying it was all Peter's idea. She would have done anything, I think, to be sure our dig didn't succeed."

Peter, from his corner, gently reminded me that he, and not the dig, had been the true target of Fabia's campaign of sabotage. "At the end of the day," he said, "it all comes down to her wanting to discredit me, to see me—as she put it—suffer."

Had she been able to see him now, I thought, she would have felt quite satisfied. The lines of suffering were still etched plainly in his handsome face, for all of us to see. Still, Peter, I reflected, had remained consistent in his actions. Saddened but unbowed, he'd spent the afternoon dispensing drinks and comfort, telephoning doctors, taking care of everything. It was, as Nancy Fortune said, his nature—taking care of things.

"Good heavens," I said, suddenly remembering. "Your mother."

David looked at me. "Whose mother?"

"Yours. We forgot all about her. She'll still be waiting for us to come and fetch her at the cottage, won't she?"

"Aye, well," David shrugged, "I can't do much of anything until Jeannie and Brian come back—I've no car."

Peter eyed him thoughtfully. "I really think, my boy, it might be best to let someone else collect your mother. You've had bad luck with borrowed cars, today."

David raised his drink defensively. "It wasn't me that wrapped the Jaguar around a fence post."

"No, but it was your fault Verity drove out there in the first place," Peter pointed out, smoothly logical. "So you see . . ."

Robbie interrupted, twisting to look up at David's face. "You didn't take the necklace," he said, as if that explained everything. "You were supposed to wear it, like."

Besieged on all sides, David drank his whiskey with a faint smile. "Aye, well, next time we're talking to your Sentinel, Robbie, you mind me to tell him why no self-respecting archaeologist wears artifacts."

"Why?" Robbie asked.

Peter explained. "Because we'd damage them. We shouldn't dig things up at all, unless we can take care of them." He was silent a moment, mulling something over. "Can he really hear us, when we speak? The Sentinel, I mean."

Robbie nodded. "He can see you and all. Only you've got to speak Latin, or he doesn't ken what you're saying. *I* can say 'hello'," he announced proudly.

"Well done," said Peter vaguely, deep in thought. The crunch of tires on the gravel roused him, and he raised his head expectantly. "Ah, here are Jeannie and Brian now."

Jeannie looked relieved to have the whole thing over with. "It wasn't so bad," she said. "It was just an identification, like."

"It did take us a while, though," Brian admitted. "Just to be sure, with the bandages and all. What the devil did your mother hit him with, anyway?"

"Teapot," said David. "Her famous tin teapot."

Peter smiled, faintly. "And I rather suspect it was full at the time."

Brian winced. "Bloody hell!"

"Will they have enough," asked Adrian, "to make the charges stick?"

"Oh, aye," Brian nodded.

"What makes you so certain?"

"Well, for one thing," said Brian, leaning back with a thoughtful expression, "the police are going to find Mick's caravan is filled near to bursting with black market vodka and fags."

David looked at him. "Brian, you didn't."

"I did. He's a right sodding bastard, and he needs to get more than your mother's blinking teapot in his eye."

Peter stopped swirling the vodka in his glass, and glanced at Jeannie, suddenly remembering. "I do hate to ask you this, my dear, because I know you've just got back, but would you mind very much driving over to fetch Nancy?"

"Of course not." Picking up the car keys, she held out her free hand. "Come on, Robbie, let's go get Granny Nan."

"And don't take her to Saltgreens. You're to bring her back here," Peter said. "For dinner. It's high time she had a look at what we've been up to."

So much for Peter remaining predictable, I thought. Even Jeannie stared at him for a long moment, and her slowly spreading smile was beautiful. "Aye," she said, "I think you're right."

"Any chance of a lift into town?" Adrian asked, rising with a self-indulgent stretch. "I have a dinner date myself, as I recall, with a rather smashing redhead."

I sent him a mildly suspicious glance. "One of my finds assistants is a redhead."

"*Is* she? What a coincidence."

"Hmm. Just see that she's not late for work in the morning, will you?"

"My dear girl," he asked me, "do I look like the sort of person who'd corrupt an innocent student?"

None of us answered him, but his words set Peter off on a new train of thought. "The students," he mused. "I must go and check on them, see that they're comfortable. I don't believe we'll have the tents set up again before tomorrow, but—"

"Aye, well," said David, stretching himself, "maybe Wally and I can go down now and take a look around at the damage."

Brian went with them. Which left only me, sitting there with the cats, in no hurry to do much of anything.

It was the telephone, jangling in the front hall, that finally got me off the sofa. With a sigh, I lifted the receiver, wishing the thing could have stayed out of order till dinnertime, at least.

"Verity?" A voice I knew. "It's Howard. You're not an easy woman to get hold of, are you? I've been trying for *days*," he complained. "Your sister thinks I'm some sort of maniac, you know."

I smiled. "Yes, well. She's a bit protective, is Alison."

"Protective," Howard said, "is not the word. I'd rather face a Rottweiler."

"She did tell me you'd called," I defended my sister.

"Well, I should hope so. I told her it was damned important."

"What was?"

"I've been feeling like an idiot all week."

"Howard . . ." I warned him.

"What? Oh, sorry. I'll get to the point. Do you remember those photographs you sent me a while back—the Samian sherds?"

"Yes."

"Yes." He coughed. "The thing is, I was clearing my desk up last Friday . . . you know how my desk gets, and people had begun to, well, *say* things . . . and anyway, I found the envelope you'd sent the photos in, and I was just about to tear it up when I realized there was a photograph still stuck inside it. Got wedged in the bottom somehow,

against the cardboard backing, and I simply hadn't noticed . . ."

"Howard." I cut him off again. "What are you trying to
tell me?"

"I told you those sherds were Agricolan, didn't I?"

"Aren't they?"

"Yes, the ones that I saw were," he told me. "Of course
they were. But this last one, darling . . . the one in the photograph I *didn't* see, it's entirely different."

Remembering the one sherd that I'd thought was younger
than the others, I gripped the handset tighter, hoping. "In
what way?"

"The rim pattern is quite distinctive, you know, and . . .
well, I'd have to see the actual sherd, naturally, before I
could give it a positive date . . . but it certainly couldn't have
been made before AD 115."

My heart gave a tiny, joyful leap. "You're sure?"

"It is my job," he reminded me dryly.

"Not before 115?"

"Not a chance."

I smiled, not caring that he couldn't see it. "Oh Howard,
that's wonderful."

"Helpful, is it?"

"You have no idea."

"You still owe me five pounds," he said. "As I recall,
the bet was that you'd find a marching camp, and the word
down here is you've found a good deal more."

He meant our digging team, of course, but the statement
struck me personally. "Yes," I told him. "Yes, I have."

"Well, well," said Howard.

"What?"

"Nothing. Look, just send that sherd to me tomorrow, will
you?"

"Right."

"And my fiver."

"And your fiver," I promised. "And Howard?"

"Yes?"

"If you're talking to Dr. Lazenby . . ."

"Yes?"

"Would you tell him I'm not interested in Alexandria?"
A pause. "Are you ill?"

"No, I'm perfectly healthy. And perfectly happy, right here."

I did feel almost ridiculously happy as I rang off. Odd, I thought, how good and bad things always seemed to come at once, as if some unseen force were seeking balance. Peter, for all his brave exterior, had suffered today as no man deserved to suffer. And now, after all that, he was about to learn that Rosehill had been twice occupied—not only during the Agricolan campaigns, but later, after AD 115, around the time the Ninth *Hispana* had started its fateful march northwards.

It wasn't proof, not concrete proof, but still it was enough to make the archaeological establishment show some respect, however small, for Peter Quinnell. Even those who mocked his theories could no longer call him mad.

Not that he was *entirely* sane, I thought fondly, when I went outside to find him.

He was standing in the field, alone, a rather tragic figure with his white hair blowing in the wind, his jaw set high and proud. Like King Lear raging at the elements, only the elements by now were fairly tame, and Peter, while he would have made a smashing Lear, was only Peter. He looked around as I approached, and smiled wistfully.

"And they say the gods don't hear us."

"Sorry?"

"I've been pondering the truth, my dear," he said. "And here you are. In Latin, truth is feminine, is it not? *Veritas*. Verity." My name flowed out in his melodic voice like a phrase from a very old song, and he turned his gaze away again. "The truth is buried in this field, somewhere. But if I fail to prove it, can it still be called a truth?"

I considered the question. "Well . . . I can't see the Sentinel, and I've no scientific proof he exists, but I do know that he's there."

"Ah, but you did see him, didn't you? However vaguely, you did see him. Whereas I . . ." His words hung sadly on the shifting wind.

"Whereas you have a potsherd that dates from the end of Trajan's reign," I said, and smiled as he turned again to stare at me.

"I beg your pardon? I have what?"

I repeated the statement, and told him about Howard's telephone call. "He said he'd be happy to give us a firm date, if we could send him down the sherd."

"Good heavens." He stared at me a moment longer, and then crushed me with a hug. "That's marvelous, my dear. That's absolutely—"

The slam of a car door interrupted us, and Robbie came running over the blowing grass with Kip bounding close at his heels. "Heyah," said Robbie. "We got Granny Nan. She's going to change her shoes, she says, and then come out."

"Wonderful," Peter said.

The collie brushed past us, tail wagging, and Robbie nodded at the field. "You found him, did you?"

I looked where he was looking, and saw nothing. "Who do you mean, Robbie? The Sentinel? Where is he?"

"Just there, where Kip is."

Not ten feet in front of us.

Peter looked, too. "Poor chap," he said. "I would have thought he'd find some peace, after what he did today. Putting things to rights, as it were. I would have thought that he could rest."

Robbie wrinkled his freckled nose, looking up. "He doesn't want to rest," he said. "He wants to take care of us."

"Does he, indeed?" Peter's smile was faint. "Well, I can understand that, I suppose."

I thought I understood, as well. And where I'd once been frightened by the thought of being watched, I now took comfort in the presence of the Sentinel. I felt a satisfaction, too, in knowing that today he had been able to redeem himself, to keep his promise, saving the life of the man that his "Claudia" loved. And he would go on protecting us, here at Rosehill. He'd see that we came to no harm. The shadowy horses could run all they wanted; they'd never come near while the Sentinel walked.

Kip suddenly sat and whined an eager little whine, eyes trained upwards, waiting. And then, as though someone had given him a signal, he broke away and bounded off to meet the older woman coming around the house behind us. Robbie turned and said: "Granny Nan's coming." And I was turning myself, to wave hello, so I might have imagined what Peter said next.

His words were quiet, very low, and at any rate I wasn't meant to hear them.

He was speaking to the Sentinel. "Thank you," he said simply, in his lovely, cultured Latin. "Thank you for saving my son."

He dropped his gaze, but not before I saw his wise and weary eyes, and knew for certain that he knew. And then his eyes lifted again, and in place of the sadness there was only a smile, as he held out his hands to greet David's mother.

David was sitting on the bank of the Eye Water, watching the swans. The harbor must have been too rough for them, during the storm, so they'd swum further upriver in search of calmer waters. They drifted now under the trees, snow-white and regal, heads modestly bowed.

I spread my anorak over the wet grass and sat down beside him. "Your mother's here."

"Oh, aye?"

"Mmm. Peter's giving her the grand tour."

"We'll be waiting for our dinner, then."

I smiled. "Jeannie says eight o'clock."

David checked his watch, and leaned back comfortably. "Plenty of time."

"I see you got your tent back up."

"Aye. The rest'll be no trouble at all, there's hardly any damage done. Tomorrow morning I'll get a few of the lads to give me a hand."

I nodded, hugging my knees. I ought to have told him about Howard's discovery, really, only I knew that if I did we'd end up talking about the dig, and I didn't want to talk about the dig right now. Instead I watched the pale swans drifting in the shallows. "They're beautiful, aren't they?"

"Aye."

"I'm glad there are two of them. The one looked so lonely, by himself."

David smiled, not looking at me. "He'll not be lonely again. They mate for life, swans do. She's stuck with him now."

And I was stuck with David Fortune, I thought fondly, studying his now familiar face—the deep lines of laughter that crinkled his eyes, the thick slanting fall of black eyelashes touching his cheekbone, the firm, unyielding angle of his jaw, and the nose that, in profile, was not quite straight, as though it had been broken in a fight. I would ask him about that nose, one day, I promised myself. One day, when we were sitting in the red-walled room at Rosehill, watching Peter and Nancy dandle their first-born grandchild, I would ask my husband how he'd broken his nose.

But till then, I could wait—I was in no great hurry. Like the swans, I had mated for life.

David, whose thoughts had obviously been drifting along the same lines, turned his head, and his blue eyes caught mine, very warm. "D'ye ken that in Eyemouth, when a woman marries onto a man, she takes his byname as well? Verity Deid-Banes," he tried the combination on his tongue, and grinned. "It's a fair mouthful, that."

"David . . ."

"Of course, you could always be just Davy's Verity."

Since I clearly wasn't going to be given a voice in this decision, I rested my chin on my knees and tilted my head to smile back at him. "Oh?"

"Aye. Davy's Verity." He said it again and nodded firmly, satisfied. "That's what you'll be."

So much for independence, I thought. Still, I took a final stab at it. "I am not," I said, setting him straight, "Davy's Verity."

But my protest had no real effect. He only laughed, and

rolling to his side he reached for me, his big hand tangling in my hair as he drew me down toward him. "The hell you're not," he said.

And proved it.

Author's Note

This book could not have been written without the expert advice and assistance of my own "field crew" of archaeologists: in Scotland, Pat Storey and Dr. Bill Finlayson, of the University of Edinburgh; and in Canada, Dr. James Barrett, and especially Heather Henderson, who guided me from the beginning and very kindly sieved my manuscript for errors. Many thanks.

Here's a preview of Susanna Kearsley's next novel, *Named of the Dragon,* coming in December from Jove Books!

I

Shine, little lamp, nor let thy light grow dim.
Into what vast, dread dreams, what lonely lands,
Into what griefs hath death delivered him,
Far from my hands?

Marjorie Pickthall, "The Lamp of Poor Souls"

The dream came, as it always did, just before dawn.

I was standing alone at the edge of a river that wound through a valley so lush and so green that the air seemed alive. The warble of songbirds rang over the treetops from branches bent low with the weight of ripe fruit, and everywhere the flowers grew, more vivid and fragrant than any flowers I had ever seen before. Their fragrance filled me with an incredible thirst, and kneeling on the riverbank I cupped my hands into the chill running water and lifted them dripping, preparing to drink.

A shadow swept over me, blocking the sun.

Beside me the grass gave a rustle and parted, and out came a serpent, quite withered and small. It slipped down the riverbank into the water and opened its mouth, and as I knelt watching the serpent swallowed the river, and the flowers shriveled and died and the trees turned to flame, and the songbirds to ravens, and everywhere the green of the valley vanished and the world became a wasteland underneath a frozen sky, and the riverbed a hard road winding through it.

And the serpent, grown heavy and large, slithered off as the ravens rose thick in a chattering cloud that turned day into night, and I found myself walking beneath a pale moon through the wasteland.

I was looking for something—I didn't know what, but I'd lost it just recently . . .

And then, far off, I heard a baby crying in the night, and I remembered.

"Justin!"

The crying grew stronger. I started to run, with my hair streaming out like a madwoman, running, but always the cry came from somewhere ahead and I couldn't catch up with it. "Justin!" I called again, panicked. "Oh God, love, I'm coming. Hold on, Mummy's coming."

But already I was losing him, I wasn't running fast enough, and then the road fell away and I fell with it, spiralling helplessly down through the dark into nothingness, hearing the cries growing fainter above me, and fading . . .

I woke with a jolt.

For a long moment I lay perfectly still, blinking up at the ceiling and forcing my eyes to focus through the stinging mist of tears. Outside on the pavement I heard footsteps pass with the brisk, certain ring of a businessman heading for Kensington station. The sound, small and normal, was something to cling to. I drew a deep breath . . . and another . . . reached my hand toward the lamp.

Light always helped, somehow.

Clear of the shadows, my room felt less cold and less empty. I rose, and shrugged myself into my robe, and crossed to the window. The sulphurous glow of a late November night had given way to hard gray light that flattened on the line of roofs and chimney-pots that faced me. In the street below, the stream of morning traffic had already started, sluggishly, as everywhere the houses yawned to life. It was morning, just the same as any other morning.

I pulled the curtain back an inch, and looked toward the fading morning star. It looked so small, so vulnerable. Another hour, and it would be forgotten. There wasn't anybody in the flat who could have heard me, but I spoke the words quite softly, all the same: "Happy Birthday, Justin," I said, to the tiny point of light.

It winked back, faintly, and I let the curtain fall.

II

Go hence to Wales,
There live a while.

William Rowley, The Birth of Merlin

"Oh, Lyn, you can't be serious." Bridget Cooper flicked her auburn hair back in a careless gesture that distracted every man within a two-table radius, and glanced at me reprovingly. "You look like death warmed up, you know. The last thing you should do is take another transatlantic flight."

With anybody else, I might have argued that I'd slept straight through the New York flight two days ago, and that my next business flight wouldn't be until the twenty-first of January . . . but with Bridget, I knew, I'd be wasting my breath. Besides, I'd known her long enough to realize this was simply preamble.

Bridget never worried about anybody's health except her own. And she never rang me at nine on a Monday, suggesting we meet and have lunch, unless she had a motive.

Bridget was a one-off, an exceptionally talented writer with a wild imagination that made her books for children instant classics, and a wild nature that drove the poor directors of my literary agency to drink. In the four years since I'd signed her as a client, Bridget's books had earned a fortune for the Simon Holland Agency, but her unpredictability had caused much tearing of hair and rending of garments among my colleagues. My favorite of her escapades—the day she'd kicked the BBC presenter—was now a Simon Holland legend. And I, who had survived four years and one week's holiday in France with Bridget, had risen to the status of a martyr.

Not that Bridget was so very terrible. In fact, if one didn't mind the occasional embarrassment, she could be tremendous fun, and time had taught me how to keep pace with her ever-shifting moods. Still, she did leave me wondering, sometimes, exactly who was managing whom.

Our lunch today had been a case in point. It had begun, reasonably enough, with a discussion of the plans for an animated television series based on the bestselling *Llandrah* books that had first launched Bridget's career. But by the time the waiter cleared away our starters, she had somehow shifted topics to the coming holidays.

"And anyway," she said, "who goes to Canada for Christmas?"

"Quite a lot of people, I'd imagine. All that snow . . ."

"There won't be snow," she told me, very certain, "in Vancouver. Their weather's much too mild." Taking another slice of bread from the basket between us, she tore it neatly into pieces. "No, you ought to come with me, instead, to Angle."

"Angle?"

"Pembrokeshire," she said. "South Wales. You know, where they had that big oil spill a couple of years ago." Bridget's sense of geography was, I'd learned, invariably linked to the six o'clock news and the Sunday tabloids. Name any town or village and she'd pinpoint its location in relation to a murder or a scandal or a natural disaster. Odd, perhaps, but undeniably effective. As it happened, I did remember the oil spill in question, and my memory flashed an image of a rugged stretch of coastline as she took a bite of bread and went on speaking. "James is minding a lovely old house down there—well, it's sort of three houses, really, but two of them have been knocked together to make one—right by the sea, with an old ruined tower in the garden. You'd adore it. Anyway, he's asked me for the holidays, and he said I could bring you along, if you wanted to come."

I didn't bother asking her who "James" was—I'd long since given up trying to keep track of Bridget's men. I simply shook my head, shifting aside so the waiter could set down my plate of risotto with fragrant spiced pumpkin. "I couldn't, I'm afraid. My brother would never forgive me."

She glanced up, clearly finding my excuse inadequate. "And how is dear Patrick the Protester? What's he on about this week? Saving the dormice? Blocking the bypass?"

"Battling the logging industry, actually. Chaining himself to trees. But only at the weekend," I explained. "He doesn't have so much free time, now he's married."

"Ah." Losing interest, Bridget took an experimental taste of her own dish of brightly colored pasta, chasing it down with a sip of red wine. "Mm, that's glorious. I ought to *marry* an Italian, they do brilliant things with food." The Italian waiter, hovering nearby, looked briefly hopeful, and I hid my smile with an effort, marveling again at the effect that Bridget had on men.

She was not, on close inspection, a beautiful woman. She had an ordinary figure, an ordinary nose dusted with freckles, an ordinary smile, and tilting eyes too impish to be called exotic. My brother, having met her, thought her "cute" rather than "pretty," though even he admitted Bridget had a certain something that was . . . well, it simply *was*. I blamed it on the auburn hair, myself. To believe a person's hair color could shape their personality might seem, at first glance, less than scientific, but I'd never met a redhead yet who didn't have the same allure—a sort of blend of vibrant energy and freshness that made those of us with brown hair feel ridiculously dull.

I smiled. "I thought you'd sworn off marriage."

"So I have," she said, remembering. "I'm thirty-four now, far too sensible to fall into the trap. And two ex-husbands ought to be enough for anyone. D'you know, that's one thing that I've always envied you."

"What's that?"

"Well, I'd rather be widowed, I think, than divorced. It's much tidier. Nobody skulking round, trying to make your life a misery. You're rather lucky, that way."

Only Bridget, I decided, would have thought to tell a
widow she was lucky that her husband hadn't lived. But her
candid words, as usual, were not far off the mark. My marriage to the novelist Martin Blake had not been the greatest
of successes.

"I sometimes wish," said Bridget, "that my number one
would drive his car into a handy tree. He's being a right
pain, lately. I'll be that relieved to get away for the holidays.
And Dylan Thomas notwithstanding, I'm frankly seduced
by the thought of a Christmas in Wales—especially the *singing* . . . d'you remember that Welsh choir we heard at the
Albert Hall? Magnificent," she pronounced them. "I mean,
how can one not admire a people who can sing like that?"

I smiled into my wineglass, thinking how my own assistant Lewis, who was Welsh, would have cringed to hear her
say that. He frequently despaired of the stereotypes attached
to his countrymen. "Singing, coal-mining, rugby and
sheep," he'd told me once, in great disgust, "are the only
things the bloody English think we know. Pure ignorance."

Bridget took another piece of bread and sighed. "I do wish
you'd come. Fond as I am of James, he can be such a bore,
sometimes. You'd be a good distraction for him."

"Oh, yes?"

"What I mean is, you'd be someone new that he could
tell his stories to. They're fascinating stories, first time round.
And I thought, since you waxed so rhapsodic about his last
novel . . ."

My fork paused in mid-air. "I did?"

"Of course you did, don't you remember? When it didn't
win the Booker, you called the judges a pathetic bunch of—"

"Bridget," I interrupted her carefully, setting down my
fork, "this 'James' of yours . . . he wouldn't be, by any
chance . . ."

"James Swift," she said, with a confirming nod.

I felt a sudden need for water. Reaching for my glass, I
calmed the tiny racing thrill along my nerves that always
signaled my professional excitement. "James Swift," I repeated the name, to be absolutely certain we were speaking

of the same man—the man whose latest novel *should* have won the Booker prize; the man who, I felt firmly, was the closest thing to literary genius that our nation now had living. "I didn't realize you two knew each other."

Bridget's mouth curved, full of mischief. "One doesn't tell one's agent *everything*," she said. "You're far too young. And anyway, I know how much you fancy his writing—I didn't want you pestering the poor man to defect to Simon Holland."

"Give over," I told her, "I'm hardly the pestering type. And I'm not so short on ethics that I'd try to lure an author from the agent he's already got."

"I see," said Bridget. "So you wouldn't want to know, then, that he's not exactly happy with his agent." She twirled up a forkful of pasta, the picture of innocence. "Or that he's thinking he might look around for a new one . . ."

"You are joking."

She smiled, sensing victory. "Are you *sure* you'd rather go to Canada for Christmas?"

"You really don't have any scruples, do you?"

"God, no. Horrible things, scruples," she said, with a shudder. "They get in the way of my fun." Reaching to refill her wineglass, she tested the weight of the bottle. "Nearly empty. We'd best have another."

"Oh, Bridget, no, I can't . . ."

But she'd already raised her hand to hail the waiter, who all but leaped across his other tables to reach ours, arriving slightly out of breath and wearing his most charming smile. Bridget, being Bridget, took no notice, though she did spare him an admiring look as he scurried off again to fetch her order. "The service here is really something, isn't it?" she asked; then, seeing my expression, raised an eyebrow. "What?"

"Nothing." I let it pass. "Only I can't drink anymore wine, I've reached my limit. Some of us," I reminded her, "have to go back to the office."

"Yes, I know." Upending the first bottle over my wineglass, she poured out the dregs. "And it wouldn't help my reputation any, if I let you go back sober."

She needn't have worried. Her reputation was already un-
assailable. So much so that, two hours later, as I leaned
against the cool mirrored wall of our office lift, my co-
worker Graham had no trouble guessing the cause of my
unsteadiness. "Been to lunch with Bridget Cooper?"

"Mm." I kept my eyes closed while I nodded. "That obvious, is it?"

"Well, at least you managed to find your way back to the
building," he congratulated me. "The last time I had lunch
with her I ended up in Soho, doing most peculiar things with
women's clothing."

"Did you really? I'd like to have seen that."

"I'm sure it's all on video, somewhere." The lift stopped
with a shudder and Graham took my elbow as the doors slid
open.

"Not my floor," I slurred.

"Yes, I know, but I can't let you go upstairs in that condition. You'll have to hide out in my office, till you get your
second wind."

Graham's spacious office, one floor below mine, was the
war room of our film and television rights department. My
bookshelves only had to bear the weight of books by my
own clients, but Graham's shelves were stacked to over-
flowing with a dizzying collection of typescripts and bound
proofs and published books, his wall-mounted schedules and
half-buried desk completing the picture of organized chaos.

Ignoring the clutter, I sank into the cushions of the love-
seat in the corner, pushing aside a stack of catalogues so I
could prop my feet up on the coffee table.

"Tea or coffee?" Graham offered.

"Tea sounds heavenly."

"Right," he said, and left me, returning several minutes
later with two cracked and battered mugs. I'd just begun to
drift, eyes closing, and the heat of the mug being thrust into
my hands came as a bit of a jolt, but the fragrant steam
revived me.

I took a sip and thanked him. "You're an angel."

"That's hardly the image I'm after," he said, with a smile,
as he settled himself in his own padded chair. "I'd rather be

seen as the devil incarnate—I get more accomplished, that way.''

''Yes, I heard you'd been terrorizing my poor assistant, lately.''

''Vicious rumors,'' he denied it. ''Speaking of which, I don't suppose Bridget happened to confirm or deny her affair with that Formula One chap? No? Damn. I've got ten quid riding on that one.'' Swiveling his chair round, he faced me expectantly. ''So, what's her opinion of the *Llandrah* series?''

''I think she likes it. She seemed quite happy they were wanting Julia to oversee the animation.'' That had been one of my concerns, as well as Bridget's. Julia Beckett's original illustrations for the *Llandrah* books had been so very beautiful that they'd become a living part of Bridget's text, and neither of us could envisage the stories being told without those same distinctive images.

''Yes, well, Julia is rather irreplaceable,'' said Graham, with a sigh. ''Horrible shame that she went and got married—I'll never understand the female mind.''

''She's very happy.''

''No doubt.'' With a shrug that dismissed the irrational nature of women, he returned to the topic at hand. ''So you think Bridget's pleased with the deal?''

''I think so, yes.''

''But you're not sure.''

''Well, we sort of got sidetracked,'' I explained, raising one hand to massage the veins pounding time at my temples. ''You know Bridget. One minute we're discussing the contract, and the next I'm hearing all about her Christmas plans.''

''Oh, yes? And where's she off to this year? Rome? Vienna?''

''Pembrokeshire.''

''I'm sorry?''

''Some little place called Angle, in south Pembrokeshire.''

''Of course,'' he said. ''That would have been my next guess.''

''Yes, well, you might laugh, but she's been asked to

spend the holidays with James Swift, of all people. And she wants me to go with her.''

Graham turned his head at that. "I hope you told her yes.''

"I told her maybe.'' To his scandalized expression I explained: "It's my brother's first Christmas in Canada, Graham—my family's expecting me there.''

He felt sure they'd survive. Turning away, he adopted a carefully casual tone. "You do know who represents Swift, don't you?''

"All the more reason not to go," I said.

"And miss the chance to lure away his blue-eyed boy? You disappoint me.'' He glanced at me and smiled, taking pity on my situation. "I've been in this position myself, you know. I once had two invitations arrive by the same post— one to my oldest sister's anniversary supper, and another to this gala West End opening—both for the same night. In the end, I found that there was only one fair way to settle it.'' Fishing in his pocket, he produced a single penny and held it up for me to see.

"What, you tossed a coin?''

"It's the tried and trusted method,'' he defended his decision. "Saves a lot of mental aggravation. Here, you give it a go.''

I caught the coin in a reflex motion, shaking my head. "Don't be daft.''

"No, really. Heads, you do the boring family thing and go to Canada, and tails . . . oh, hell,'' he said, as the ringing of his telephone cut in. "I'll have to take this, Lyn. Won't be a minute.''

As he swung around in his chair to take the call, his back to me, I frowned, considering. He might be right, I thought— a toss of the coin did seem the only fair way to decide where I ought to spend Christmas.

And it only took four tries to make the penny come up tails.